Mary, EVERYTHING

Cassandra Yorke

Cassandra Yorke

ISBN: 978-0-578-68036-1

Edited by Jorden Ridenhour
Cover design by Cassandra Yorke
Maps and artwork by Cassandra Yorke
Fonts used: EB Garamond, Goudy Bookletter 1911, Telegram (HPLHS).
Library of Congress Control Number: 2018675309
Printed in the United States of America

The Flapper Covenant series

Mary, Everything

Keepers of the Veil (TBA)

To Mary and Nettie
My first friends in the 1920s
And the grain of truth at the heart of this story.
All my love, always.

And to Lindsay
Who never stopped believing in me - or Courtney.
I love you, darling.

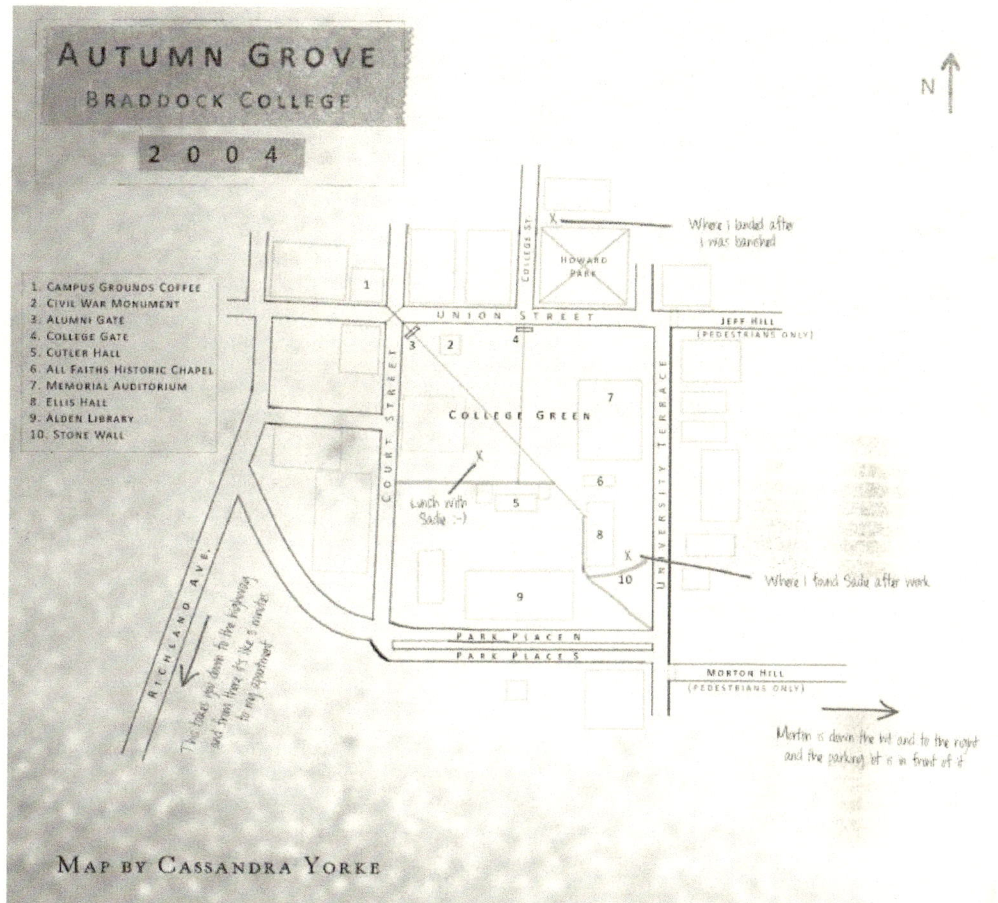
AUTUMN GROVE
BRADDOCK COLLEGE
2004
N
1. CAMPUS GROUNDS COFFEE
2. CIVIL WAR MONUMENT
3. ALUMNI GATE
4. COLLEGE GATE
5. CUTLER HALL
6. ALL FAITHS HISTORIC CHAPEL
7. MEMORIAL AUDITORIUM
8. ELLIS HALL
9. ALDEN LIBRARY
10. STONE WALL
COLLEGE ST
HOWARD PARK
X
Where I landed after I was banished
UNION STREET
JEFF HILL
(PEDESTRIANS ONLY)
COURT STREET
3
2
4
7
COLLEGE GREEN
X
Lunch with Sadie :-)
6
5
8
UNIVERSITY TERRACE
X
Where I found Sadie after work
10
9
PARK PLACE N
PARK PLACE S
MORTON HILL
(PEDESTRIANS ONLY)
RICHLAND AVE.
The trains go down to the beginning and from there it's like a minute to my apartment
Morton is down the hill and to the right and the parking lot is in front of it
MAP BY CASSANDRA YORKE

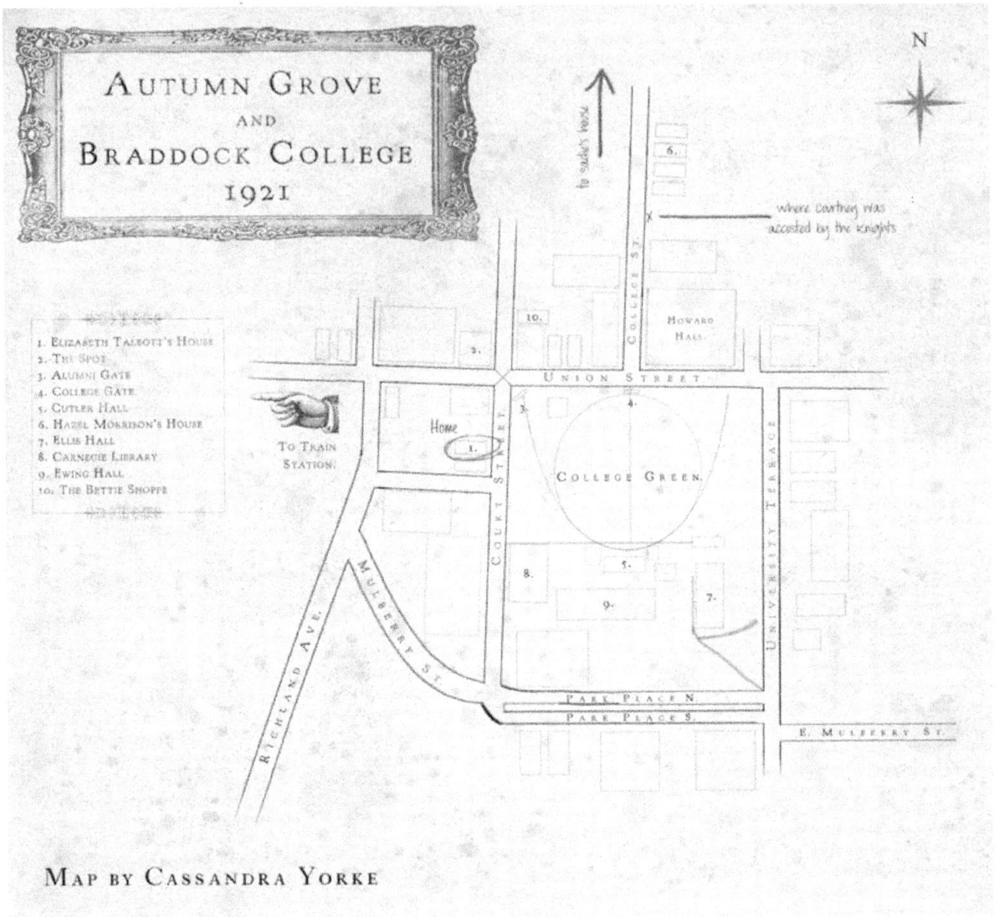

MAP BY CASSANDRA YORKE

AUTUMN GROVE
&
ENVIRONS
TRAEBURN RIVER
THE MONOLITH
GREVETT'S CROSSING
(UNINHABITED SINCE 1729)
BLACKSTEAD FOREST
THE CLEARING
OLD TRAEBURN
ASYLUM
BRADDOCK
COLLEGE
AUTUMN GROVE
TO STANHOPE
53 MILES
TO PARKERSBURG, WEST VIRGINIA
48 MILES
MAP BY CASSANDRA YORKE
N

If Light Is In Your Heart,

You Will Find Your Way Home.

-Rumi, 13th c.

Wednesday
September 7, 1921

Blackstead Forest
10 miles from Autumn Grove city limits
Before dawn

Courtney

"I shall not remain alone...I shall try to scale the castle wall farther than I have yet attempted...I may find a way from this dreadful place. [...] And then away for home! Away to the quickest and nearest train! Away from this cursed spot, from this cursed land, where the devil and his children still walk with earthly feet!"
-Bram Stoker, *Dracula* (1899)

The best years of my life begin like an execution, far from home.

A trail of my blood leads out of the woods for a half mile in the dark. Then into an empty state forest, and a parking lot, and a highway you drive for ten minutes to get you back to the apartment where I was almost butchered by someone who wanted to kill me just for the fun of it. A place where my bones ached with loneliness, a place where I became convinced I had more good reasons to die than I ever had to live.

Imagine everyone who ever wanted to hurt you, every accident and near-miss, every cold look and hurtful comment, all of it rousing itself for one purpose - to kill you. Now, a lot of people feel like misfits, but imagine that you were never meant to exist. You spend your whole life getting told that, and *knowing* that, but then one day it becomes real in a way you never imagined. Menacing smiles in the distance. Hate mail written in blood. The fabric of the world itself, the pavement and buildings and signs glaring at you like an unwanted guest. You feel it swirling around you - something bad is about to happen.

And then one night, it does. A thick, curved knife in the failing dusk. Someone who hates you with an inhuman ferocity for the sake of hate alone. They invent some reason to come to your apartment, and they've got about eight friends as big as phone booths and they hold you in place so someone with black eyes can cut you open, spill your blood all over a dirty parking lot on the edge of town. They want to slice you up, do horrifying things to you, leave you to bleed to death all alone. That's what they want, but nobody is totally separate from their universe, and they don't know they only want it because the *universe* wants it. You were never meant to be there. You were never meant to exist. And that universe wants you gone.

But sometimes, when reality breaks down near the end, there's an escape window - one last chance to get out - and if we make that leap of faith into the dark, it takes us home. Where we should have been all along. If you're quick and smart and really lucky, you can beat the odds and end up happier than you ever imagined. Beating the odds is the hard part, though - especially when someone comes into the picture and decides they'd like to try their hand at ending your life.

Right now, I have no idea how I got this horrendous cut on my shoulder, or why I can't stop bleeding. Pieces are missing.

The worst part is knowing that none of this should be happening anyway, and if I'd done things a little differently in 1915, I wouldn't be out here in the woods running from God knows what. I've had a lot of years to sit alone and think about that.

But here I am. I still don't know how I could have done it any differently. I'd have *died* to keep that sack of shit away from Mary. I still would.

Right about now, you might misunderstand what's going on and ask what it's like to travel back in time. It's not *exactly* time travel, *per se*, but it's the simplest way to explain what's happening, so let's roll with it.

Imagine running forever through endless woods in the dead of night, through tangled thorns, across deadfalls hidden in the leaves, waiting for you to trip and kill yourself. Your arm is useless and numb, slathered in thick coats of old blood. Your fingers are stiff and sticky with it, brown and red. Something sliced your shoulder open hours ago, and it never stopped bleeding. You've been on the edge of passing out for as long as you can remember. You're getting more lightheaded all the time, but the blood won't stop. No matter how far you run, the forest never ends. No matter how much blood you lose, you keep losing more.

Off in the distance, a long gash cuts open the horizon, and it bleeds red sunrise over the hills. The sky is a massive violet bruise, but dawn will break it into pieces and wash it away in a flood of molten orange. You wonder if you'll still be alive.

You taste it in your throat, coppery and tangy, from your tired lungs. A glowing hot ache spreads out of your airways and across your chest, and there's no way to breathe fast enough or deep enough to satisfy the heart pounding its way through your ribcage. Every wheezing breath is a burst of stars across your vision. Every heartbeat is a flash of lightning in your eyes.

Some nightmare scorched your brain like a hot iron, but you can't remember that, either. Whatever you saw, it engaged your fight-or-flight and sent you scrambling into the night-black wilderness, crazy to survive. Even though you can't remember exactly what it was, some animal terror urges you to keep going. *Don't stop.*

Something is out there.

A face, a triangle of rotting holes in the fog. Something from the distant past, not meant to be seen with human eyes.

Did something out here drive me insane?

Rocks. There was supposed to be a clearing at the top of a hill, and it had rocks or something. That's what they told me last night. I clamber up the side of this forested hill deep in the woods, layered eight inches high with old dead leaves. It looks like there might be a clearing up there. And two or three big rocks-

A flash of white-hot pain across my shoulder. The wound throbs with heat, and my right hand has been numb for a while. It feels like this cut is infected. *God, I hope this works.*

Just get to the rocks. There they are, toward the far side of the clearing, just like

Nothing.

There's a voice, off in the distance - a girl, screaming my name.

I'm nowhere, and I like it. No more pain. The searing gash on my arm is a distant memory, like a bad dream fading off your brain after you wake up.

Oh, god, no, I think she says. Somehow, the voice is familiar. Oblivion pulls me back down, like ocean currents out to sea. Then the voice again, waking me up just a little.

"Courtney! *Courtney!!* Oh, no. No, no, no. Is she...?"

Long moments, then another female voice - young, competent. She sounds familiar; I talked to this chick recently.

"No," she says at last, very quietly. "But she may not have long. She's lost a lot of blood."

"Courtney!" The girl's voice is shaky with tears. "Oh, dearest, what have they done to you?" A soft, cool hand brushes hair from my eyes.

Feeling washes back into my shoulder, like bleach on raw tissue. Nerves curl up like hair singed in a fire. Alarms in my head, flashing.

Aaaand, we're back.

I gasp and moan and whimper all at once.

"Courtney!! Oh, thank goodness!"

It's a young, pretty voice, full of energy and enthusiasm. I know her. My chest aches with anguished relief. My eyes sting and I can't cry since there's not enough fluid in me but I want to throw myself into her arms. I love her so much right now.

I open my lips a little, try to speak. But my throat is dry, and all I can manage is a pathetic moan, like wind through a doorway.

"S...Sadie?"

A wet sniffle. Was she crying?

"Yep! It's me! You're safe now. Everything's gonna be jake."

I grope for my best friend in my twilight darkness and find the soft cotton hem of her dress. She takes my blood-sticky hand in both of hers, kisses it.

"We'll get her to Professor Talbott's house, and I'll call for a doctor." The other chick's tone becomes businesslike. "Courtney? It's me, Hazel Morrison, Sadie's friend from last night. Can you hear me?"

I groan, try to swallow, but my throat is cement. I give her a weak nod.

"Good. You made it, sweetheart. We're gonna get you back to town." She rummages through a bag. "We brought you some water."

There's a glass jar near my lips, and I raise my good arm to hold it. I'm fumbling, trying to drink it with dirty fingers. Some of the water makes it past my lips; I even manage to swallow some. Then I'm sputtering and coughing, and Sadie's arm is around me, propping me up, rubbing my back.

"Easy, honey, easy." Hazel's voice is gentle. She places a cool, steady hand on my shoulder, right above the wound. She's checking it, probing very gently.

"It's probably not the best time to say this," Sadie admits with a hint of a smile. "But you look awfully pretty for a girl that almost got herself killed." She runs her hand over my hair, smoothing some of the tangles. "Lovely blonde hair and soft pale skin, even when the worst happens."

Her words bring a smile to my face. "You're sweet to say so." I still can't help but cringe from embarrassment; I wish a girl as cute as Sadie wasn't seeing me at my worst - and this *has* to be my absolute worst.

I started out today looking clean and nice, the typical preppy girl who smells good and might even be able to model for a Delia's or Aerie catalog if my eyes weren't so piercing, didn't see through people like windows. If there wasn't a giant sign hanging over me that said *She's not supposed to be in this world!* And now here I am, from preppy to roadkill in twenty-four hours.

Yesterday. Holy shit. I force myself to sit up a little more, gasp with the effort. "Is this actually 1921?"

"Sure is," Sadie says. "And this time it's absolutely for real."

I sag with relief. "Good - 2004 can go die in a fire."

"Well, you're here now, and it can't hurt you anymore. You made it." Hazel touches my lower arm, avoiding the actual wound. "I know it's a lot, but can you stand?"

No matter what's going on, I am *not* going to be killed by a cut. I give another quick nod, reply in a weak voice. "I'll make it work."

I take a moment to summon my reserves, then heave myself up, leaning back against a tree. I open my eyes, blink into the flickering orange sunrise. The sun's almost up. It's my first morning in 1921, the first morning of a new life. That feeling is back, the one where my arms tingle and turn warm, and that warmth turns into absolute joy. My world explodes in vibrant, euphoric color in spite of the searing agony in my shoulder.

We're deep in the woods, and all around us are uncharted miles of huge trees and thick undergrowth. Behind me, away from the sunrise, the forest is thick with purple twilight. I'm a little amazed that I managed to come that way all on my own, plunging up and down all those ridges, through all that undergrowth. Sadie's familiar face is next to mine, her eyes soft. Over next to her is the chick I spoke to last night. Hazel. She looks a little more grown up than me and Sadie, probably in her mid-twenties. She's got light lipstick and blush, sandy brown hair done in loose curls around the bottoms of her ears. She wears a chocolate brown cloche hat and matching summer dress, and she stands poised and erect, holding herself with easy confidence. She looks at me with heartfelt concern but she wears a faint smile, like she's happy to see that I'm alive.

Wow. She's an actual legit flapper. This is crazy.

We're in a clearing somewhere, a nice little open space that might be good for a campfire, a few tents, some music and some marshmallows. But there's nothing here, no reason to think that human eyes have ever seen this place. And it's alive with noise, all around. The birds are up, chirping like crazy, fluttering across the leafy canopy above. And over it all is a loud mechanical rattle. There's a black Ford Model T idling maybe ten feet away, the headlights round and brassy, the engine making an old-fashioned clattering sound that I find oddly comforting. The way the clearing is, it almost feels like the trees are leaning in toward the middle, and it makes the engine that much louder, like we're in the middle of an amphitheater. The car has thin spoked wheels like a bike, and they're sitting on a dirt path, ready to drive right back the way they came in.

The morning sun has vanquished the horrible night. I almost laugh at myself. So many references I'm never gonna be able to share with anyone ever again.

I give Sadie my good arm and she ducks under it. My best friend is a little thing, no bigger than me, but she's surprisingly strong. Her slender almond-shaped eyes blaze with fierce determination, a promise that she's gonna *make sure* I live. The arm she's got around me never wavers, even for a second.

Now I know I *will* live, at least for a while. I *have* someone - someone who honestly cares about me.

And not just *one* someone, apparently. I don't know how it's possible, but *they're* here, too. It's too weird to even wrap my head around, but then again, what about this last week *hasn't* been? It all started with them anyway; seeing *her* picture again was like pushing the big red button you always see on cartoons, the one next to the sign shouting at you not to press it.

"Attagirl," Sadie says quietly, helping me into the back seat of the Model T. "There you go." She deposits my messenger bag and backpack on the empty passenger seat, then climbs in the back next to me.

I'm really here; all this is *really happening*. A smile comes uninvited to my face, even through all the pain.

It's *actually* 1921.

And this time I'm staying here, no matter what, even if I have to fight. Because if the last few days are any indication, I'll probably have to.

Hazel climbs into the driver's seat, closing the door and quickly shifting the motor car into gear with levers behind the steering wheel. The Model T swings around and onto the dirt path with a rattle of shifted gears, and we start down the hill. The nameless clearing where I almost died vanishes quickly from view, and nobody dignifies it by glancing back.

I look at myself in the bright morning sun - I'm a disaster. Short denim shorts around the tops of my thighs, ankle socks hidden in black low-top Chuck Taylors. My legs are a mess, but they don't look as bad as I thought - a bunch of little cuts from shrubs and brambles, little brown rivers of dried blood, lots of dirty smudges. I'm wearing a burgundy camisole with tiny polka dots and shoulder straps of red ribbon. My red Abercrombie hoodie has been cinched around my waist since last night, smudged with blood but okay otherwise. And my arms? Yuck. A whole bunch of little scratches, just like my legs. An improvised tourniquet - some rotten old white t-shirt covered in patches of crimson and brown - that I must have tied around my bicep at some point with one hand and some teeth. Countless layers of rusty blood across my right arm like grisly war paint. Dirty little rivulets down my pale white wrist. I used my left hand to put pressure on the cut, and it's coated in so much sticky blood that it's hard to move my fingers.

"How did that happen, Courtney?" Sadie squints at me, auburn hair tossing around her slender eyes in the open breeze. She nods once at my arm.

I glance at it, taking in the full grotesque vision in the morning light. A long, thin stripe, from the soft part of my bicep and then up across my shoulder. It looks like it's been coated in about ten messy layers of hickory-colored wood stain. It's not bleeding much now - this waterproof layer of filth is finally doing its job - but an ominous trail of bright red runs up the wound. I almost feel like it's glaring at me, like *I'm still bleeding, bitch, and I can start back up anytime I want.*

By this point, most cuts stop hurting. The body adjusts to the damage and starts healing. But something's different with this thing. The whole injury aches with a sick chill that just feels *wrong,* like toothpaste smeared into the wound. It's throbbing, scorching hot on the surface, but underneath it's like waves of ice throbbing in my bones.

Nothing. I blank out and stare at it like an idiot.

Sadie cocks her head a little. "Courtney?"

I look up into her pretty eyes, almond-shaped and sparkling green in the sunlight.

"I have no idea," I answer quietly. That's weird; I have an excellent memory. I've never just blanked out before.

Hazel glances into the rear-view mirror. "You don't remember?"

I shake my head helplessly.

"What's the last thing you *do* remember?"

"Well..." I begin. "You and Sadie. And before that..."

I travel back the best I can, into the lonely trauma of those woods. I remember waking up, Sadie's face, her voice. Hazel giving me water. Before that, just running, traipsing up hills, through brush and leaves. Images are patchy and dim, like the undergrowth at four in the morning. Somewhere in my head, the vague concept of mindless terror. Something in the pitch black. And before that, just...nothing. Nothing at all.

What the hell?

What's the last thing I remember *before* the woods? Distant flickering memories, hazy images of campus in 2004. My job at the Archives, the dry rot smell of the black and white book where all this started. Glaring sun, a hot car interior like an oven in the summer heat. A cold, lonely apartment. Sadness, rejection, despair. I wanted to die. Was I really there yesterday? It feels like another life. It *was* another life. Trying to remember feels like grabbing handfuls of water.

Hazel reaches into her handbag. After rummaging a moment, she produces a small flat makeup mirror about the width of a tennis ball and hands it to Sadie.

"Sadie, would you check Courtney for concussion?"

"Oh. Sure."

"You think I might have a concussion?" I ask blankly.

"Concussions can cause retrograde amnesia," Hazel informs me. "It would explain why you know certain things perfectly well - like who we are, who *you* are, where you're at - but why more recent memories are missing."

"Okay." Sadie speaks quietly to me. Her voice is as soft and cool as her hands. "Look at me, sweetie?"

She holds the mirror up, shining reflected sunlight in one of my eyes, then the other, then back again.

"Her pupils look normal enough," she tells Hazel over the breeze and the loud rattle of the motor, handing the mirror back. Then she turns back to me, holds up three fingers. "How many fingers am I holding up?"

I hold up three fingers.

"And the last thing you remember?" she prompts.

"Before you and Hazel found me?" I ponder. "Flashes, pieces of my old life."

"Why don't you start at the beginning?" Hazel brings the Model T to a clattering stop at a dusty intersection of two unpaved roads. Pools of orange sunlight spread across the dirt as the sun rises, and all around us the forest is green and cool. She glances both ways, then swings the big steering wheel toward town.

I glance at Sadie. "How long ago did we have lunch?"

"Early yesterday afternoon."

"Okay, um…" I glance at the roof of the car, pondering. "If I started at the beginning, that would have been, what, three days ago?" Three days. It feels more like three *years.*

"If you remember having lunch with Sadie," Hazel says, "then I think we can safely rule out any significant brain damage for now. But I'd still like to hear your version of things. There's a great many important things I'll need to know."

I lean back against the seat, glancing out the open window. We're coming down out of the thick woods now, and the treeline is receding, making way for wide green fields full of mown hay. Lazy brown cows sprawl in the pastures, chewing mouthfuls of cud. It's still early; dew lays thick on the grass.

"I guess if you really wanna hear," I tell her.

"I do." Hazel looks at me in the rearview mirror. "All you can tell me."

"Me too," Sadie chimes. "Give us the score."

"Okay," I say uncertainly. "Well, if you told me about all this stuff a week ago, told me I'd be *here,* I'd have thought you were wacked. I was in a whole different place."

part one

S U M M E R   2 0 0 4

One

June 2004
Autumn Grove, Ohio

Courtney

"For Courtney, it was always about Mary, long before it was about any of the rest of us."
-Alice Thatcher, *Memoirs of an Accidental Arcane*, 1927

One week ago

It's the summer of 2004, and everything is ending. The days are hot and wide under a blinding sun. Distances go on forever; you're at a crossroads, and every direction looks the same. Everything is ending, and there are no beginnings after.

Autumn Grove is a busy little college town nestled in the foothills like crumbs in a messy blanket. The sun rises slow at old Braddock College, to the tall round cupolas above the roofs, into the wavy glass in the high windows. The sun sparkles like ale in the high green canopy. The Appalachian mornings are cool and moist and they smell like the forest floor, like grass and moss and mushrooms. The Georgian buildings are all done in red brick and they've been here for centuries, watching lazy mornings roll into long afternoons, before they stretch out like an old cat waiting for evening. The sunsets are long and golden over a bright green campus and you don't know a soul for sixty miles. You're all alone here with your brand new start among ancient oak trees and little brick streets.

Braddock has been here since the 1760s, built as a kind of academic outpost on the edge of the wilderness. It was named for the British general who marched out this way and fought the first engagements in the French and Indian War. People were going to class here when the tea was trashed in Boston Harbor. Antiquity lays heavy on Autumn Grove. Hundreds of people you've never met go about their busy days, oblivious to your presence. Just out of sight, countless more people, the ghosts of professors and students that came before you.

You're all alone here. Nobody knows you enough to hate you. Loneliness seeps up from the cracks in the street, between the bricks, across the sidewalks. It drifts low along the grass, through the middle of campus, among the squirrels and acorns. Maybe the loneliness is as old as Braddock itself; maybe it's the original loneliness of eighteenth-century scholars in the wilderness, desperate for a new start, a world away from New England. But Braddock calls to its own. If you're a lonely young person, desperate for a new start far away, Braddock will turn its gaze on you. Its attention is cool and scholarly, but not unfriendly. As you stroll its well-kept grounds and look inside its antique windows, it'll have already begun to seduce you with images of old libraries and old desks and quiet study. And from the first time you visit, maybe still in high school, it's already got its hooks in you. Its lonely, studious solitude will haunt you like a murdered ghost until the day you enroll. That's when you'll realize that Braddock College chose *you*. It had you from the moment you first laid eyes on it.

Most students go to Braddock, graduate, and leave. Maybe they reflect fondly on their time here, and all the students and alumni are kind of a big, loose family. But if Braddock called to you, haunted you, then it's different. If you leave, it'll *always* haunt you. One way or another, you're part of the campus now, like all those restless students that came before. And when you die, your spirit will go back to walk those beautiful old grounds.

Just out of sight, you'll whisper to students just like you, beckoning them to study at old Braddock College.

In Autumn Grove, the solitude really hits in the evening. A brassy sunset over endless emerald grass, strangers jogging the bike path by the river, and it looks just like it did in the brochures. You savored that image for years and now you're all alone in it, just like you always imagined. During the school year, students move across the quads, home to the dorms, out to the dining halls, uptown for a drink. When June arrives, all the paths and walkways are vacant, and those milling crowds are a fading memory. Clouds drift high above and songbirds twitter and everything looks just like it did a few weeks ago, but it's empty and abandoned like a ghost town and it reminds you just how alone you really are. Up on College Green, in the middle of campus, the pretty white lamps flicker on by the walkways, cool and eerie like will-o-wisps in the night. Cars drive by every now and then, orange and red taillights coasting down streets, stopping at bright red lights, turning, headed down campus streets with fast food joints and green awnings and a few grad students here and there. The restaurants are still open, the neon lights and street lamps are on, the traffic lights keeping the same faithful routine. It's lonely and cozy and you're all alone here in this little college town in the Appalachian foothills, an island of civilization far from your hometown. And high above in the night sky, impossibly distant stars flicker and you can't help but look at them and dream of all the things that might be.

Because down here on the ground, something's not right. And I don't mean with the world; the world's just fine. Something's wrong with *you*. Something went sideways a long time ago, and you're living on borrowed time. The clock is coming back around, and you can only run for so long. It's almost time.

You have no idea how you know any of this, but you do. You know it the same way you know when you're hungry or thirsty or tired. And on these breathless, waiting summer nights, staring at the sky by yourself never feels quite right. You're alone and exposed, full of questions you're powerless to answer.

As for me, I can't help but gaze up and wonder if there's someplace where second chances are possible. Maybe it's possible to un-fuck everything. Maybe we can seize what was offered, one more chance to get out alive. Before it's too late.

And if I wish hard enough, just maybe...

Alone on campus during the day, Spitalfield keeps me sane. I've had *Stop Doing Bad Things* on repeat since it came out right at the end of spring quarter. I'm glad I have an iPod Nano, because if I were listening to my CD copy I'd have already worn grooves in it. If I don't listen to this album at least once a day, I feel empty and sad. They're my favorite band for a reason - they keep my head above water.

When the clear summer evenings fall over my apartment way out on the edge of town, the TV is the only company I've got - cartoons and anime on Adult Swim, and the volume feels hushed no matter how loud it is. The silence is the absence of everything, the ache where a bad relationship was less than three months ago, an empty void without friends or family. It's another calzone night; I hardly ever cook anything anymore. Dinner for one, you might as well eat out. Braddock College is home. It's all I've got. Because it doesn't matter how hard you wish on those twinkling stars or how much that purpling midwestern sky squeezes your heart like a cramp. You'll be staring into it alone when the last evening light is gone. You'll make the drive back to your apartment alone, turn off the light in the silence of an empty world, and fall asleep alone.

Alone sucks, but alone is still better than surrounded by enemies. They're closing in, too.

It's 2004, and everything is ending. And in 2004, out here on the edge, I go to bed every night wondering if I'll ever have another chance. One more chance to escape, to be safe, before the monsters close in for the kill. Before all that's left of me are lies written by people who have always wanted me dead.

Two

Wednesday
June 2 2004
Autumn Grove, Ohio

Courtney

"That miserable tenement of a verse is an awfully strange place to stumble on a loyal friend, to say nothing of the shining heroine to whom we owe our lives. But that's where they found her, sitting all alone, waiting to die."
-Alice Thatcher, *Memoirs of an Accidental Arcane*, 1927

June 2004. The beginning of the end.

Every morning is bright and sunny. I'm out the door at seven thirty for the short drive down to campus. The Ataris have been on constant repeat for the last week, but they're *so perfect* for right now. For whatever reason, "Boys of Summer" is so fitting that I feel like I'm in a movie.

Park down in front of Morton Hall, then up the empty walkway that winds up the hill toward the middle of campus. We call that path "Morton Hill" or just "Morton," and it's one of the main arteries that pump students from class to class during the school year. Now it's empty and shady and quiet, and the lonely stillness pierces your heart. But I'm one of the lucky ones; the college gave me a summer job, and I get to stay in Autumn Grove. I don't have to leave campus.

I don't have to go back *there*. Not yet, not without fighting for my life. Stanhope is a hellhole. Stanhope and Kenny are one and the same.

You can get away with just about anything if you're charming enough. It's true. Haven't you ever just wanted to beat the shit out of your kid? I mean, just let loose, go to town, just pound her into the floor? Have you ever watched her get off the bus on the way home from school and noticed she's in a really good mood? Have you ever watched her make her way inside, still laughing about something, happy and totally innocent? How's that make you feel? Does it make your fists itch? Don't you stand there in the doorway, stripped naked down to your boxers, and feel that manly rage coursing through your big trucker arms and think, "Oh, that insolent little pissant. It's gonna feel so good to beat her into a pulp."

Yeah? Do you let yourself do it? Or do you just sit there on your bowed couch, smooching a cigarette as you watch John Wayne kill some Indians? Watch the uppity little rugrat come inside *your* house with her infectious enthusiasm and do nothing to show her you're the king? What the hell's the matter with you? She's in *your* house, eating *your* food. And look how insolent she is, all happy like that. If you just sit there giving her eyes like hot venom and don't do anything, you're seriously missing out. And if the only thing stopping you from turning her into a greasy spot on the carpet is the fear of punishment, don't worry about that. All you have to do is practice your charisma. Trust me, if you've got enough old-fashioned country charm, nobody will *ever* believe her. Everyone will take your side, all the time. Here's what you do.

Let it all out. Let her know how righteously angry you are. Remind her that she owes you for *everything* - letting her stay under your roof, providing food and electricity, letting her breathe your smoggy, cigarette-choked air. And get really good and hot about it. Bellow it out like the strapping six-foot-six man you are. Maybe a bill collector called, or someone was rude to you on the road, or you're annoyed at your wife, or maybe you're just furious that this little eleven-year-old *bitch* is able to laugh and she doesn't make a point of thanking you every day for letting her live under *your* roof. Whatever it is, it's alright, because you're the king in this house, and everything you see is your personal domain, and you can do any goddamn thing you want because you pay for the goddamn shit. Dontchee? So work yourself into a towering animal frenzy. Hit her in the head with your hand, twelve inches long and brown with decades of cigarette tar. Make sure you're wearing all your ugly rings, too. It's so satisfying because it makes the little slut cry - instant tears - and the best part is that she can never prove you did it.

And if you're *really* worked up, then by god you can just go right to town on the little cooz. Just knock her clear into next Tuesday. Use your fists if you want, or if you're feeling really sadistic, take her up and show her your collection of snakeskin belts, make her choose the one you get to lash her with. It's *your* goddamn house. You can do what you goddamn want to, and it ain't nobody's business, goddammit.

But this is the clencher, right here. After it's over, since it's your kingdom, you get to decide that it didn't happen. Isn't that brilliant? If she - or anyone else - ever brings it up, you can say, "Awh! I ain't NEVER beat you!" Poof! Never happened! And since you're king and god, you can tell her teachers that, or god forbid, the children's services if they show up. She don't have no proof, does she? Though it's usually best to tell her you'll kill her if she calls the cops. You have to cover your bases.

Once the sniveling little cunt is back upstairs in the bedroom you provided, you can pick up the phone and call one of your trucking buddies. How about that grizzled, dirty new owner-operator you met last week at the truckstop? Sit there on your smelly couch and call him up and blush and giggle because he's so funny and charming, just like you! And if anyone even *hints* that you're effeminate or that you might be fantasizing about sucking his dick, get loud and angry and tell them, "You're damn right I'm homophobic - I'm scared t'death of 'em!" Let them know how much you hate faggots and queers. You can't have that hot piece of trucker ass thinking you're some kinda fairy.

It's all about charm. If you can smile enough with your servile, fawning little grin where the corners of your mouth turn up and shiver like you've got a bad case of diarrhea, people will never, ever believe you capable of doing the things your daughter accuses you of. Because - *oops!* You didn't, did you? Wink! Your secret's safe here, you tall glass of nicotine, you.

You have the ultimate power. You can inflict scars on her that will keep her awake at night for the rest of her life, and you can do it any goddamn time you feel like it. And if she ever *thinks* about trying to become confident or pretty, or she won't come home from that college and get a REAL job, then you really *can* kill her. Because you're a suave sumbitch, aintchee? You have that good ol' down-to-earth country charm, and if you beat that little slut to death out in the woods somewhere, nobody will ever believe it was you, not in a hundred years. Because you're Kenny, and you're such a nice guy, and you always introduce yourself to strangers by making them laugh. You're just not capable of doing such horrific things. Kenny don't have it in 'eem.

Courtney musta gotten herself into trouble somehow, pissed off the wrong person. Probably had it coming, anyway. Uppity little bitch, with her nose stuck in a book or on a computer screen all the time. I don't know how Kenny stands her acting that way. Such a nice guy, being treated like that. Don't tell nobody I said so, but if he did kill her, I can't say I'd blame 'eem. I'd probably kill her too.

Alden Library is an uninspired eight-story block of Vietnam-era concrete towering over the middle of campus, its study desks and reading rooms overlooking the green parkways and shady streets. I work up on the fifth floor, the college's Archives and Special Collections. When you step off the elevator, the first thing you notice is how quiet it is. The silence is profound, even out at the front desk. Wind your way back through the STAFF ONLY door and into the Archives proper, and the silence rises to a roar. It's almost like you can reach out and touch it all around you, soft and thick. Up there, the silence isn't the absence of noise, or the absence of anything. It's a *something* - a rich substance that fills the air, fills every corner, the space between objects. It cushions every word you speak and it's in every breath you draw. There's people that get fancy job titles and run the place from day to day, but silence is the real master up there.

That silence is where it all starts.

I've been working up there since fall of last year, passed around to whoever needs the help. The Archives is pretty much what it sounds like, a place where you can go back through old records, yearbooks, census data, whatever you can't find in the stacks. We've got hundred-year-old records from the asylum up on the hill, we've got old academic journals written by long-dead professors, valuable memorabilia, even the original charter document that incorporated Braddock as a college back in the 1700s. My bosses tell me scanned digital documents are still way off in the future, so if you want something, you actually have to come up and get it. Some days - if we're busy or on weekends - I might even be the one working out front, helping you find what you're looking for. Call the front desk and you might hear a girly teenage voice answer, *"Braddock Archives and Special Collections, this is Courtney."*

The thought of having to leave is unbearable.

I have a whole cubicle to myself, and it's not one of those little rat holes like in a call center. It's big - as big as an office. I'm only a sophomore and I have my own workspace - a computer, a desk, and a six-foot-long table to spread stuff out on. I stop at my cubicle - no, my *office* - and smile. It's all mine, and I feel so grown up and important and necessary. I've barely started my summer quarter up here and Dan has already given me my own assignment. A big one, an important one. I stand there for a second, chewing my lip in thought, staring at the heavy box sitting on my desk. I have no idea how to start this monster of a project. And something about that dusty old box promises that everything will change when I open it. And I'm right. If I'd had any idea what was about to happen, I'd have at least put a warning label on it.

Yesterday was my first day working for Dan. He's the collections curator here at the Archives, the guy with the desk in the back corner piled high with clutter, like a rampart to keep him safe from the outside. He's not what you usually think of when you picture an introvert; you look at him and you can tell his heyday was in the early 80s. Thick red moustache, big glasses, the slight drawl you can only get by using a lot of fun substances at a formative period in your life. And of course, big into music, which turns out to be what we bond over - the fateful detail that got me my assignment.

"You like music, don't you?" He asked me right away. "Do you know who Rex Williams was?"

I had no idea.

"So you probably don't listen to a lot of big band. That's okay. He was one of the most important swing artists of the twentieth century, famous all over the world - and he went to Braddock." Dan stopped at one of the shelving aisles, all compacted together into a solid wall of boxes and old documents. He pressed a red square button and the shelves started moving. After a minute, an aisle opened in front of us. The smell of dust and old cardboard boxes greeted me as soon as the shelving unit stopped. I followed Dan back into the shadows, most of the way back the aisle, until he stopped. There was dust in the air; I wiggled my nose against the urge to sneeze. All the boxes looked the same to me, but not to Dan; he knew exactly where he was. There were no distinguishing marks here, just rows and rows of boxes and empty spaces. But soon I'd know the spot where we stood as well as I knew my own living room. That was the idea, anyway.

"Where are you from, Courtney?" He scanned the aisle with thick glasses and a squint. "I don't think I ever got to ask."

"Oh, um...Stanhope, originally." I don't lie about where I come from, but I do my best to forget. I'm not proud of that shithole, and it's not proud of me.

"Wow, really?!" he turned his eyes halfway in my direction. "I would've never guessed."

"Really?"

"Yeah. You don't sound like it at all."

I smiled a little in surprise. I mean, I kinda knew that, but it's still nice to hear. "I trained it out of my accent before I got to junior high. What do I sound like?"

"I'd have guessed...Cleveland? New Stafford, maybe?" He reached up, touched the side of a box, reading some numbers written in black marker. "Definitely up north somewhere - way north. You don't have an accent at all."

"Oh!" That was definitely a compliment. "Well, thank you!"

After a minute, he started to get his bearings. "Most of these boxes are sheet music, I think," he said, pulling one down and lifting the lid. It was full of folders crammed with loose yellowed paper, and a cloud of dust drifted up and peppered my nose. I dug a tissue out of my pocket and got it in front of my nose just in time to catch my sneeze.

"Bless you." He replaced the lid and hoisted the box back onto the shelf, preoccupied with finding something in particular.

"Ah," he said. "Here we go." Inside this new box were a few trophies and awards from forgotten events, sitting on top of some books. "I'd like you to go through and catalog the sheet music, but I'd also like you to go through this box. Learn as much as you can about Rex. You'll be writing the biography of his early life."

I blinked, a little stunned. "His biography? Me?"

"The first one ever written," Dan said. "You're the first person to have access to this collection, so you're the first person that will know anything about his time here at Braddock. Think you're up to it?"

Most employers won't even trust you to find your way to the bathroom when you're my age, so I was floored that Dan had given me such an important task.

"I mean, yeah, sure!"

"Great," he said warmly, handing me the box. "Take this one." It was heavy, but it looked light compared to most of them. He grabbed one overflowing with yellowed sheets of paper, easily hoisting it down and following me out of the aisle with it.

"Here you go," Dan plopped the box down on my desk and patted the side. "Good luck, and I'll be right back here if you need me." He disappeared behind the cubicle wall and left me in the silence. And that was that.

And now it's the next morning, my first full day alone on the job. I'm still flabbergasted; I have no idea what I did to deserve a responsibility like this, and I'm still not sure where to start. Dan suggested I start with the yearbooks - look at them, get some context, get to know Rex Williams' class, get a feel for Braddock in the 1920s, go from there.

I'm hesitating in front of that old box, and I'm telling myself that it's because it's a big project and I have no idea what I'm doing, or I'm overwhelmed and floundering without clear instructions, or that I don't want to touch the cardboard too much because it's covered in decades of dust and my hands are already filthy from touching it. But deep down, I'm struggling with the truth, that I'm getting one of those deep sensations that make absolutely no sense, like you're hearing a faint echo in some ancient part of your DNA. You know that feeling you get when you walk into a building that's been there for centuries and you can feel earlier times the place has seen? It's like that. There's something about this box, something odd. Not sinister or anything, but my spine is tingling and I've got goosebumps on the back of my neck.

But Dan was right - I do like music, and this feels like an Afghan Whigs kinda project. There's nothing to be afraid of as long as I have the Afghan Whigs with me. I go ahead and cue up some streaming radio on my computer and play it out loud on the speakers - it won't travel any more than five feet in this all-encompassing silence.

Then I take a deep breath and open that box.

A stack of yearbooks, each one unique, sits inside. "Expedition" is stamped on each one in a different font and style - 1922 is red and 1923 is a brownish color with a lot of Nordic-themed art. But 1925 - right on top of the pile - is the one that stands out the most. 'The Expedition' and '1925' are embossed in silver leaf on a black faux-leather cover. It looks classy. I lay it aside; I'll start in 1922 and follow the class from the beginning.

The first thing you notice about eighty-year-old yearbooks is the smell. It hits you as soon as you crack them open, a heady cloud of mold and moisture and ancient binding. You can smell just a touch of the book's original odor there, changed a bit with long decades. If a book's fragrance is part of its voice, these artifacts welcome you like a staticky, muffled phone call from the 1920s. I've never smelled anything like it, oddly sweet with ripe decay. A lot of people would hate the smell and they'd say I was crazy. But then, a lot of people have jobs in offices and watch reality TV and wear the same tropical fruity floral lotion all the time. Maternity Leave Mango. Heterosexual Hibiscus. Water Cooler Wisteria. Malicious Gossip Grapefruit. Baby Shower Bahama Breeze. Fake Tan Flip-Flop Fruit Sangria.

That lifestyle isn't something I can relate with. I feel like something happened along the way to leech the soul out of humanity, and I've always found so much more joy in the past. Old books, old signs, old clothes - the smell of years draws me like smoke into a chimney.

The pages are a kind of eggshell white, spotted with age and turning yellow around the edges. The pictures are all a little eerie at first, all those stern-faced faculty members with their perfectly round glasses, the severe old matrons in the club pictures. Then there's the students. At first glance, it's hard to imagine them as students - they all look ten years older than me. Not everyone smiles, either. The boys all wear suits, their hair slicked back like old-timey stockbrokers, and the girls wear old lady dresses with short hair done up in finger waves. Every photo you see is black and white, everyone peering at you from the distant shadows of Prohibition. With the rotting book smell wafting up from between the pages, it's hard not to feel like you're in an old haunted library.

But then something shifts. You notice them having fun, making memories with each other. The girls aren't wearing old lady clothes - it's the height of fashion for 1925. And they're rocking it, standing near their old cars or walking down the street with their cloche hats. The clothes are glamorous and sexy, and they've got a vanished sort of class you can't find in the twenty-first century. And most importantly, the more girls you see, the more you see that they *are* your age. Some look old before their time, and some are really, really pretty. They're wistful and happy and looking at them makes you a little sad somehow - the perfect flappers.

So you follow their adventures for a while. It's part of your assignment, right? A group of girls crowded on the back of a Packard roadster, with the caption "Searching for rushee material." A cluster of boys pelting each other with snowballs in front of a big house. Another photo with the campus buried in fresh snow, the wind cutting and howling under a heavy midwinter sky. Some familiar buildings, some you've never seen before. Everyone's smiling at you, having an amazing time, making memories. Those memories are wafting up from the cracks in this book, in the smell of this moldy binding.

It sneaks up on you, long before you're aware of it. A sense of wistfulness. When you reach the end of the book, you hang on to the last few pages, reluctant to say goodbye. But why? They're just really old photos. Your hand lingers on the last page and your eyes drift to the computer screen, Microsoft Excel, and the blinking cursor. Part of the project is data entry; you're the curator now, and you have to make a file listing everything in it. That's not a problem, exactly; it's easy work and it makes the time go by. But maybe that's why you pause. Maybe the thought of any more time going by is what bothers you. Something deep and warm and familiar has a hold of you now; maybe you'll just do one more pass through the book. It's all part of the job, so it's not like you're slacking.

So you go back and visit it again. It feels good, like some exclusive club that's welcomed you, someplace where the doors are always open to you. You're wrapped in a warm embrace, and you're back on familiar ground again. The photos of campus life, friendly smiles, cozy Gothic buildings you've never seen before, it's all so close to your heart. It's such a familiar feeling - warm times long gone and far away, a bittersweet ache in your throat. Sad, longing.

Nostalgia. It's all too familiar. But it can't be yours, can it? Can you really be nostalgic for a time and place that was there decades before you were born? And if it's not *your* nostalgia, then whose is it?

The question loses more meaning with every time-spotted page you turn. Faces that stuck out when you first opened the book have become old friends, and names stick on the end of your brain like peanut butter on your tongue. Memories weigh a little more with each page you turn until you're sodden with them, and turning pages takes longer and longer. Your heart becomes so heavy that you fall back in your chair with it, staring at that book with an ache you didn't have when you woke up this morning.

I'm starting to feel like I've lost something, some treasured piece of myself, and it's just a vague notion until there's an ache behind my eyes and the sting of tears. What could I have lost, and why would some old yearbooks tell me that? Are these just psychic imprints I'm picking up, left on these pages a long time ago? No, the emptiness is inside me. Something is gone, something I didn't realize was missing until now.

We have a simple relationship with pain; when something hurts, the first thing we do is try to get away from it. I think that's healthy. The problem is, there's no escape from what I'm feeling right now, no cure. My heart droops like a bowling ball in my chest and I'm driven by one single need - find my way back to this place, back to my friends. But time sits in front of me like a solid granite boulder. I could hammer that rock with my fists for the rest of my life without leaving a mark on it. Every blow, every scream, every tear I shed, all gone without a trace. And there it would sit, indifferent to me, never knowing I was there.

This bittersweet longing, this desperate need, has become my entire world. Nothing else exists. The people I miss are all here, frozen in time, and the closest I can get to them is lingering in the pages of this yearbook like a ghost in a window. If only I could go back...

But it's 2004, and I'm looking at these pages at my desk, under the floodlights at work. If there's a way to get back to my friends, my treasured memories, then the universe is as silent as the gravestones marking the final resting places of everyone in this book.

I want to cry, just bawl my eyes out right here, but I can't.

I'm not sure how long I'm wandering through that yearbook before I spot one face that snaps me back into myself.

Her eyes. That's the first thing to pierce the veil and grab a hold of me. Her eyes.

It's not her normal yearbook portrait. The first time I see her, it's a more spontaneous photo. The photographer caught her in the middle of campus, among trees and bushes and grass. The way her body is positioned, it's like she was going somewhere and agreed to stop long enough to get her picture taken. Her face is turned a little bit down, eyes fixed on the camera from under the brim of one of those bell-shaped cloche hats. She's wearing half a smile, a kind of secretive grin like the photographer caught her unaware. There's something so natural about her, something so vulnerable and open in her huge soft eyes. Whoever took that picture, she trusted them with her life. It's only when I feel the tightness in my chest that I realize I've been holding my breath, staring at this girl - Mary Carlyle, New Stafford, Ohio, Class of 1925.

Mary Carlyle.

A deep shiver goes through me, all the way to the core. The first girl I ever had a crush on. The first girl that reciprocated my feelings. My first kiss.

The girl that transformed everything forever.

It's her.

Three

Courtney

"I've heard people say that what doesn't kill you makes you stronger. That's a bill of goods, at least where Displaced are concerned. You see, trauma makes a person weaker, not stronger, and if she hadn't had to endure those soul-breaking years in Exile...we wouldn't have to consider these drastic measures.

Oh, how I wish we could have known. I'd have simply tied that silly girl to a chair for a day, and she'd have thanked me for it. We'd all be thanking me for it right now."
-Nettie Talbott, personal memo to Hazel Morrison,
Autumn 1921

Mary.

She's always been there, in the back of my mind. The girl I fell in love with. The girl that made everything so beautiful it hurt.

Mary's world was one of breathtaking beauty and innocence. I say "world" because I really think it *was* a different world. The mornings sparkled and the evenings glowed. The air was always just a little chilly and the people always warm. They didn't have TV or stereos or video games or anything, but they did have a really old Victrola phonograph, the kind in a polished wood cabinet with the big horn on top. Mary's dad drove a really old Ford Model T, but it was polished up and looked brand new. All the pictures on their walls were black and white photos. Mary and Nettie dressed in really old jumper dresses and ankle boots. I used to call them my "Titanic Girls" because they looked like the girls in the old pictures from the *Titanic*. I have never felt more at home in my life than I did when I was there with them, or felt the same kind of warm euphoria filling my chest. Every moment was pure bliss, and I never, ever wanted to leave.

Somehow Mary's mom was the opposite of what I had at home - she was lovely, kind, inclusive. Marian *wanted* me there, wanted me to be a part of Mary and Nettie's little gang as much as the girls themselves. She had nicknames for us when we were all together - Mary was Sugar, Nettie was Spice, and I was Everything Nice. I wanted to fly into her arms and cry and never let go.

I don't talk about this very often, as you can imagine. I've only just started to work up the courage to tell my friend Tiffany about it. How would you even bring up something like that? How do you explain it? For my part, I guess it just *was*. Sometimes, on a certain kind of day, I just knew I could go to Mary's house. I would go outside, wander out of my yard and back into the woods, and before I knew it, I was in the yard of Mary's three-story Victorian house with its bay windows and wrap-around porch. I would see the Model Ts rattling down the street and the nice people would honk their quack horns at me as they passed. And Mary and Nettie would see me and get excited and run up and hug me, and I would play with them until dusk. And if it was a weekend, I got to spend all day with them. Like the night with the fair, the night everything changed.

Mary gave me something that afternoon, and it meant the world to me. I kept it close to me forever, kept it hidden from my parents...what was that...?

Two red ribbons! Like the kind you put in your hair. I've still got them; they're the most sentimental things I have. Mary's mom put my hair up in pigtails and tied them with those ribbons. She made me wear one of Mary's dresses and I thought I'd die from euphoria - they kept telling me I looked like a princess. I *felt* like a princess! Then, with the three of us looking our prettiest, they took us to the fair. It was the day they found out who I really was, where I'd really come from. It was the first time I ever heard anyone call me "Displaced." The day when Mary's mom told me she wanted me to stay with them, that she would keep me safe no matter what. The evening when Mary and I had our first kiss. When I almost moved to 1915 forever...

I had a monster crush on Mary. She had such soft hands, and her smile was so sweet it gave my heart cavities. I thought about her every moment for months and months. I always wondered where she was, if I'd ever be able to see her again. A year later, I realized I was in love with her, that I'd been in love the whole time.

And I know it was love, because when you love someone you're willing to sacrifice yourself for them. Which is exactly what I did.

Mary Carlyle, New Stafford, Ohio.

A chill goes up my spine when I read the name again, etched in an outdated font. Time stops; it's just me and her and the smell of rotting books. Her round face, her big soft eyes, her perfect nose, her soft little lips.

Did I *know* they lived in New Stafford, two hundred miles from home? Sure. Did they know I lived in Stanhope, at the other end of the state? Yeah. But we didn't waste a lot of time worrying about it. We were together and that was all that mattered. I never really gave it much thought; who needs to look at a map to make sure they were really with their friends the night before? Still, every time I looked at a map of Ohio, my eyes always sought out New Stafford...

I need to go somewhere and think, puzzle some things out. Voices up front; one of the faculty leaving her desk and talking to someone up in the office. I look up at the clock on the wall above my cubicle; 11:04. Lunchtime. I get up, grab my purse, push my chair in, and make my way out front. The feeling in my chest is growing into a pleasant warmth, and I'm almost on the elevator by the time I realize what it is.

Excitement, anticipation.

What could I be excited about? I have no idea, but I've got a feeling in me, *around* me, like I'm on the fast road to a new life, and it makes no sense.

But then again, neither did moving to 1915.

Interlude

"For the thirst to possess your love
Is worth my blood a hundred times."
-Rumi, 13th c.

"You know that old saying 'love moves heaven and earth'? Anyone who thinks it's just a figure of speech has never met Mary Carlyle."
-Alice Thatcher, *Memoirs of an Accidental Arcane*, 1927

It wasn't until the moment Courtney was gone that I realized I loved her, that my affection wasn't just the whims of childhood puppy love but some deep, resonant thing in my chest, hot like flowing blood. When she was gone, I slumped to the floor and I cried and cried, just cried to beat the band. I cried the rest of that day until the moment I finally collapsed from exhaustion late that night, then started up again the next morning as soon as I remembered what had happened. It was days before I could think of eating anything, and days more before I could carry on a conversation.

Her sweet face, her warm smile, her delicate scent when you get close to her. Sure, we were going together, but I think it must be rare to love someone at that age as deeply as I loved Courtney, to want to be with her every waking moment, for every day to be a bright new adventure whenever she was with me. She has that effect on a person, I suppose. I loved her then and I love her still. You must understand that I haven't stopped yearning for her a single minute since that chilly fall day in 1915, when a delicious life was rolling out before us like brand new carpet, fresh as an ice-crusted mint julep in the summer.

New emotions, new feelings. We began to grow up, you see, and I began to yearn for Courtney in whole new ways. Exhilarating ways that left me thrilled every moment, that made me see her differently, that left her lingering on my mind late into the night the same way the taste of candy lingers on your tongue.

I hadn't begun to lust for her - yet - but I *had* begun to *need* her. Thoughts of holding hands on the playground slowly became thoughts of stolen moments alone, warm slow kisses; thoughts of passed notes became thoughts of confessed love and promise rings. The fall of 1915 became sweeter than anything I'd ever tasted, and every moment rang with the delicious thrill of all that was possible now that she was with us. All the things that might be. All the things that certainly *would* be.

On late evenings, in the privacy of my own thoughts, I began to think ahead. I decided that I should like to wrap her around my finger - just as she'd already wrapped me around hers - and that I should have her always. Courtney was going to be mine and mine alone. And my long childhood dream of a white wedding? I might just decide that Courtney would be the one I wanted for it. She would have a say, of course - but I should have the *final* say. She was agreeable by nature - I knew she'd be a sport about it.

Oh, how sweet life was about to become.

Then Courtney had to go and do the thing she does best - she had to be heroic. And her heroism stole her from me.

It made it all the worse that when she fell on her sword, she did it for me alone.

Her visit was the first time I ever heard the word "Displaced". Nettie's Aunt Elizabeth is the real versologist, but her mom knew enough to bring over a versocular, look at Courtney, ask her a few questions. At first, Nettie and I just thought Courtney might have been some kind of time traveler; that alone would have been perfectly screwy. But I overheard the conversation downstairs. Nettie's mom said, "The poor dear is Displaced, sure enough. And it's coming off her in clouds - why, if I showed these readings to a versologist, they'd be down here writing a book about her before supper."

"What should we do?" My mom asked.

"Well, we mustn't let her go back there. Her energy signature matches our universe. She belongs here; she should have been here the whole time, but someone over there stole her away. And that's consistent with what she told you about her parents, about how they're treating her."

"I think the poor child might be in danger," my mom said.

Nettie's mom said, "As do I."

So it was agreed that Courtney should stay with us. We would help her build a new life in 1915, she would go to school with Nettie and me, and she would be safe. I wasn't entirely sure what Displaced meant at the time, but I always knew she belonged here, with us. Her being over there with those horrid people was a mistake that never should have happened, you see. Well, perhaps *atrocity* might be a better word. She'd been cursed to live in a world that was not her own, a world that would grow more hostile with each passing year until one day it would kill her. She was in even more danger than I knew at the time.

If she'd known what kind of danger she was in, would she have still thrown herself back into the lion's mouth to keep that brute away? Something tells me she would have. Even then, Courtney was ready to sacrifice herself for me at the drop of a hat, the darling little fool. I found myself loving her so much more deeply for it, so deeply that I ached day and night. Oh, how it hurt, and for so very long.

Once I could think properly, I knew the only thing to do was to find some way to see her, find out if she was all right. I needed to know, one way or another, or I should go mad.

That's when I discovered divination.

When it comes to divination, the rules don't seem to apply to me. Aunt Lizzy was astonished to see the things I could do, and said I was a natural prodigy. Everything that's supposed to be impossible, I could do, right from the start. Extraversal divination is supposed to be almost impossible unless your own verse is in direct conjunction with the one you're trying to reach. Not for me, though. I reached out across immeasurable nothingness to find Courtney, and I found her.

My heart broke to see how savagely she was being treated, but at least she was alive. And as long as she was alive, I still had time to devise some way to bring her back.

To bring her home.

Four

Courtney

"Displaced persons sometimes find themselves phasing between realities, a process entirely beyond their control. Before the 17th century, superstitious folk attributed this to witchcraft or demonic intervention, but the science of versology has discovered a very simple mechanism behind this strange phenomenon: that of resonance caliber. Individuals with especially high resonance caliber are liable to distort and weaken versal barriers, especially when those barriers are acted upon by outside versal forces such as conjunctions and various transits. The mechanism is not unlike a magnet with a magnetic field; some magnets are stronger than others and thus exert a more powerful influence on their environment.

However, this is a difficult phenomenon to observe in nature, as most versal barriers are impervious to a resonance caliber of six or less, and persons with a resonance caliber above six are exceedingly rare. So rare, in fact, that scholars can definitively credit perhaps five or six individuals having such abilities since the time of the Norman Conquest."

-Professor Vivian Halloway, *Collected Lectures on Versology and Applied Versal Theory*, 1889

11:33 a.m.

I step out of the cool library into the sun-scorched oven of early June. I squint hard, trying to get my bearings in this bright noonscape, and stumble off down the brick pathways, through the shade, toward the street.

We were eight, playing together, having so much fun. Little simple stuff: hide-and-seek, tag, sitting around in the fall and telling ghost stories. Mary's mom treated me like she'd known me since I was a baby. *My* mom responded to stories about Mary with heated alarm.

I came in one evening about six, cheerful as could be. That was my first mistake, right there - when I was completely happy and relaxed, when my guard was down, *that's* when my parents attacked.

There was a TV dinner sitting on the counter next to a half-finished can of Budweiser sweating into a beer cozy. A cigarette wafted tan smoke into the air.

"Where the hell have you been?!" Her eyes were a little wild. "I've been callin' you for a half hour."

I blinked at her. "I didn't hear you yelling."

"Yeah, right," she dismissed me. "That's bullsheeit. You just didn't wanna come home."

"I really didn't, I swear!" I really *hadn't* heard her yelling. I hadn't heard anything except for whatever had been going on with Mary and Nettie.

"Don't lie to me." Her words oozed, slow and noxious, through gritted teeth. "You were grinnin'. You were out there ignorin' me and you were laughin' about it."

"No!"

"That's alright," she spat. "Wait'll your dad hears about this. *Your ass is grass.*" She grit her teeth again for the last sentence.

She was a very masculine redneck named Nadine. And that was even *before* she joined the Marines to "prove herself" to her psycho parents. Maybe she also wanted to get away, but

I don't know why she bothered since she was gonna be a big country music star - or so she always told me, anyway - and she'd be playing in Nashville if *I* hadn't decided to ruin everything by getting born. You could tell she was a star in the making, too, because of those really dark songs she wrote about light bulbs shooting knives into her brain. Serious Grand Ole Opry material. She even had a whole routine she did - write and practice some oppressive tune that sounded like a tragic medieval ballad from Russia, drink a tall can of Bud, and hurl pots and pans at the wall for a half hour at a time. She'd have fit right in with Reba and Dolly.

"Why would you do that to me?" I demanded. "Why do you like seeing me get beaten?"

She went on like I hadn't spoken, reaching for her beer can. "That's just fine. He's in Memphis. He'll be home by tomorrow night. Just wait and see what happens."

My elated joy was souring quickly into despair. Happiness never lasted long on Old Toll Road.

Nadine had this shit-brown hair that was *made* for the '80s, the way it naturally sat tall on her head, the way it curled up and out like a fountain shooting muddy water into the air. She'd always grit her teeth and say "I need a *purrrrm*," jabbing a finger at whoever she was talking to, one foot way ahead of the other in this really aggressive stance. She never needed a *purrrrm*; her hair was already stacked and ready for a Mötley Crüe video because it grew in that way. The one thing she always needed more than a *purrrrm* were pills, and a trip to buy, beg, or barter them would take us out of the trailer, day or night. And later on in life, when I started needing ibuprofen, I learned that I couldn't just go looking for it in the cabinet. I'd pick up a bottle that I thought was ibuprofen and she'd swoop in out of nowhere and seize it out of my hands. *"Whaddaya lookin for?!"*

She was a pharmacist without a pharmacy, and she was better at it than she was at anything else. Her favorite book was the navy blue PDR (Physicians' Desk Reference) she kept by her bedside, and she would read it like a novel. Maybe she ate pills like candy because she'd been in the Marines at one point and they screwed the jar on really tight. The first eight years of my life were like one long boot camp, and the reason I know that is because she'd rent war movies sometimes with drill sergeants and it was just like being at home. Then again, she could have also been intersex, and instead of going inward and pondering a solution to her discomfort, she'd just started raging when she was a toddler and kept raging. I was told she tried to drown me in the bathtub when I was two. I have no idea if she was on pills that night or if she was dead sober. Honestly, neither would surprise me.

"Dinner's cold." She threw the tin TV dinner onto the table; it landed with a *smack*. A cloud of steam rose from the long planks of cheap Salisbury steak, from the sludgy brown gravy. It looked hot enough to me. "I hope you're satisfied. Who were you out there with, anyway?"

I hope you're satisfied. One of her favorites; she kept that one on repeat. She had a very strong chin.

"Mary and Nettie."

She drew a deep drag off her cigarette, a long gray ash growing off the end. She flicked it into an ashtray. "Who?"

I repeated myself.

"Who's that?"

"I dunno. Some girls I met. We're friends. We play together sometimes."

"Where?" she demanded. "You went to one of these girls' houses?"

"Yeah."

She kissed another, shorter drag off her cigarette and crushed it in the ashtray. She daintily blew smoke into the kitchen, and I got really creeped out at how such a macho man could randomly switch on these little feminine gestures. "I don't know these people."

I shook my head and shrugged a little, not knowing what to say.

"I don't want you hangin' out with people I don't know, you hear me?"

My face collapsed in a look of helpless protest. Alcoholics are pathological control freaks, but I wouldn't learn that until college.

"I don't know those people, and that's it. You stay around the house from now on. And your dad's still gonna hear about this. Now eat your goddamn supper."

And he did, the next time he called home from the road. When he stormed in the door three days later, a massive row of crooked chipped teeth swallowing his bottom lip, I'd forgotten what crime I'd committed to offend Nadine so much. All I saw was the Behemoth of Old Toll Road, with the teeth of a horse and the body of a sasquatch, bearing down on me, fists clenched.

He beat me, and beat me, and beat me. Whenever he came in from the road, I could always rely on either fists or snakeskin belt.

"You like that?! Huh?! *HUH?!!*"

Nadine watched from the kitchen, her face flat and hard. Deep in her stony eyes, a faint glimmer of satisfaction.

I find myself walking back down Court Street with a paper bag and a cold drink in my hand. I have some vague recollection of having gone in somewhere, ordered a salad, and left, but I don't think I was there to witness that firsthand. I must have been watching reruns of childhood when that happened.

So now I'm back in the blinding summer sun, headed for the middle of campus. It's time to dispel this gloom. Out comes the iPod, on goes Spitalfield. I need *Texa$ with a Dollar Sign* today.

A deep breath, and I shiver - the opening chords hit hard and drive away the bad vibes.

The crosswalk is the busiest place in town any time of the year, and even if Braddock has a fraction of the people in the summer, it's still bustling. As I'm coming up, I spot a girl approaching from my left. She's ghostly pale like me, with auburn hair cut in a short bob around her soft jawline. The most striking thing about her is her narrow, almond-shaped eyes. I've always thought chicks with eyes like that are really cute. They catch mine as I approach, and there's a kind of click; two people in a crowd with matching energy. She greets me with a narrow, witty smile. I return hers in my usual unintentional way, soft and genuine and a little bit sad without ever meaning to seem that way. And we stand there for a minute, waiting for the traffic to clear.

"Say, is it gonna be dry like this all week?" she asks.

"Um…" I wish I had a better answer ready. "I think so? I haven't really checked the weather."

"Why, I sure hope it is." She stares back across the street at the shade of College Green. "Anything I hate is rain in the summer."

Roll my eyes in agreement. "Ugh, totally."

I sneak a look at her. She's wearing a brown bell-shaped hat, the kind that were popular in the 1920s. She's wearing a 20s style dress, too: green, knee-length, with a round-cut neckline and loose cap sleeves. She's even wearing old-fashioned brown stockings and brown heels. It catches my eye and I stare for a second or two; it's a hot day for stockings, especially the old-fashioned silk kind like that. And her shoes are *really* retro, like old church grandma shoes. She must shop at that vintage thrift store all the way up at the far end of Court Street; it's the only place around here where you could get clothes like that unless she goes thrifting in Columbus.

She's standing here next to me, watching the street, not self-conscious at all. Like she wears stuff like that every day without even thinking about it.

Then she looks at *me*, glances away, looks at me again a little longer. Her eyes linger on my top and on my legs, and she looks away again, blushing. I've always been a little bit empathic and I can feel curiosity in her glance. And...*attraction?*

Nah, that can't be right - girls are never into me. Maybe I look too preppy, I don't know. I'm a D&D nerd, raised on video games from the age of five, but because I wear an Abercrombie hoodie or Hollister shorts or flat iron my hair, people assign me a whole package of expectations - *Courtney is a bitch, Courtney's stuck-up, Courtney's a backstabbing gossip, Courtney's rich. Courtney is heterosexual...?* Look, I'll be honest with you, I'm gonna have a hard time living up to all of that. Maybe not the bitch thing - because yeah, I'm probably a bitch - but the rest of it? Sorry, no can do.

The traffic finally stops from the other direction. I give her one last smile - which she returns warmly - and step onto the street. A few quick steps take me to the other sidewalk. I stop and look at my slender Fossil watch, making a pretense to turn in her direction again for one last look. She's awfully cute, and I love her chic vintage style. I wonder if she'd think I was creepy if-

There's nobody there. I glance around to see if she took off in another direction. Nothing. There are plenty of people around, walking dogs, wearing flip-flops, riding bikes. But no girls with vintage clothes.

She's gone. It's like she was never there.

But she totally *was* there! I talked to her!

Unless I'm finally losing it?

I rub an eye with the heel of my hand, not really caring that I just stamped dry mascara on my skin. Maybe I need to get out more. Maybe I need friends. I stand on the busy sidewalk for a moment, completely disoriented, before remembering that I was looking for a place to sit down and eat my salad. But even as I make my way onto College Green and up toward the Civil War statue, looking for a place to sit, I can't get that girl out of my head. Not just because she was cute. Something about her, that weird click when we saw each other.

Eh, maybe I'll see her again. I shove a straw through the lid of my drink. Nobody just vanishes.

I *wish* you could just disappear.

Though I guess if you *wanted* to disappear, this would be the place to do it. Outside the city limits, the nights are dark and old, and people who vanish are never seen again.

Blackstead Forest

It's not hard to go missing in Autumn Grove. People have been vanishing every year since the town was founded. Go uptown to the courthouse and you'll find missing persons cases that have been open since 1851. If you want to go beyond that, you'll have to come up to the Braddock College Archives, where I work. That's where you go from the block print forms of the Civil War era and wade into crumbling pages written entirely by hand with colonial cursive. When you get to the 1700s, more and more words have weird spelling and the writing is peppered with long '*s*'s that make it harder to read. The language changes a bit, gets fancier and more eccentric at the same time. You start getting the eerie feeling you only get with historical research - the feeling that you're not reading about the past anymore. You're *in* it. The town clerks that wrote these pages are long dead. And they weren't just funny-looking people in a history book.

They're right in front of you. Looking at you.

And yet, the strangest thing about all of it is that they wrote these records for the local courts, lived out their lives, and then died, and the people they were writing about never turned back up. The missing people - everyone *they* ever knew died a long, long time ago, but the people were still missing and they're still missing today. I mean sure, they're dead - they've gotta be after more than two hundred years - but nobody ever found out what happened to them. There's just an empty space on the page. The earliest names listed here go all the way back to 1763, at the end of the French and Indian War, when Autumn Grove was founded. That means these cases are older than the United States and they're still open. Still unsolved.

Before the first white colonists, the Shawnee, Delaware, and Erie all avoided the area. Native scouts and traders urged the first settlers to do the same. The Shawnee claimed that it was the hunting ground of the "Wandering Pilgrim" and they wouldn't venture anywhere close. Before that, when the Erie were here, they refused to even talk about it.

Some people think there were earlier attempts at settlement before Autumn Grove was established. If there were, there's no hard proof. Did people cross the Alleghenies, come down into the Traeburn valley, and disappear? Could whole groups of settlers go missing? A whole village? Just *poof*, without a trace? Who knows.

The only other thing we have - other than court records - is a letter written the year after Autumn Grove was founded. It's from some guy named Israel Wallingford, sent to a relative in Philadelphia. This Wallingford guy says that *"this new settlement"* in the Traeburn valley *"progrefses nicely"* but *"we knowe not what befell thofe earlier inhabitants."*

There's an old folktale in Autumn Grove about the Blackstead Forest, where these settlements are supposed to have been. This oral tradition is so old, so long forgotten, that I've never seen it mentioned on any of the "Haunted Autumn Grove" websites. But rarely, you'll find someone mention it in writing.

Before the end of that letter, the author says, *"there was some talk in the taproom on the evening of Wednefday laft that the Tricorne Man still haunts this place. The subject was quickly clofed & none have dared speake of it since."*

People still go missing on occasion, and usually it's out in the Blackstead. The usual leaflets go up around campus, with Have You Seen Me? in bold black letters. The local cops just shrug and file a missing persons report. Volunteers search their last known locations for about a week. Nobody ever finds anything, and eventually the case gets buried. The Blackstead Forest is a huge state wilderness that stretches across five counties, from the outskirts of town all the way east to the Ohio River. With an area that big, you have to expect a missing persons case every now and then; it happens in every state and national park in the country. But here's the thing - when someone goes missing in the Adirondacks or Yellowstone or somewhere, someone will eventually find a body, or the person will wander out, half-starved but alive.

That doesn't happen here. Nobody ever comes stumbling out of the woods with stories about kidnapping or surviving on wild berries. Hikers don't discover badly-decomposed remains. Nobody ever finds anything - no clues or confessions or witnesses or murder weapons. Nothing at all. It's like the person just evaporates into thin air.

Remember how I said that Autumn Grove was built as a kind of outpost on the edge of the wilderness? It was, and it still is today. Outside the city limits, modernity starts to lose its hold. Pretty soon you start to feel like maybe things haven't changed all that much since the British were here.

Honestly, the Blackstead isn't some huge deathtrap, even if it's got that reputation; most of it is a fairly typical state park. There's a paved bike trail that goes through the western edge of the woods, and plenty of people use it every day; serious cyclists ride it all the way north to Mecklenburg and beyond. Hikers use the trails and have lunch among the big rocks; this is where the Appalachian foothills start. It's quiet, it's beautiful, and the air is clean. If you go out there and don't know what you're looking for, you're probably gonna miss it. That's because the really troubled places are all in one wide patch called the Blackstead Triangle.

The triangle starts at the edge of the state park ten minutes out of town, goes fifteen miles east to the village of Grevett's Mill, and all the way north to Haydenville in Traeburn County. The abandoned town of Grevett's Crossing sits at the far eastern edge of the triangle, and if anyone claims they've seen an abandoned town, it's probably that one. Nobody knows much about anything else in the Triangle. All anyone knows is that the monolith is in there, along with some terrible place called The Crossroads that nobody knows anything about.

As you can imagine, the Triangle is what attracts most people; every undergrad at Braddock and half the urban explorers in Ohio are self-proclaimed authorities on it. Everyone knows someone whose roommate's best friend's classmate's ex ventured into the woods and brought back a souvenir from Grevett's Crossing - a brick, a piece of wood, a pair of tongs from a forge. Everyone's so brave; nobody is afraid to leave the trails, pass into the forest, and begin their own adventure - even at night. But it's a whole different story when you actually get out there.

Cops are usually everyone's first concern, which makes sense. Braddock County sheriffs are bored, over-funded, and they have a special hatred for college students. Signs are posted at the park entrance and in the parking lots, written in huge official letters like the booming voice of a moustached cop: PARK CLOSES AT SUNSET. TRESPASSERS WILL BE PROSECUTED. They love to catch people and verbally abuse them forever, lecturing them on all the people that have gone missing in the woods, calling in fifteen backup cars and police dogs to search you for drugs - whatever they feel like. Officially, they have jurisdiction over the park, all the way to the county line. But in the real world, their jurisdiction ends at the treeline. I've never heard of anyone being arrested on the trails at night - not once. That's because the cops are no less scared of the forest than anyone else, and those trails are terrifying after dark. *Leaving* the trails is unthinkable.

Since a lot of the park's disappearances are officially thought to be suicides, the park put up signs back in the 70s begging people not to kill themselves, that life is worth living, call this number. I guess some people think that the Blackstead is like a mini-version of that suicide forest in Japan, which is a strange conclusion to reach about a forest where no bodies are ever found. Still, it's a little unsettling when the first thing you see on the trail is a sign begging you not to kill yourself.

By the time you step onto the trail, you've probably noticed that something is really off. There's a feeling in the air, in the night itself, that prickles your skin like needles all over. An unwelcome feeling, a sense of hostility, like a cruel ancient old man watching you with an icy glare from deep in the trees. You're about to cross over onto his property, and he's waiting.

The hostility rolls across you like nausea, growing heavier every minute you stand there looking up at the endless black woods blocking out the moonlight. You've stumbled across something old beyond reckoning, and you're nothing more than a blink in its lifespan. It hammers you with a wordless message: *You don't have any business being here. You're not welcome. Turn around and leave. Now.*

Some people press on - frat boys scared of looking weak, or spiky-haired reality tv hosts with night-vision camera crews. They reach the top of the first rise and pause. They peer down the trail as it meanders into the distance, grazed by the skeletal shadows of tree branches. And they look off to the east, into the darkness. On a clear day, you can almost see what's left of the old Grevett's Mill Road leading away from this saddle in the trail; at night, it's just a menacing contour in the ground, a long snake of leaves leading away into the dark.

This is where everyone's courage runs out. Loud machismo types stop at this spot, an uneasy smile on their faces, shift their feet and cross their arms. Or maybe they stare into the dark, slumping around in little circles like an adolescent cheetah trying to work itself into attacking a porcupine. They have two choices. They can grin and say, "ah, fuck this, I'm not goin in there," and they can turn around and walk back down the trail with the uneasy laughter of their friends rising around them. When they reach the parking lot, they'll be shoving each other and joking, their laughter just a little shrill, and maybe they don't fully notice how fast they're walking as they make their way back to the car.

Or they can tense up and step off into the woods. A few cautious steps will take them down a slope as they look for the barely-visible wire fence fifty feet from the trail, the fence that separates the safety of well-used paths from the uncharted interior of the forest. Most people don't make it to that flimsy little fence since hardly anyone mentions it in their stories. But it's an important barrier, because they're always on the near side of it when they come running back. They never walk, never make remarks. They *sprint*, full-tilt, back onto the path and down the hill, and they don't stop until they reach their cars, where they're begging their friends to hurry the hell up and open the door so they can get the fuck out of there. They don't smile or make jokes. Whatever sent them scampering out of the woods, they don't want to talk about it. Maybe they turn on music or something on the way back, but they're not talking. Not for a long time. Not till they're safely back in town.

If they step off the trail and don't come running back in a minute or two, nobody will ever see them again.

Five

Courtney

"Our society has become a cult of skepticism, promising that it is safer to ignore our higher senses than to risk being seen as deranged. Thus we obtain conformity at the cost of perception, wisdom, and insight, to say nothing of those deeper intuitions that routinely save our lives.

As I have said many times, I say again to you now: there is no such thing as 'I just imagined it.' In some few cases, these signals might be the product of lunacy. However, for most people, such insight is genuine. Our senses were not developed over countless eons for the purpose of self-deception. Newtonian physics is no longer an adequate model for understanding the natural world, and must therefore be discarded, or we shall stunt our growth, inhibit inquiry, and halt progress indefinitely while we wait for society to give us permission to follow more advanced insights."
-Professor Emeritus Elizabeth Talbott, former Professor of Versology, Braddock College
Commencement address to the Class of 1915

12:02 p.m.

My head is a whirlpool when I get back to work. I wake up my computer, then wheel my chair back over and open the yearbook.

The damp smell of rotting pages welcomes me and I'm back in familiar settings, back in the old book where things make sense. I've barely gotten started on this project and I'm already so invested. It's not just Mary and Nettie; the faces are *all* a little familiar. Braddock in 1921 means more to me than my own hometown, even more than present-day Autumn Grove. It feels like a part of me, and I have no explanation for it. Somehow, it's *my* friends in that yearbook. The memories wafting up from those mildewed pages are *my* memories. The people in those pages, I'm part of their games, their classes, their weekend adventures.

I can't stop looking at Mary's sparkling eyes. I miss her so bad.

The weird part is that there aren't that many pictures of Mary in this yearbook, and the pictures in here are blurred by distance or motion. It's really odd the way she stands out in a sea of faces, how she always manages to hone in and look at me. I'm near the back of the book, turning pages, when she pops back up. It's just her in this picture, standing on a path on College Green. It's fall, and there's leaves everywhere; even through the blurry black-and-white of the picture, you can still make out the long golden light of an autumn afternoon. She's wearing a bell-shaped cloche hat, a dress that goes just past her knees, heels. The way she's facing the camera, the openness of her face, it's obvious that she trusts the photographer. Her smile is thick with joy, her eyes wide and vulnerable. She's staring right at me. It's only a picture, but I'm getting a little self-conscious as I sit here. I can't stop staring at her.

My whole right leg is numb and tingly, so maybe a stretch would do me good. I honestly have no idea how long I've been sitting on it. Now that I'm thinking about it, I don't know how long I've been sitting here, period. I stand up and stretch. I can't feel my leg; I rest my weight on it and it buckles under me and I crash into my computer. I catch myself with both arms, and a cloud of darkness passes through my eyes. I stood too fast. Close my eyes, take a few breaths, don't fall over.

Once my vision clears, I look up at the clock - 4:45. Fifteen minutes until I leave for the day.

Seriously? Wasn't it just lunch? How...?

I've got a cheap ink pen woven through my restless fingers. My notepad is covered in ugly swarms of dark blue scribbles. Two mouldering books lay open in front of me, tabbed with a growing mess of pink Post-Its I've used to mark the pages. A rough index system is forming on pages of brusque notes, circled with arrows and tiny edits. I vaguely remember looking at a lot of group photos and student life pictures with a magnifying glass; at least the past four hours haven't been a *complete* blank. I leaf through the notes and see there's not much here about Rex Williams - just Mary and Nettie and a couple of other girls I've made references to.

Up toward the front, a chair scoots out, then back in again about a minute later. Footsteps walk away, out the door, headed up front toward the lobby. I look up at the clock again; it's almost time to go home for the day. Usually I'm pretty Jenny-on-the-spot with knowing what time it is. I never get so lost that I'm not watching the clock, waiting to leave. But today, time has been playing games with me, running circles around me, doing what it wants. I need to get out of this office, get some sun. I shake the cobwebs out of my head, grab my jacket and purse. I just need to shut down my computer and I'm free to go.

Back outside, then down Morton like a water slide, no stops. Then down to the car, then home. No excuse to loiter on campus in the hazy late afternoon, no real way to avoid going back to my tomb of an apartment. I wish I had a reason to linger here in town for a while, someone to hang out with. The shitty thing about these yearbooks is that leaving work for the day feels like stepping out of a cozy hot tub into a bitterly cold night. I slouch in my chair, shooting an accusing look at that dusty old book. Inside is my welcoming new world, cozy memories of those golden years I spent with my dearest friends.

On an impulse, I scoot my chair over and grab the book. I'll take it home tonight. Part of me reminds myself that it's only a book; the other half of me replies that it's one book more than being alone. It's not like I can just call Tiffany and see if she wants to hang out. She's back home in Cleveland and I'm down here in Autumn Grove, by myself. Alone with the yearbooks and the ghosts and the memories of the 1920s.

Tiffany Cheng is a preppy Asian girl with big-city emotional detachment and friends on the lacrosse team. We lived in the same hall freshman year, two doors apart. We were the first girls to move into our hallway, so naturally we were the first people either of us met. Tiffany's mom loved me from the start (unlike most people), and when she found out my fridge was broken she insisted that I keep some of my cold drinks and stuff in Tiffany's fridge until I got a new one. We never really stopped sharing our fridges and we'd keep stuff in whatever room we'd been in last, or wherever we planned on hanging out.

We've got the weirdest friendship, and it's because Tiffany's so cool and detached all the time. At first I thought she was gonna be too cool to even associate with me; there was no warmth in her voice when she'd ask, "hey, I was gonna grab some dinner or whatever, you wanna come?" And she's one of those chicks that's effortlessly gorgeous all the time, one of those chicks that's always got new clothes every few months or so - really nice, expensive stuff, too. So because she looked intimidating and because she never really acted warm, I was never sure if she liked me, even though deep inside I really wanted her to. She was everything I wanted to be.

But every time I thought she didn't like me she'd come around, invite me to dinner, invite me uptown to hang out. Before long, she started saying, "Hey Courtney, do you like this sweater? Here, try it on. I have to clean out my closet or I'm gonna die. Yeah, that looks way cuter on you than it did me. It's yours. Yeah, no, seriously - please take it or I'm not gonna have room for new stuff." And as the weeks went by and fall turned into winter, we spent more late evenings together, watching Adult Swim or movies or painting nails, or just hanging out reading beauty mags with music playing. Oh, and of course, Playstation. She loves *Tekken*, and she turns psycho when she plays.

I don't know if I've ever heard her refer to me as her friend, but she was so excited when she found out I read tarot - and read it really well. She started coming to me for readings at least once a week, and within about a month of moving into the dorm those readings became late-evening confidences. In hindsight, I realize that as freshmen in college we need friends possibly more than any other time in our lives. No matter how together Tiffy made herself seem, she was still a freshman living on campus, far from home. And so was I. She hung out with the lacrosse girls sometimes - and usually brought me along - but when she really needed to spill, she came to my room. And we got closer all the time. So whether or not she's ever called me a friend to my face, we both know we're close. It was Tiffany who saw how vulnerable and unprepared I was for college. She taught me about beauty, about fashion, and it was her influence that started making me a little more detached, a little cooler, and a lot more confident. It was Tiffany who said, "Girl, you're smokin' hot. You better own that shit." So if some people think I'm a preppy bitch, it's because of Tiffany's influence - and you know what? I love that about myself. I love the way I am now - the way I act, the way I look. And it's all because of her.

Tiffany is probably the best judge of character I've ever met. She's seriously never been wrong. You know what she said about Kenny? "Wow. What a piece of shit. Someone's either *really* gay or they've got a serious case of vagina envy. Whichever it is, they are *not* happy about it, and they especially don't want *you* to be happy." Nailed that. And Krystal? Tiffany curled her lip and said, "No offense, Courtney, but you are *way* outta her league." Two for two.

Before she went home for the summer, Tiffany looked at me and said, "Hey, so...are you gonna be alright down here, all alone?"

"What do you mean?" I asked.

"Well, just, you try to pull off this whole Edgar Allan Poe thing, like loneliness is some natural state of being for you or something, but I know it's not."

I grinned at her. "Are you trying to tell me I'm not goth enough to spend a summer alone in Autumn Grove?"

"You're about as goth as I am, you fucking poser." She narrowed her eyes. "Seriously, are you sure you don't wanna come chill with me for the summer? My mom *loves* you and she'd love to have you there, and Tyler will be gone half the summer, so you don't need to worry about him."

I smirked. Tiffany's slightly younger brother gawks at me whenever I'm around and never manages to hide the fact that he has a "serious boner" for me, as Tiffy puts it.

I gave her a warm smile. "It does sound fun, but...nah, I'm good. I'd have to move out of my apartment and everything, which would be a serious nightmare. But you should come down and spend a few weeks with me, whenever you want. I admit that it's probably gonna get pretty quiet."

"Alright," she said breezily. "I'll see about coming back down a few weeks early. But seriously, Courtney - be careful, okay?"

"What's the deal?" I asked her. "You're never worried about me. Ever."

"I dunno." She got serious all of a sudden. "I'm just getting a weird vibe. Just be careful."

That was only last week, but it feels like forever. I'm all alone in Autumn Grove and I'm even lonelier than usual - I guess I never realized how much I rely on Tiffany. I just hope she was wrong about the vibe she was getting.

Monday
September 5, 1921
New Stafford, Ohio
11:07 a.m.

Mary

It's one of those shady summer days where morning stretches over into mid-afternoon, and you can't tell what time it is just by looking outside. The shade is deep and cool, and it sways back and forth across the wood-paneled floor. Little white sunlight flickers through the old leaves outside, and a chilly breeze on my arms tells me that fall is on the doorstep. Low noises drift by outside; the lazy buzz of a faraway motor car like an old tired insect, birds fluttering in the branches. A distant high-pitched orchestra plays very softly on the Gramaphone. I was sitting in the easy chair in Nettie's front parlor, leafing through the *Saturday Evening Post* without any real interest, and I must have fallen asleep against the back of the chair, my head on my wrist.

What pops into my head must only be two or three seconds long, but the intensity of it certainly makes up for its shortness. I see a couple of fellas in their early twenties, and they're standing around next to some crazy-looking red car. It's a low thing - rounded, with a lot of curves - and the headlights are small and round. I never saw a car like that before, but from what I could see of the street there were more like that. There's a monstrous howling from inside the car - some frightful mixture of a growl and a scream - and I think some poor creature is trying to sing, though it sounds as if he's trapped in some hellish dungeon. The animalistic snarls are accompanied by horrific noises that sound vaguely like melody, so perhaps this is what these boys listen to for enjoyment. It takes all kinds, I suppose. Anyway, I only get a good look at one of the fellas by the car. He has filthy jet black hair and it hangs in greasy strands over half his face, down to his chin, like nobody ever taught him how to clean up. He has several piercings in the bottom of his lip, with little chrome studs stuck in them. And his eyes - I don't like to think of them, even now. They're clammy gray with pitch black pupils, and they look more like the round mouths of two repulsive worms, with jagged irises like horrific needle teeth. Those eyes are completely devoid of humanity. Cruelty is all there is.

"Krystal wants to stop by that bitch's house tomorrow for some clothes or somethin'. I'm good with breakin' in if she's not there."

"That's cold, bro," the other fella says. *"And what if she is?"*

He smiles; his eyes stay dark and cruel. *"That's what I'm hopin' for. I can fuckin' take that bitch out! Haa!"* His laugh sounds like the 'a' in apple, and the only time he ever really smiles is when he does it.

"Man, what'd this fuckin' bitch do to you, brah? Steal some drugs or some shit?"

"Nah, brah." He's got a vague grin, and his face is like an icy fog. *"I think her name is Courtney or some shit, some fuckin stuck up preppy bitch name. She dated Krystal for a minute. But she was always goin' out to bars and pickin' up guys and shit with her stuck up Barbie girl friends. And she went and told all these bitches all this shit about Krystal, like about her eating disorder and shit, and they came to her place one night when Krystal was there and were makin' all these snotty bitch comments about it. So I told Krystal I'd stab 'er in her fuckin preppy bitch throat! Haa!"* He lifts up his elbow and smacks it, and he's got some cruel knife in his fist with a handle made of horn or bone or something. The blade is a good six inches long, with a bend in the middle. Some kind of hunting knife.

What the hell is this imbecile talking about? I know Courtney better than he ever will, and she doesn't go with guys, or pick them up at bars, or tell somebody's secrets to a stranger. Though I get the sense that it's not really important to him whether those things are true or not. Even if it's all a complete bill of goods, what's important to him is having an excuse. I'm getting that impression from him very strongly.

"Whoa, bro, so you're actually gonna shank this bitch? Ah, that's cold!" Laughter.

"Fuck yeah, brah. I think I'll probably do it tomorrow night. Tonight I'm gonna chill, smoke some purple zoom, tear up some pussy, know what I'm sayin'? Get it while I can, cause I dunno if Krystal's gonna flip out or some shit when I knife that bitch in the throat. And then tomorrow, when I'm mellowed out, feelin good, then BAM!" Brings up his elbow

again, smacks it, flashes the knife in his fist. He's got really low, small fingernails that are dirty around the edges. *"Haa! Stick my grandpa's huntin' knife right in her fuckin' throat a few dozen times. I think I might hit that tight fuckin pussy too, while it's still warm, before she goes all cold and shit."*

"Duuuude! Man, fuck, dude, you are one psychotic motherfucker!" His friend laughs nervously; he sounds a bit frightened.

The dirty fella with the creepy eyes that look like bugs, he just lifts up his knife and looks at the long shiny blade, at the curve in the middle, and I flinch a little at the thought of it going into Courtney's soft belly.

The way he looks at that knife, his face hasn't changed a bit. No facial expression, just a fog over his eyes and a vague smile on his face.

That disgusting creature really is going to try and kill her.

Like I said, all this hits me in just a few seconds - all the psychic impressions, all the clear details, all my own emotions. I come gasping out of my nap with a terrified moan in my throat, and I almost fall right on the floor. I grab the arms of the chair, steady myself for a moment until I catch a few breaths, and process what I've seen. That vision really did happen to me. I don't believe I've ever had a divination that clear before - and I've certainly never had premonitions; I don't get those.

I blink the disorientation out of my eyes and remember where I am. In New Stafford, with the quiet clipping of grass outside, with the shouts of children playing in the street, with the sunlight and the swaying shadows of leaves.

I catch my breath. "Courtney."

Then I'm up and running down the hallway, looking for Nettie. She's at the kitchen table with some magazines open. Her finger trails down the page looking for something - one of her crazy research tangents. Her chestnut brown hair is pulled back in a bun and a few frazzled strands have come free, floating around the sides of her head. Her pale freckled skin glows in the sunlight.

"Nettie, we need to go. Right now."

"Good *lord*, Mary, where's the fire? Slow down and tell me what on Earth you're talking about."

I take a breath and get a hold of myself. It's not easy. "Your Aunt Lizzy."

"Yes?"

"Her offer. To come down and stay for college. Is that still good?"

Her eyes shift. "Why, I don't see why not. What for?"

"Well, we gotta get packed and leave."

Nettie blinks. "When?"

I've already turned to run back home and pack my own things. "As soon as we can catch a train."

"Mary, wait! Just...explain, won't you?"

I give her a very serious look. "Courtney's in trouble. Someone's trying to kill her. If anyone wants to help her, they have to be near a versal aperture, and there's a conjunction going on right now, right? Your aunt lives near several hotspots for versal transits, which means a versal aperture somewhere, which means Courtney can get to us. I fear we're all she has, and if we want to help her we have to hurry."

Nettie's whole attitude changes. She's cleaning up her mess, the magazines sliding into a neat pile and being tucked away. Nettie trusts me. She knows how sharp my gift for divination is, knows what I see is always true. I run down the hall and out the screen door, onto the sun-dappled street. I'll go home and pack, and I know Nettie will come down after me when she's ready. We'll be on the next train to Columbus. Hopefully if we play our cards right, we can be in Autumn Grove by tonight.

I've been waiting and planning for this moment for five agonizing years, but I never imagined it might happen like this. Courtney's smart and quick - she always has been. I just hope she can stay one step ahead of anyone that tries to hurt her. I hope to all the goddesses that this isn't the start of a resonance purge. It might not come to that. I think we might still have some time.

I pray that we still have time.

Six

Courtney

"Nettie and Elizabeth both insist that time isn't linear. That makes me all the more certain that sometimes blood covenants are forged before you even meet the person."
-Sadie Van Tassel, private letter to her sister Sylvia, 1924

5:03 p.m.

The revolving door makes a sucking noise as it drops me outside on the shady library front porch. I squint into the sun and draw the first scalding breath of summer heat into my lungs. Right in front of me, across the library courtyard and behind some trees, is Cutler Hall. It's the oldest building at the college and it sits smack dab in the middle of campus. It's flanked by two equally old buildings, all of them facing north across College Green. They've been there since the 1760s, built before anyone was mad at England.

Maybe if I walk slow on these sloping brick pathways, I can spend an extra three or four minutes on campus. Even if it's less busy in the summer, the sparse evening bustle is better company than the silence at home. I cue up The Ataris on my iPod and make my way down the winding shady path, staying on the side so I'm not in anyone's way. I want to get lost in my head. I'm usually too on edge to let myself do that, most of the time.

It feels so nice, relaxing back into that alpha wave part of your brain. It's where we go when we watch TV, read a good book, trance ourselves out. I guess it's where I've been when I'm in the yearbooks, too. It's nice to not be so hyper-aware and tense all the time. It takes me a minute or two to notice that it's quieter than usual this afternoon. So quiet that I stop my music, pull out one of my earbuds, let it dangle while I listen to the open air. All I can hear is a gentle summer breeze, maybe the distant sound of an old motor rattling far away. It's one of those lovely days you get familiar with when you grow up in the country, the ones where you can smell the rich dirt from some distant farm. That smell is one of the few childhood memories I'm able to treasure.

An old Ford Model T putters down the street and back toward campus, and I watch with numb astonishment. Wow. That's an odd sort of coincidence. I wonder who it belongs to; probably just some old collector guy. A few more steps, and I hear what sounds like a sniffle. I stick my earbuds in my tank top and pause my song.

This curvy brick passage winds down around Ellis Hall, then a straight shot down to the street. Where I'm at right now, Ellis is above me and to my left. There's a little brick wall, maybe six feet high; if you climb on top of that, you're right on the building's wide, shady lawn. Above that is Ellis itself: a three-story building from 1910 with a wide rotunda and big pillars, all nestled in the drowsy shade of huge oak trees. That emerald lawn is scattered with fallen leaves and pocked with acorns. That's where I find her, sobbing her eyes out next to one of those trees.

College is an instructive experience for a small-town girl. One of the most important things I've learned at Braddock is how *not* to stare; when I first came here, I stared at everything like a yokel. It's so freaking rude - and a little creepy - so I've trained myself not to do it. I glance at the girl sitting on the blanket for as long as I dare, probably only about three-fourths of a second, trying to take in all the information I can, as quickly as I can. Her hunter green dress and dark hose look familiar - could that be the same girl from earlier? Her bell-shaped hat sits next to her on the ground, and her reddish mahogany hair hangs loose and wavy around the apples of her cheeks, like it was pulled back and then came undone. She's sitting there all alone, a white handkerchief in her hands, and even at this distance her eyes are puffy and bloodshot. Sadness lays on her thick, like a cloying smell.

The poor thing! What's got her crying out here all by herself? My heart aches for her - I want to run up to her and hold her and let her ugly cry on my shirt and make her feel safe. But no matter how much I want to do that, or how much I want to ease her pain however I can, that's not how it works in the real world. People prefer to wrestle with their problems alone, and I'm basically a stranger.

I guess I won't bother her. It's probably part of some unspoken social contract; if someone's alone, they probably *want* to be alone.

But something about her sticks out. It's nothing I can put a finger on, not even her style; she's probably just a thrift store junkie, the kind of girl *I* might even be if I knew how to wear vintage clothes and stuff. No, it's something intangible, almost like it's her presence itself. There's something *sweet* about her, deep in my awareness, pulling at me. Maybe I should...

No, Courtney. That sounds like some skeevy pickup line. Keep walking. She won't want to be bothered.

Still, I glance up at her as I pass. Knees together to cover the basics of propriety, teasing out her handkerchief, sniffling and dabbing her cheeks with it. Very ladylike, even old-fashioned. Yeah, that's definitely the same girl from earlier. Maybe I'll just see if she's okay; I can't just walk by and leave her all alone if something's wrong. She'll tell me she's fine and thank me, then I'll go. I won't be creepy or hang around.

"Hey," I call out to her, standing on tiptoes to see her over the wall. "Sorry to bother you, but...is everything okay?" *A tight, grateful smile – 'yeah, I'm alright, someone's on their way to pick me up, thanks anyway.' 'Yeah, no problem, hope you feel better-'*

She looks up - a little startled, a little embarrassed. She sniffs and wipes her eyes a little more aggressively. She chuckles through her tears, looking at the mascara smeared on her handkerchief.

"Gosh, sorry. Yeah. I'm alright. Thank you for asking." She smiles at me and it's sweet, even through her sniffles. "Say, we met earlier, didn't we? Crossing the street."

"Yep, that was me!" I grin at myself. "Aaaand now I realize how creepy it is that I'm showing up like this. I'm *really* not stalking you, I swear."

She pauses, not comprehending. Then she laughs. Like, *really* laughs. It's pretty, like little silver bells. "That would have never occurred to me."

I flash an uncertain grin. "Small town, I guess?"

"Or destiny, you never know." Her smile and tone are ironic. "The fates punishing me by making me cry in public."

I give her a sympathetic smile. "Hey...do you need a tissue or anything? I've got some in my bag."

"Tissue...?"

"Yeah, just...you look really sad, and it sucks to be all alone with no tissues."

She sniffs again. "Oh, I'd hate to impose."

"Pfff," I wave it off, then scamper over the wall and approach her. I swing my backpack around with practiced ease and produce a couple of tissues from the front zipper pocket. She watches, eyes fixed on my backpack, the band patches safety-pinned to the front pocket. I've got my Spitalfield patch - the one with the red silhouette of the girl with the short dress - and my Ataris patch right under it. I had my black square Nirvana patch on there until last semester; apparently I'd had it too long, put it through too much abuse. I hand her the tissues, and she looks at them.

"What...what if I ruin these?" she asks.

I squint, not quite following. Finally, I reach in and produce the puffy pack I got them from.

"No worries," I assure her. "I gotcha covered."

"O-oh. Right." She puts one of the tissues to her nose, blows delicately into it, then dabs her eyes. She smiles a little at me. "Thanks awfully. You're an angel."

"No problem." I swing my backpack around and onto both shoulders. I store my hands in my zipper hoodie's pockets and hope I don't look awkward.

She hands me the other tissue. "Here. I don't want to take all your hankies from you."

I wave it off. "Seriously, no worries. I've got tons."

"Oh." She glances at it again. She seems a little happier already. "Well, golly, thank you!" I smile at her, a little baffled. She's kinda making a big deal about a couple of tissues. But I guess there could be all kinds of reasons for that. Maybe someone really treated her like crap. Maybe she's lonely like me. *Yeah, Courtney - believe it or not, you might not have a monopoly on loneliness. Imagine that.*

"Forgive me," she apologizes. "I'd shake your hand, but..."

"Pff, like I care." I extend a hand. "Courtney."

Her smile returns. She's got a cute smile; it's thin and sharp like her eyes. She extends her hand.

"Sadie."

Her hand is soft and warm, a little moist from her tears. When I touch it, I feel a satisfying click in my chest. Something right. We both look at our hands, just a soft casual girly handshake, but whatever it was, she felt it too.

"Sooo," I crouch in front of her, and my words tumble out before I've had a chance to think. "I really don't mean to pry, but...is everything okay? Like, you seem really sad."

"Oh," she laughs a little. "I don't know. Maybe it's a lot of things. I'm probably just being a baby."

I narrow my eyes. "I doubt that's it."

She toys with the wet tissue in her hands, and after a moment she looks up at me like she's surprised I'm still paying attention. She starts again. "I suppose it's just...I've been so frightfully lonesome since I got here."

"Why is that?" I ask. She's got a curiously old-fashioned way of talking, too - I guess it's not just the ladylike way she sits.

"Well, you see, Sylvia - that's my big sister - she's a senior here at Braddock. I'm just starting as a freshman this year, so I thought I'd come down early and spend the summer with her before I start this fall. But a few weeks ago, our parents asked Sylvia to join them in Europe. Now she won't be back till the start of the semester, and..." Sadie draws a shuddering breath. "Back in New York, I couldn't wait to get down here. Now I'm all by myself, and I guess I'm a pretty sorry fish."

I'm not sure what that means, but I'll roll with it and pretend like I do.

"You're from New York?" Sadie's warmer and more vulnerable than the people I've met from New York. Though I'll be the first to admit that I haven't met all that many.

"Yeah," she sniffs, folding the tissue. "Buffalo."

Ah, that explains why she sounds midwestern, why we have pretty much the same accent.

"How long have you been here?" I ask her. "On campus, I mean."

She makes a face at the tissue in her hands. "A little over a week, maybe?"

Wow, no wonder. She's probably never really been away from home or family before, and now she's all alone four hundred miles away on a campus where the loneliness tests you even when you have a ton of friends.

I carefully sit down across from her, still worried I'm intruding.

"God, I'm so sorry." I give her a hurt, sympathetic look. "That really sucks."

She smiles a little, grateful and self-effacing. "Then some dumkuff walks by a few minutes ago - real low lid, if you ask me - and says some real mean things about my clothes. I don't know what I ever did to her; why, I never even saw her before."

Dumkuff? There's another one that just flies over my head. I hope it's not obvious that I'm totally blanking out. I'd like to seem at least *half* cool.

I sigh and roll my eyes. It doesn't happen a lot, but sometimes some bitchy hipster cunt will come out of nowhere, like a psycho with a shotgun. I know the type: short hair, light canvas bag with Sonic Youth or Pixies buttons, and clothes she dug out of a damp closet - skintight stone-wash asspants or cut-off shorts from about 1980 and stinky old Puma gym sneakers with the velcro straps. You could imagine her digging them out of some box and laughing the whole time with one of her constant hanger-on friends, probably some twinky gay boy named Elliot with huge square nerd glasses who wears an expression on his face like he's walking through an open sewer when he has to talk to anyone but the bitch he's next to.

One time, I had a run-in with a couple of cunts like that - twin sisters. They both had the exact same dykey haircut, both dyed bleach white like flour. They listened to this stupid new wave shit. They randomly decide to not like certain people (like me) for some unimaginable reason, and whenever they see you in passing, they make sure to make the nastiest remark they can - about you - to the person next to them. It baffles me. I can almost imagine doing that to someone that really hurt me in some really personal way, but I don't understand doing it to someone you've never met, just because they listen to different music or because you found some shoes that should have been burned by the time Reagan was elected. Maybe it makes them better than everyone else.

I'd love to find whoever hurt this sweet girl and bash their face in.

"Where was this?" I ask Sadie, my tone flat.

She gestures vaguely up the walkway, pointing at the building looming over us. "Over by the back door to...is it Ellis Hall?"

Uh huh. That figures. Some stuck-up cunt from the English Department.

"Just the worst ragamuffin you ever laid eyes on," she goes on. "Dirty blonde hair, but not bobbed. It looked like someone went and hacked it all to pieces with some dull scissors. Real tight shorts with threads hanging off the legs - not nice and clean like yours. Her duds looked old, like she dug them out of a dumpster. And she had a whole buncha outlandish pins and buttons, like with wings and stuff, on a green musette bag. You know, the kind like she might have brought home from the trenches."

I try not to laugh. I really like the way this girl observes things.

"I wish I'd have been there." My voice is tinged with blood. "I'd have made her kill herself. Bitches like that make me...*urrgh!*"

She looks astonished at the venom in my words. I get that a lot. But she's smiling.

"Anyway, nothing she said is true. Remember when we ran into each other today at the crosswalk?"

She nods.

"I thought you were one of those really classy thrift store chicks with the awesome style that was too good to talk to a girl like me."

She gives me a baffled look. "Whatever for?"

I shrug. "You're so..." I search for the words. "Poised and put together."

Her face glows with hope and gratitude, then reverts to self-doubt. "Why, you're an angel to say so, but I've always been the ugly little sister. Everyone in my family says so - except my sister, that is. But she's always been nice to me."

My mouth falls open; I can*not* believe what I'm hearing. The girl in front of me is a picture of effortless beauty, some crazy mix of Edwardian grace and honest, expressive midwestern friendliness that comes together to make this delectable gourmet piece of art. She's petite and cute, with her soft milky white skin and round face and delicate features and slender narrow eyes. The upright way she holds herself; it's not like overconfidence or arrogance. It's more like an old habit, or maybe something she picked up from people around her growing up. The really genuine, unironic way she wears her knee-length flapper dress and the short brown scarf tied around her throat. She's exactly the kind of girl I'd love to be.

Or exactly the kind of girl I'd love to be *with*.

Stop it, Courtney.

"Are you serious?!" I demand. "They say that to you?"

She sniffs a little; the worst of the tears have passed. "They have before."

"Okay, no offense, but screw your family." She blinks at me, startled, like I smacked her in the face. "And I know I just met you, so please don't get creeped out by this, but...you're *gorgeous*. Like...do you know how many girls would kill to look like you? To *be* you?" She stares. "You're *hot*. Your eyes, I love your eyes. They captured me right away. And you've got the perfect body - you're petite and cute but you're not like, rail skinny, you know? You're soft. And there's something else about you, too - something I can't put my finger on. You're..." I struggle for the words. "*More*, somehow. There's something almost aristocratic about you, the way you hold yourself. But it's so attractive because you don't act bitchy or stuck up. You're genuine and friendly and sweet, and you care about people, I can tell. I've never met a girl like you. You're kind of a big deal."

She stares at me, mouth agape. "I..."

"And by the way?" I drive it home. "Your clothes? They're sexy. You *rock* the flapper thing - not many girls can do that. Everyone else feels ironic, but somehow it's really natural with you. You've even got the language down! It's like you're *actually from the 20s*." I've been working up to the most significant thing I've noticed about her, the thing that defies words or logic. I have no idea how I'm going to put it into words, so I just launch in. "I think the biggest thing I've noticed about you is your presence. There's something really *alive* about you, something really energetic. And that makes you..." I don't really know how to put it, so I just gesture vaguely at her with both arms and exhale something pathetic. "Just really special."

The look she's giving me tells me that nobody's ever said anything like this to her, ever. She's totally lost for words.

"I..." She's breathless for a second. "May I hug you?"

I smile, and she wraps her arms around me; we're a perfect fit. She's delicious in my arms, and my heart is doing this annoying thing where it's thumping into her boob and I know she's gotta be able to feel it pounding. I wish I could tell it to chill the F out.

Ungh. I am such a creep. She was crying, and now I'm all checking her out and hugging her and stuff.

My guilty side is like, *I told you that you were skeevy.*

And I'm like, *you're totally not helping.*

Now that my heart is next to hers, I can feel her energy; she's alive with something that reaches out to me, feels familiar and right. I don't want to over-hug her, and I think she must be nervous about over-hugging me, but we stay like that for a few seconds before we pull slowly away.

"Why, that was posilutely the sweetest thing anyone's ever said to me." She looks directly into my eyes. "Thank you, *oh*, thank you *so much!*"

My guilty sarcastic side is all *Hey, there's an opening, playa. Why not just be like, 'that's alright, baby. Just gimme some of that sweet sugar and we'll call it even.'*

And I'm like *Why don't you go fuck yourself.*

I give her another hug wrapped in a smile. "That can't be true. But, you said you kinda grew up in the shadow of your sister, right?"

She nods. "Sylvia is beautiful, graceful, like a fairy tale. Everyone loves her."

I'm dubious. "Maybe she's pretty, and I've never seen her, but I'm guessing that she looks like a lot of other girls. *You* don't." I grab her eyes with mine and add, "The realest beauty is unique - and genuine."

I knock the breath out of her lungs again, but she recovers. "Say, I know I'm a complete stranger, so please don't think me too forward, but I'm awfully glad I met you, Courtney. You just turned my world upside down, and it's posilutely the best thing that's ever happened to me." She smirks a little. "But then, a girl like you probably rescues damsels in distress all the time. You've probably heard it all."

I laugh out loud. Wow. If she knew me just a little, she'd see what a flaming disaster I am. Still, I've never heard something so heartfelt and amazing from a stranger. Come to think of it, I don't know if I've ever heard something so heartfelt and amazing, period.

I give her a confused smirk. "You...have no idea how *not* true that is."

We snicker a little bit together. "Well," she says, "if everyone here is like that dewdropper with the dumpster shorts, I could see it. Maybe Braddock isn't the place Sylvia said it was."

"I'm sorry that had to be one of your first experiences here," I tell her. "I really hope we can make it up to you."

"Don't worry," she says. "I feel a thousand percent better now."

"I'm glad I could help do that, at least."

A breeze kicks up, rustling a few crispy leaves on the lawn. The wind hisses through the green canopy high above, and the long golden rays of evening sparkle through. Normally I'm hyper-aware of every passing moment when I'm hanging out with someone. I'm always awkward and on edge, feeling like it's up to me to keep them from getting crazy with boredom and leaving me. But I feel really comfortable and happy sitting here with Sadie. I'm enjoying her company so much; there's a warm, easy silence between us. This girl is awesome and I'd love to hang out with her again, but I'm half afraid to ask. I don't want to mess it up, and I *really* don't want to seem like I preyed on her misery just to get her number. Yuck. Because she's totally my type and I feel gross for thinking that when I honestly just wanted to help.

"Say," she says, looking at me. "Do you work here on campus?"

"Oh. Yeah. Up at the Archives."

"We have Archives?" Her face is a little blank. Well, she *is* new on campus.

"Yeah." I warm to the subject; we're all a little nerdy up there, even the students like me, and I love my job. "Up on the fifth floor of the library. You can't miss it."

She's drawing a blank. Sadie and I seem to have a lot in common - we even have the same vacant stare when we're confused. "Oh. Right."

"What about you?" I try to smooth it over.

"Oh, no. Not yet, anyhow. Maybe once things get more settled for me." She dabs at her face and turns a sunny smile on me. "Why, what I was gonna ask is, would you like to meet me for lunch tomorrow? I always feel like such a canceled stamp, having lunch by myself."

Canceled stamp? I should start keeping a list or I'm gonna end up looking like a dumbass.

"Yeah, totally!" I'm relieved and excited. "I usually go around noon-ish, but I can take my lunch whenever. My boss doesn't care. I can meet you...I guess in front of the three buildings in the middle of College Green?"

"Ducky," she says happily.

"Oh." I swing my backpack into my lap, unzipping and reaching in for last quarter's notebook. I take my pen from the top of the notebook's rings and flip to some blank pages. "Do you use AIM?"

She pauses. "AIM?"

"Instant messenger?"

"Uhhhh…"

Okay, that's new. I've met a few people on campus that don't use messenger - not many - but I've never met anyone that didn't know what it was.

"Ah, okay." Let's roll with it. "Email?"

Her mouth hangs open, eyes blind in my headlights.

"No email?"

"I'm afraid not." Her voice is slow and uncertain.

Wow. Alright.

"Well, I can give you my phone number, even though we won't be able to reach each other tomorrow during the day, if I'm at work." Her face brightens a little; okay, at least the girl has a phone. "And I'll scribble my screen name and email on here, just in case. It would be nice to hear from someone I actually like, for once." She smiles a little, hopeless and lost. I write everything in my skinny, tall handwriting that's just a little loopy, the handwriting that I wish was softer like a lot of other girls so it wouldn't stand out so much. Then I tear off the bottom of the paper and hand it to her.

Courtney :)
AIM: HistoryOfNow
email: historyofnow @ braddock.edu
Phone: xx7-4729

And a little heart symbol at the bottom. She takes it and looks at it, her face a soup of conflicting emotions. She's flattered and happy, but she's looking at the paper with that horrified, inadequate look, like she walked into an expensive store to buy a gift for someone, only to get told that it costs five times more than what she's got in the bank.

She looks up at me, dreading the confession she's about to make. "I...don't-"

"You know what," I brush it off. "Don't even worry. I'll just meet you tomorrow."

"Well, I can at least give you my telephone number," she says, borrowing my pen and notebook. She glances at them a moment, looking the pen over, before remembering what she was doing. She writes her name and number in lovely, feminine cursive.

Sadie Van Tassel
385

I stare at her paper for a second, totally baffled. I've never seen a three-digit phone number in my life. It's not an abbreviation - even if I assume the first three digits of her number are the same as mine, I'm still missing one number.

Sadie felt lost, and now it's my turn. She's a natural flapper with gorgeous handwriting and a lot of slang I've never heard before. But she's sweet, and we vibe. Like, a *lot*. Maybe if I just-

"Say, Courtney?"

"Hmm?"

Every word is careful, like she's stepping into a dangerous swamp.

"Sorry, but…what did you mean earlier when you said that it was like I was really from the 1920s?"

I open my mouth, close it. Images of the yearbook trickle across my vision, fast then gone, like pixels on a screen. Something feels a bit off.

I stare at the ground, feeling kinda awkward. "Um, just…"

Then I look up. All her tears are gone, one arm is holding the other under her knees, and she's really sober and serious. I don't like the idea that it might be really important how I answer a question, or that someone might wonder if I'm out of my mind. Her look isn't critical or threatening, really, but she's definitely paying attention. I speak slowly. "You don't wear your clothes like you bought them at a thrift store, or like they're a novelty. It's like you're the real deal, like someone that's actually from the 20s. You even talk like it. And I think it's probably the coolest thing I've ever seen, and I'd love to be like you."

Now she's quiet and shocked, her mouth agape like someone coping with the most intense mindfuck ever. But maybe I can talk to her. Maybe there is someone I can open up to about what's been happening to me.

Screw it.

"Hey," I begin slowly. "Could I share something really weird with you? It's just, you don't seem like you'd judge me."

"Please do." She sounds a bit desperate.

"Sorry if the 20s thing was weird or it freaked you out or whatever," I tell her. "The last few days have just been...*insane*. They put me on this new project at work, and since I started, life has been, like, *really freaking weird*. It's like nothing makes sense anymore."

Big eyes. "You too?"

"Wait, you're not serious?"

"I'm sorry," she says. "Please continue."

"Oh, no way," I grin. "You can't just do that and then leave it. You *have* to tell me now."

She smiles, her eyes a little reluctant. "Oh, alright. It's just that I've had the queerest sensation for the last day or two. Sometimes it's, I don't know, as if there are two versions of the same town, and one is laid over top of the other. And I've been getting a bit mixed up-"

I lean forward and smack the grass with both hands. "Yes!! And you start losing track of which one you're in, and it's hard to concentrate because it's like your body is in one place but your eyes are somewhere else-"

"*Yes!*" She leans forward. "Oh, Courtney, I thought I was loony for sure! Today, at lunch, on the street. That person earlier, and then, you. I thought maybe you were just quirky at first, but...you're really swell. Different clothes, that little wire on your shirt. You act and talk different, but in a comfortable way - like you've done it for ages."

We stare at each other, two kindred spirits in an impossible scenario. Then the doubt hits me. No way. She's gotta be playing me.

"You're totally messing with me," I tell her, my face cracking in a self-deprecating grin. I lift my backpack, get ready to leave. "I know, I'm a weirdo, it's funny-"

"No!" Her voice goes through me, vibrating every nerve in my body like the noise of a jet flying right overhead. It's not loud but it *feels* loud when it thrums inside my muscles and my stomach. She's emphatic, deadly serious.

She continues more gently. "No. Honest to goodness, Courtney, I'm not being cruel. And - on the level - things have been screwy all week. I really thought I was cracking up. But even with all the weird stuff on the paper you gave me, you're still as real as anything - and I hope you *are* real, because I really like you and I sure could use a friend." Her expression is more serious than ever. "I'm not pulling your chain. Weird things have happened to me my whole life, weird things I could never tell anyone about, but this week has just been plain loony." Her eyes plead with mine. "Please believe me."

We share a look, two damaged girls expecting to be hurt, expecting to be left alone. "I believe you," I tell her. "Sorry. I guess things have been so bizarre that I couldn't imagine how anyone could believe me, and maybe that makes me vulnerable. But I guess you're just as vulnerable as me right now."

"Then let's swear right here, this instant, to be totally open with one another," she declares. "We'll swear to believe each other entirely, without question, because we've seen things nobody else could possibly understand."

When I smile at her, I feel the warmth radiating from my eyes. "Deal. I swear to everything you just said, because I know you'll believe me."

"Deal," she says happily. "And at lunchtime tomorrow, you can tell me all about your crazy project."

"Definitely." But I can't help worrying about her; seeing her crying really bothered me. "Hey, are you gonna be alright?"

She beams at me. "I am now. Because now I know that if I'm going loony, at least we're going loony together."

"Hey, that's totally a promise, right?" I grin. "You gotta take me with you."

Her eyes are earnest, staring into mine. "I wouldn't dream of leaving you behind."

S e v e n

```
WESTERN UNION TELEGRAM
INTER-CONCLAVE MEMORANDUM
1921 SEP 6  AM  9  59
NEW YORK NY 1012A

SECRETARY ARCANA ETHEL KRAUSE
SEVEN TOWERS CONCLAVE
CINCINNATI OH

READING CALIBER 8 THERIC SIGNATURE PHASING IN AND OUT NEAR AUTUMN GROVE
CHANNEL LINE CONFLUENCE HAVE NOT BRIEFED ASSEMBLY WANTED TO ASK YOU FIRST
PLEASE ADVISE BIG READINGS HAVE US WORRIED UP HERE

ELLA MAE HANNEGAN
VICE PROVOST ARCANA
NEW AMSTERDAM CONCLAVE

RECEIVED AT 1023 A
```

6:26 p.m.

The yellow light of a fading evening stretches across my apartment when I finally walk in. The hot air is a solid object and it burns my lungs. Motes of dust drift across bars of light, and I can't figure out how things can move across a room when the air is hot and solid like pound cake in the oven.

But my apartment smells sweet, a blend of a hundred nice smells - all my perfumes and lotions and shower gels and laundry detergents - that have combined to make something new. It's how every place I've lived has smelled since I left Stanhope. I guess it just smells like *me*.

I walk over, drop my backpack next to the couch, and turn on my window air conditioner. Then I plop down on my little couch as the A/C blows its first hot, garage-scented breath in my face before it turns cool.

It's dead silent in here, almost as quiet as the Archives, but this is a different kind of silence; this is *empty* silence. There's a sadness in this place, this heavy loneliness that came with the apartment. It's this sweet mournfulness that attacks your heart when you're alone. Sometimes I come back here in the evening and out of nowhere I feel like crying, even if I had a decent day and nothing's wrong. I mean, I know you're probably like, "Hey, Queen Obvious - you're lonely. *You're* the problem. There, I fixed it." Thing is, I've been lonely most of my life. I was lonely pretty often when I lived in the dorms, and it was nothing like this. This is a whole different thing. There's something in the paint, in the walls, in the apartment itself. It's a sadness that comes on you and drinks your joy like some freaking vampire. When you bring people in, you can feel it waiting at the edge of the room, watching you. When you're alone, it curls up next to you. At night, it seeps into your chest and tears out your heart from the inside.

I used to think it was just me, but it's not. Nowadays, everything in my reality takes on the same basic flavor of bittersweet aching lonely *bullshit*. People and products and stores and classrooms all glare at me with this frozen exterior, and everything I look at makes me lonelier. My fingers are slipping off the edge - but what that edge is, I have no idea.

And then one day, you wake up and realize that you never belonged in this reality at all. This black curtain of despair falls over you, this sense of impossibility like a burial shroud. What the hell are you supposed to do? What *can* you do, other than lay down and die?

My computer isn't much comfort. As soon as I turn it on, the usual *UH-OH* squeaks at me. Ooh, lucky me - I have a message. I bet it's Krystal's scuzzy boyfriend. Ah, here we go.

URDEAD120932: Im comin 4 u bitch

He's just following up regarding his previous memo, left on my front door on Monday morning:

YOUR DEAD BITCH

YOUR gOINg 2 PAY

The writing was rusty brown, cracked and flaky. Blood. The penmanship would be pretty impressive if the author were in third grade, but if the person writing it was an adult you'd be moved to pity. Especially since he used real blood - either his own or someone else's - just to tell me about my "dead bitch" or my "gOINg 2 Pay." I don't own either of those things, and I don't know what they are, but he must have thought it was pretty serious if he used his own blood to tell me about it then drove the hour down here from Stanhope to give it to me. What a good little trooper.

It was stuck to my front door with a rock of old chewing gum. I tossed the disgusting thing in the trash on the way to my car, only to discover a silver streak about a foot long running across my drivers' side door. I touched it absently, reflecting that not even Krystal is skanky enough to key someone's car. You need a whole other level of scrub for that, someone who never bathes and might be inbred. Enter Derek, the loser that my ex is sleeping with.

So I dated this girl named Krystal for a month or two last year. I was really lonely, and I have no idea what even drew me in. It must have been her natural genius for sweet-talking - she'll get you online and bathe you in affection and warmth, and then pepper those messages with cute pictures of herself. She doesn't overdo it; just the right amount. It wasn't until she was out of my life that I knew what the word "narcissist" meant.

Whatever. It's not like we slept together or anything. She'd be all sweet on messenger, but when she came down here - she lives in Stanhope, my hometown an hour away - she'd sit on my couch and watch stuff with me and act really tense and awkward. She must have only dated me as some kind of queer cred. "Hey, look how edgy I am! I'm dating a girl. Isn't that *sexy?*" She's as straight as a razor, and she only turns on the tits when men are around.

Men like Derek.

One time on the phone, Krystal told me that Derek was a trust fund baby or something; I guess someone died and left him a ton of money, so he started living like a prince. Krystal said she met him on a Greyhound bus and they started swallowing each other's faces within a half hour of "hey, how's it going?" Next thing you know, Krystal's shacked up with him in some fancy hotel in Stanhope, and he's buying her all this expensive stuff. And she's returning the favor by fucking him fourteen times a day...and feeding him heartbreaking tales of her shallow, cruel ex, some fake preppy bitch named Courtney. And he snorts it up like coke - which he also sells, by the way. She made sure to tell me that one, because it's impressive.

So since the end of spring quarter, I've been getting anonymous messages on AIM from names like URDEAD129803 or DIEBARBIE8237, describing all the ways I'm going to be stabbed to death or hacked up with machetes. At first, it really scared me. But it happens so often now that it's just another part of my week, like the totally unnecessary account balance statements you get from the electric company when they tell you your bill isn't due yet. All I've been able to gather is that he and his friends and Krystal hate me because...well, actually, that's not entirely clear. It's either 1) because I have blonde hair - sort of a coppery blonde, really; or 2) because I shop at Abercrombie and wear sweaters and hoodies. I'm definitely not a "preppy bitch," though. Sorority girls treat me the same shitty way they treat everyone else, and the band logo patches on my backpack are kind of a no-brainer, right? I thought punk rock wasn't supposed to be about how you dressed, but the way you thought, the experiences you've had, your attitude toward life. But that's not how it works. The punk kids treat me like a sorority girl, and sorority girls treat me like a punk kid.

Just ask Tiffany's friends, they'll tell you. "Courtney's sweet, but she's definitely no preppy girl. She's way too weird."

And why would they lie? It's the truth. I *am* weird.

Some days I'm convinced I'm from some completely different reality, and somehow I got trapped here by mistake. All I know is I damn sure don't belong in *this* one.

It seems like more and more people are driving that home recently.

The way my feelings are a raw nerve right on the surface, the way everything is dark, I can tell it's a dream.

But even when you know it's a dream, it doesn't always help.

It's evening - the sky is fading orange and deep violet - and I'm on a street corner. It's not like any place I've ever been, but it's familiar in the dream - I live around here, I walk these streets all the time. I belong. It almost looks like the crosswalk in uptown Autumn Grove, right across from College Green, except this is a three-way intersection and I have a clear view of the horizon, the blaze of orange where the sun was.

I'm alone out here - the last few people in this part of town are making their way home, disappearing behind buildings down the street. Fear crawls up my spine as the last sunlight fades. Twilight vanishes from alleyways and shadows spread onto the street, devouring the last purple light of evening. It's okay though, right? I mean, soon the streetlights will come on and I'll be able to find my way home.

But wait, hang on. Do I have a home? I'm not sure, now that I think about it. I'm a local, but I must not actually live here. How is that possible? There's a vague idea of a home, but it's more of a concept, a possibility, and it's really far away. Like twenty miles or something, way down this street and across the railroad tracks, way out past where the neighborhoods get dark and dangerous, past where people shamble half-dead in the orange glow of barrel fires, flames flickering on menacing eyes. Way out past the decaying ruins of 1950s bowling alleys and fun parks with big ostentatious plastic signs with rockets and strange angled curves and big letters that used to light up. Now they stare into the black night like long-dead husks. Beyond those places, the very edge of town, darkness - dangerous woods with sharp things and trash and lurking predators in the dark. Then, beyond that, the countryside - wide empty expanses, gentle rolling curves of cornfields backlit by the orange glow of distant cities in the night. Out there, people sleep comfortably in farmhouses and you journey alone across great distances. Then across some nameless creek. Familiar faces wait on the other side, and they'll know me when I get there, but no living person has ever crossed that stream. Going across means death, and there's no coming back. Over there, I'll be white and pure, gliding over the ground.

I have to go through all of that to get home, and it's a home I've never seen but there's a place for me there. Here in this college town where I don't live, streetlights flicker on with noisy hums and swarms of gnats. Their light is weak and there aren't as many of them as there should be - there's a lot of dark shadowy gaps between them. There's a streetlight on the corner where I'm standing, and the dim light is the color of an apricot smoothie and it's just enough to see a messy smattering of papers posted to the big metal pole of the streetlight itself. These are mostly obsolete things: ticket scraps, unfriendly-looking handbills for punk rock shows, played in red-lit basements full of strangers. Advertisements with shadowy outlines of people, vague two-toned smiles in some forgotten time, photocopied over and over until there's nothing left except grainy fuzz.

Then, in the middle, a notice. It's half-covered by some other paper, and when I peel it off to see what's beneath, I startle. Bold letters, all in caps, leap at me in the night like a ghost. It's faded in places, smudged and runny in others, and it looks like it's been here a long time.

MISSING

COURTNEY (last name smudged by printer malfunction)

BRADDOCK COLLEGE SOPHOMORE

BIRTHDATE 8/10/84

(There's a faded picture of me in the center of the page, taken on some forgotten sunny day. I'm standing on the corner of a busy campus street, a backpack drooping from both shoulders, and I'm wearing a white pullover hoodie with a red Braddock College seal, jean shorts, and white sneakers. My features are a little blurry and distant, the way details look with a disposable camera. I have a grave, serious expression on my face, and my eyes are afraid. I totally have no memory of this picture being taken.)

LAST SEEN LEA I G WORK ON THE EV NING OF JUNE [ink runs], 2004. DISAPPEARED SOMETIME BETWEEN SUNSET ND 1 AM ON THE NIGHT OF JUN . VEHICLE FOU [ink got runny and wet here, and page is ripped] BLOOD. [long trail of ink runs unevenly down the page] SET OFF INTO TH [gash] ALONE AROUND MIDNIGHT ON UNE [smear of red marker] AND VANISHED [smudge], NO REMAINS HAVE BEEN FOUND.

[someone has taken a knife to this part of the page - a sharp, jagged line of silver shows where the pole got scratched underneath] WANTED FOR QUESTIONING IN CONNECTION WITH THIS D SAPPEARANCE.

IF YOU HAVE ANY INFORMATION REGARDING THE WHEREABOUTS OF [my name has been slashed out] PLEASE CALL BRADDOCK CAMPUS POLICE OR THE BRADDOCK COUNTY SHERIFF'S OFFICE.

My face goes numb with terror. Everything about this poster scares me to death - how it appeared so suddenly from beneath other papers, the idea that I could disappear and never be seen again. Mostly it's the page itself, with its huge, terrifying dead-black letters; just the sight of it makes my heart twist up inside my chest. Even my own picture, where I look like I'm in one of those fucked up Japanese horror movies, like I'm watching the angry corpse crawl out of the well and shamble closer and closer with the promise of horrific death.

Every pore on my body tingles with dread, and I take a step back. I start to wonder what's behind me; I never thought to check, but I'm scared to look now. I'm all by myself, stranded out here in the menacing night. Just because the streets are empty doesn't mean I'm alone.

Behind me is the past, troubled places haunted by the shadows of unfixable mistakes. An evil man waits beyond the light - Kenny. Beyond him, far off in the pitch black night, something else; much older, too powerful to ever face or kill. He sits on the wreckage of my worst regrets, the wreckage I've always wanted to fix more than anything. Things that broke me, left me half a person. Far away, out there in the dark. Looking this way.

Trapped here on the street with my terror, I look to the sky, hoping for something. Anything. The moon has come out, big and white above the trees ahead of me, in the one direction I never considered - toward the nicer part of town. The moon is the same as it's always been - distant and untouchable, friendly but indifferent. A white star sparkles in the sky below, like a little jewel hung as a Christmas ornament. There's a silent knowledge in my head, the way you always know things in dreams. That star smiles upon me with a calm promise - *If you can get to me, I'll gladly give you my power - you'll always be safe. You'll never be afraid of anything ever again.*

A cynical thought - *Yeah, that's awesome, but how am I supposed to get all the way up there? Even if I do, it won't be now, and I'm alone out here, in real danger.*

One more calm assurance - *You will.*

I get that dumb song in my head they used to play every ten minutes in the 90s - the one about not going home but not staying here. I can't loiter and wait for something to come out of the night. I'll catch a glimpse of some unspeakable face as the light starts to reveal its features, and I'll go insane. No, I better get moving. Kenny won't follow me into the nicer parts of town. Even though I've got nowhere to go and no one will have me, it's at least a little safer there. There's streetlights up that way, and hills and clean sidewalks. I can at least keep moving. Maybe something will present itself.

I start walking and catch one more glimpse of that MISSING poster. It's gonna stay here forever; time will pass, and it'll get covered up. Whatever happens, I won't be coming back. My terrified long-ago face will be buried and forgotten, and this campus will move on without anyone ever knowing I was here. The poster stares; it's menacing and I'm scared of it, but I try not to look as I walk by. I feel safer once it's behind me, and I keep moving toward the streetlights in the next part of town. I'm not exactly welcome, but I'm not *un*welcome either. As long as I stay on the move, I should be alright.

Without even doing anything, somehow that star feels a little closer. I have no idea how that's even possible, but it's true.

I open my eyes. My room is deep in shadow, and the window blinds slice the moonlight into silvery bars on the carpet. I'm lying on my side, and I huddle up with my arms over my chest. That dream lays on me like syrup, and I feel like I'm still in it just a little bit. It really made me aware of how silent, how still this apartment is in the dead of night. Like a corpse.

Okay, stop. I shiver. I want a drink of water, but my kitchen is at the far end of my apartment - a vast, terrifying distance, all alone. My cold, familiar living room is a stranger at this alien hour, and the moonlight looks obscene and threatening in its huge pools on the floor. I don't know if I really want to make the trip.

I glance at my alarm clock - 04:24 a.m. in red numbers. Ugh. I need sleep if I don't wanna pass out at work, but I'm a little scared to go back to sleep after that dream. But there's something sweet on the edge of my mind; if I could just remember-

Sadie.

Warmth spreads from the thought of her, down through me, quenching the nightmare's shadows like morning sunlight. I barely know the girl, but I've never vibed with anyone the way I did with her. She wouldn't want me to be freaked out. I'm so excited to see her today.

I'm all warm inside as I roll over. Soothed. I don't think I'll have a problem sleeping now - all I did was think of her, and now I don't feel alone anymore.

E i g h t

T h u r s d a y
June 3 2004

6:22 a.m.

Courtney

"And thus, realities...take unto themselves that which harmonizes, and cast out what does not harmonize. Thus every (verse) becomes a kingdom of HEAVEN, and HEAVENS beyond number and mortal reckoning drift together across the fathomless void, each contained, a kingdom unto itself. Thus is the perfect form and nature of GOD maintained."
-William Halle, *VERSOLOGICA PRINCIPIA*, 1639
Early versology text

"Will you come travel with me?
Shall we stick by each other as long as we live?"
-Walt Whitman, *Leaves of Grass*

Sunlight flickers on the window blinds, and I blink as my pupils adjust to the light. That freaky dream feels distant this morning, driven far away by sunshine and peaceful sleep. My bedroom is familiar again, with its cool, sweet-smelling air. There's a sweet feeling in my chest, like something went right yesterday...

Sadie.

So that *was* real.

I'm out of bed and halfway through my shower before it really hits me. What amazes me is the fact that I made such an awesome friend yesterday. I can't remember the last time I met someone that I clicked with so perfectly, and I'm a lot more amazed by *that* than the fact that she was talking like a flapper and wearing clothes from the 1920s, which is oddly kind of an afterthought. Somehow her presentation doesn't seem as explosive as the fact that I could vibe so exquisitely with another human being. But now that I'm thinking about it, she looks and acts like she walked off one of the yearbook pages at work. I guess it never really clicked until now. I wipe shampoo off my face and squint into the stream of water. Is this what it's like to go crazy?

I don't think so. "Crazy" still makes sense. "Crazy" is still of this world.

I roll down my window on the short drive down to campus. Moist with dew, heavy with the smell of green, the breeze is too chilly to enjoy without a jacket. Early morning air has a way of cutting you to the bone if you're lonely, and I can't remember the last time I enjoyed it like this.

I'm not really sure what's making me so happy. Maybe it's the heavy, sweet sense of anticipation. I can feel the machinery of fate moving into position like some huge clock. Something is coming. That always feels good, whether or not you fully realize what's happening.

When I park at Morton and start my walk uphill toward campus, I realize something else. I feel like one reality is superimposed on top of another. Let me see if I can explain it. Like, have you ever used a typewriter? You know how you can write one line, then push the carriage over and type back over it? You've got two sentences there, jumbled up, one on top of the other. The first line of text doesn't go away; they're both there now. That's sort of how I'm feeling right now. Except it's not words - it's a whole reality. And it all started with those goddamn yearbooks.

One thing is clear - this isn't just some project at work anymore. I feel like I'm being pulled in. Or like what's in the books is spilling *out*.

At the foot of Morton Hill, I stop and turn around. The sun is higher in the sky now, burning away the morning mist, and the air is starting to get hot and sticky. I'm the only person in sight, standing here on the brick walkway, just outside the shade of East Green. In the distance, my green Chevy Cavalier sits in the middle of that empty parking lot, floating on a sea of rippling heat waves. It looks small and flat, like a plastic cutout seen from far away. Almost fake. I turn around and head uphill, toward work.

I make a point of leaving a little bit early for lunch so I have time to go up and get something. I'm a nervous wreck.

I've been excited about lunch with Sadie since we made plans last night, but I'm also scared. Part of me is a little bit worried I'll walk outside and she won't be there and I'll be standing around on College Green like a loser, except a hundred times worse because I got ditched by my own hallucination. So I come back across the crosswalk and onto College Green with a knot in my stomach.

But there she is, all the way up by the middle building, just like she said. She's sitting in the shade, on those brick steps, and her face lights up when she sees me. She waves.

Oh, thank goodness. I breathe a sigh of relief.

"So I hope this isn't weird, but I'm really happy to see you," I tell her as I walk up.

"What for?" she tilts her head just a little. "Is something wrong?"

"Maybe I'm still a little worried that none of this is happening, and I'm just…"

"Screwy?" She smiles.

"Screwy." My lips pick up her smile.

"If I'm a hallucination," she says, "I'm a darn good one, because I've even got *me* fooled." She looks around, her gaze lingering on a grassy spot nearby. "You wanna have a seat?"

The world is changing. Colors are blooming. Everything is *brighter*, and everything I look at makes me happier. A sense of euphoria falls over me, and I have no idea why. It's just like that day in October of 1915, when I wandered out of the sparkling coppery woods and into Mary's yard. I was filled with absolute bliss and a sense of peace, like everything was right for the first time in my life. I was home.

I'm getting that feeling again right now.

"Yeah, let's."

As I follow her onto the lawn, I notice that there's actually people coming out of Cutler, the big building in the middle. A man and a woman are headed this way, both middle-aged, and the first thing I catch is a glint of reflected sunlight from the man's perfectly round wire-rimmed glasses. He's got thin hair combed over a bald patch on his head, and he's wearing a dark blue bow tie with a white shirt and suspenders. The woman next to him has dishwater blonde hair pulled back and flattened into a frumpy bun at the nape of her neck. She's wearing a really interesting dress; it's plain white cotton with long lapels that point down, and the dress is long enough to reach the middle of her calves. They're deep in their own conversation, but they smile and wave at Sadie as they pass us by.

It takes a minute or two for it to hit me - those two were dressed really vintage. As in *too* vintage, as in *authentic*.

Like Sadie.

Something feels weird in the air right now, and I keep it to myself while I ponder it. I *feel* things before they actually become visible to me. I feel a boxy, rectangular motor car clattering its way up Union Street, way up at the front of College Green; then I hear it a few moments later, and only *then* do I see it. It's a bit like hearing things underwater at first; it's muffled and the vibrations reach me before the sound does.

When I look back at Sadie, she's giving me a funny look, like she's right on the edge of a question. I start first.

"You told me I could say anything and you wouldn't judge me."

"Yep," she replies.

I squint at the muffled impressions of people walking nearby. "So, let's just get this out of the way. What year is it?"

"Oh." She almost seems relieved. "1921."

"1921." I draw out each syllable. "Okay."

Holy shit. It's real.

"And you?" she presses.

"2004." There's an actual horse and wagon headed up Court Street, and I'm gawking.

"*Jeez Louise.*" She's quiet and emphatic, and her eyes are wide.

"Hey," I say suddenly. "Before we get into the really crazy stuff, do you want some fries? I think they messed up and gave me a large. There's no way I'm gonna eat all these."

Right after finals were over at the end of spring quarter, I treated myself to a trip to Columbus one afternoon, just for me. Malls are lonely places when you're all alone, but I needed this. I always used to love shopping, and I didn't want to think of Krystal's slutty ass every time I came here. This was one of her favorite places to try and pick up guys. At least *that* wouldn't be a distraction anymore.

My main destination that day was Barnes and Noble. I was happily browsing books and at one point I found myself in the science section, with all those books about space and time and stuff. I happened on a book by this guy Brian Greene, all about the structure of time and why he thinks there's other universes. This stuff usually goes way over my head because it's got so much math, but I found the topic fascinating anyway. I managed to find another couple of books on time and probability and brought them back to the cafe. I ordered a Frappuccino and sat down with hungry curiosity.

I couldn't read the whole book in one afternoon, obviously, so I skimmed. Maybe I got some really botched understanding of everything, but what I learned lined up pretty well with my astronomy class last fall. Time flows forwards, and scientists don't really know why it goes that way and not backwards. Something about expanding chaos and entropy - I didn't understand that part. Anyway, the important thing is that you can't travel backwards in time, at least according to Einstein. You can travel into the future, if you can accelerate to a fast enough speed, but you can never actually go *back* in time. That's just the way it works, I guess. If you wanted to travel back in time and go to the Middle Ages - or the 1920s - you'd have to find a parallel universe where it was the Middle Ages or the 1920s and go there. So then you're not breaking the law of probability, you're just stepping around it.

And no, apparently that's not science fiction. There's this doctrine, the Many Worlds Hypothesis, and it's becoming science orthodoxy now. Physicists have good reason to think our universe is only one of countless, infinite universes out there, all with infinite possibilities. So, there's a universe where you're a criminal mastermind, or a comic book hero, or a comic book villain. There's a universe where you met totally different people, made totally different decisions, went to a different school, were popular or some hopeless outcast. There's a universe for every single possible variation of your life, or anyone else's life, or of anything at all.

So that's where I stopped with a blown mind and an empty Frappuccino. There was a lot the author couldn't answer, a lot of things physicists don't know yet.

At least in *this* universe they don't.

So maybe that's why I'm sitting here with Sadie right now, having what looks like a normal lunch and not completely freaking out. I've read a lot of fantasy and sci-fi - I've even written some, which could also help in being more flexible and open-minded. That's a good thing, because where I'm at right now, what I'm seeing, I think a lot of people would snap. Then again, maybe I snapped a long time ago, who knows? Maybe it's easier to take something like this in stride if you're already a little crazy.

But Sadie is pretty flexible and open-minded, too. So we pick at our shared lunch - me with a salad, fries, and Coke from Wendy's, her with a grilled cheese sandwich and tomato soup - and we try to get some sense of what's happening to us. It's kind of a relief to say *us*, because she's right there with me, having strange experiences she can't explain.

"So," she glances at me over her examination of a soggy french fry, "you're a...time traveler?"

I sigh a little, putting my drink down. "I dunno. Maybe? I mean, I always thought if you traveled in time, you *traveled*, you know? It almost seems like I'm phasing back and forth without even realizing it. And sometimes I'm halfway in my time and halfway in...1921, I guess. Or wherever. It doesn't really make sense."

She puts the fry back in the box and wipes her fingers on a napkin. "Well, it happened to me, too. Remember that *person* behind Ellis?" She puts an insulting twist on the word. "She looked like she might have come from your time. She certainly didn't come from *mine*."

I grin a little. "Yeah, that's true. You had a run-in with my world." I deadpan. "Sorry about that."

"It's not your fault, sweetie. Why, if I can be honest, you don't seem like you belong there at all." She gives me an apologetic wince. "I hope that doesn't sound offensive."

I'm not offended - more like stunned. Her observation makes me feel like someone shoved me onto the ground and knocked the wind out of me.

"Golly, I'm sorry-"

"No, no," I smile a little. "You didn't, really. It's alright. It's just, I guess I never thought of it like that. Or maybe I have, and nobody else has noticed before."

"People seem pretty self-centered where you come from," she says, a little resentfully.

I snicker. "*That's* an understatement."

She leans in, smirking. "Ever think about running away?"

I give her the full brunt of the wonder in my eyes. "I wish I could."

She glances around for a second, and her mischievous grin has a harder edge when she looks back at me. "Maybe you can." She was only joking before, testing the water. But now she's actually thinking about it. I am, too.

"Oh, Sadie. You have no idea." I look around too, amazement blooming in my brain with all its bright shades of hope and possibility. *Don't get your hopes up, Courtney. Don't get your hopes up, Courtney.* "Actually, that's something that's been bothering me for a long time."

"What do you mean?" She picks up my Coke, takes a sip.

"I don't want to take up your whole afternoon, though," I tell her. "It's...complicated."

"I *think* I can make room in my schedule." Her lips twist in a sardonic grin.

I give her a glance from the corner of my eye. Maybe she *would* get it.

"Well, remember how I told you about that project at work?"

She nods, taking another sip. "I'm drinking your Coke."

"Have all you want, sweetie."

So I start telling Sadie about the yearbooks, about Mary and Nettie, the 1915 Fall Festival, the attack, how my world felt close to Mary's, then far away again. I tell her about high school and constant regret. I tell her about the visions, the loss of time, wandering for hours through euphoric memories of the 1920s. How right now, sitting here with her, is exactly like it was with Mary and Nettie. Sadie listens to every word, her face grave as she takes it all in, forgetting our lunch in my insane story. She's not a condescending shrink, a cold scientist, or a terrified acquaintance. She's invested. She's a collaborator. She's with me.

"Gee whiz," she breathes when I finish. She blinks, trying to decide where to start. "Listen, I think all this is happening to you for a reason. To *us*. I haven't told you my story yet, but I'll tell you one thing - I don't think we're like other girls, Courtney. And for the record, I don't think either of us is screwy. I think we should just forget that idea right now, because it's not gonna get us anywhere."

She turns her face into the breeze, and it tosses her bobbed auburn hair around the bottoms of her small ears. She's so pretty. Her small lips look soft and alive and delicious, and I wonder what it would be like to kiss her. I push that out of my head before the blush can spread over my face.

"There's things about me you don't know yet, things I can do that other people can't. So take it from me that there's stuff in the world that science hasn't addressed." She catches me looking at her and suddenly she's embarrassed. "I'm sorry, I tend to ramble-"

"No, please," I tell her. "You're helping. A lot. So thank you."

"Well, that's a relief."

But what does she mean, *things that other people can't?* I want to ask her, but I don't want to push her before she's ready to tell me.

"Oh, listen," I suddenly remember, reaching for my backpack. "I'm totally over on my lunch, but I brought this to show you and I totally forgot." I reach in and pull out the

Expedition yearbook for 1922. I bookmarked the page with a purple Post-It note, and I flip gently to it once I've rubbed my fingertips clean with a napkin, careful not to touch the pages. "So I think I may have found you?"

I point at "Sadie Van Tassel" and flip the book around so she can see. She finds what I'm pointing at and her eyes slowly widen.

"Get outta town!" She's quiet, awestruck. "How is this possible? Why, I haven't even started class yet!"

I just shake my head. She stares at the page for a minute.

"Why, that's definitely me, all right." Sadie creases her eyebrows. "But I don't recognize that dress."

I lift my eyebrows. "Maybe you don't own it yet."

"Pff. Golly. Talk about a..." she searches for a word. "Something that really blows your mind. 'Humdinger' doesn't cut it."

"Mindfuck?"

She gives me that thin sideways grin again. "I love how you talk, Courtney." Her teeth are pretty and not *quite* perfect in that adorable way some girls have.

"I really like how you talk, too."

She smiles at me a minute before her glance returns to the pages she's absently flipping. Then she narrows her eyes at the book. She pulls her head back with an incredulous expression.

"Say, isn't this you?"

"Huh?"

She flips the book around again, stabbing the top of a page with her index finger. *Courtney Ashford, class of 1925.*

That girl has a different last name, but I'm fascinated. I've never heard of anyone having the name Courtney before the 1980s; definitely not the 1920s. I don't know how I managed to overlook this chick; she's gorgeous, *radiant*. Like Mary, she's got lovely eyes that look right into you from eighty years away. But where Mary's eyes are soft and enticing, Courtney's gaze is daring. With her bold half-smirk, the hair framing her lovely youthful face, she almost looks modern. Something about her is familiar and it's bugging me...

Then I see her necklace. It's three little sparkly hoops sitting together, like little silver Cheerios crusted with diamonds, on a delicate chain. For a fraction of a second I get this falling sensation, like when you're falling asleep at your desk.

I have that necklace. I'm wearing it right now.

I don't mean I'm wearing a necklace like it, I mean I'm wearing *that exact necklace.* I'd recognize it anywhere; I got it for myself last Christmas. The gems are tiny white sapphires set in silver, and the style is definitely early 2000s minimalist. And those little silver hoop earrings she's wearing, I have those too. The more I look at her face, the more familiar she becomes. It feels like looking in a mirror and seeing a happier version of myself in black and white. A cold trickle rolls down my spine as I stare at her.

She's wearing a fairly plain flapper dress with a plunging neckline; she's definitely not making any effort to hide her postmodern jewelry or razor-straight hair. But it's clear she belongs; she's not out of place among her classmates, and her oddly anachronistic style compliments her. She holds herself with pride and there's real happiness in those clever, sparkling eyes. Looking into those eyes fills me with hope and courage and strength, this sense that I can *do anything*. I get that rising sensation in my chest you only get when you discover something you want more than anything in the world, that perfect click that tells you that it's for you. *I want to be her.*

That eerie chill lingers on my spine, and a strange notion pops in my head: *maybe you already are.*

For a second, my world stops.

"Courtney?" I snap back to Earth; Sadie is looking at me. "Is everything alright?"

It's early afternoon and the sun sparkles in the green canopy of trees high above College Green, moving around on my shoulders with the whims of the breeze, warming patches of my skin wherever it touches. Everything is colorful, even the old black Ford Model T parked over on the street.

"I-" My throat is dry all of a sudden. I reach for the Coke, take a sip, choke on it, sputter and cough. Sadie leans in to help me, but I manage to catch my breath. I finally speak in a pathetic croak. "That's not my last name, but...look." I hold my necklace up.

"For crying out loud!" she breathes, leaning in to stare at the gems. "Why, that's the exact same necklace!" Our eyes meet, and we're wearing the exact same expression. Mutual terror.

I draw a breath of fresh air and try to calm myself. There's a lot of ambient noise around me. Birds chirping, fluttering in the branches above. A woodpecker drilling away at a hollow tree somewhere with that rattling wooden machine gun noise they make. The roar of wind in the trees, louder than normal. Leaves blowing across the curving brick paths. A single clattering motorcar engine, rattling its way up the street.

Curving brick paths. *Hold on.* There's no curving paths on College Green. They're all straight, and they streak their way across the green like a nerve cell. They're more concentrated over in the east corner, over by the auditorium and that tall church over in the corner.

"What the...?" I stand up.

"What's the matter?"

The web of walkways, all lined in brick, aren't there. There are two big brick pathways, curving around either side of the green. The paths I'm looking for are just trails in the summer dust, meandering across the grass.

"They're gone," I tell her. She waits for me to explain.

Those dusty little campus trails *do* converge in front of the church, on the top left of the green. But the buildings up here in front have big Victorian porches, lined with tall columns.

Those buildings haven't had porches for decades.

I take a couple of steps through a few fallen summer leaves. The church is there, and Ellis is there, but the front campus buildings have changed. When I look to my left, down toward the street, there's just a small grove of trees and empty grass. The auditorium is gone. When I turn around, Chubb is, too. There's nothing between me and Union Street except a wide expanse of sunlit grass and old trees.

I turn to Sadie very slowly. On my way, I actually *see* the scattered few people crossing College Green this time of the afternoon. Nobody's invisible or "almost" there. They're *there*, as real as me, and they're wearing flat newsboy caps or long dresses with the pointed lapels.

"Courtney, you're starting to frighten me. Please say something."

I look at her helplessly. "Hey, Sadie? So...if I got stuck in 1921, could I maybe crash with you?"

Her eyes flash with sudden, fierce hope.

Nine

Tuesday
September 6, 1921

3:19 p.m.

Courtney

"Captain Morrison's later forensic divination would uncover several rather cheap tricks that must have been employed with no other purpose than to intimidate a young college freshman, and which would not have impressed even a middling arcanist in the slightest. If Pearse had attempted to use his enscrived pocket watch eight months later on any of the Keepers of the Veil, they would have laughed him off the street, for the cheapness was not in the theric reaction itself, but the intent behind it. Captain Morrison, in her official report, would call it 'a childish example of carnival charlatanism.'"
- Edith Winthrop, *Flapper Sorcery: American Arcanology in the 1920s*

"Say, I was gonna take care of a couple of things uptown..." Sadie seems uncertain. "Would you like to come with me?"

I look at myself, all tank tops and zipper hoodies and jean shorts and Chucks. I look back at her with a grimace. She catches it right away.

"Your clothes," she remarks. "Hmm. Say, why don't you go on down to my house. It's quiet down there, and that way you won't be gawked at."

I nod, following her train of thought. "Okay, yeah."

"You'll need my house key, of course," Sadie says, after I scribble her address at the top of an old syllabus.

"No, wait." I stop her with a hand as she's reaching into her purse. "You better keep it for now. I don't know if this is for real, or..." I glance around, pulling my hoodie closer around my shoulders.

"Or if you're gonna phase right back," she finishes.

"Exactly."

There's a strange tingle on my skin. The tingle gets more intense and reminds me of static on an old TV, until the tingle spots grow larger and merge into each other. Those spots soak into me, into my spirit, and turn warm, before they burn into me and seep pure bliss into my being. My whole world is consumed in intense joy, a storm of vibrant colors. Euphoria. For the first couple of seconds, it kinda burned, but now it's subsided into a nice, warm glow. It's a really strange sensation, like I'm becoming a part of this reality. I'm starting to feel "locked in," I guess, in a way I didn't just a few minutes ago.

Sadie bounces a little, her face lighting up like Christmas. "Oh, Courtney, this is just the cat's particulars! We're gonna have so much fun!"

We share a quick, excited hug, my chest vibrating with excitement. As she pulls away, she takes both of my hands in hers and we share this ecstatic look.

"I hope..." I shake my head a little, unable to finish my sentence. There's too many things I'm hoping for, and I'm worried I could still jinx myself.

"I will see you as soon as I finish," she says, face split with a smile. "I shouldn't be any more than an hour."

"I can't wait," I tell her, my heart in my eyes.

"Me either!" She turns toward the crosswalk. "See you shortly!"

"Okay!"

With that, I turn toward the sun-drenched entrance to College Green, drawing a deep breath of this new air.

Sadie called it my "new life." Wouldn't that be nice? It almost feels like too much to hope for.

Have you ever looked at really old pictures of your town from a long time ago? You ever notice how, if you go far enough back, the town becomes harder to recognize? I guess miles and years can both take you away from home, and the farther you go, the less familiar things are.

It's still Autumn Grove, but it's not the Autumn Grove I know. The light is slanted differently. The town looks different. It smells different. It *feels* different. It's like the sibling of someone you know really well, or maybe a family member. There's a resemblance, but they're still a different person.

The streets are still paved with ruddy bricks, but all the buildings along those streets are different. Campus buildings share the sidewalk with Victorian houses and porches. The shade-dappled curbsides are bare; I think I see one Model T sitting along the street at the front of College Green. Uptown, most people get around on foot, though there's at least two brown horses I can see pulling wagons up Court Street a block away.

I almost pull out my iPod and turn on my music - purely out of habit - but the gentle, breezy silence stops me. I can't cover up this beautiful quiet. Not today.

Then a flash of alarm through my brain, startling me back out of my thoughts: how will I survive here? Where will I stay? Sadie is the only person I know.

Sadie is the *only person in the world* I know.

The way I've been phasing back and forth, I don't think I'm gonna be able to control it. This time travel thing, if that's what you want to call it, it's not like walking down a hallway and choosing a door; it's more like being blown around in a gale, tossed around at the mercy of some kind of crazy cosmic weather. If this is anything like when I phased into 1915 that time, there was a short window where it was strongest, almost like the way the moon's pull is strongest when it's full. Then that window starts to close, and it becomes harder to phase back and forth. So I'm not gonna be able to just come to 1921 every night after work, hang out with Sadie for a while, then go back to 2004 and sleep in my apartment. I'm gonna need to make a choice: 1921 or 2004.

That's something else. Sadie. I barely know her. I just met her yesterday! Talk about a mindfuck - I feel like I've been best friends with the girl since junior high. She might be okay with me crashing on her couch for a couple of nights, but then I'll probably need to move on so I don't wear out my welcome. The last thing I want is to ruin the one

121

friendship I have. Besides, she said her sister would be back at some point. What if her sister doesn't like me? What if Sadie herself decides she doesn't like me? I'm amazed she likes me at all, to be honest; usually nobody likes me.

And I don't have any clothes! It's almost like being naked. No money - I have like five dollars and some change from 2004 in my wallet, and the rest of my money is on my debit card. Most of my transactions are electronic. God, I don't even have any ID! No birth certificate, no identity. I don't officially exist.

Well, whatever. First things first. I'll go to Sadie's place tonight, and we'll talk when she gets home. Maybe she can help me figure something out. And if not, I'll go back.

Back to 2004, where the clock is ticking. Soon I might not have a place to stay there, either.

Deep breath. Onward.

I stand at the very front entrance to College Green, looking north up College Street. I snicker to myself. The student center should be just across the street in front of me, diagonally to my left. Instead, there's a couple of old two-story houses. Across the street to my right is an aging three-story academic building with one of those Greek Revival front porches, the kind with the big pillars in front. A plaque above the front entrance reads HOWARD HALL. Seeing it there is messing with my sense of reality; I'm used to seeing an open park space there with a few paved sidewalks. Beyond it, just down the hill, is the clinic I go to at least three times every winter and crowd into the waiting room with a hundred other people with the exact same illness. Who knows if that clinic exists here.

I start across the brick street, taking soft, careful steps without even meaning to. The campus I'm used to might be pretty, but it doesn't compare to the old beauty of this place. Oaks and maples, tall and ancient and deep green, tower over the north side of campus. Here, you can go all the way up College Street, as far as you can see, and never step out of the shade. Tall, narrow Edwardian houses nestle along the shady narrow street, broken once in a while by a sorority house with white pillars on the porch. I can only imagine how beautiful this big green campus must be in the fall, with the smell of dry leaves in the air.

There's something so welcoming in the air this afternoon. I breathe the comfort into my lungs and it radiates into my stomach and warms me like coming home after being gone for a long time. Not that I'd know firsthand, but I've got a pretty good guess as to what that must feel like. These dusty old streets, the dry clatter of old cars making their way up the street behind me. Tidy little stores with wood-paneled floors and a handful of candy for a dime. Pop from soda fountains. The sharp smell of wood smoke on the air and the dry scent of fallen leaves rolling down the brick street. The smells of a warm cozy parlor, and the crisp new pages of one of those really tall magazines they used to sell. I randomly get the taste of home-cooked food, of iced tea with fresh lemon dropped in. Just down the street, at one of these cozy Victorian houses, someone's got the door propped open and a staticky old record plays onto the street. A chick just a few years older than me appears in the doorway with a long maroon skirt and matching blouse, her dark brown hair pulled up in a bun. I instinctively flinch, remembering that I'm dressed in shorts and t-shirt and a zip-up hoodie. But when she sees me, she waves and gives me the sweetest, most heartfelt smile. I must look pretty crazy when I return it with this look of desperate relief on my face. It's because there's so much simple affection in her greeting, and I feel it soothing aches inside me I never knew I had.

I'm starting to feel like I've come home to a place I never knew was home. I walk a little faster, my legs suddenly feeling naked and conspicuous. Not because I don't feel like I belong, but because I *want* to belong. Being stuck here might not be so bad.

I almost allow myself a smile as I make my way up this shady street. I glance back once to make sure I haven't attracted too much attention. That black Model T is going on its way; it seems like they didn't see me.

That's when I catch it - a dark spot. A man stands at the corner I just came from, staring in my direction. He's a black speck at the edge of my vision, a horsefly marring the perfection of my gorgeous painting. He's big and solid, rooted like a light post in concrete about a half a block away. He wears a dark suit, pinstripe trousers, and a round black derby hat. He's staring right at me; I feel his gaze on my clothes, my skin, like a Doberman that's just sniffed out its prey. Like a prison spotlight, exposing me, nailing me in place.

Got you.

He's so out of place in the comforting beauty of his surroundings that I can't help but stare in horrified fascination. His eyes are wells of blackness, absorbing everything, giving nothing back. Holes. He holds himself upright, solid shoulders set in the relaxed confidence of someone who's never been wrong in his life. He looks like he's in his late thirties, and the easy hardness of his face suggests someone born cruel. He's never aged a minute from stress or worry because he can't feel those things. No compassion, no empathy, no pity; a machine. I've only known one other person like that, and my ex is dating him. I shiver, suddenly cold despite the summer warmth. I wither under his inhuman gaze; naked, defenseless. Only one thing goes through my head, over and over - an overwhelming need to get as far away from him as I can, as fast as I can. I take a faltering step back.

He wiggles a finger back and forth like a metronome.

Bad girl. Don't do that.

Icy terror freezes my blood. I need to get out of here, *now.*

Ten

Sadie

"The history of arcanology in America is woven inseparably with the history of the great rogue arcanist circles of legend. The American heart is ever infatuated with the noble outlaws, the swashbuckling gunslingers of the Old West, with the free folk of every age who refuse to be ruled, whether by kings or religion. Perhaps there is something in the American character that lends itself to informality, plain-spokenness, independence, and mistrust of authority. America was a frontier nation for much of its history, and our arcanology reflects that; America attracted the disdain and even alarm of the long-established circles of Europe and Asia throughout the 17th and 18th centuries, both for our cavalier attitude toward theory and practice as well as for the innumerable rogue arcanists that haunted the frontier. Americans, in turn, mocked the stuffiness and snobbery of their counterparts in the Old World...

...However, just as in every mythic age, the truth in back of the legends is less romantic. If one finds honor and inspiration in the free spirit of American rogue arcanology, in the age of 'Howitzer Henry' Beaumont and Seven-Gun Sallie, the Bitterroot Desperadoes and the Whiskey Fire Rangers, then one must also blame the Knights of Augustine for sounding the death knell of that heroic age."
-J.M. Devon, *Taming the Frontier: The Decline of Rogue Circles in America 1900-1945*

I can scarcely keep a handle on myself as I hurry about my errands. No matter how fast I walk, the street doesn't pass quickly enough. Courtney's absolutely here! She's waiting for me!

I remind myself that I've only known the kid for what, twenty-four hours? I just can't get that through my head. We finish each other's sentences. Nothing we say can throw the other one off. Something in me is drawn to her, and saying I barely know her almost makes me want to laugh. I feel that's quite beside the point, and not fully true besides.

Just because we only met yesterday doesn't mean we don't know each other. On the contrary - I think we know each other really well!

Maybe she'd think I was a sap if I said that. Maybe I *am* a sap. Though I honestly think that's just my insecurity talking. The vibration in my chest says she feels exactly the same way.

I finally get out of the grocery, back into the warm sun, quick steps taking me home. I'm full of pep; moreso now than any time since I've been here. I'm nervous the whole way back; everything inside my ribcage vibrates like a tuning fork. At one point I begin to wonder why I'm such a nervous wreck. Why, it's almost like I'm going on a first date with the biggest crush of my life. Gee whiz, *do* I have a crush on her?

Dry up, Sadie. Don't even entertain the notion - there's no way a doll like her gets a crush that fast, especially not on the ugly Van Tassel sister. You'll end up embarrassing yourself.

She *is* awful pretty, though - dainty and feminine. Flawless face, just a few freckles smattered across the bridge of her nose. That rosy blush that lights up her cheeks when she laughs, that adorable sparkle in her soft eyes when she's relaxed and trusting. And her eyes, *oh*. They're like little windows into a bright blue sea, so deep you could never see the bottom but you could easily spend hours gazing, watching. Lovely pale blonde hair, her delicate feminine scent, just a hint of sweet perfume on her soft ivory skin. The way she looks so soft and delicate when she looks at a book, the way her deft fingers sweep locks of hair behind her tiny ears. A sweet smile, so open and full of wonder. Soft lips of cherry red, moist and glossy, begging to be kissed.

My chest is tight and I'm short of breath. *Stop it, Sadie.*

Well, we're gonna have a swell time, regardless. We'll stay up talking way too late, and we'll figure out how to get her started on her brand new life. We'll make a regular flapper out of her, and it'll be the happiest occasion of her life.

Just thinking about it makes me happier than I've been in as long as I can remember. She deserves a fresh start. She deserves people who care about her.

I come around the corner, trying to spy her from the top of the street. It should be easy, her red sweater jacket, a flash of white from her t-shirt. But there's nothing. Maybe I need to get closer?

But sure enough, I get to my house - and nothing. Maybe she's around back, waiting on the back porch? That would be the smartest thing; I can't believe I didn't think of that myself. Surely she's there-

Nope.

I stop, look back and forth, confused.

"Courtney?"

I'm answered by a slight breeze, a hint of evening closing in fast. I call her name again and again, go back and stand on my front porch, stare into the coming twilight.

She's not here.

But where else could she have gone? She hasn't anyone, anywhere to go. Could she have gotten lost? Could the cops have found her and taken her in because of her clothes? Could she have phased back?

Could she have just decided she didn't want to pal around with *me?*

The grocery bag slides from my hands, lands upright with a *plop* by the door. Then I slump down, knees together, on the steps of my concrete porch. An enormous cloud descends over me, heavy and opaque. There's so many things that could have happened to her, and I feel I should do something but I simply don't know what. What if she's in trouble? Should I go out looking for her? Should I go to the police, or back up to College Green? Why, she could be absolutely *anywhere,* and I haven't a clue where to begin.

What if she's relying on me?

What if she's simply avoiding me?

Indecision crushes me, pulls me in a dozen directions at once, and I feel more alone than ever in this lonesome town so far from home. I rest my face in my hands, feeling the ache of tears.

A sudden presence in front of me. Before I can look up-

"Miss Van Tassel?"

Three men in front of me. One dumpy and plain in nice clothes, the other one a withered little fossil in outdated tweed, and in the middle a two-story bruiser with a face that could break rocks. The old man scowls at me. The big one in the middle just stares at me, his face full of terrible things I'd rather not imagine.

I sit up a little. "Why, yes, that's right."

"We're a civic interest group called the Knights of Augustine," the fat one says. "I'm Mr. Hodges. These are my associates, Mr. Pearse and Mr. Eastwicke." Their faces are cold gravestones. "We're here to talk to you about a friend of yours. One, ah," he flips through a notepad. "Courtney."

"What's happened?" I stand up. "Is she all right?"

"What is the nature of your relationship with this young woman?" The fat one asking the questions, he talks like a police detective. Official, in charge. But the other two stare at me like I'm some kind of working girl in an alley. The old one scowls like an angry preacher right on the edge of screaming an hour-long sermon in my face. The other one wears a cold sort of smile, like a wolf in the dark, like some prowler seeing through my clothes.

I glance back at the fat one. "Are you with the police?"

He ponders that. "Perhaps it might be best if you thought of us in that manner."

"Answer the question." The big one glowers at me. He's got a jutting brow bone that shades his eyes like a porch awning.

I take them in again, this strange trio. They'd make a great comic strip - Grouchy, Goofball, and Goon - but they aren't police. There's something *off* about them. They make my blood run cold, like bugs crawling on my skin. I'm overwhelmed by a sense of loathing, of unease, and all I want is to get away from them.

"Why, no," I say after a moment. "I don't think I will."

The big one steps forward, black eyes staring holes in me. "You sure about that?"

Then it hits me. I'm so dumb - why didn't I see it before?

"You've done something with her, haven't you?" I ask, my voice quiet and sharp with accusation.

Nothing. They just stare. Clearly, it's still my move.

"What have you done with her!?" I demand, a lot louder this time. The big one makes my skin crawl, but something in me has snapped. There's an electric outrage in my veins and it's keeping me going.

"Dose her with laudanum or chloroform or something," the old bluenose growls. "We need her calm and compliant. We won't have any success with a raging little harpy like this."

The round one, Hodges, flashes him a look, commanding him to be silent. But the damage is done. I'm seeing red and my blood is boiling.

"*Dose me!?* Did you *hurt my friend,* you filthy old pervert!? If you touched a hair on her head, why, I swear I'll *kill you myself!*"

The huge one glides onto my porch like a glacier, presses me back toward my front door. "You'll what?" He's quiet, almost whispering, as he looms in close. "Pardon me, I didn't catch that last part."

He's arching over me, forcing me to back up and crane my neck just to keep my eyes on his. He's pushing me backwards without touching me, this thick barrier of intimidation that will bend me over, send me flying off my feet and onto my rear end where I'll be at his mercy. He wants me sobbing, begging to spill anything I know.

This monster is capable of anything. Anything at all. What have they done with Courtney?

I shouldn't have let the poor thing out of my sight for a minute. I should have insisted she come with me, and to hell with anyone that had a problem.

Oh, Courtney...

Eleven

Courtney

"So looke with kindly eyes
Upon the Displaced hounded by lyes
For 'tis widely knowne
Devils seek not their owne;
Virtuous blood be their prize."
-17th century versologist's maxim

"I think all of them were destined to come together in a great tale of friendship, sisterhood, and love. But the road that led to the Keepers of the Veil, or the 'Flapper Covenant' as people have taken to calling us, began with three bullies, two hard-boiled flappers, and a war heroine."
-Alice Thatcher, *Memoirs of an Accidental Arcane,* 1927

There's a little T-shaped intersection coming up on my left - Washington Avenue. From there, it's a short block over to Court Street and the very busiest part of town. I should probably stick to more populated areas until Sadie gets finished. Maybe I can even catch up with her. But that'll involve being seen by everyone, won't it? Aren't there laws about what clothes women can wear in the 1920s or something? Ugh, dammit. So now I have to choose. I can go up to Court Street and loiter in a more public area and risk being arrested for indecent exposure or something, or I can take my chances on the back streets with some creep job following me. Awesome. Even in 1921, in a time and place where life is supposed to be simpler, I manage to bring plenty of complexity with me.

I'm staying on the right side of the street, where I started; if someone's watching me or following me, I want to avoid spooking them until the last minute. That will give them less time to react, and it might give me the second or two I need to get to safety. Washington is coming up on my left, a sunny corridor spilling light into the shade of the street I'm on. I turn really quick to see if that guy started following me or anything.

He's behind me and he's a lot closer, like maybe a hundred feet. Wait, what? How the *hell* did he catch up with me that fast?! Even if he'd taken off at a dead sprint the moment I saw him last, he'd still only be halfway to where I am right now. And he's walking - strolling, even. He's grinning, like he's enjoying this.

The side street isn't far now. I'm about to break into a run when I see a figure waiting at the corner, across the street from me. An old man in a brown tweed suit fixes me with an icy glare of disapproval, like I toilet papered his lawn. He's got a gray goatee and mustache and bushy eyebrows like smog above his beady eyes. Is he just offended by my clothes? The more I look at him, I don't think so. If he'd just stumbled on me by chance, he'd go through a few seconds of shock and dismay before settling into moral outrage. This geezer's face has been locked on mine since he arrived. He was waiting for me.

These guys are obviously interested in me for some reason. I could try to run - the street is still open in front of me. But this makes two men who look like they're seeking me out on purpose. And if there's two, chances are good there's a third one lurking somewhere. I might as well face them, find out what they want.

I stop at the intersection, turning a little so I can face them both. I try to relax and look confident, hoping they can't see my guts trembling inside my ribcage. This is starting to feel like one of those true crime shows on late-night TV.

The guy following me, the one in the black suit, slows down as he approaches. Deep black eyes set in a face full of edges, jawbones and cheekbones poking out of his skin like a skeleton cuddled up in a bag. But for as bony as his face is, he's awfully big, with a broad, flat chest. He towers over me, blotting out the sun when he gets close, like an obelisk in a black pinstripe suit. He reminds me of some assassin you'd see on the X-Files. His cold smile spreads as he draws closer.

Sometimes those true crime shows have interviews with people in prison - serial murderers, sex traffickers, pedophiles. The worst of them are devoid of anything resembling humanity. Dead eyes, monstrous smiles. He's starting to give me the same kind of vibe.

I call out to him, not bothering to hide my annoyance.

"Um, can I help you?"

He doesn't reply, just tilts his head. He purses paper-thin lips, looks hard at me like a menu at a fancy restaurant, gears moving. He looks tempted and skeptical, the way someone might look if you begged them to take a free tray of gourmet chocolate and they weren't sure if they were hungry. Flat eyes drift down my neck, linger on my chest for a second, then fall down and drink the rest of me like a glass of water he gulps down without thanking anyone. Those eyes scale my body again, back to my chest, up to my face. He sucks something out of his teeth, balancing things in his mind like someone about to haggle on a price.

Revulsion churns in my stomach. Nobody has ever dehumanized me like this. He's wondering if he feels like sampling what's on offer, how I compare with the fifty gorgeous women that throw themselves at him every day.

I've never felt so violated, so naked, so disgusted. So *angry.* He's everything I've ever hated about men, distilled and concentrated and amplified. They see everything in their environment the same way they see food at a buffet - there to examine, to weigh, decide on, take or pass. Almost every man I've ever known has this deeply programmed assumption that the world - and everything in it - is theirs for the asking. Or the taking. I never asked to be accosted and here I am, stalked and tracked down, weighed and judged, in one righteous motion. Like I asked for all of it.

"I don't know," he says after a minute, smiling at himself. "Can you?"

I squint in confusion, my lip curling in disgust. I'm shaking my head, ready to ask what exactly that means, when he finishes. "Yes. You need to come with us."

The old man has crossed the street and now he's next to the black suit in front of me. They want me to come with a creeper who just undressed me with his eyes and a crotchety old stalker that cut me off at the intersection to stop me from getting away.

As if.

I level them with an outraged stare. "And I'm gonna need you to go fuck yourself."

"She's got a mouth on her." The old man's voice is a death rattle, and his expression is a burning Bible.

"I'll handle this." A chubby man makes his way across a neighboring lawn, approaching from my left now. I was right when I wondered if I'd be accosted from three sides. I shoot a twitchy glance over my shoulder, making sure nobody's coming up behind me.

This new guy is flabby and round, taking wide, careful steps across the grass in shiny leather shoes. He's wearing a nice black suit and black bowler hat like the man in front of me, but this new guy looks like a bureaucrat, some paper pusher in an accounting department who gave up on getting a date years ago so now he makes fun of women on the internet and jerks off to girly anime. They both look like they're in their late thirties, but now that I'm looking at them it's kinda hard to tell. It's like they don't look old but they don't look exactly young, either. They don't really look *anything.* Even the old one with the brown Victorian hunting tweed has something vague about him that makes details hard to guess.

"Miss?" Chubby guy makes it to the sidewalk, brushing something off his dark trousers. "Please excuse my colleagues. They can be...undiplomatic."

I raise my eyebrows.

"I intended to speak with you first, but it seems they beat me to the punch. Now, then. My name is Jeremiah Hodges, and I'm Vice Castellan of the Knights of Augustine. You've met my associates, Mr. Pearse," he nods at the six-foot-eight tower of bones and meat. "And Mr. Eastwicke." The wheezing old cadaver.

Vice Castellan of the Knights of Augustine? Either I've died and gone to LARP-land, or I'm in some purgatory full of creepy clubs for old dudes that throw fund raisers and march in parades.

"Hi." Sorry, but it's really *not* nice to meet you. "Courtney."

"Courtney. Pleased to meet you."

"So...who are you guys?" I ask. "And why are you following me?"

"Ah," he says, almost regretfully. "We're what you might call a public interest group."

My eyebrows rise again. "A what, now?"

"I'm afraid it's all rather complex," he says, waving his hand dismissively. "Nothing you need concern yourself with. But more to the topic, Miss, we're not here to harm you. In fact, we're here to rescue you!"

"Rescue me."

"That's right." He smiles encouragingly. "Do you know where you are?"

My eyes dart around, taking in my surroundings. "Is this a trick question?"

He seems taken aback. "No."

"A poll?" Then I snap my fingers, point at him. "No! One of those annoying Israeli guys in the mall! With the moisturizer."

"Miss," a hint of frustration in his voice. "Have you any idea where you are?

I smirk, just a little. "Last I checked, I was in Autumn Grove."

"Autumn Grove, yes," he says, excitement in his voice. It feels rehearsed, like a sales pitch. "And do you know *when* you are?"

I squint at him. Things have been weird as shit, but these questions, these *men*, definitely take the prize. Obviously, if he's asking me that, he knows it's possible to be in another time, too. Or another place entirely. "Um. I dunno. It was 1921 a few minutes ago. Has it changed?"

A flicker of confusion across Hodges' face. Meatface and Bedpan share a quick glance. I allow myself a second to gloat; I put them on the back foot. Score one for Courtney.

"N-no," Hodges stammers. "No, of course not. The situation is quite serious, Miss. I hope you appreciate that."

He's not sure if I'm being flippant or serious. That must mean he doesn't know everything about me. I let myself grin a little. "Oh, I agree. See, I know *exactly* where I am, and when. I'm not an idiot." Eastwicke snorts; it sounds like a nursing home patient snoring themselves awake, lungs rattling with lethal congestion. I ignore him and go on. "You guys really don't know what's going on, do you?"

Hodges' eyebrows crease in annoyance. "We know the details perfectly well, Miss. Unfortunately, you're in a place you don't belong. We came to help you with that, to send you home."

"Home?" I lift my eyebrows. "I don't have any idea what that word means. All I know is this happened to me once before. You didn't know that, did you?"

He shakes his head. "That is immaterial-"

"I'm sure," I tell him. "You don't give a rat's ass, but I've spent my whole life hoping it would happen again. That *place* you want to send me back to? That's not my life."

Hodges chuckles. "That's absurd."

I'm getting really bored with these guys. "Yeah, so it's been great talking to you, but I have friends I have to go see, so...*later!*" I raise a hand, wave a little with my fingers.

"You have one friend," Hodges declares to my back as I turn away. "A Miss Sadie Van Tassel. And yes, we're watching her, too."

My blood turns to ice water when I hear him say Sadie's name. I turn to face them. "*Watching* her?!" I demand. "Are you stalking my friend, you fucking creep?!"

Pearse, the monolith with the hard face, smiles a little. He must like emotional reactions. He pushes back the side of his coat, revealing a little black sap on his belt - those black leather dildo things that cops carried in the 1800s, or like you see in gangster movies from the 1930s. It looks ridiculous on such a huge person; his fist alone is half the size of that thing.

"You're outside your natural realm of existence," Hodges insists. "That makes you dangerous. So yes, naturally we keep a close eye on any associates you may have."

"You stay the hell away from her!" My words are hot venom, and I take a step forward. "Or I will fucking *end you!*"

The old one, Eastwicke, has listened to the conversation with growing outrage, and the white bristles of his goatee tremble with suppressed fury. His bottom jaw cocks to the side in blind rage.

"Come here, you little hussy! You need to be taught some manners!"

He makes a few awkward swipes at my arms with gnarled fingers and long yellow nails. Before I can back up, he latches his skeletal claws onto my right arm.

I had this gym class in junior high, taught by one of the head coaches who was too busy to actually teach the class most of the time, so he let us pretty much do what we wanted. I had a couple of older classmates in advanced karate who passed the time teaching me basic martial arts. They drilled me on how to block punches until it was a knee-jerk reaction, and they spent two whole class periods on breaking holds. They drilled me over and over until I could do it all by reflex.

So I'm as surprised as Eastwicke is when I realize I've twisted out of his grip and jabbed him in the throat. Rheumy eyes bulge out of his head and long, gnarled fingers clutch at his baggy neck skin. He's coughing, hacking, wheezing. I hate that my first instinct in times like these is to make sure the person is okay, especially when I realize that I've caused harm. But I shake off my compassion. These men stalked me, and they stalked Sadie *because* of me. I have to get out of here, right now.

I turn and run as fast as I can. Maybe I can lose them in the little streets north of campus, then I'll double back and wait for Sadie. I can't go to the police, not with how I'm dressed. In a weird kind of way, the thought drives it home that I'm really in the 1920s, but it also reminds me how alone I am. I don't have anywhere to go, anyone to trust.

One of the basic things they teach you in self-defense is that, if you're being attacked, make as much noise as you can. You want to draw attention to what's happening; a lot of attackers will second-guess themselves if they're afraid of being seen. But I don't have enough breath in my lungs to shout and run at the same time; I have to choose one or the other. So I run. And if you've ever worn Chucks, you'll know they're not quiet shoes if you're flat-out running as fast as you can. *Smack, smack, smack.* I lose myself in the steady rhythm of my shoes hitting concrete, finding an odd sort of comfort in the repetitive *tap-tap* echo between houses.

I can't hear anything behind me, so I sneak a quick look over my shoulder. They're all standing there, not chasing me, and that's all I can tell. I can't risk slowing down to take a longer look. I have to keep running.

They haven't moved. Maybe I bought myself some time when I punched the old guy? My eyes are quick, scanning in front of me; nobody has come around to intercept me, at least not that I can see. So far, so good. If I can just mak-

Smash.

My whole body hits the bricks at full speed. An explosion of white light and ten thousand stars where my head hit the wall, a single coughing grunt, and I'm flat on the pavement. It takes me a full second to realize that *I* made the sound; it's the sound you make when you get the air knocked out of your lungs and it passes through your vocal chords. I'm choking, I can't breathe. The need for air overrides everything else, but the warning lights are still flashing in my brain. *Get up! Keep running!*

I struggle to rise, palms against the hot brick pavement, pushing myself up. I take a moment to glance in front of me, looking for the wall I ran straight into. I'm pretty alert; I don't just run into things. The wall I hit was at least as tall as me, and I'd have definitely seen that.

There's nothing there. I hit a wall, and I hit it with my whole body. But there's *nothing there*, nothing at all except empty street. I blink, my brain fumbling the conflicting information, trying to piece it together. *How...?*

A long shadow over me, then a huge fist grabs the top of my arm like a twig. The hand is big enough to wrap around my bicep the way I'd grab a strap on my backpack. My brain is starting to work now, and I know whose hand this is. Pearse may not have talked much, but it's easy to tell he's a man of action. His fist is hard as granite, and scorching pain erupts in my arm as he grips the underside of it and hauls me into the air. By his practiced ease, I'm guessing I'm not the first girl he's intercepted with those Frankenstein hands of his.

I'm dangling above the pavement. He leans in and smells the side of my neck; air hisses through his long hairy nostrils. I cry out against the fiery agony in my muscles and bone, and whimper in terror when he scrapes my neck with bristle like steel wool.

"Get off me, you fucking creep!!" My voice sounds shrill in my ears. I try to twist my arm out of his industrial grip, knowing it probably won't matter anyway. There's no escaping him. There was never any hope of escaping these men.

"Off the street, Pearse," the fat man says quickly. "Let's use the courtyard behind Howard Hall. We need to make this quick."

They're gonna kill me. These wackjobs are gonna take me into a back alley and kill me. In an instant, I realize this is it. This is how my life ends. Twenty years old, still technically a college sophomore. Murdered.

Pearse grunts some kind of filthy approval against my neck. He puts his other massive hand against my collarbone, runs his palm down the front of my tank top, staying on top of my clothes but pressing his hand against my breast. I watch it happen with mute horror and a numbness comes over me, that sense of moving out of your body and watching things happen to yourself from the outside. Cold, observing, unfeeling; life tastes like mineral oil, like smooth nothing, while you watch a horror movie happen to you in the next room. I feel something hard poke into my ass, and when I realize what's happening, I clench my teeth in revulsion.

I might as well do it now; it's not like I need to save my air. I draw a breath and scream this blood-curdling, ear-splitting shriek.

"GET OFF ME, YOU FUCKING ASSHOLE!!"

The hand on my chest clamps over my mouth like a steel trap, aching and bruising my face. His huge fingers block my nose, and I can't breathe.

"Now, Pearse!" the fat man commands. "This job was your idea, and we're going to carry it out. Amuse yourself on your own time."

My captor grunts, carrying me forward again, hand still over my mouth.

A searing pain in my arm before it starts to go numb. He carries me like that most of the way, not bothering to let me walk on my own; my shoes scrape the sidewalk as I try to gain footing.

"Let him do it, Hodges," the old man wheezes, rubbing his neck. "Teach that little trollop some manners. Or let me have her, so I can give her a good spanking."

"We have one simple job," Hodges says firmly. "And it doesn't involve rape, or spanking, or anyone else's goddamn perverted fantasies. Foul this up, and I'll see that you both answer to Kluivert for what happens here today. And if someone reports us to the police, or you bring that meddling Seven Towers witch down on us, I will see you both cast out for your incompetence - especially you, Pearse. You brought us out into the open just to banish one little Displaced girl. You went *on and on* about how powerful she is, how essential it is that we send her back. It's starting to look like you set it up for your own amusements."

Powerful? *Me?* Did I hear that right? They definitely have no clue what they're doing. The only power I seem to have is being a magnet for abusive men.

Pearse stops carrying me for a second, and the air goes tense. I feel stony glares being exchanged, even if I can't see them. He continues on. I'm being carried behind Howard Hall, the really old Victorian building across from College Gate. They're taking me into the alley behind it; in my time, the edge of the park you cross to get down to the clinic. The alley is dark and narrow and secluded enough. A perfect place to get murdered.

"There, in the open space behind that wall." Hodges points a finger further into the alley, to a kind of alcove tucked into a corner of the building. "And let her breathe, for Christ's sake."

Pearse still lets me hang by one arm, but he releases the hand from my mouth. I shake my head, clearing it away from my face.

"You don't have any right to do this to me," I tell them, and I'm ashamed at how feeble my words are, how pathetic I sound. I can still feel where Pearse's huge hand grabbed my chest, the hot moisture clinging to my skin.

"Semantics, my dear," Hodges says calmly. "And perspective. We're doing what we must to protect this town."

"You're out of your fucking mind," I tell him. But I might as well be talking to a wall.

"Oh, make no mistake, sweet thing," Pearse says, right into my ear. "If it were up to me, I wouldn't send you back." He takes another whiff of my neck, his bristly face scratching my chafed skin like steel wool. I grit my teeth against terror and revulsion boiling out of my stomach; an anguished whimper escapes my throat, and I'm furious and disgusted with myself when I feel his lips curl into a smile against my skin. I just gave this piece of shit something he wanted - a taste of my fear. "And I wouldn't let you live."

He lingers a moment by my neck, then throws me onto my back on the hard-packed dirt. As bruised and beaten up as I am, I feel a ray of light pierce my awareness. *'And I wouldn't let you live?'* That means they're *not* going to kill me?

Still, a mournful ache rises in my chest. Worried as I was about being here - where I'd stay, how I'd live - it's starting to sink in that I don't get to be here at all. These men are going to do something to get rid of me, and I won't get to live in 1921, and I don't get a say.

I watch them, helpless. The scowling old man. The fat, professional bureaucrat with the bowler hat. And the monstrously large rapist blotting out the sun. All of them completely indifferent.

"Nice wall, Hodges," the old man croaks. "I'll just let you take care of the versal banishment."

Hodges reaches into a front pocket and produces a monocle on a gold chain. He places it to one eye and removes his hand, the lens staying in place like he stuck it there with glue. Then he reaches inside his jacket and pulls out what looks like a long black ink pen. He flicks it once and it extends, now two feet long and capped with a silver tip. He's wearing another silver tip on the end of his index finger; I didn't see him put that on. Maybe he had it the whole time.

"Don't worry, doll face," Pearse says with a slight grin. "Before we've finished with your pretty little friend Sadie, I'll pass along your regards."

Despite a whole body full of throbbing aches, I'm on my feet in an instant. They're going after her, and it's all because of me.

"Stay away from her, you piece of shit!" I throw myself at them in one last reckless, heedless attempt to break through them and get down the street. I hit the same wall as before, and this time a shock sends me flying back. I hit the ground with a pathetic *thud* and a weak groan escapes my lips. Pearse and Eastwicke laugh.

"Stupid little split-tail," Eastwicke says.

I've been at the mercy of men my whole life. I've been beaten by them and controlled by them. I've lain awake at night, dreaming of what it would be like to have powers - like in video games or comic books - that I could use to protect myself from abusers and bullies. Savoring the looks of astonishment on their faces, watching as they become less sure of themselves. Turning the tables on them. Kicking the shit out of someone that came to hurt me, watching their faces collapse when they realize they can't hurt me ever again, no matter what they do.

What I wouldn't give to have abilities like that right now. But wishing never did me much good. So I sit in the dirt, pathetic, watching these men do whatever it is they want to do to me. They're the ones that get to decide what happens to me. All I can do is sit and wait.

Hodges, his face dry and serious, draws designs in the air with that long pen. The silver tip leaves light trails on the backs of my eyelids, like blind spots from a camera flash. As I watch in mute fascination, those light trails take on complex geometric shapes that I can *almost see* floating in the air in front of me. There's more of them on the ground, too. I'm sitting inside a razor-thin circle. Is it a circle? If I stare hard, sometimes I think I can see it. Slender lines, four geometric patterns around the edge, etched into...*something*. Not exactly into the ground, because there's no depth like there would be if you stamped something in dirt. The best way I can describe it is to say that it's etched into reality itself. It's just *there*, rock solid but untouchable, and even though I can't touch the designs or the circle with my hands I can *feel* them on some deeper level.

What is he even doing? How is this possible? He must have conjured those invisible walls, too. But how? Sadie's words pop into my head. *'There's things about me you don't know yet, things I can do that other people can't.'* Did she mean like this? Hodges touches points in the air above the circle, lighting them up like bright little stars. There's a weird, intense sensation inside me, all around me, like I drank way too much caffeine. My brain burns with it, and I'm filled with this ugly, cranky feeling. The light gets brighter and brighter, and the caffeine feeling in my nerves gets more intense. A nasty upward pull adds itself to the sensation, in the air and in my body at the same time, like being sucked up by a giant vacuum cleaner. But something inside, entirely beyond my knowledge or control, is fighting these guys. Some part of me feels heavy and solid, like a lump of iron weighing me down.

"How is she resisting that?" A wheezing voice demands. "Is there something you neglected to tell us, Pearse?"

"No, I told you everything," a deep voice replies. "She's not arcane, I'd swear on it."

"I'll just add another layer of abjuration formula," Hodges says quietly. Or maybe he's further away. "It's not a problem. A to B, and...ah, here we are." His voice has been fading, and I can barely hear him. I'm being turned into tall, jagged pieces of light, like frequency waves on some audio display. My world is washed in a blinding white glare that burns to the core.

A short falling sensation, then bricks. And pavement. The world is a whole lot louder, and after I manage to tune my brain in, I recognize it. The roar and hiss of traffic, an occasional car horn, a distant soaring airplane overhead. The sky is blue above me, and a bright yellow afternoon stabs my eyes.

I look at my hands, pocked and strewn with tiny gravel. My knees, skinned and scraped and dirty and bleeding. My backpack is on my back, my clothes just like I remember, my arm wrenched and sore like it got caught in some machine.

I'm still me, and I'm back where I started. In 2004. It's only now that I feel how wrong this place is. It's like I got acclimated to really warm water and it was starting to feel *really good,* and then someone yanked me out and threw me in an icy river.

I touch my tender arm, puffy with new bruises. Then the breast he touched, hard, with his disgusting hands. My chafed, sore neck. I feel filthy, and violated, and used.

An ugly feeling all around me, on my skin. Imagine a whole bunch of really gross, uncomfortable sensations all at once. Shocks that go through your teeth when you chew a foil wrapper. Five iron nails scratching a chalkboard. Slugs crawling on you. That horrible feeling in your veins when you haven't eaten anything for twelve hours but you've had enough caffeine to keep you awake for days. All of these feelings at the same time, compounded when I look at anything - trees, buildings, cars, people. That passenger jet flying overhead. That dipshit driving by in an old dirty white Honda Civic, and it's deafening with its broken muffler and tricked-out stereo system blasting Limp Bizkit through a bass amplifier. Sights, sounds, smells, curling up in my nerves and making me cringe.

Wrong. Everything that exists is *wrong*.

I'm sitting up now, weakly brushing gravel off my knees and arms. A straight couple walks by, sandals and shorts and sunglasses, and they've got a Golden Retriever walking ahead of them on a leash. Their lips curl in disgust when they see me, and they maintain this really thick, awkward silence until they're a good ten feet away. Even the dog looks at me like rotten meat.

I felt like I was home for like, ten minutes. *Really* home, like I belonged more deeply than I've ever belonged anywhere in my life. But I was used and tossed out like last week's garbage. And now that I've been thrown away, everyone *else* sees that I'm garbage, too. Wow.

This is the worst feeling ever.

Tears sting my eyes, but I can't bring myself to cry. Not yet. The hurt is waiting deep beneath the surface, saving itself for tonight.

It feels like it's been days since Sadie and I had lunch together, but my world reels when I realize...I think it's the same afternoon. That means I technically have to go back to work. Then when I'm done, I have to go home and watch the sun go down, alone. More alone than ever.

I was going to spend the night with Sadie. But that was a dream. All I did was put her in danger. She'll think I flaked on her without an explanation.

I want to die. I was so afraid of those men killing me, but now I almost wish they had. The best day of my life just turned into the worst, and I'm not sure I ever want to get up off the sidewalk.

Twelve

Sadie

"The Knights of Augustine could scarcely have chosen a worse enemy than they found in Autumn Grove; indeed, they may have fared better if they had simply moved to Cincinnati and operated directly under the noses of the Seven Towers Conclave.

Sorceress (Captain) Hazel Morrison, whose nom de guerre *is "the Bloodstaff", received numerous decorations for valor in the First World War and is most famous for destroying a German fortification at Soissons, on the American left flank, in the Battle of Chateau-Thierry in 1918. This is the same battle in which Morrison, then only a lieutenant, bested the feared German ace arcanist Colonel Klaust von Schwarzenheim and received the red staff that bestowed Morrison's famous nickname. For this, she received the highest American award for battle sorcery, the Congressional Order of Valor, and went on to further acts of distinction and bravery before the close of the war. Germany never again produced an arcanist of Von Schwarzenheim's talent during the First World War, and those remaining German arcanists on the Western Front fearfully dubbed Captain Morrison 'die rothexe' - the Red Witch."*
-J.M. Devon, *Taming the Frontier: The Decline of Rogue Circles in America 1900-1945*

"One should never bite off more enemies than she can chew."
-Gen. Molly Bradford, 1783
Verse: Tranquility Dawn

In an instant, I know all I need to know about the meathead in front of me.

The image comes back, clear as yesterday. Tommy Kelley, the bully that kicked my shriveled, useless legs when I was fresh out of bed with polio. Laughed when I screamed with the white hot blade of searing pain chopped into my bone. Mocked my tears.

Followed me. Shoved me. Threw me on the ground, knowing I couldn't get back up. Tried to pick me up by my leg braces.

I've always had a power in me, but one day it got unleashed. It changed everything.

Tommy, on his back on the pavement, screaming. His hip bones shattered like fine china. Tommy survived, and he's spent every day since then wishing that he hadn't. I was never the same after that, and neither was he. This power is a part of me, like my lungs or kidneys, and I've learned to use it in small ways. A year later, I was walking again like I'd never been sick. The polio was gone. Tommy Kelley will *never* walk again.

I never set it loose again, not like that. I'm eighteen now, and this energy, there's so much more of it. I could hurt a lot of people. Maybe worse - a *lot* worse. But that's what I'm so terrified of - I don't want anyone to get hurt because of me. My skin crawls when I think about what I did to Tommy. I've never forgotten the sound, never forgotten how it felt. I've never forgotten his first blood-curdling scream. I can still hear it.

This stony-faced mug has eyes just like Tommy's. Cruel, empty eyes. Black. Inhuman. I don't want to hurt anyone, but I'll defend myself if I have to - and I *will* protect the people I care about, damn the consequences.

Anything I hate is some bully throwing his weight around.

I've backed up a few steps, yielding space to him, but never yielding my resolve. I remember Courtney's soft face, the way her eyes light up when she's excited, the energy that fills everything she says. She doesn't judge, doesn't look at me funny, no matter what I say. Nothing surprises her; her eyes are always warm and full of compassion. Nobody has ever understood me like she does.

These degenerates did something to her, and I need only think of her for my eyes to bloom with hot tears and fury. I stop backing up, let him loom in close. I let my eyes scorch his, and I speak each word with quiet ferocity.

"I *said* that if you hurt my friend, I will kill you myself."

His eyes are smooth and hard as granite, impassive in the molten stream of my anger. Some incomprehensible thought crosses his features in a blink. His face remains stony, expressionless.

Then he lashes out and grabs a fistful of my hair, white fire torching my scalp. He jerks my head to the side, his face on the side of my neck, smelling my skin. Countless rusty iron nails scratching me - his stubble.

A flare of agony, a scream howling from my throat. He hauls me over to the side of my porch by my hair, bends me over the railing. What is this bastard going to do to me? Is this what he did to Courtney? Even the thought makes me sick and nauseous all over, like a bad case of the flu. I'm blind with hatred. I want to kill him.

"You're all alone," he murmurs next to my ear, his voice a resonant baritone that makes my skin crawl. "Scream all you want, you little cunt. Nobody can hear you."

Boys will be boys. I stared at Tommy and knew that I could never undo what I'd done. I destroyed him. The older I got, the stronger that power became. If I used it again, people could die. This power terrified me so much that I pushed it down, tried to forget. Sometimes I almost managed to convince myself I was normal, that I wasn't a bomb waiting to go off.

But it hasn't gone anywhere. It comes right to my hand.

He's hauling me around by the hair like an animal. The roaring inside me gets louder, more intense every second. It's as if a giant powder keg was lit in my chest. I have no idea what will happen if I relax, if I let this power out. Will these men die in a single deafening blast, their bones liquefied in an instant? Blow the inside of my house back out onto the street? I lose control with every second, but I have to hold it back. I *have to*. I don't know what will happen if I don't. That horrific feeling - bones grinding into dust - a memory that sticks to you like grease for years and years.

"Pearse, enough!" The fat man shouts uselessly. "You're dismissed!"

I'm losing control of it, fingers slipping from the edge of a cliff. I'm hanging on by my fingernails.

He barks a sudden exclamation and lets go of my hair in an instant. A drip of that energy escaped my skin as a slight peppery tingle, something I barely felt. He curses, standing back and clenching his numb fists. I must have put his hands to sleep by accident. I redouble my efforts, wrap myself around the energy dying to escape.

I turn around to face him, and back up against the edge of the porch. He clenches his meaty wrist, shock turning to outrage.

His eyes blaze. "The hell I am." A wolf, eyes on my throat, ready to kill.

He reaches out with two great hands the size of dinner plates; strong, knobby fingers eager to snap my neck like a twig. He'll choke me to death, I just know it-

Before he can grab me, he's gone - tumbling through the air, tossed into the breeze. He flies back over the steps and onto the street, lands hard with a wet *plop*.

A woman stands at the top of my porch steps where there was only open air just a second ago. She stands with her back to me, guarding the narrow entrance to my porch. She's tall and slender in plain boots, a long skirt, and a short green summer blouse; the smell of rose water lingers gently around her. On her head, a dark green cloche hat. She faces my attackers, holding a staff out and behind her so the steel head points down the street. The staff is metal, the color of glistening wet blood.

"You should listen to your master, Chisel Face," she says. Her voice is calm, alive with danger. "Because if you touch this girl again, you'll spend the next week coughing your balls out of your throat."

My brain is numb with surprise as I try to piece together what just happened. I don't know who this lady is or how she got here so fast, but golly, am I ever glad to meet her!

The one they call Pearse is on his chest, on the street, licking blood from inside his lip. He flashes her a look laced with sadistic pleasure and hate.

The woman half-turns to look at me. She's young, not quite ten years older than me, and she's very pretty in a sharp-eyed kind of way. Her face is white porcelain, smooth and flawless.

"Are you all right, Sadie? Did these men hurt you?"

I rub my sore scalp, making sure all my hair is still in place, not fully understanding what's happening. I'm still back in the few seconds before the big oaf flew off and crash-landed on the street. I assumed I was all alone; I never imagined anyone would be asking about me today. I have absolutely no idea how she knows my name, either. Or where she came from. Or how she appeared out of thin air. Was she nearby without me seeing her?

"Oh, I'm all right." It's a bit of a lie, but I'm not about to whine when Courtney could be in worse trouble.

The fat man keeps a solid, measured gaze on her. "Are you Conclave, then?"

"I'm what happens when you cross the line," she says. The civility in her voice wears thinner every second, revealing more of the razor edge underneath. "Special Agent Morrison, Seven Towers Conclave. Busy day for you fellas?"

Understanding dawns in Hodges' eyes. "Of course. Captain Hazel Morrison, 'The Bloodstaff.' Sorceress, Congressional Order of Valor. A battlefield legend, the Alvin York of the arcane world." He smirks, almost impressed. "And to think your Conclave keeps you exiled in this backwater."

Sorceress?! Who are these people, and what fairy tale have I stumbled into?

She dismisses it all with a brief smirk. "Why, if I didn't know any better, I'd think we had a new gang of bullies in town, beating up kids for their lunch money."

The fat man wears a hard look. "The situation is unfortunate, but necessary."

"College girls being assaulted by giant middle-aged perverts and tobacco-stained geriatrics is unfortunate, but it's far from necessary. Don't you think?"

"What did you do to my friend?!" I demand. The lady listens to my question, then turns back to face them.

"Why, that's an *excellent* question!" she states. "Why don't you go on and tell her. Go on!"

"A simple class two banishment," Hodges maintains. "Quite harmless, I assure you."

Miss Morrison snorts, stepping onto the sidewalk, toward the men. "Harmless? The banishment itself, perhaps. But you let your pet gorilla fondle her for about five minutes beforehand."

So it's true. Bile scorches my throat and my stomach lurches; I feel like I might be sick. I'm filled with the ache of powerless rage and heartbreak and guilt. I never should have taken my eyes off her.

He opens his mouth angrily. "That is-"

"*And* she's Displaced," she goes on, talking loudly over him. "Which has turned your 'harmless' act of intimidation into a death sentence."

They're tossing around all these strange words I've never heard before, but for some reason "Displaced" is one that I find unsettling. What on Earth does that mean, and why would it kill Courtney?

"That's entirely conjecture," he scorns.

"Perhaps." Her voice is the wind going dead before a hurricane. "We'll need a versologist to tell us for certain, which I'm sure I can arrange. Anyhow, it's immaterial now the damage is done. My most pressing concern at the moment is the safety of this young woman here."

My safety? She's here for me?

He raises his head a bit, an indignant look on his face. "The situation is under control," he huffs.

"*Clearly,*" Hazel says expansively, her eyes ablaze. "You're all doing exactly what you came to do: playing cop so you can bully and rape and intimidate your way across town."

The old man, the one who glared at me like some Baptist preacher, stands a few feet from Hodges. He mutters to himself, getting louder, then softer again. He twirls his finger around in a circle like a clock.

"That young woman is more dangerous than you can possibly realize." Hodges points a wobbly finger at me. "And *she* is an accomplice."

"Bullshit." Hazel steps forward, her tone freezing. "An accomplice is someone who knowingly assists in committing a crime. Neither of these girls have done any such thing. Why, the girl you banished was minding her own business and you *assaulted* her!"

"You clearly have no idea what you're dealing with, *Captain*." Hodges is sarcastic with her military rank. "An anima signature like hers could easily set off the Blackstead

Anomaly. Murders and disappearances every day for another century. Is that what you want?”

“You are an imbecile and a bastard,” Hazel says flatly. “Anima is anchored to the body. That means it’s localized, like a magnetic field. That kid could no more wake up your anomaly than your snoring can wake up my granny in Vermont. You need to read some books written after 1300.”

“I’m tired of listening to you, quim.” Pearse rises to his feet, wiping a smear of blood from his lip with a wrist. “Maybe I’ll just enjoy both of you right on that porch before I kill you. Or after. Doesn’t matter much to me.”

“*Ohhh,*” Hazel breathes rapturously, eyes narrowing to slits. “I *beg* you. *Please try.* You are a disease, and I’ve been waiting for the chance to exterminate you for a *very* long time.”

There’s a roaring in my ears, slowly getting louder - a whooshing kind of sound, like listening to the inside of a seashell. Now there’s a pressure inside my head like a sinus headache, and a strange pressure in my bones, too. Uncomfortable, like putting on tight clothes when you’re sopping wet. It rises and falls and rises again, a little more each time, corkscrewing upwards in intensity and volume. I glance at the angry old man on the street, and every last little variation in the pressure matches something he does with his fingers or lips.

Hazel holds her blood-red staff out to the side, feet planted, body tensing. I can’t see her expression, but I’m sure I wouldn’t want to be in front of her. She lifts a hand to a pocket in her skirt, and with the very same motion, tosses a kind of silver bracelet at Hodges. He flinches back but the bracelet lands on his arm and claps itself shut, instantly, with a final *snik.*

"Jeremiah Hodges?" Hazel's voice is the sound of a cell door slamming shut. "You're under arrest for attempted murder, arcane kidnapping, criminal abjuration, and arcane intimidation. You will submit to arrest and trial by Conclave. Do you understand?"

I draw an excited gasp. This lady is the real thing! There's actually someone who can stand up to these bullies!

"I won't!" Hodges' voice is shrill. "I won't go!"

"End of the line, pal."

The roaring in my ears has been building the more the old man swirls his finger around in the air. The pressure in my chest is getting uncomfortable.

The old man grins at Hazel like a hyena. He traces patterns in the air, punctuations of pressure in my ears. His hands move too quickly for me to see the imaginary pictures he drew.

"Miss, look out!" I'm surprised to hear my words in the air, to see Pearse and Hodges turn to me. Hazel pivots - too slow, too late.

The power in me is waiting to be released. I don't fully realize it until I stretch my arm and let go, unleashing it at the old man. An explosion of pure energy blasts out of my hand, a delicious tidal wave that leaves a shimmering trail of pleasure. Even as I bask in the intense tide, I hope I'm not too late. Even now, I feel Eastwicke releasing the energy he so carefully built up - some elegant tower of multiplication - aimed straight at Hazel.

He wears that smug grin until an instant before my wave reaches him. For a fraction of a second, his face goes sour like someone biting into a raw grapefruit. Then he's gone, and there's only a tiny, dusty howl of protest flying away on the wind. *Where did he go?* I spot him a moment later, lying on his back halfway up the street.

Hodges stares at me in open-mouthed horror, his face white as a sheet.

Before I can move, the blood drains out of my head. My vision goes dark, stars bursting in my eyes like fireworks, and I collapse.

Miss Morrison yells my name, and then a series of loud waves erupt in my ears. *Whoosh, whoosh. Whif, whoosh, whip.* I'm pathetic, weaker than I've been since I had polio. The thought of falling asleep right here on the hard cold porch sounds posilutely divine. But I can't. I'm in danger, and this Hazel lady is too. I groan and swallow the sour knowledge that I'm gonna have to get up in a moment.

I roll onto my belly to see what's making that unearthly sound, like birds flying past my ears at hundreds of miles an hour. What I'm seeing is incomprehensible.

Miss Morrison and Pearse are a good twenty feet apart, and somehow they're brawling despite the distance. It's like no fight I ever imagined. Pearse wears a set of brass knuckles, hammering away at open air. I would think he'd gone completely loony or that it was some strange dance, but I hear his fists flying and I feel a dull *thump* as they land. Those brass knuckles project some kind of force as he strikes.

I feel the blows, feel her blocking, feel everything. Hear everything. It's a brand new sense, some strange combination of sound and touch.

Pearse brawls like a back-alley thug, throwing punches with nothing more than rage and brute strength. Hazel's elegant staff stops the thrusts of energy thrown at her with a series of twirls and parries. Some she deflects, throws aside. Others she blocks directly, and those land with a bone-crunching *thud*. It feels like a doctor flicking the side of my ear, sounds like bombs exploding underground. I feel the force in the air, feel it *thump* inside my chest when it connects.

This is insane. He keeps coming on, powered by strange energy and hate, fighting and grappling against open air. Any one of those long right hooks would be enough to break this skinny jane in half, and I flinch a little with each blow; but she's holding her own, narrowing her eyes, moving smoothly. Cool and patient. Pearse will eventually mess up, and she's waiting for it.

He stops for just a moment, rubs his nose with the back of a hand, glares at her. He hikes up his sleeves, winds back like a man trying to split a log with his fist.

I cringe, try to get up. This one's gonna be bad-

Hazel steps calmly aside, twirling her staff to the side. Pearse flies across the pavement as if he's been grabbed and thrown, hitting the ground and rolling with a grunt. Hazel swiftly brings her staff around, as if to bash his skull with it. She hits something I can't see; a dull *whump* goes through my chest with the impact.

She twirls her staff back into position. "Nice shield, Chisel Face. You must have expected to run into me right along."

He glares at her from a half-crouch, then lunges forward. Hazel tries to deflect, but she's too late. A cruel thrust hits her full in the stomach with a dull *crump*. She flies back, hits the street and rolls.

"Miss Morrison!"

I'm frightened by Pearse's predatory grin, by the eager way he gets up and moves forward for the kill. Hazel props herself up just a little, head hanging. She utters a low, injured moan, punctuated with a cough.

I scream at him. "Stop it, you bastard! She's had enough!"

If he hears me, he doesn't react. He moves forward, sneering at Hazel. He winds back, clenches a huge fist. Everything in me wants to stop him, to unleash my strange power at him without any regard for what I might do, but I've nothing left. I'm empty. All I can do is watch helplessly as he bears down on her. He's still ten feet away, closing in. His cruel smile promises to beat her the whole way as he approaches.

His expression turns to pleasure and he raises his fist high-

And Hazel lunges, holding her staff with both hands.

The impact explodes with a deafening vibration. I clap my hands against my ears. The unearthly noise-that-isn't-noise pierces my head, wobbling my eardrums like a tuning fork. I clench my jaws and close my throbbing eyes and try not to scream.

Wummm, wumm, wum...

I slowly open my eyes as the vibrations begin to subside. Hazel strolls toward her opponent, and she doesn't look nearly as hurt as she sounded a minute ago. Pearse picks himself up and starts to laugh.

Hazel cocks her head a bit. "What, you enjoyed that? What kinda lunatic are you, anyhow?"

He raises a hand almost conversationally, waving away her comment as he continues to laugh.

"No, no. Just remembering that little blonde."

Hazel comes to a stop a few yards away, staff planted at her side. Eyes frozen.

"Oh, yeah? What about her?"

He shakes with laughter, sitting up. "Oh, I wish you could have seen it, Conclave. Wish you could have watched. You and that sweet thing over there on the porch, both watching. That would've made it so much nicer."

What did he do to her...!?

Hazel's jaw moves inside her cheek as she clenches it. "Watched what?"

He leans his head back at the sky a moment, smiling, before answering. "She's spirited. Feisty. The way she struggled when I grabbed her chest, the way she fought and screamed when I grabbed that sweet little titty of hers. You're a little bigger than she is, just a bit. A fella can look at your tits and see you're a grown woman. But her? Mm. So young." He levels his gaze at her, still smiling, eyes black and empty. "I've always thought fruit was sweetest when it's not quite ripe."

My whole body feels sick. It feels as though someone took my heart out of my chest and put it in the freezer, then coated my skin in motor oil and set it on fire. For a moment, I forget where I am. I've never felt this before, this combination of loathing, heartsick grief, and blind rage.

"You *son of a bitch!!*" My words are in the air as a scream before I even realize my mouth is open. I stumble down my porch steps in a frenzy. None of my strange energy is left, but I've still got a bit of adrenaline. My knuckles clench white with blind fury. I need something - an axe, a hatchet. There's a loose brick over by the street; I'll bash his goddamn brains in with it-

Hazel holds up a hand in my direction, urging me to wait. She never takes her eyes off Pearse.

Hodges, kneeling on the ground, slumps and casts his subordinate a look heavy with disgust and personal guilt.

Hazel's face is twisted with hatred; she nods a little at Pearse. He smiles back and whispers, "What are you gonna do? I could perform an encore, if you want." Then he glances at me.

Hazel is quick. Fingers in the air, touching different points only she can see, then tracing two quick designs.

"Brittle-" Conversational tone, but I'm sure I could hear her down the street.

"-and-" Each word, a different movement of her staff.

"Snap!" She thrusts her staff forward, both hands clenched in the middle. A different shockwave this time. A wave of bitter cold washes over me, like the icy wind off Lake Erie in the wintertime, back home. For just a moment, it cuts through me and deep into my being, and then it's gone. It moves away down the street, carrying flaky, paper-thin pieces of Pearse's shield.

The goon clenches his eyes with an ugly grimace, holding the sides of his head. It looks like he's got brain-freeze, like you get with a mouthful of ice. He opens his eyes and charges at her with a howl of rage.

Hazel holds her staff horizontally in front of her; she lets him get within about six feet, then thrusts.

Pearse flies back and up, flipping end over end in the air, and lands on the street with a flat *plop*.

He snarls, rises to a crouch, reaches for his ankle. He pulls an evil-looking knife from his boot - the kind that doughboys bring home from the trenches. It's one of those brass-handled affairs with a hole for each finger around the hilt, like a set of brass knuckles attached to the top. *Oh, gracious. If he could punch her from a good ways off with those brass knuckles, what's he gonna be able to do with that knife?* I want to help her, but I've no idea how. I hate standing here like a sap, powerless to do anything but watch.

"Playtime's over, pal." Hazel's fingers dance again; she traces a sign in the air, then touches three distinct points in front of her. He's up and rushing at her, closing the distance quickly.

She thrusts again, clenching her staff in both fists.

A series of wet, insulated sounds - *snap, crunch, crack*. One of Pearse's arms twists inward at a sickening angle, then the other. Then his right leg snaps, folds inward. *One, two, three,* and it's over, like the snap of a finger.

The big goon collapses to the street, a long grunt rising into a gravelly howl of rage and pain. Hazel approaches him, her face impassive, producing another shiny bracelet from a bag at her side.

"This didn't have-"

Something explodes in the air and my brain scrambles. I'm not sure what I'm seeing anymore. I'm foggy and stupid, like a baby looking at the world for the first time. I'm not even sure I *can* see, or what seeing *means,* exactly. My teeth tremble and buzz, and I cover my head in my arms to stop everything from rattling out of my skull.

Slowly, haltingly, my senses come back. I know what a house is, then I know who *I* am, then *where* I am. Then the vibrations stop. Hazel's on the street, eyes flashing with anger and frustration as she looks around. She doesn't seem to have been affected by whatever that was. Hodges crouches at her feet, still in the same place.

But the old man and Pearse are gone, as if they were never there.

I stumble off my porch, toward the street.

"Miss Morrison?" I blink. "What...*happened?* Where'd they go?"

She doesn't look at me right away. "Last minute jailbreak, looks like. Someone threw a disorientation cantrip. I doubt we've seen the last of them." She looks at me, face brightening like she's seeing me for the first time. She reaches out, touches my arm. "Are you all right, honey?"

I nod quickly. "Yeah, I'm jake. What about you? He got you real good!"

"Naw," she waves it off. "Not quite as bad as I made it seem - just a little battlefield drama to lure him off his guard. But thank you for asking." Her face softens and grows warm. "By the way, thanks ever so much, Sadie. Why, that old coot's arithromancy mighta cooked my goose if you hadn't stepped in with that kinetic blast!"

I haven't any idea what she means, but I'm at least able to tell that she's grateful for me unleashing my power at the old man tracing imaginary clocks in the air. "Aw, ishkabibble. Least I could do, you coming to help me and all."

She places a warm hand on my cheek, then she turns, glances down the street for a moment. Her face is heavy with concern when she looks back at me.

"Say, I hate to ask this of you, seeing as how you don't know me, but I really wish you'd come stay with me for a day or two. You're not gonna be safe here, and I really don't feel right leaving you by yourself."

I glance back at my comfortable house, sitting quiet and empty. I haven't even gone inside yet today. The evening sun will be casting long rays across my dining room table, where I eat so many disappointing meals alone. This morning's dirty dishes are still in the sink; I promised myself I'd clean up tonight. No matter, Miss Morrison is right. Evening isn't far off, and I *really* don't want to be here after dark, all alone.

"All right." I glance back at her. "Can I go in right quick and pack some things?"

"Please do, but make it snappy. We should blow as soon as we can."

I nod and hurry onto the porch. I get my door unlocked, put my bag of groceries on the table, then rush straight to my bedroom. I barely notice the clothes I gather, but the silliest thought occurs to me: *I want to look nice if Courtney shows up.* I smirk at my own foolishness as I take a few changes of clothing and stuff them in a messenger bag.

As I close my door behind me and turn to lock it, I snicker at myself. How silly I was, to think life had already gotten as weird as it could get. Everything got turned upside down, but at least I'm alive, and I've somewhere safe to go. *It's more than Courtney's got,* I reflect miserably.

"My machine is just at the end of the street," Hazel says as I arrive. "We'll have to take Hodge-Podge here with us, but I'll make arrangements. You won't have to sleep under the same roof with him."

He glares at her, but remains silent.

"Why, that's a relief," I tell her, as we begin making our way down the street toward her waiting motor car.

Poor Courtney. Please be okay...

Thirteen

Thursday
June 3 2004

4:45 p.m.

Courtney

"There's a single cold, terrifying moment when the world goes silent around you and your own unspeakable loneliness descends over you like a frozen shroud. You've certainly been lonesome before, but this new loneliness is absolute. You are now a world unto yourself, and you begin to drift further and further away from the world you have known. This is how the resonance purge begins, and the short downward march to the grave."
-Alice Thatcher, *Memoirs of an Accidental Arcane,* 1927

When the elevator doors slide open, the fifth floor is silent. All the lights are on, but nobody's home. Sometimes this happens - the Archives staff step away from the front desk - but today feels like the end of the world.

I glide into the front office, a ghost in an empty house. The reading room is as still as a mausoleum, and a mostly-empty coffee mug sits on the front desk, like one of those stories about abandoned cabins with the meals still on the table. I pass through the copier room in a rustle of denim shorts, back into the Archives with the deafening roar of its silence. My tread is noiseless; I pass unseen. Unknown.

My desk is waiting; I dread the thought of going back to it. It's full of 1921, full of pictures of that cozy world, full of eighty-year-old emotions sealed in the pages, ready to be inhaled. It's too much to handle right now. I hurry by the entrance to my cubicle, trying to avoid the warmth that reaches out as I pass. I need another human being. Anyone. Just a few warm words, a little small talk. Maybe Dan is at his desk in the back corner. I'll ask him how life is, I'll ask him, I don't know. Something. Anything.

His chair is empty, crouching behind walls of stacked papers and clutter. Computer on, screen off. I turn and peek down the long corridor between the shelves and the wall; nothing, just tall windows and glaring sun. I stop and listen for the sound of shifting feet, a scuffling shoe, a moving box.

Absolutely nothing. I'm by myself.

Because of course I am.

There's nowhere else to go; I have to go back to my cubicle, padded stiff with warm memories. I trudge back up to the entrance to my little makeshift office, backpack slumping in my hand. My notebook is just where I left it, scribbled with hasty notes in blue ink, connections looped and arrowed. I kept those notes in an attempt to navigate a sea of memories that filled up my workspace, a world more real than my own, a world that swallowed me whole. A warm place where dreams I couldn't identify, dreams I didn't know I had, were busy being realized.

I thought I was hallucinating at first, but it was all real - 1921, Sadie, all of it. The only thing that *wasn't* real was my part in it. Some things aren't meant to be. Some *people* aren't meant to be.

I wasn't meant to be.

It was a nice dream, and for a little while I felt like I'd really come home. But no dream can survive the scorching summer of 2004. Everything is ending.

I swing my backpack around, unzip it, pull out the faithful old 1922 *Expedition* yearbook. I run my hand over the cover, savor the ripples of its textured binding under my fingers. I open the fragrant pages one more time, age-browned and soaked with heartfelt nostalgia, and gently remove my Post-It notes from the marked pages.

Sadie's freshman photo jumps off the page and grabs hold of me as I pass. Her eyes are bubbly, like that candy that crackles in your mouth; lively, energetic, ready for adventure. Her smile warm and sharp, cutting through the gloom. My lip trembles a little at the sight of her, but again the tears won't come. I've never felt so safe with anyone, never clicked so well with a person. She made me feel alive in ways I never dreamed possible. I run my fingers across the smooth old page, touch her photo.

I flip to the last Post-It with a feeling like being hit in the face; it's that photo of me, in black and white. My eyes are those lights you see in rich people's swimming pools at night, glowing, tantalizing. I'm leveling my gaze at the viewer, head tilted forward, my smile a warm challenge. The girl in this picture has everything.

So it can't be me - or at least it can't be my future, right? Because even with all the weird shit I've seen over the last few days, I still can't imagine any way of getting from here to there. Not when the only door was slammed in my face.

I take one last measure of this girl, the girl I wish I could become, and I gently close the book. I'll take my notebook with me, but I'll leave the yearbook here on the desk. It belongs to the Archives and I won't be needing it where I'm going, anyway.

I think what hurts the most is that this is 1997 all over again. Or 1915, however you want to look at it. I almost got free. I was almost loved, almost safe. And then more men came and forced me out, just like before. I'm not meant to be safe, and I'm not meant to belong. Every time I try, there's always some man there waiting for me, telling me that my only purpose in life is to suffer because he wants me to.

Well, I'm done letting men decide where I belong, decide where I get to live. I tasted happiness - twice - just for it to be taken from me. I want to die. And it just so happens that's one thing I get to decide for myself. Men have taken my life from me - twice - but they can't take my death from me.

I don't have long, anyway, even if I wanted to live. The walls are closing in. You can't see it from in here, inside the padded softness of the Archives with its temperature-controlled air and nostalgic smells of decay, and you couldn't see it outside in the blazing summer heat. But it's there, just under the surface, just beyond the curve of the horizon. The end of things. Death.

Not the gentle Death of the tarot, a turning of the seasons, a bridge between present and future. This is another kind of Death entirely - this is apocalypse. There's no life in the wake of this pale horseman; no regrowth, no springtime.

When you stare into that darkness and finally catch a glimpse of his terrifying cadaverous face, that's when it's too late.

Dead.

A single tear spills down my cheek as I caress that yearbook, those warm memories, one last time. Then I sniff, rub my nose, and leave the Archives forever.

Fourteen

Tuesday
September 6, 1921
4:49 p.m.

Sadie

"It remains a mystery why so many naturally aspected individuals came together in the same place at practically the same moment, but eighteen-year-old Sadie Van Tassel's cheerfulness and affability must have certainly cemented their bonds, ensuring lifelong friendships and romances among them."
-Edith Winthrop, *Flapper Sorcery: American Arcanology in the 1920s*

"Miss Morrison?" I ask as she pulls her rattling touring car onto my street. "I'm awful sorry you had to get mixed up in, you know. All this."

"You've nothing to be sorry for, sweetheart." We're headed back toward campus, bouncing along as the machine rattles up the street. My house is quickly swallowed by trees behind us. "Blame *him*. He's the one who got us all mixed up in this." She raises her voice a little, shouting into the rearview mirror. "You got a lot to answer for, pal."

He snorts and shakes his head, watching the street go by. His expression is heavy and distant.

"Thank you. For coming to help me, that is." I look at her sadly. "Why, I don't like to think about what might have happened if you hadn't."

She smiles warmly. "Think nothing of it! It's my job. But I'd have come to help anyway, even if it wasn't."

"Well, I'm grateful anyhow. And it's awfully good of you to take me in for a day or two," I tell her sadly. "I'm obliged loads."

"Not at all, dear. I wasn't about to let you stay down there all alone after that mess. Besides, like I said, you saved my bacon! I think I owe you a great deal more than a night or two in my guest bedroom!"

My heart slumps in my chest, and I don't know what to do with myself. When I woke up this morning, everything was so bright. Now, everything's gone so terribly wrong. Miss Morrison glances at me, her face gentle and kind.

"I know you have a great many questions," she says, eyes on the road, arms on the big steering wheel. "Because I have lots of questions, too. Maybe we can take turns?" When I look at her, she's prompting me with a soft smile. I return it and sigh.

"Why, I don't even know where to start," I confess. Thinking about it a moment, I start at the only place I know. "What happened back there, anyhow?"

Hazel smirks, her eyes darting up at her rearview mirror.

"Hey, you. Hodge-podge. How 'bout we make a deal. If you cooperate - fully - and answer all of our questions, I'll request leniency from the Conclave."

He snorts again. "You will not. You've no reason to grant me leniency, any more than I have to assist the Seven Towers Conclave in extending their dominion eastward."

"Sheesh. Dominion?!" She turns onto College Street, and the sunset is blotted for a moment by a thick canopy of green leaves. "Why, that's about the wettest thing I ever heard! We couldn't rule a city block, let alone the whole state. We do what we've always done - we keep our eyes peeled and our ears to the ground. We advise, we teach, and we train. Occasionally we act, if we have to. Like tonight."

He chuckles. "So you're spies. How upstanding."

"If you say so, pal," she says into the mirror. "But we're a lot more than that, too. And we do a heck of a lot more good than *you* jackasses ever did."

He doesn't reply. Even I know she's right, and I don't know anything.

"So, you wanna cooperate or not? You put two innocent girls through hell and condemned one of them to death, all for some fool idea that everyone knew was all wet by the time the Pilgrims landed. It's gonna take years and years to make up for that, but you can start tonight, right here, by telling us what we want to know."

He doesn't reply, just stares out the side of the car. We make our way up the street, and I've already resigned myself to the idea that he's not going to help, when he finally speaks.

"Very well, Sorceress. I know when I'm over a barrel. Information for leniency - I accept. Ask your questions."

Hazel smiles triumphantly. "That's the first smart thing you've said all day, Hodges." Then she looks at me and nods. I feel humbled; important adults have never wanted my opinions before. I'm really starting to like Hazel.

"Why were you and your goons laying for my friend?" I ask him, unable to keep the bitterness out of my voice. "She wasn't bothering anybody!"

He draws a breath, forcing himself to be patient. "It's going to be difficult to explain this without your knowing the basics of arcana or versology, and I refuse to be your tutor. You can do that job if you like, Captain, but I'm a witness - not a school teacher."

"Just answer the darn question, sourpuss," she tells him. "I'll translate for you. None of you dumbbells knows the first thing about teaching, anyhow."

He sighs a big gust of wind, then takes off his pince-nez spectacles and rubs his face. "Several days ago, Pearse brought it to my attention that he'd been observing the local omniversal cluster through our lab, and that someone with a high theric resonance was straddling the barrier between our verse and a neighboring one. He wanted to apprehend her if she came through and then send her back. He argued to Kluivert and myself that her level of power would disturb the Blackstead Anomaly."

"*Pearse* brought it to your attention." She looks hard at him in the mirror. "*Really.*"

"Yes, that's right."

"What, is Chisel Face the loan shark suddenly a master versologist?"

Hodges actually chuckles; I gather he doesn't like Pearse much. "Why, no, I should think not."

I'm glancing back and forth, completely lost. Hazel catches it and explains. "All living things have a life force. We call it 'anima.' Just like everything else in nature, it's energy - and we can measure it to some degree. 'Theric' is just another word to describe the energy that makes up anima, so someone's 'theric resonance' is just the amount of that energy they carry around, as well as its particular properties. And it looks like Courtney's is really powerful." College Gate is visible in the distance at the very top of the street before we begin to slow down. "You see, back in the Middle Ages, when people thought the world was flat and doctors slapped cow shit on infected wounds, they had another funny idea. Back then, versology hadn't been invented yet, so the people who studied this kinda stuff - with anima and everything - were called Scholastic Magi." We pull up across from a cozy two-story brick house with little pointed gables on the upstairs windows. "Now, along with flat worlds and doo-doo dressings, these 'magi' had another sparkling idea: they said that if a Displaced person had a strong enough anima, they could burn holes in reality so that demons would come through and devour everybody."

My laughter comes out in snorts, despite how hard I'm trying to hold it in. Hodges levels a disgusted glare at Hazel. She turns the car off and opens her door.

"Now, about the time versology was invented in the mid-seventeenth century, we figured out that Displaced aren't demons or fairies or little goblins. Displaced are normal people, just like you and me, only they ended up in the wrong universe. If you've the right instruments, you can see it on them; their energy always matches the verse they get pulled into, and never the one they escaped. Every time, a hundred percent."

Hodges looks sullen as he steps out of the back seat and onto the sidewalk.

"Golly." I close the car door behind me. "So this is what happened to Courtney? She's supposed to be here in this world like you and me? Except *her* world kidnapped her?" I remember noticing how much she belongs here, how it seemed so wrong to see her among the hostile indifference of her world.

Hazel looks impressed. "Now you're on the trolley! That's a good way to look at it, Sadie."

"And," I can't resist finishing my thought, shooting an accusing look at Hodges. "The minute she finally makes it home, *they* send her back out into the wilderness."

Hazel nods grimly. "Exactly. That's one reason it's a criminal offense in our society."

"How *could* you?!" I exclaim at Hodges. "Why, she doesn't belong over there any more than you do! She was *home!*"

"Young lady," Hodges sounds frustrated and condescending. "Do try to see the bigger picture. You may not know this, but a great evil sleeps in the woods not ten miles from town. In Colonial times, people disappeared routinely from both town and countryside, in significant numbers. That forest is - for lack of a better word - *cursed*. That young woman stormed in here like a tornado on two legs. I acted in the interests of this town and all who live in it. Had you more maturity, you might be thanking me instead."

Hazel rolls her eyes, poking him in the back with her staff, urging him toward the house.

"We don't cure the common cold by slicing open veins anymore, and lives are ruined when we act based on superstition. You better hope that kid survives. If she doesn't, you're looking at a first-degree murder charge."

"Miss Morrison?" I ask as we approach her front door. "How will we know for sure if Courtney is, you know. All right?"

She pulls a house key from a pocket in her long skirt. "We'll enlist the help of a versologist. Tonight. Then we can decide on a way to proceed."

"We?" I ask, self-conscious and surprised.

"Why, of course," she says like it's the most obvious thing in the world. "You're Courtney's friend - a darn *good* friend, I think. In the absence of family, that entitles you to act on her behalf in every matter that concerns her." Hazel's door opens, and she steps into her shadowy parlor. "You're effectively her next of kin, her attorney, and the executrix of her will. Whether she's dead or alive, you're all she's got."

I'm all she's got. Jeez Louise. I can almost hear Courtney now - *"no pressure, right?"*.

Hazel's house is tucked cozily among neighboring Victorian houses and shady trees. A spicy odor greets me as soon as I step into the front parlor, reminiscent of exotic wood and artifacts from far away. The smell of books and scrolls peppers the air among the rich odors of dry tea and oriental rugs. Her parlor feels cool and pleasant, almost chilly, despite the summer heat outside.

Rich red mahogany is everywhere, on tall thick bookcases lined with volumes, on polished tables and desks. Heavy bookshelves sit against the left wall, stacked with countless volumes and a few rolled papers. A polished table sits in front of me, topped with a thousand half-finished ideas. An antique globe, tanned and faded, perches among stacks of papers. Over on the wall to my right, a plain secretarial desk topped with a green banker's lamp and a small stack of antique books hunches in seclusion between the bookcases. A black candlestick telephone hides at the back corner of the desk, almost like it feels self-conscious. Long lazy sunlight streams through a front bay window - it's wearing on toward evening.

"Sadie, darling, make yourself at home," Hazel tells me, shutting the door behind us. "There's a sofa on the other side of that table in front of you. Feel free to browse, read anything you like. I'm just going to make arrangements for our guest here. I shouldn't be a minute." She lifts her slender red staff in one hand, twirls it into place across the door, and punches the door very lightly with it. I feel a clicking sensation inside my skin, hear it distinctly just behind my ears.

"You needn't lock the guardhouse door, Sorceress," Hodges says, sitting himself down in front of the door. "I've gone turncoat, betrayed my brothers. I've nowhere to run."

"Brothers?" Miss Morrison leans her staff on the wall next to her desk.

"Yes. At our core, the Knights of Augustine are still a monastic order. The church abandoned us, but we never abandoned our traditions."

"Monks, huh?" Miss Morrison sits at her desk. "You learn something new every day."

I stroll over next to her, glancing at her desk, with her cozy green lamp and her books from last century so casually stuck between bookends. Miss Morrison has a warmth about her, a sense of safety, and I like being near her.

"Say, Miss Morrison?"

"Yes, dear?"

"Why do they call you Sorceress, anyhow?"

"Oh, that." She makes a wry face. "They pinned some medals on me during the war, and one of them came with a rank and title. It's just like when people call me 'captain', or when you call someone 'professor' or 'doctor.' Just an honorific."

"Should...*I* call you that?"

She puts her hand on mine. "Oh, darling, I wish you wouldn't. All that stuff does is put barriers between people. And please, call me Hazel."

I smile. "Hazel. Okay."

She gives me a warm smile, pats my hand, and picks up the earpiece from her telephone. I decide to give her some space, so I wander back over by the door and listen as she dials three numbers on the rotary.

I'm still trying to figure out what to do with myself when I catch Hodges looking at me from where he's sitting.

"Miss Van Tassel?"

I look at him.

"I..." He struggles with the words. "I am sorry for the way Pearse treated you. For the way he treated your friend. You must understand that is *not* the way we operate. We have principles, though I could hardly blame you for not believing it." He swallows. "Pearse is a beast, though I didn't fully realize it until today. I should never have considered bringing him along." He closes his eyes and heaves a regretful sigh. "Perhaps I shouldn't have considered his scheme at all. Perhaps it's not my place to care what the Blackstead does."

Over at the desk, Hazel starts talking to someone. "Hello, it's me. Say, remember what you said earlier, how you wanted to help? Did you truly mean it?" she pauses. "Well, it's only that I've a small favor to ask. Well, maybe a big one." She pauses again, listening, smiling a little into the phone. "Why, that's not true! Still, I've no one else to ask. All right, well, how would you feel about a trip to Cincinnati? Tonight." A long pause. "I don't know where to start. Maybe you should come over here and see for yourself."

I haven't the first clue what to say to Hodges. Maybe he's trying, and I appreciate his apology, but so much has happened today. And in the end, it's all because of him. So I don't say anything. I just stand back against the wall next to her door, looking out the tiny windows into the hazy September evening. Out there, the low screech of crickets starts to rise. In here, stillness and quiet.

"I also realize that I'm the prisoner here," he goes on, "and I have no place asking anything, so I understand if you don't wish to answer. But there is something I would very much like to ask, if you and Captain Morrison would permit it."

I glance at her; she's holding the phone up in front of her face and the bell-shaped earpiece to her ear. She shrugs at me.

"How did you *do* that?" he asks quietly. "Back there, in front of your house. When Eastwicke was building his arithromancy reaction and directing it at Captain Morrison, you..." He shakes his head, searching for a word. "*Unleashed* something. Some kind of spontaneous energy blast. I've never seen the like of it."

There it is. My oldest, strangest secret. The reason I was always different than the other kids, the monster I had to keep tame. The thing that almost killed Tommy Kelley, the thing I prayed nobody would ever learn about. And now, this man wants the straight dope on it, this man who banished the only friend I've ever felt I could share this secret with. Hodges will have to forgive me for feeling a bit reluctant to discuss it with him.

"What, you never saw a natural arcane before?" Hazel says to him, holding her hand over the receiver. "The bigshot expert that knows everything? Imagine that!"

A natural *what?*

Hodges' eyes travel slowly back to me, wide and disbelieving. He rises to a crouch, as if he's about to stand. I flinch away from him without thinking.

"How is that possible...?" Hodges asks me. He glances at Hazel, then back to me, like he's not sure where to direct the conversation. He licks his lips, reaches for his pocket handkerchief, and mops his brow with it.

A male voice on the other end of the telephone exclaims something. Hazel smirks. "That's right. It's been quite a day. You simply won't believe what arrived on my doorstep." A pause. "Well, I'm not about to spoil the surprise."

"At first I hardly believed my own eyes," Hodges continues. "A theric detonation on that scale didn't seem possible. But then I remembered how many primary sources before the fourteenth century make references to spontaneous reaction." Hazel, watching him, nods her head in my direction. "Er, that is, natural arcanes, such as yourself."

Hazel covers the telephone again, looking at me. "The things I did today? People who can use energy that way are called arcanes. But being able to pull off what you did is mighty unusual. You're what's called a natural arcane, or a Type A." She turns back to the receiver and rolls her eyes. "Okay, fine, but this is all you get. Remember the Displaced kid? Well, I got her friend here with me right now."

So that means Hazel is like me? There are others that can do these things, too?

I'm not alone?

She pulls her head back, gives the telephone a funny look. She flicks the switch on the side a few times. "Hello? *Hello?*" She sighs and hangs the earpiece on the switch. "Sadie, we'll have a visitor in a short while, but don't worry. He's a friend."

"I always believed the accounts from the Middle Ages and antiquity were just folktales, myths," Hodges goes on, glancing at Hazel. "No different than tales of dragons, or blue children from the sea, or Saint Patrick commanding all the snakes to leave Ireland."

Hazel crosses her ankles. "Well, that's the problem with you fellas. A bit reckless to paint everything with a broad brush, dontcha think?"

He turns back to me, looking at me with something almost like wonder. "Extraordinary. A real, live Type A, in the flesh. One of the first in centuries - and a woman, no less." He shakes his head. "The Lord truly works in mysterious ways."

Hazel and I share a baffled, incredulous look.

"Oh, that's right," Hazel says. "You fellas are all a bunch of celibate woman-haters."

"We most certainly do *not* hate women!" Hodges huffs. "On the contrary. We believe women are pure, and exist to be protected. Granted, women are very different from men - your intellectual capabilities differ drastically from ours. Women are ill-suited for science or academics, because you're designed to be subservient to men and provide us with children. That's just biology. But we hold women in high esteem."

I honestly don't know whether to laugh or not; it doesn't seem real, and I have to remind myself that these fellas actually *believe* this stuff. Courtney's face appears in my mind, one eye bigger than the other as she listens, her mouth open. Golly, what would *she* say to him? The thought of Courtney here beside me, reacting to this, is like touching a candle to gunpowder. The laughter chortles out of me before I can stop it, and it's rolling and rolling and I can't keep it in. And now I've got Hazel laughing too, leaning over her desk, forehead on her hand, shaking uncontrollably.

Hodges withdraws into a sullen pout. Hazel and I share a long, amused look as we try to stifle our laughter.

"Well," she says, dabbing a tear from her eye. "I just don't know *how* we'd manage without you. You protected *two* young women today, kept them safe from a quiet day minding their own business. And that Chisel Face fella is a real model of chivalry; why, when you fellas are around, it really feels like being stuck in the Dark Ages!"

A little while later, I'm sitting on Hazel's sofa with a small cherry-red book she brought me - ESSENTIAL PRINCIPLES OF ARCANE SCIENCE. is stamped in gold leaf on the front. Paragraphs of dry text and weird geometric diagrams drift past in a blur as I leaf through the pages; I couldn't concentrate right now, even if I wanted to. Too much is going on. Hazel sits at her desk, busily scribbling something with a pen.

A sudden knock at the door doesn't startle anyone; our heads fly up at the same time, and Hazel is on her way to answer it. I turn around, craning my neck to see who it is.

A man stands on the porch in the growing evening, glancing up at her with something almost like shyness. He's handsome, with twinkling eyes and a sharp, prominent nose. A moustache and goatee the color of mahogany soften his sharp features and wan complexion.

"Thanks for coming, Johnny," Hazel says. "Truly, I mean it."

"Well, I haven't learned how to say no to you yet, and I doubt I will anytime soon." His voice is a warm, nasal soprano; the voice of a country doctor or tractor salesman. Just occasionally, above certain words, there's a hint of Boston and Cambridge, a faint echo of the lazy patrician accent I heard so much as a child among friends of my family. But mostly he sounds midwestern, like everyone else in Autumn Grove. Today it looks like he's opted for comfort over elegance - he wears a vest and flat messenger cap of matching brown tweed. He's rolled up the sleeves on his white dress shirt, and his only concession to style is a crimson bow tie. The gold chain of a pocket watch hangs from his vest pocket.

I stand politely to acknowledge our caller, just as my parents taught. It's reflex by now. He steps inside, doffs his tidy brown cap, and stares at nothing for a moment as his eyes adjust to the darker room. Then he gives me a cordial look.

"Ahh, so you must be Miss Van Tassel."

Hodges' eyes turn to flint. He stands up, glaring at our visitor.

"The very same," Hazel confirms. "Sadie, this is Doctor Johnny Forsythe, an old friend."

I step across the room to greet him, shaking the hand he offers.

"It's wonderful to meet you, Miss. You must forgive me if I seem over-enthusiastic, but…" He maintains his warm handshake a little longer than I'm accustomed to. "I just wish to say that I am *very* pleased to see you safe. Very pleased indeed."

"Oh." I finally withdraw my hand, glancing at Hazel with a little confusion. "Why, that's very kind of you…"

"Doctor Forsythe was the one who warned me that you might be in danger," Hazel explains. "His warning prompted me to begin my investigation. That was when I saw what happened to Courtney - and that, in turn, led me to you."

"So it *was* you," Hodges' voice is almost a hiss. "*You're* the filthy double-crossing spy!"

Forsythe looks over and sees him for the first time. "And *you* must be my train ticket to Cincinnati on the red-eye special! Good to see you, Hodges."

"I'd find a way to tell the Knights this minute if I weren't tied up in this fiendish binding cuff." Hodges shakes his head, his voice turning almost sad. "Why'd you do it, Johnny? Why did you betray your brothers?"

"Someone had to stop you, didn't they?" Forsythe looks him dead in the eyes. "I only wish I'd done more, and done it sooner. Things could have gone on like they were, but you just had to cross the line."

Hodges curls his lip. "I was wise to you all along, you know. But it seems you covered your tracks a little too well for Kluivert to catch on."

"Well, so did you fellas. But not quite enough." Forsythe turns away, handing Hazel a leather folio. "My preliminary readings. They're only eighty percent complete, but it seems we were right."

Hazel opens the folio, eyes desperate and deadly serious as she looks up at him. "Do you mean...?"

Forsythe glances at me, a clever expression on his face. "Say, what do you say we start Miss Van Tassel's education by telling her what the word 'interloper' means?"

Hodges stumbles a half step back, eyes bulging, like he's been impaled with a bayonet. "H-how..."

Hazel's mouth falls open, her shock turning to grim satisfaction. "On the level?"

"As sure as sunrise," Forsythe swears. "You wanna tell her?"

"Tell me what?" Whatever it is, it's clearly good news. I could use some good news right now.

Hazel pauses, dazed and happy, and takes a moment to gather herself. "Sadie, we think these dumkuffs and their little stag club, the ones going around banishing innocent people, aren't even from this verse to begin with."

It comes on me slow. "You mean Displaced, or whatever the word is? Like Courtney?"

Hazel grins at Hodges like a cat with a cornered mouse. "Nope, not Displaced. An interloper is someone who forces their way into a verse they know they don't belong in and then stays there with malicious intent."

"We had to, we were running from the Inquisition!" Hodges protests. "Your verse had the most passive resonance, it was the best place to hide-"

"Aw, tell it to Sweeney." Hazel narrows her eyes at him with grim pleasure. "I hope you're sent right back to whatever cesspit you crawled out of, and they add a temporal spin to make sure you end up right back at the same time you left."

"I'll...I'll talk, I'll do anything, just please, please don't-"

I can *not* believe my ears. This bastard came here from a hostile verse, hid here on purpose right under everyone's noses, then turned around and banished someone who *belongs* here?

"It didn't bother you too much, doing it to someone else," Forsythe says coldly.

"I hope you burn," I hiss. "And if I can, I will *make* you burn."

His face screws up into an ugly grimace and he slumps to the floor, crying like a baby.

Hazel glares at him a moment before looking back to Forsythe. "When shall we have something concrete?"

"By morning, if I stayed in town," Forsythe says. "But seeing as how I'm taking this little side trip with Jeremiah, do you think Kline will act on an eighty percent dissonance reading?"

"Why, she'll have to," Hazel says firmly. "That's at least enough to open a formal investigation. I'll send her a telegram as soon as your findings are in my hands and I can verify them. Then all that's left is for someone to go in and put an eviction notice on the door."

"You can't do this," Hodges says very quietly, his voice shaking. "Who are you to just...just...*throw us out*, like a bunch of vagrants?!"

"Your medicine doesn't taste very good, does it?" Hazel asks, stepping forward. "Imagine doing that to a *kid*, one who can't protect herself. Women in high esteem, my ass." She kneels down, right in his face. "Once we get that girl back, maybe we'll leave your fate in *her* hands, and in Sadie's."

Hodges looks slowly toward me with bulging eyes, cheeks slick with tears. I can't summon an ounce of pity for him. He's just another bully who invaded my life and tried to wreck it. I hope these Seven Towers people have the spine to make him answer for what he's done. Heck, someone's gonna need a backbone pretty soon - that other lunatic is still out there somewhere, and I can't imagine he's going to let any of this go.

193

I still have a great many questions about that brawl earlier. Right now, Hazel and Dr. Forsythe are filling out some paperwork, so I take advantage of the quiet to get the straight dope on this...*arcane* stuff.

"Say, Hazel," I ask. "I hope this isn't some kinda secret knowledge or something, but...earlier, when you were fighting that Chisel Face fella, you said three words to him and he crumpled up. Were those some kinda magic words?"

Hazel's grinning, and her smile splits into open laughter. She's got a sweet, elegant laugh, even if it does make me feel like a rube. "Oh, forgive me, dearest. I don't mean to laugh at you. It's just that sometimes I forget what all this looks like to someone who's never seen it before." She tilts her head to the side and rubs the back of her neck. "For one thing, you mustn't worry about secret knowledge or anything like that - we're practical scientists, not Freemasons. And secondly, no. 'Brittle and snap' aren't magic words - they're simply words."

Dr. Forsythe takes over the lesson as Hazel scribbles something with a fountain pen. "What we call 'arcanology' - the use of theric reactions to manipulate our world - starts in the mind. First, we must understand what we want to do, and with training and practice your mind will recall the right formula to accomplish that. Then it's a matter of focusing that intention out into the world and forcing it to happen."

Hazel caps her pen. "What Johnny's trying to say is, knowing your apples is one thing, but throwing them is another. That's where your theric body - which some call the anima - comes into play. You project theric energy through yourself and into the wo᜔᜔ ᜔᜔ you conjure the formula you want." She folds her hands in her lap, turning to face me. "Since it all starts with the mind, different arcanists use different tricks to get everything moving, up here," she points at her head. "So for me, 'brittle and snap' is just a simple mnemonic device to help me recall a reaction I've already stored in my staff. A shortcut, if you will. That's important when you have a bunch of reactions stored in a device or something."

"So," I wonder aloud, "if it all just starts in your mind, does that mean there are no, um...magic spells you have to memorize? You can just make it up on the spot?"

"Not...entirely," Dr. Forsythe says. "You do have to memorize the occasional formula, since formulae are written to cause a certain specific effect. But to fully answer your question: there are no 'magic words' or any other such thing, merely words that have meaning for *you*. And in a manner of speaking, yes, anyone can build a formula to make something happen, but this often takes time and research. It's not something you can do on the spot."

"Unless you're a Type A like Sadie." Hazel gets a mischievous look on her face.

"Now don't go confusing the poor girl," Dr. Forsythe scolds her. "It's true, Sadie - you are a natural arcane, but that only means you operate under somewhat different rules. You're attuned to a particular aspect - or element - and you can unleash a handful of powerful reactions. However, learning to do more *within* your aspect often takes some training."

My head is swirling. "But, can I still use those...formula things?"

"Yes," Hazel replies. "Certainly. Though the same condition applies - Type A arcanists must work a bit harder to attune themselves to different aspects before they're able to cast reactions properly. Put simply, you're more powerful than a learned arcanist - or Type B, as we're called - and those reactions you *can* do easily are much simpler to cast than they are for others. Essentially, you point and shoot. However, it takes you a little more work to branch out."

"I think I begin to see," I say uncertainly. My head still feels muddled.

"It's a great deal to learn," Dr. Forsythe says with a smile. "But I sense very strongly that you shall outclass us all. And very soon, I should think."

Hazel just smiles at me in agreement. I don't know how they get that idea - why, I'm still stumbling over what "theric" means.

But it *is* rather fascinating, isn't it? I never knew there was so much science behind something I'd tried so hard - and for so long - to keep wrapped inside myself.

"Say," Hazel interjects, "I guess we should probably find out what the kid's made of, shouldn't we?"

"Why, I think that's a splendid idea," Dr. Forsythe says.

Find out what I'm made of? Lordy, that doesn't sound good - I hope they don't start pummeling me with fireballs or something.

Hazel reaches for a little shiny black scope, stuck among a few small volumes on her desk. It looks like something you'd see on top of a marksman's rifle, except much smaller - this is about the length of a hot dog and a little wider than a dime. It's an elegant-looking device, nicely polished and probably rather expensive. It's lined with a number of gears and tiny dials, which Hazel starts fiddling with like an expert. She rotates something at the very end of the scope, like something you might use to focus a set of binoculars. She then lifts the scope and peeks at me with it. After a moment, her face drops.

"Why, I never!"

"Aw, now don't do me that way, Hazel," Dr. Forsythe says. "Spill the beans!"

She gives him an incredulous look for a moment, then simply hands him the scope. He sticks it to his eye and squints through the lens.

"Holy mackerel!"

"You're starting to frighten me," I tell them. "Am I in some sorta trouble?"

They're dumbfounded for a moment, but Hazel snaps out of it first. "Oh, heavens no, darling! Quite the opposite!" She shares one more sidelong glance with Dr. Forsythe. "It seems that not only are you a Type A arcane - which is itself rare enough - you're also one of rather..."

"Exceptional power," Dr. Forsythe finishes.

Hazel flashes me a look of almost girlish enthusiasm. "Why, you're a full caliber seven, Sadie!"

I blink. "And that's...good?"

"Allow me to put it in perspective for you," Dr. Forsythe says. "Sorceress Morrison here is a war heroine. She defeated Kaiser Bill's most powerful arcanist, blew up a whole German fort with the snap of her fingers-"

"Now don't go filling the girl's head with all *that* baloney!" Hazel rests her fists on her hips.

"-and *she* is a caliber six," Forsythe finishes. "Which is quite the normal limit. We're not sure why, but most humans can't contain a theric signature above caliber six." He fixes me with a direct stare. "You, my dear, are a caliber seven."

My mouth falls open. "So, what does that..."

Hazel claps her hands together excitedly, giving me an infectious smile. "A caliber seven kinetic aspect. Type A. Darling, once we train you up, nobody - and I mean *nobody* - will ever mess with you again!"

Excitement rises inside my chest, and I pick up Hazel's grin. That does sound wonderful. Even Hodges, distraught and sitting in a shadowy corner, looks at me with awe.

"And...Chisel Face...is he a powerful arcanist, too?"

They share a laugh. Hazel shakes her head. "Heavens, no. He's just a brute with some fancy toys. The arcanist who made those toys had to be powerful, but Chisel Face himself? He's a caliber two, soaking wet. Without his toys, he's little more than a common thug. And you, Sadie - once we train you, you'll be able to break him in half, in your sleep, with your eyes closed and one hand tied behind your back."

The thought brings a grin all by itself, and I feel my face glowing.

Hazel was right! By golly, nobody's gonna mess with me - or Courtney - *ever again*.

It's after dark now, and I'm sitting on a bench at the train station, watching as Hazel and Dr. Forsythe talk on the platform. Hodges sits alone on another bench, slumped, defeated. I asked Hazel why Hodges didn't just try to run away or cast something. Apparently, that bracelet she put on him stops him from channeling any energy at all; he can't perform the slightest reaction. It's also really hard to break, even by the most skilled arcanist; the only safe way to get it off is to have it unlocked by someone with the right key. It can do other things, too - for one, it's a kind of homing beacon that tells her exactly where the subject is any time she wants to know. She also said that if he strays any more than two hundred feet from her, it'll explode.

"That cuff is wired with an interphased charge equal to forty full sticks of dynamite," she explained. "That's enough to replace him with a crater the size of three cars."

"Interphased charges," he snickers bitterly. "The self-righteous Seven Towers. You're all a pack of savages."

I didn't understand all the fancy words, but I understood the thing about the big hole in the ground. And Hodges has stayed pretty close.

I'm close enough to Hazel and Dr. Forsythe to hear them talking quietly.

"No, Johnny." Her eyes are far away, lost in the gloom. "I made a bad hash of things. I failed."

"How did you fail?" he asks intently, leaning in just a little. "You just apprehended the Knights' second-in-command. One of the bosses behind a rogue arcane circle, I should add. Why - if it were me, I'd give you a commendation!"

She shakes her head very slightly. "There won't be any commendations. Nor should there be. All I did was catch the easiest prize. Hell, he practically gave himself up." Her eyes dart over to Hodges, sitting a ways off. "His heart wasn't really in it today. That stunt he pulled wasn't even his idea to begin with; it was Pearse's."

Understanding dawns across Dr. Forsythe's face. "Of course. Hodges is a fussy busybody and he likes to poke his nose in where it doesn't belong, but I don't think it would have occurred to him to mess with some Displaced college girl unless someone put him up to it." He turns and looks back at their prisoner. Hodges leans back against the bench, arms crossed, staring out into the night with a clouded expression. "That's a pretty queer scheme, even for him. But Pearse isn't half bad at talking people around to things, if he really wants something."

"But I don't understand," Hazel persists. "*Why?!* Why would Chisel Face Pearse care about some Displaced girl he's never met? I don't get it." She leans in, voice intense. "And when did he become a versologist? Hodges told me Pearse was spending time in their lab - though I can't imagine what kind of half-baked versology lab they've got over there," she adds glibly. "But anyhow, he'd been watching Courtney for *days*, phasing off and on around the versal barrier. He knew she was phasing in, and he knew when and where." She pauses, her eyes hard. "Pearse had this *planned*, Johnny."

"God dammit." Forsythe stares into the night, hands on his hips. He runs a hand over his face. When he speaks again, he's almost too quiet for me to hear. "All right. I'll nose around, see what I can find out. But I can't make too many promises. If Hodges was onto me-"

"No," Hazel shakes her head. "I don't think we can risk it. I think it's time to get you out of there."

"Hazel, something rotten is going on over there. You said it yourself - why would Pearse care about something so inconsequential? We're close to finding out. I just need a little more time."

"I think you're *out* of time," she tells him firmly, arms crossed. "Your cover is wearing thin, and if you're compromised, you know good and well they'll kill you. We must abort your mission."

Forsythe closes his eyes and sighs deeply. "Very well. You're the boss. But what do I say?"

Hazel shrugs. "You could tell them that this business of kidnapping and intimidating defenseless young women isn't sitting right with you, and you refuse to abide it anymore. Or you could tell them that you're gonna skip town while you can. The Seven Towers never arrested any of the Knights before, and now that it's started it means the noose is closing. One of the ringleaders is in captivity now, and it won't be long till they're on the doorstep with armed agents. You're not about to make some heroic last stand to protect Kluivert's ego and a few rusty antiques."

He nods, digesting that. "It's not a lie."

"One more thing," Hazel says. "Have you any idea where Pearse and Eastwicke are?"

Forsythe shakes his head. "I haven't been to the Hall since before I called at your house this afternoon. Though I'm assuming they're both in recovery. Between you and the young wildcat over there, it sounds like you cleaned their clocks good. I doubt they'll be bothering anybody anytime soon."

"I'd like to make sure of it," Hazel insists. "I don't think Pearse is seriously hurt, aside from a few broken bones, but Sadie snuffed the arithromancer's lights out." She glances at me, and I look away as quick as I can. She continues, her voice low and emphatic. "Why, I still can't believe it. A real Type A! A *caliber seven* Type A!"

"Truly remarkable," he agrees, glancing at me. "What'll you do? Train her yourself? A little young for the Seven Towers to get their mitts on. Just starting college, isn't she?"

I feel Hazel's eyes on me, contemplating. I try to keep my gaze averted. "Yes, she is. And I'm not sure yet; maybe I will. Hell, someone's gotta train her, and soon."

"And keep her safe until the Knights are put away," Dr. Forsythe says.

"Yes," Hazel agrees. "Though if she's properly trained, she'll be able to look after herself far better than I could."

A warm glow of hope tingles in my chest. They're talking about my power - not as some freakish curse, but as a gift to be embraced. When I glance their way again, I find them both watching me. Hazel offers me a warm smile.

As they wrap up their conversation, Hazel hands Dr. Forsythe a small stack of papers lined with her tall, flowy handwriting. Finally, she hands over a small yellowish crystal. It looks like a smooth glass vial without a lid.

"This is the forensic divination record," she tells him. "Keep it safe. That's what's gonna send every last one of these shitheel bastards away."

The train hisses.

"I know, Hazel. I promise." He places the crystal carefully in an inside jacket pocket. "And I'll take him to the conclave immediately, as soon as the train gets me to Cincinnati. I'm not as fearsome as you are, but I can at least mind a cuffed prisoner."

"I know you can, Johnny. I know you can." A deep breath. "This whole rotten business just has me on edge."

"I know, it's perfectly all right." Forsythe smiles. "Look, I'm not the one you have to worry about. You're the one in the lion's mouth right now. Just keep yourself safe and mind your young pupil over there." They startle when the train whistles - it's shrill and it splits the night. "Seems we're both on edge."

"Yeah. I guess so." She steps in and embraces him. Forsythe stops, stunned, as if he's not sure what to do with his half-extended arms. Finally, he returns the hug, very warmly. He steps away after a moment, eyes a little bit downcast, a tight sad smile on his lips.

Hazel's face is clear, set with intense purpose. She gives him a cool smile, nods. "Watch yourself, will you? And have them contact me immediately."

"You shall have your telegram tomorrow afternoon." He gives her one more lingering, sad smile, then offers his hand to me again. I shake it. "Good luck, Miss Van Tassel. Don't take any wooden nickels, all right?"

I laugh. "I won't."

He winks at me, almost a blink, then looks to Hodges. "Rise and shine, Jeremiah. We're off to Coney Island."

"You're no good at levity *or* sarcasm, Forsythe," Hodges says, slowly rising and straightening his jacket, summoning the last of his dignity. "And your bumbling attempts to combine them just make me despise you more."

"Aw, quit being so grumpy. You're like some rich old widow." Forsythe says, waiting for Hodges to step onto the train in front of him. "We'll get you something from the dining car."

The rest of their conversation is lost as they board the train. The locomotive belches one last restless shriek as I come up next to Hazel. She puts her arm around my shoulder, giving me a comforting rub as the station attendant closes each compartment door. Forsythe appears at a window after a minute, and Hazel and I wave as the train slowly chugs away into the night.

Looking at Hazel's face makes me sad. Her mouth is tight, her green eyes a little too quick and alert. I don't need to be a mind reader to know what she must be feeling, watching that train crawl away from the station. She's all by herself now, the only agent of her conclave in a dangerous town. Pearse and the old man, Eastwicke, they got away; she couldn't catch them. She blew it, or so she believes, and they're still out there.

I feel it in the tense arm around my shoulder, holding me close like the edge of a cliff in the night. She's determined to keep me safe, but she's not sure she can. They could come back at any time, ready and laying for a fight, with more men. She'll be facing them all alone.

And Courtney, somewhere out in the void. To Hazel, my life and Courtney's hang in the balance. *I have to do this alone,* her face says. *I have to. But how?*

Naturally, she'd never admit any of this to me; she's a war heroine, an important sorceress, and she'll keep it all inside. Any self-doubt she's got, she'll hide so that I feel safe. But I'm stuck in this rotten mess, too, same as her.

"Miss Morrison?" I ask. Hazel shoots me a quick look, her face tense, a mask of painted confidence. "Until today, I thought I was all alone. With this...*arcane* stuff." It still feels strange saying it. "But you showed me I'm not."

She smiles. "Why, of course you're not, dear."

"Well, I just wanted to say, neither are you. I don't know how, but everything will be all right."

Just for a moment, her mask softens, and she looks vulnerable. Then she pulls me close, summoning her resolve.

"You're a darn good egg, Sadie. Such a darn good egg. And you're absitively right." She smiles, and the sunlight is back in it. "Come on. Let's go find a way to bring Courtney home."

Fifteen

Sadie

"There's no such thing as "coincidence" or "odds" in versology. If the universe needs something to happen, it's damn well gonna happen. It's that simple."
-Harriet Stokeley, Provost Arcana
New Amsterdam Conclave, New York
1919

This has absolutely been the longest day of my life.

It's nine o'clock in the evening by the time we reach Professor Talbott's front door, and my brain is numb from all the stuff I've learned in the last two hours. Why, just a month ago, I was sitting at home in Buffalo, bored to tears - I couldn't wait to get down here and start a new life. Now that I've got my wish, I almost envy the old me.

Almost.

As it turns out, the world goes a whole lot deeper than I ever imagined. I've learned that I'm not some freak, either. The hazy summer night is alive with excitement and danger as we make our way uptown.

Hang on, Courtney. Help is on the way.

Professor Talbott's house is uptown on Court Street, right in the middle of campus. College Green is alive with crickets just across the street from this porch. Earlier today, Courtney and I had lunch over there; it's dark under the shade of those massive trees, but I could still point you to the exact spot. Then I sent her back to my house and into the hands of a monster.

Professor Talbott's front bay window glows with lamp light. The muffled sound of a woman's voice leaks through the door. Then the murmurs of a higher, younger voice. Has she guests?

Hazel stops at the front door, squaring her shoulders and taking a deep breath. She closes her eyes for a few moments then opens her eyelids, head held high.

"Is everything all right?" I ask her quietly.

"Just ducky," she says, almost to herself. Then she half-looks at me in the timid moonlight. "Well, it's just, Professor Talbott is scary."

"Scary?" I'm a little incredulous. Hazel was in the war, right? Why would she be scared of a professor?

"It's silly, I know, but honest to goodness, I'd rather fight every last one of those brutes from today than to get on *her* bad side - and I think I've been on her bad side for a long time." She heaves a sigh. "Still, she's the best versologist I know of, and she happens to be right here in town. She's got to help us. She's just got to."

One more breath, then she raises a hand, knocks.

A moment of stiff silence before a shadow flickers across the parlor. Then the door opens, revealing a tall, gangly young woman. She's got crinkly mouse-brown hair tied back in a bun; a few wiry strands have flown loose around a rather homely face. Hazel offers her a warm smile, like a conciliatory gift.

"Yes?" The tall kid is friendly and a little bit hesitant.

"Hello," Hazel sounds perplexed. "Is this the home of Elizabeth Talbott?"

"Yes, that's right."

"I don't believe we've met," Hazel says. "I'm-"

An older woman, nearly as tall as the mousy girl, appears in the doorway.

"Hazel Morrison?" She narrows her eyes, and there's a question in her glance.

"Professor Talbott," Hazel says meekly.

The woman peers at Hazel with curiosity and suspicion. With her little round glasses rimmed in copper wire and the outdated dress of ruddy brown that falls to her ankles, she looks more like a harsh schoolmistress than a renowned versologist. There's something cool and detached in her eyes, and something impetuous in the way she stands. I certainly understand what Hazel meant when she called Professor Talbott "scary."

"What brings the Seven Towers calling at *my* humble door? At-" She cranes back, looking at something in the parlor, "nine of an evening?"

"Professor, I-" Hazel bites a lip, just a little. "*We.* Need your help."

"*My* help?" A small laugh. She's got a rich voice. "What could the Cincinnati Conclave possibly want from *me?*"

"Not the Conclave," Hazel replies quietly. "Just me. Please, we've nowhere else to turn."

The professor leans back, contemplating. Her steely gray eyes soften when they catch sight of me, and she relents. "Oh, very well. You'd better come in."

"Thank you," Hazel breathes, and we step inside. The woman gives me a soft smile as I step past her, into the parlor. Once inside, Hazel stands nervously, hands clasped around the top of her staff, now shortened and resting on the floor like a cane.

The tall kid closes the door behind us. A stained glass lamp sits near the front bay window, shaded in morning tones of peach and rose, and it bathes the room in radiant light. Another girl about my age sits on the couch, cramped and awkward with all the commotion.

"Hazel, I don't think you've met my niece, have you?" She turns to regard the lanky girl with an easy, familiar smile. "Nettie, this is Captain Hazel Morrison, part of the American Arcane Expedition during the war - and before that, an undergrad at Braddock, just like you girls. You might say we go back a ways."

The kid steps forward, greeting Hazel with more openness and more awkwardness than her aunt showed. Her royal blue satin blouse looks comfy, worn above a plain gray cotton skirt and brown oxfords. She fidgets and gives Hazel a self-conscious smile. "Lovely to meet you, Captain Morrison."

"The pleasure is mine," Hazel says warmly. "And no need for that rank stuff. Hazel is just fine, or 'Miss Morrison' if you really want to be formal. But I prefer first names, don't you?"

The girl smiles. "Hazel."

Nettie. Why does that name sound familiar?

"And this is Nettie's friend, Mary Carlyle, who might as well be my niece, too, since she's been as much a part of my life as Nettie has. Inseparable, these two, and they'll both be freshmen at Braddock this year."

The girl rises from the couch and offers a slight, nervous smile. She's shorter than her friend; actually, I believe she's a bit shorter than me, too. This kid has a soft, milky pink face with delicate rounded features and big eyes the color of cocoa. Light brown hair, too, cut in a fashionable bob around her soft jawline. She looks so petite in her pink summer dress with the matching sailor scarf. She's posilutely precious.

"Very nice to meet you, Mary." The way Hazel's eyes twinkle, I can tell she thinks the girl is cute, too.

"Nice to meet you." Mary speaks softly, and her eyes fall to the carpet.

Mary. That name rings a bell, too. It's common enough, but it sticks in my ears anyway; it seems like I heard it somewhere recently.

Hazel turns to me. "Ladies, this is Sadie Van Tassel. She's a Braddock freshman as well, and she's all the way down from New York. She's all alone on campus; maybe you girls could keep her company?"

Nettie and Mary flash me looks of gentle alarm.

"Why, sure!" Nettie exclaims. "You poor thing, all alone down here?"

"Aw, s'all right." I wave it off unconvincingly. "But sure, I'd love some company!"

Nettie beams triumphantly, and Mary answers me with a lovely smile.

Professor Talbott's eyes grow warm as she approaches me.

"Elizabeth Talbott," she says kindly, and she offers me a weathered hand. "Though you may call me Elizabeth. I suppose there's no sense standing on formality when I'm retired, anyhow."

"Hello." I shake her hand, not sure if I was even loud enough to be heard.

"New York, you say? You haven't a New York accent - why, you don't sound that different than Nettie or Mary. Where are you from?"

"Oh. Buffalo."

"Ah, the lake," Elizabeth says. "That explains it; you're practically a midwesterner like the rest of us. So you three have something in common already! As I said, Nettie and Mary are inseparable, but they're not the kind to wall themselves off. I'm sure you three can find plenty of mischief to get into."

We all exchange the kind of awkward, uneasy smiles that happen when older folks make arrangements that involve you with people you've just met.

"Say, speaking of inseparable," Mary says softly. She's half-pointing at me, mouth open, like a thought is about to leap out at any moment. "Your friend. Where...?"

What does this girl see? My mouth drops. "How...?"

"Why, you must be a diviner," Hazel realizes.

Mary nods shyly, and her eyes find their way back to me. "Where is she? Your friend, the girl you lost?"

"I-I..." I don't even know how to begin. Maybe it's the soft compassion in her voice, or maybe it's the acknowledgment that I've lost someone, but something provokes a sting of grief in my chest. I'm having trouble forming a response.

"As it happens, that's exactly the reason we called," Hazel tells Elizabeth. "We're trying to find her."

"And that's why you needed a versologist," Elizabeth realizes.

"What happened!?" Nettie asks, frightened.

Hazel hesitates, looking at me for some reason. After a tense moment, she responds. "A group called the Knights of Augustine happened."

Elizabeth's eyebrows shoot up in alarm.

"You're certain?"

"I got in a scuffle with them," Hazel replies. "They showed up at Sadie's door to take her away or do heaven knows what, and fortunately I arrived in time to prevent that. But I wasn't able to keep her from getting mixed up in the scrap that followed, and I'm awfully sorry for it."

The girls look at me in wild astonishment. They'll surely be full of questions.

"Nettie, Mary," Elizabeth says after a moment. "Would you go upstairs and dig out my collection of arcana books? Nettie, you were asking about *Fundamentals of Higher Sorcery* - I believe that's in there. You'll want to become familiar with it, I should think."

For a tense moment, the girls don't move. They look startled, like they just watched a hold-up man jump in a car and take off. But Elizabeth quietly stares at them until they snap out of it and make their way upstairs. Once their footsteps have faded down the hallway above us, Hazel turns to Elizabeth.

"Nettie's arcane?" she asks.

"I couldn't say for certain," Elizabeth says, quickly dismissing Hazel's question. "I'd rather she not get mixed up in all that business, regardless. And I'd like to insist that the Seven Towers stay away from her so that she can focus on college."

"Why, certainly." Hazel's confusion turns to hurt. "I'm sorry, I was just curious. And I'm sorry if I've given the impression that my motives were dishonest. I wasn't posted here to recruit students."

I should probably keep my mouth shut, but there's a point where I can't anymore.

"Hazel saved my life, Professor," I tell her. "Those lousy, rotten goons did some awful things to my friend, and then they came laying for me, just because we're pals." Remembering everything that happened is getting me worked up, but I continue, my words tumbling out faster.

"You wanna know what they did to her? That monster, Chisel Face, they call him, he..." I try to hold back the tears but they're filling my eyes. "He put his filthy hands all over her, touched her. And he'd have done *worse* if he could have! The only reason he didn't is because they were too busy trying to banish her!" The tears trickle down my cheeks. "Courtney was *home* - they threw her out like some drunk bum on a corner."

Hazel watches me, eyes heavy with compassion and sadness. She comes over and sits me down in a chair, her arm around my shoulders. I'm a mess, crying all over the place. I remember Courtney's tissues, a blob of white peeking out of the pocket of my summer cardigan. I reach for one, very gently, and examine it before raising it to my face. It still smells like her; delicate and sweet, like the perfume she wore. It breaks the dam; sobs come rolling out of me.

"If Hazel hadn't shown up when she did, heck, I don't know what they'd-a done to me!"

Hazel pulls me close, rubbing my back, comforting me. Elizabeth's face is pallid and shocked, like someone stabbed on their way to the grocery store. She raises a hand to her mouth like she's going to be sick.

"Did you really think I came calling at nine in the evening so I could shanghai your niece for the conclave?" Hazel raises an eyebrow.

"Why, I suppose I don't know what I thought," Elizabeth confesses. "I at least assumed that's what you were in town for. So you could recruit students."

"Well, it's not," Hazel says flatly. "You know me, Prof. Or I thought you did, anyhow, back in my college days. I'm a supervisory field agent for Seven Towers Intelligence now. I'm here to keep an eye out for anything that might threaten this town. Including rogue arcane circles." She props her staff next to me. "Earlier today, one such group - and you know who I mean - illegally banished a Displaced girl. I failed to protect her once, and I'm damn well not gonna fail her again. *That's* why I'm here." She approaches Elizabeth. "And I can't help her without a skilled versologist. Won't you help me?"

Elizabeth nods very slightly. "Why, yes, of course I'll help you. I'm...I'm frightfully sorry, Hazel. I owe you an apology."

Hazel sighs, relieved. " 'Sall right. Whatever misgivings you have about the conclave, I'm sure you have your reasons."

The professor nods, staring off with clouded eyes. But then she collects herself and looks at me. "Well, anyhow. Something's troubling me. Sadie, you said her name is Courtney?"

I nod at the floor. She's awful quiet, so I look up after a moment. Her eyes are narrowed in thought.

"Would you describe her for me?"

I sniffle. "Soft blonde hair, razor-straight, with just a hint of copper. Lovely blue eyes. Sweet, kind. She's about my size, maybe a little bonier." I toy with the tissue in my hands. "She wore a kind of, um, red camisole, I think, with a hooded sweatshirt over it. It had a logo on it, started with an A, I can't remember. Short denim shorts, black canvas sneakers. She's from 2004."

Elizabeth goes pale and her fingers cover her mouth. "Good lord."

"What is it, Prof?" Hazel asks. "You look as though you've seen a ghost."

Elizabeth's eyes flick over. "I believe I may have."

There's some commotion upstairs, and then a whisper at the top. *"Mary!"* Then footsteps on the stairs, noisy and fast. When I look up, Mary's leaning over the banister with desperation in her eyes.

"That's Courtney!" she exclaims. *"My* Courtney!"

Her Courtney? What does she mean *her* Courtney?!

Elizabeth turns to Hazel. "Our ghost, Miss Morrison."

Poor Mary is quite flustered. She's interested in everything - lunch, the yearbook, the moment I last saw Courtney, anything I know. Nettie is deeply concerned but calmer than Mary; she asks careful questions about the banishment, about our encounter with Chisel Face and the others, about their alleged motives.

"You girls are terribly invested," Hazel points out, early in the discussion. "May I ask why?"

"Courtney is our friend too, if you can believe it," Nettie says, before Mary can speak. "As strange as it sounds, the three of us have been friends since we were little. We'd be here all night if we told you everything, but let's just say that nothing's ever been easily explained when it came to Courtney. We didn't think much of it back then, but there's a lotta things that don't make any sense." She looks at her aunt. "Heck, Aunt Lizzy was the only person we could tell any of this to."

Mary and Nettie! Of course! That's where I heard their names - Courtney told me! How is that possible? We run into Courtney's oldest friends the first place we come to? I've never really bought into the idea of fate or anything - that's a more Christian idea, and me and sissy are American Church of Venus Welcoming - but I'm getting this crawling sensation in my spine, and I'm certainly starting to feel things being orchestrated around me.

Elizabeth nods. "Courtney's situation was a puzzle. I tried to make sense of it and help the child the best I could, but the matter taxed even *my* capacity for versal conundrums."

It's ten o'clock before we finish explaining everything that happened.

"Good grief!" Mary cries, standing up and stomping a foot. "She just *phased?! Today!!?*"

Nobody really knows what to say. Mary stamps over by the entrance to the kitchen, puts her arms on the wall, and leans against it.

"*UUUURRGGGHHH!*" Her voice comes out muffled from under her arms. "I've been chasing her since seventh grade only to miss her by a *few hours?!*"

"I'm ever so sorry, dear," Hazel sounds mournful. "I'm sorry I didn't get there in time to help her."

After a moment, Mary gives a wet sniff and turns around, resting her back on the wall. Her face is rosy with tears. "No, Miss Morrison, *I'm* the one who's sorry for getting worked up. It's just so incredibly frustrating!"

Nettie goes over and tries to comfort her.

I look between them. "So is that why you're in town? To find Courtney?"

Nettie looks right at me. "As it turns out…"

All the blood drains from my head and goosebumps stand out on my arms. "Chase yourself! *Really?!*"

Elizabeth's still looking at Mary. "What's more, we believe she may be in real danger now."

Hazel's expression turns grave. "How so?"

Elizabeth nods at Mary. "Mary received a precognitory flash this morning."

Mary's sitting back on the couch now, looking at a handkerchief in her fingers. "Some fella. He looked like some sorta Satanic apple-knocker. He kept playing with this long knife and saying the most-" she sniffles, "the most dreadful things. Oh, I can't..." She leans into Nettie, who takes her in her arms and gently rubs her back.

I walk slowly over to Mary, not sure if I'm intruding, but I really hate seeing the poor darling cry like this. Nettie holds out a hand and takes mine, and I feel welcomed right away. I take Mary's hand with my left, and she squeezes. She has such soft hands, warm and moist with tears.

"Thank you, Sadie," she tells me very quietly. She sniffles. "Both of you."

Elizabeth watches Mary and Nettie, but her eyes are sick with dread and hate. "What Mary saw was a psychopath in the truest sense. The precognition allowed her to listen in on a conversation where this repulsive beast revealed detailed plans he'd made for Courtney."

"What kind of detailed plans?" Hazel's face looks sick and grim, and her words sound more like a statement than a question.

Elizabeth's soft gray eyes dart over to her. "The sort of plans no young woman should ever have to hear, especially not about someone she loves." She shakes her head very slowly. "We are dealing with a monster vile beyond description, Hazel. And Courtney's banishment has raised all manner of unpleasant possibilities."

"What kind of possibilities?" I ask her. My voice sounds bleak and hollow in my ears.

The knocking pendulum of the grandfather clock is the only sound in a silent room. Somehow it feels as if it's gotten darker in here. Elizabeth looks right at me. "Miss Van Tassel, has Hazel told you what a resonance purge is?"

Black dread rolls up my shoulders, and terror stabs my heart. I'm not sure what's got me so scared, whether it's the way Elizabeth asks or the term she used. But I scoot a little closer to the girls.

"I'm afraid I don't know what that means, myself," Hazel confesses, lightly sitting down in a chair opposite Elizabeth, folding her legs to the side.

Professor Talbott takes a deep breath, and she seems almost reluctant to answer the question. "Most Displaced live on borrowed time. There comes a time when the verse can or will no longer tolerate the presence of a Displaced - usually some threshold of growth or maturity in their lives. This varies from person to person, but it has been suggested that the return of a Displaced, especially after they've begun to resonate with their true verse, will accelerate the process."

I'm trying hard to follow. "Please forgive me, Professor, but I'm not sure I understand."

Mary speaks quietly, her voice bleak. "It means that Courtney is supposed to be here and she'd-a been fine if she'd been allowed to stay. Because when she came here, she began to settle into our universe, and that changed her. But *then* she got thrown back, and now that place is going to see her as some kind of disease and kill her."

The words knock the wind out of me. "*Kill her?!* B-but surely..."

Hazel turns a very serious look on the professor. "Are we powerless to intervene?"

"Not necessarily. But that's dependent on a number of factors, including how far the purge has progressed and the state Courtney is in. You must understand that if we *can* intervene, we mustn't sit around and hope she can phase over as completely as she did today. We shall need the fastest, most reliable transit possible from that verse to our own."

"You're talking about a versal aperture, aren't you?" Hazel asks.

Elizabeth nods. "Precisely."

"Well, how can we guide her to one? She won't be able to find it on her own."

Elizabeth looks back at Mary. "That's where Miss Carlyle can help us."

I chime in. "But I still don't understand. What do all these *processes* have to do with the fella that wants to hurt Courtney?"

The professor nods. "You see, Sadie, a universe is nothing less than everything in it. People, plants, rocks, air, energy, all of it. And if a universe wants to kill you, the entire thing will turn against you - and it will throw anything at you, anything it has, until you are dead."

I jump as the grandfather clock clangs the quarter hour. Hazel closes her eyes and lifts her hand to where her green cloche hat flattens against her forehead. Her hand is trembling; it must have startled her, too.

The fading chime of that clock is the only sound in the room. Elizabeth sits up and looks over by the stairway, reading the time.

"Hazel, you said you performed a forensic divination?"

"Yes, that's right."

"What time was the banishment complete?"

Hazel pulls a little notepad out of her handbag, flips it open. "Why, about...two-nineteen this afternoon."

Elizabeth nods. "Then I would assume that, by this hour, the resonance purge will have entered its terminal phase."

I turn a terrified look on Hazel.

Mary looks up. "What do you mean, terminal?"

"It means," Hazel says, "that if we don't get Courtney home before sunrise, she's dead."

"Mary," Elizabeth gets up. "You know how to make a type one standard scrying basin?"

"Sure thing, Aunt Lizzy."

"Okay, sweetie - go cleanse and prepare one. I've purchased a vial of extraversal amplifying solution since you were last here - add a drop or two of that, won't you? Nettie, Sadie, would you girls fetch my external versocular? Oh, and Nettie, be a dear and fetch the cal-sextant and the resograph, too."

"Certainly," Nettie gives me an encouraging look. "Sadie?"

I get up and follow Nettie, happy to be useful. She takes me back through a cozy kitchen and off into a side hallway. We reach the closed door of a back room and Nettie flicks on the light as soon as we enter.

It's like being in a different house altogether. Instruments of polished brass crowd the middle of the floor, propped on tripods or sitting askew on wall racks. Some look like telescopes, set with brass gears and gauges and dials in strange places, and they come in all shapes and sizes. Some look like nothing I've ever seen, and I can't imagine what purpose they could serve. There's a few posters and charts on the walls, like in a doctor's office, but these show planets and trajectories and who knows what else. I haven't a clue what any of it means.

Nettie goes right for a big one in the middle of the room, glazed in a shiny black exterior. It's got a funny L-shaped telescopic lens on the back end, and it sits on a wheeled tripod.

"Here we are," Nettie says. "It seems like an awful lotta truck, but it's not too heavy if you use the wheels. Here. You can carry these." She reaches onto a rack and pulls down a copper device that looks like a naval sextant, except it's got two scopes sitting crosswise on top and some funny geometric designs along a moving scale. Then she gets another one with two sliding scales, one sitting on top of another - again, crosswise - topped with a single scope. She hands them both to me.

Nettie smiles. "All this screwy stuff has a purpose, and I can tell you about it later if you're curious."

"Sure, I'd like that!"

When we get back to the living room, they've got a black blind pulled down over the window. It's a strange, opaque kind of black fabric I've never seen before; it absorbs all the light that falls on it. Nettie doesn't pay it any mind as she wheels the big cauldron of a telescope into the middle of the parlor.

"Thank you, girls," Elizabeth says. She takes the strange devices from me and proceeds to calibrate and align the bulky machine. Rotating dials make a series of snaps and clicks, and scopes rise slowly into place.

"Say, you really know your onions," I comment to Nettie.

She smiles. "Aw, just the basics. But the stuff Mary and I know, we learned because of Courtney."

I'm intrigued. "How so?"

Nettie looks at Mary, who's just stepped into the room. "Care to explain, Mary?"

"When Courtney disappeared, I couldn't possibly just let her go. I knew I needed to find her again, no matter how impossible anyone said it was. So I started learning divination."

"And my aunt is a versologist," Nettie supplies. "So I guess all this stuff was already in the family. She happens to have a few old books on arcane science, so I figured if Mary was studying divination, why, I'd study arcana."

"Now then. I believe we're in business." Elizabeth leans over and peers into the L-shaped lens. Nettie produces a notebook and pencil from under the coffee table, and the way she flips it open and starts making notes, it looks like she's done this before.

"Okay," Elizabeth says, slowly. "We're in a trinary conjunction with arcs Servant and Hierophant." She adjusts a small dial on the side, squinting. "And I believe Arc Servant might be our culprit. Nettie?"

Nettie steps up and bends over the lens. "Uhhhh-huh. 92293 looks like an angry bedsore." She raises her head and scribbles something on her notepad. Elizabeth clicks a single small dial on the side as Nettie puts her eye back to the lens. "Ah, gotcha - Verse Servant Languish. Sounds like a nice cozy joint."

"Please forgive me for interrupting," I say, suddenly self-conscious. "I'm just trying to understand. What exactly is it we're doing?"

"That is an excellent question, and I'm glad you asked," Elizabeth tells me, her hand on the side of the big round device. "We're trying to get a fix on Courtney's location. Once we've done that, it'll be easier for Mary to contact her."

Mary stands near me, gives me a self-conscious smile.

"And she's there?" I continue. "That...Servant Languish place?"

Instead of answering me, Elizabeth looks at Nettie. "Nettie?"

"Why, I'd say it's looking more likely." Nettie stands up and rubs her eyes. "Mary, Sadie? Wanna have a look and see what you think?"

Hazel looks at me, a touch of teacherly excitement in her eyes. "Why, yeah - come through, Sadie! Solve the puzzle for us."

I hesitate. "Ah, maybe Mary should go first." My smile steps aside and offers courteous surrender. She sees it, and her big brown eyes give me a warm sparkle. Golly, she's got pretty eyes; no wonder Courtney was goofy for her.

"Nah, Sadie, 'sall right. I betcha never looked through a versocular before."

"Why no, I haven't!" I can't hide my excitement.

She smiles. "Go ahead, then! We're a team."

I give her a grateful smile and approach the instrument.

The lens shows me a glowing, moonlit sky without stars; little worlds follow colored lines across the horizon, and the worlds have clear text right alongside them, just like in some old book. Two lines cross my field of view, almost parallel, crossing at a single point and going on in separate directions. One is dull yellow, with the word HIEROPHANT. The other is dark red, topped with SERVANT. A small ruddy sphere like a dirty pearl floats along the latter, up past the crossing lines at the middle-right of my view. When I strain my eyes and focus on that sphere, it seems to grow before my eyes; but that's not possible, is it? I blink, trying to clear my eyes, and the circle looks just like it did, but it's as if it's bigger inside my mind, somehow. It's an angry shade of red, pulsing more on one side than the other. A tiny + is barely visible inside the reddest patch of the orb.

A bit of text floats in space next to the sphere; it looks like a page from an old textbook.

(SERVANT) LANGUISH.
MV-92293-B206.
SIDEREAL TRANSIT: 39 DEGREES.
THERIC PROPERTIES: NONE.
THERIC PULSE: 0.000043.
DEAD VERSE.
ARCHETYPE CLASS: PATRIARCHAL, DOMINATION.

RECENT INTERVERSAL INCURSIONS: 1.
PRESENT EVENT: **ONGOING, INTERMITTENT.**
RESONANCE PURGE IN PROGRESS – PHASE 7 (TERMINAL).
ESTIMATED COMPLETION: 7 HOURS 19 MINUTES 39 SECONDS.

TRINARY CONJUNCTION IN PROGRESS.
FIELD DECLINATION — ARC TRANQUILITY: 1.5 DEGREES — OPTIMAL.
ARC SERVANT TRANSIT SPEED: 590 HU/HOUR.
ARC EXIT LOCAL INFLUENCE: 19 DAYS, 4 HOURS, 11 MINUTES.

"I'm afraid I don't understand," I confess, still staring into the device. "What does all this stuff mean?"

"Oh, all the numbers and stuff?" Nettie asks. "Don't let that get you mixed up. Focus on the verse itself. And that round piece where your eye is? Rotating that sharpens the image, and the big dial up here zooms in and out."

"Ah, thanks." I focus on the angriest-looking patch of red in the bubble, rotating the eyepiece slightly. Just like Nettie said, the image sharpens. The '+' fades, replaced by 'PURGE EVENT IN PROGRESS', blinking very slowly in dark red letters.

"So how do we know we're looking at Courtney's verse?" I ask. "And not some other Displaced?"

"Well, let's add another piece of the puzzle," Elizabeth says, moving a dial, making several clicks. More text appears next to the verse.

> JUNE 5, 2004.
> 7:14 P.M. EST.

"Holy cow," I breathe. "It's seven in the evening over there. And it's...June?"

"June?!" Hazel exclaims. "Why, she'll be in for a frightful shock, won't she?"

"Time flows differently between verses," Elizabeth points out. "It might be seven o'clock over there now, but in another hour it could be two in the morning. The time differential is important, but we'll have a better handle on it once Mary makes contact."

I search the surface of the verse, rotating the big dial; I seem to be zooming by scenery. Something comes into view - college buildings, seen from a hilltop? They're barely visible; the sun is still up over there but there's a dark shadow over everything. White lights, pinpoints moving in pairs through the haze; car headlights, headed down the street? A lot of other lights, too; red and green lights above the streets, blinking orange lights on the corners. Hazy shadows moving in the dark beneath the streetlights - are those people?

I never imagined such a thing in my wildest dreams.

"Where are you, Courtney?" I whisper. Out of nowhere, the view swings away from what I'm looking at, like when you move fast with a pair of binoculars.

"Yikes, what did I do?" I jerk my head up in a panic. "Oh heavens, did I break it-"

"Did it move on you?" Elizabeth demands. "That's all right! Keep your eye on it - sometimes these devices react to the presence of arcanes."

I do as she asks, still not quite able to grasp that I'm arcane. In a moment, I'm in front of a long, rectangular building. Strange, rounded motorcars are parked in a row in front of it. Everything seems darker, somehow.

"Say, why does everything look so dark, anyhow?" I ask. "Is there another setting I need to adjust?"

A moment of silence. I look up to find everyone glancing at each other.

"No," Elizabeth says, quietly. "Nothing's wrong with the instrument. What you're seeing is a sign that we might be running out of time."

"The zoom will take you inside, through the wall," Nettie supplies, tapping a big round dial in front of me. Hazel and Elizabeth take a few steps aside, sharing a quiet word away from us. The three of us share a nervous look. When they continue to talk, I return to the lens, using the rotating zoom like Nettie showed me.

The view moves through the wall and into a wide living room. It's got tan carpet and sterile white walls, and a girl sits on a couch in the light of a dim lamp. She has a fatally-wounded look in her eyes, and she lays her blonde head on the arm of her sofa, staring at nothing. Even though the room is lit by daylight, everything looks covered in shadow.

"Oh, god," I whisper.

"What?" Mary and Nettie crowd close. "What do you see?"

"I found her."

"Where is she?" Mary pleads. "Please tell me she's all right!"

I give her a bleak look from just above the lens. "That depends on what you mean by 'all right.'"

I understand now. Someone's verse doesn't manifest hands out of nothing and strangle someone, or kill them with a lightning bolt. If it wants to kill you, it kills you however it can, even if it means getting in your head and making you kill yourself.

And judging by the look on Courtney's face, that's exactly what's on her mind.

My heart is pounding. "We must hurry."

S i x t e e n

T h u r s d a y
June 3 2004

5:05 p.m.

Courtney

"If you're smart and mighty lucky, you can still make a clean getaway, even if a Resonance Purge has already got started. Just keep an eye out for any disagreeable fellers that might be layin' for you, 'cause if they got a grudge, that's when they'll come a-callin'.

"Then the boy, he says, 'hey Jack, what if it's the seventh hour? Or the seventh phase, or whatchamacallit?'

"'Well, son,' I tell him, 'Then you're in the valley of the shadow of death, and you don't have too long. Best make your peace and get ready for the end, or get ready to go out fightin' like a rabid wildcat. 'Cause one way or the other, your earthly days are done.'"

-John "Wandering Jack" Pollasky, *Traveling Journal of a Versal Wanderer,* 1908
Book last seen - Versal Arc: November

Breezes like this one are rare in the summer. Shriveled brown leaves clatter around my ankles as I pass, rolling and bouncing down campus walkways. When I got banished back here earlier this afternoon, noise was everywhere. It was like noise was all there was - roaring jets and car horns and the low roar of traffic rumbling down brick streets.

But now there's none of that. Hardly anyone walking the paths, and only the occasional car drifting by. Barely a sound as I pass down the hill where I met Sadie, the trees swaying in a silent breeze. Leaves roll by like cicada shells on the sidewalks. *Clak, clak, clic-clic.* A daffodil sunset over the still summer grass. I pass by the diner cafe that squats at the top of Morton Hill, this ugly dive that started as one of those big food trailers like thirty years ago and has been growing like a fungus around its original walls until it grew an ugly green awning and a permanent sour odor of old cigarette tar. Hippies and hipsters have this militant attachment to it, and they'll fight people for it like some violent recluse that's been saving his scabs and toenail clippings in a jar. There's a TV inside on a nicotine-tanned wall, and on it is a red CNN banner and some bald old fuck with an evil beak, and then some explosions in the desert and some soldiers. Oh, that must have been Cheney, talking about his fucking war. Oil and profit and theocracy. The war on terror, the war on queer people, waged on TV. Praise the lord and pass the fucking ammunition. The brutal charade passes by in silence, and the only thing I hear is the roar of the breeze in my ears as I start down Morton.

I may not have gotten my happy ending, my ticket back to my real home, but that doesn't mean I have to wait for my enemies to close in and have their way with me. I'm a Braddock student, and Braddock students always have one last way out.

The breeze lifts, hissing away overhead. I feel a cold, hard grayness settle in my features and in my heart - and just like that, I've decided.

I'll journey to the Blackstead Forest tonight - alone - and take my place among the missing of Autumn Grove. I used to get a chill down my spine when I read about everyone who vanished in the woods, but it always snagged my curiosity and kept me reading in fear and fascination. Maybe, in a way, I always knew it would end like this.

My parents are trying to torpedo my college career, and I'm out of ways to fight them. A psychopath with a crusade has me in his crosshairs and wants me dead. One way or another, my life is over. If the Blackstead takes me, then at least I got to make a choice.

YOURDEADBRITNEY1238: read the nam bittch

That's what pops up on AIM after my computer gets booted up.

My dead Britney? Seriously, *Britney?!* Of all the stupid fucking things to call me. I hung out backstage with Spitalfield last summer at Warped Tour. When I was sitting on a secluded stairway and I thought I was gonna pass out from heat stroke, Justin from Anti-Flag was the one who came over to make sure I was okay - I got to talk to him, too. This assclown must be calling me Britney because I don't listen to that god-awful screamo shit. Sorry, I can't stand it - if I wanted to listen to someone howling and shredding their vocal chords in a medieval dungeon, I'd play *Diablo.* Ugh, this window licker seriously gets on my nerves. I block him, and he just makes a new screen name. Does he honestly have nothing better to do than sit around and harass me? I thought Krystal was supposed to be riding his dick all day long - that can't be true if he's up *my* ass constantly. I sigh and block him - again.

My black flip phone is blinking with a voicemail, so I reach over and grab it.

The automated voice first. "You have...ONE...new message." Then it switches to a girl's voice, attractive and sultry. "Courtney. Hey, it's Krystal. I just...wanted to see what you were up to. I'm gonna be down your way tonight, so I'd still like to stop by and find my top."

Freakin dumbass. I told you that your skanky ass top isn't here.

"I've looked all over." A bored sigh. She sounds languid - probably oxycontin. "I've torn the place apart like five times and it's not here, so the only place it can possibly be is with you. And I'm going to a party this weekend, and I'd really like to have it. So yeah, we'll probably come by, maybe around seven. Cool? Alright, well...see you then!" A little pause. "Bye."

I thumb the red button and frisbee the phone back onto the table. My eyes dart to the bottom right corner of my computer screen - 5:39 p.m. That means I've got a little more than an hour until she *says* she'll be here, but honestly there's no telling. Skanky pill-poppers with homicidal drug dealer boyfriends - you have absolutely no idea when they're gonna show up. It could be in the next seven seconds or it could be eleven tonight when they roll in, chugging cocktails of 4-Loko and NyQuil. And maybe *they* don't know when they'll show up either, but they like the idea of keeping you on edge, making you wait around, like cops outside the interrogation room. It's a power play, a psychological tactic to keep you off balance.

Well, I'm not down for it. I showed Krystal screenshots of the messages her boyfriend sent me and she called me a liar. "Derek wouldn't do that. Stop being a drama queen and grow up." And she's gonna show up in his Slipknot-mobile tonight and just expect me to let her and Derek and ten of their lowlife friends into my apartment? Not likely.

I could stay here and woman the gates. I've still got my lightweight aluminum bat that I spray-painted red and keep around for emergencies. I could simply refuse to let them in, and tell them if they don't leave I'll call the cops and talk about the god-knows-how-many kilos of coke they're carrying around. But that might piss the psycho off, and I doubt my door would hold up if he and his bulky friends decided to pile on it, which they'll do anyway if they're convinced I've got Krystal's hooker shirt. I could leave the apartment and just not be here - but again, they might decide to break in and rob me blind. They might even set up booby traps or something for me - I wouldn't put anything past these nutcases. And even if I left, where would I go? Back to Stanhope? There's nothing there but horrible things I want to forget, and that's where Derek and Krystal are coming from in the first place - a whole town full of people like them. That could be even more dangerous than staying here. Not campus, either; there's nothing down there but sadness now, and I'd be all alone with it in the dark.

The only place that leaves is the Blackstead. I guess I hadn't thought out how I wanted to do this yet, but if I'm going to a haunted forest and into a missing persons file, I guess it doesn't really matter how I do it. Death is death.

Death is the only option I have; the only *choice* I have is how I want it. There's being stabbed to death, hanging myself back in Stanhope once my parents take everything from me, or however people die when they disappear in the woods. I lean my head back over the couch and swallow a sad tingle in my throat. I didn't mean to remember but the images are there. Roadsters, round headlamps, bobbed haircuts. Sadie's sparkling slender eyes. That photo of Mary, doe-eyed and vulnerable. That place itself - or that time, whichever it was - was so sweet to me. It was like the fabric of reality itself was loving, but only for us. Like I was one of them. Like I'd always belonged.

My eyes ache, and I swallow another noisy lump in my throat. When I was with Sadie, a choice between three deaths would have been completely ridiculous. When she hugged me close, when we shared our confidences, I was safer than I'd ever been. It was the essence of belonging. I fit into place just like a puzzle piece, and I was important to someone for the first time in my life.

A hazy mist floats in my eyes. The setting orange sun looks foggy, the color of those frozen orange sherbet things you have to push out of a white round toilet roll. I've never felt so alone in my life. I miss Sadie so much already. Everything was right with her, everything made sense. Here in this cold, silent apartment, the years fall away and I remember Mary and Nettie, too, how safe and warm I felt with them so long ago. I belonged. I was a vital part of something that wasn't the same without me. I was safe, and I was loved.

I love each of them - *all* of them - so much. But they're so far away now, and I have no idea how I was able to be with them in the first place. If I *was* really in the past, then that means they're probably all dead now.

I wipe the milky tears out of my eyes; the sun is setting just outside my apartment complex, across the highway, beyond the trees. Soon I'll be dead, too.

A little noise, like ears ringing, like the squeal of brakes a mile away. Then it's gone, and it was nothing but a trick of my ears in the dead silence. The sun is behind the neighboring building now, and the sky is the color of rose quartz shot through with daggers of violet. Those daggers will bleed and darken and cover the world in night. The last night of my life.

Courtney!

Hearing my name causes a twitch reflex; pupils flare, body tenses. It was a girl's voice - it sounded like Sadie.

Well, of *course* I'm hearing echoes of Sadie's voice. It's probably my auditory nerves doing...I don't know. Sorting information, or whatever it is your brain does when you're alone in a quiet room. This is the first time I've gotten to sit down today, so now that I'm relaxed - if you want to call it that - it's able to-

Courtney, I know you can hear me, you silly goose. I'm looking right at you.

Okay, what the hell? My eyes instinctively dart to the window.

Hi! Yep, that's where I'm at, but you're not gonna be able to see me. And you're not losing your marbles. It's really me.

"Sadie?!"

Hello, dearest! Whew, thank goodness this thing works!

"Wh-how...?" I think I'm about to cry again. "I thought..."

Quiet for a second. I get the impression that she's talking to someone, even though I don't hear it.

"Did you think your connection was severed?" she asks.

"I...yeah!" My eyes are aching. I'm legit ten seconds away from bawling.

"Fortunately, it wasn't. Those idiots weren't that thorough. Listen, we haven't much time, but we're working on a way to get you home. Hopefully tonight."

This. This can't be happening. Can this be happening?

Home. She called it *home.*

"Are you...? For real? Wait, who's 'we?'"

I feel her smiling. *"Why, I made some new friends! And I'd like to introduce you."*

A vague image pops into my head - an impression of an attractive chick in her mid-twenties. She's poised, confident, but she has a fun smile. It's not all that clear and the picture is just a few dark colors, like when you're having a dream. *"Hello, Courtney. It's such a relief to hear your voice! My name is Hazel Morrison, and I'm here to bring you home."*

A tear falls from my eye. "Wow, it's...yeah. Hi, Hazel!"

"I won't hog the oracle. There's someone else who's dying to say hello."

She steps away, and there's a sense of nervous hesitation in the air. Or inside me. Wherever this is happening.

An impression of a girl my age approaching. Soft features, a pretty round face, bobbed hair. She's got a sweet aura, and something about her is deeply familiar...

"Courtney?"

The cute voice knocks the wind out of my chest, and I'm not even sure who it is I'm talking to.

"Do you remember me?"

Oh, god. Oh holy fucking shit-

"Mary?!"

She smiles. *"Oh, thank goodness. I was worried you'd forgotten all about me!"*

My soul surges out, reaching for her, and my chest aches with the attempt. It's all under the surface, on some instinctual level; it happens before I can think about it.

"I...*god*, no. Are you kidding? Never, not for a single day."

She beams at me - this warm, beautiful smile that fills me up inside. Oh, god. I forgot she could do that.

"Me either, honey," she says quietly. And there's a nice, rosy silence between us before she continues. *"Nettie's here, too."*

A tall girl appears in the periphery of my mind, and she smiles.

"Courtney?"

"Nettie!!"

"Say, you really got yourself in a fix this time, didn't you?"

She gets a wet, soppy laugh out of me.

"Yeah. It has been one epic freaking disaster of a day."

"Well, it's about to get better. We think we know how to fix this whole rotten mess."

"But wait. Those assholes that did this to me. Won't they just try again?"

Hazel appears again. *"Jeremiah Hodges, the one shaped like a soft-boiled egg, is in custody. He's on his way to Cincinnati, where he'll stand trial for what he did to you."*

A surge of hope in my chest. They can do that? I didn't imagine anyone in their right minds would have ever believed me if I'd told them what happened.

"Hazel arrested him," Sadie says. *"Oh, Courtney, how I wish you'd been there! It sure was something to see, and how!"*

"I'm sorry I wasn't there when you needed me, Courtney," Hazel says. *"Truly, I am."*

I smile. "Oh, that's okay. I mean, I'm just glad there's justice for this kinda stuff, you know? I'm glad I'm not all alone."

"You are most certainly not, darling," Hazel assures me. *"These girls would tear their hearts out for you."*

"The feeling is mutual," I say emphatically. "I love all of you. So much. Please know that."

A warm silence. Everybody is glowing, and nobody knows what to say. What's weird is that I'm an empath - I've always been able to feel emotions around me. But however they're communicating with me, it's amplifying that - Sadie and Mary, especially. From

Sadie, I feel excitement, anxiousness; something even sweeter, I can't put my finger on it. And Mary - warmth, a rosy pink sensation. Hope. Shyness, short of breath. Stiff with nervous terror. A million unsaid things. Desire.

"I think they get the message, lady killer." Hazel smirks, and there's a silent roar of a whole bunch of voices raised in protest. I feel their voices on my skin, even if I don't hear them with my ears. *"And you can tell them yourself - in person - once you're safe back here, where you belong. But right now, you're in a lot of danger."*

"I am?" Well, I mean yeah, I know someone wants to hurt me, but she's making it sound pretty ominous.

"Yes. Your universe is trying to kill you, and I'm afraid we haven't much time. So I'm going to give you some very clear instructions. I can tell you're a smart kid, so you're going to be just fine."

"Alright, what do I do?"

"Okay," Hazel begins. *"First, pack your things. Pack light, and make it quick. Can you do that?"*

"Yeah." This isn't my first rodeo. When you have an abusive, violent father, you learn how to pack fast and keep a cool head. "Definitely."

"Good girl. Second, I want you out of that apartment as soon as possible. Get in your motor car and head east, for the Blackstead Forest."

A chill goes down my spine. "Okay?"

She's quiet a moment; she's getting directions from someone. *"Head for the main visitor parking lot, you can't miss it. Get out of your machine and make your way up the main trail till you reach the top of the hill. At the top of the hill, there's a slight dip in the trail for about thirty yards. When you reach the first bottom of that dip, I want you to turn directly to your right. Break off the trail and head straight into the woods."*

I get goosebumps on my arms just thinking about it, but I put on a brave face.

"If you're confused about where, look for a marking on a tree - something like the letter M with a line through it. If you see that, or you see the letter C with an X through it, you're headed the right way. If you find those markers, you'll be on the old Grevett's Mill Road. Even if it's covered up in your time, it's still there. You'll know it when you see it, and it'll take you straight through where you need to go."

I'm skeptical about there being markers on trees after all this time; who would maintain them? But I put my faith in her.

"So, please forgive me for interrupting. But...couldn't I just phase over? Like I did earlier?"

"Not this time," she says. *"We're bringing you through something called a versal aperture. I'll give you the score later, but in a nutshell - we're making sure it's a one-way trip this time. You'll never phase again, and nobody can banish you. You'll be here for good."*

A deep thrill goes through me, mingled with nervous apprehension.

"For good," I confirm. "So...just so we're clear. You mean I'll be stuck in your time for the rest of my life?"

"Yes," she says. "You will be stranded here forever, with no way back to 2004. You will have to start a new life in September of 1921. So it goes without saying that you must be absolutely certain that this is what you want. Because once you're here, that's it - there's no way back."

I take a deep breath. No pressure, right?

"I don't really have a choice, do I?"

"You always have a choice," Hazel says. "But frankly, I suppose you haven't much of one. You can live here or die over there."

Another sigh.

"Alright. Once I'm on the old road, what then?"

"Get a move on. You'll be looking for a clearing at the top of a hill with a couple of big funny-looking rocks. You'll know them when you see them. Go toward the rocks and keep a clear picture in your mind of what it looks like here, in our time. The aperture should take care of the rest." She pauses, and her tone turns serious. *"Courtney, it is imperative that you do not proceed beyond that clearing. You mustn't wander any further into the woods. Do you understand?"*

"Yeah," I say, a little subdued, a little freaked out. "I won't. I promise."

"Good. We mustn't tempt fate. That forest is ancient, powerful, and evil. Stay on the trail, don't proceed past the grove. I'll be waiting for you right on the other side. You're a brave girl. Do this one thing alone, and you'll never be alone again. All right?"

"Alright."

"Okay. Your friends would like a word with you before you leave." Another pause. *"Good luck, Courtney. And godspeed. I'll see you soon."*

"Thank you, Hazel."

She's gone, and Mary returns.

"I'm really glad I'm able to see you again, but I'm awful sorry it's gotta be like this."

"No worries," I smile at her. "This is worth it."

Silence. Something heavy and painful under the surface. She's dying to say so much more.

"Courtney, I..." She freezes, gets control of herself. *"Just, be careful? Stay safe out there. And I'll...see you soon."*

She's rich and warm and heavy in my heart, her warmth filling me all the way to my fingertips. I forgot what kind of power she had over me. "I will. I promise."

"Okay." She lingers another moment, her presence heavy, before she fades and Sadie appears.

"Courtney, listen. Like Mary said, be careful. Watch yourself out there. Find your way to that aperture and come home. I'll be there."

I wipe a tear away, sniffle. "I don't know what to say. I owe you my life, Sadie. All of you."

"Aw, phooey. You don't owe me squat. Just bring me a fun souvenir."

"I will totally hook you up."

"Ducky. What's that you said yesterday? You got this."

"Yeah. I got this. Thanks, Sadie."

"I'll be right there, waiting for you. Come back to me."

Then she's gone, and I'm all alone again just like before, with my ears ringing in the silence.

I sit there a moment, struck dumb by everything that just happened. My friends found me, somehow. And Mary - after all this time, what was she doing there?

But I've got a stupid smile on my face that won't go away. It's time to get up, get packed...

Hazel's words echo in my ears. *Make absolutely certain this is what you want. There's no way back.*

Is this really what I want? Am I ready to live in the 1920s? Forever? Can I do it?

I get up, go to the window, and peer out the blinds at my parking lot. As I watch, the purple streaks in the sky grow and deepen, sucking the orange out of the atmosphere. Nectarine hues fade to blue, then freeze into violet. Is it really getting dark that fast? I glance at the clock on my DVD player. 7:05. 7:06. 7:07.

An icy shaft of fear through my chest - the digital clock moves right before my eyes. And as it moves, evening falls away into night. I take a step back, watching to make sure that I'm actually *seeing* this and not lapsing into weird catatonic trances that just make it *seem* like time is flying.

7:09...7:10 p.m.

Oh, hell no. Hazel wasn't kidding. Time to get my backpack and get the hell out of here.

I dump it on my bedroom floor, watch a cascade of papers fall out, class handouts long forgotten and folded into narrow, weathered strips by weeks in my backpack. Grab my notebook, put that in there. iPod Nano charging cord. Red Game Boy SP, folded up; the games are in the pack, just grab the charger. A few random things from a drawer. Mary's ribbon, sitting on my bedside table. Changes of clothes, folded and smelling like laundry. Extra socks and underwear. My bottles of Chanel *Chance Eau Tendre* and Abercrombie *8*, a few pieces of jewelry I like, my good lotion. Mudd combat boots - they're super comfy. Extra pair of Chucks, my comfy white Adidas sneakers with the pink stripes. Basic stuff from the bathroom. My old mini-disc player from freshman year and all my discs - Sadie needs music. A couple of books Nettie might like. That spare tarot deck for Mary - I bet she'll like that.

Grab my brown canvas messenger bag, dump it, pack the clothes away. 7:19 p.m. *Zip, snap, snap.* Backpack on, shoulder the bag.

I stop and take one last look at my bedroom, soft and quiet under lengthening shadows, then turn and make my way back into the living room. I tear a sheet of used scrap paper, and I write a simple note in black ink.

It's time for me to go. I'll never go back to Stanhope, and I'll never surrender. I've never belonged here. I've been exiled from my true home. I'm going back, or I'll die trying.

I'm on my way into the Blackstead Forest. Tell Tiffany I'm sorry.
Goodbye.
-Courtney

My apartment is cool and silent; it smells a little bit sweet, like it always does. I take one last look at this wide, lonely living room where I spent so much time alone, soak it into memory. This is how I'll remember it - quiet, chilly, with the last evening light casting shadows through my blinds onto the carpet. Fading into dark.

I take one last deep breath, trying to relax, and reach for my car keys.

People make a big deal about saying goodbye, but when you're wrapped up in the flow of events, pulled along by a current, these things happen by themselves. You're a passive observer, watching yourself close your door, lock it, everything quick and efficient. It almost feels like someone else's footsteps taking you into the parking lot, like you're just along for the ride.

And even though I'm freaking completely out, my brain all tense and smooshed up, I have just enough cognition to realize one thing - I didn't think this out beyond the parking lot. It's just now sinking in that I'm completely alone. It was easy to overlook that when I had my friends talking to me - however that happened - but I have to drive all the way out to those hellish woods, by myself. Then I have to go in and stumble around in the dark, by myself, trying to find a magical doorway to get back to 1921. And it's only when I start thinking about how crazy it is, how all this could have been a hallucination, how there might not actually *be* anything at the end of this trail, that it becomes truly terrifying. Because, in a weird sort of way, cursed forests and evil wraiths aren't half as terrifying as the thought that all the things that have given you hope may not be real at all.

Shit, there it goes again - this horrid universe, trying to get in my head.

Fact check: it's a whole lot more likely that all this *has* been real. I've seen solid evidence - I've still got the bruises on my arm, bruises I got in 1921 before three skeezy douchebags banished me with some 10th level wizard spell. And now I'm driving out to the Blackstead by myself, then I'm going into those woods - in the dark - by myself.

It's the only chance I have. Time is running out.

Everything is ending.

PART TWO

SEPTEMBER 1921

One

Wednesday
September 7, 1921

7:04 a.m.

Courtney

"Oh, how I wish I could tell you half the dangers and hardships she's suffered. But the story hasn't a sane word in it. If I breathed a word of it, even to tell you where she has been these many years, I fear you'd think me mad and despise me. I value your friendship and long years of affection far too much to see how you'd react if I told you the truth. But my Mary knows. The experience has been burned into her heart."
-Marian Carlyle, letter to Jennie Ashford, 1915

"The experience of versal displacement would define and prepare the Keepers of the Veil - and thus, define countless lives in the 1920s - in ways a Conclave education never could have."
- Edith Winthrop, *Flapper Sorcery: American Arcanology in the 1920s*

The morning sunshine is the color of peaches, flickering through the passing trees as we drive uptown. It blinks on and off my shoulders, leaving little patches of warmth on my skin as we make our way along.

The house we're headed for sits in the shade on Court Street, across from the campus green. It's tall and elegant, the color of beach sand, and it's so Victorian with its rounded turret on one side and sharp gables on the upstairs windows. It's my first time seeing this house - it's not there in 2004.

Three people on the porch, waiting. One is an older lady I've never met, sitting on a porch swing. The other two I'd know anywhere, no matter how long it had been.

Mary and Nettie.

"Oh, my god."

Sadie looks over, smiles uneasily.

"There's your welcoming committee, Courtney," Hazel says over the clatter of the engine.

"Don't leave me," I beg Sadie.

She smirks. "Not a chance." Her hand slips across mine, holds it. She's so soft and gentle when she does it that on a normal day I might get nervous and short of breath. But I'm covered in a second skin of blood and filth, and I look like I just walked off a medieval battlefield, so I'm guessing she just feels sorry for me like most chicks probably would. I mean, *I* can't imagine finding me attractive right now.

And Mary. Just the thought of her would twist my stomach into balloon animals until I reached high school. I didn't know if I'd ever see her again. Now, here she is out of nowhere, waiting for me. This thing on my arm? I don't know if I told you, but it hurts like freaking *crazy*. I don't need my stomach balling itself into some pressure orb like the core of one of those stars from astronomy class. Because Mary was a little cutie even when we were kids, so I can't even imagine how ridiculously hot she's gonna be now. Even Nettie, all tall and skinny, is probably gonna be hella cute. And I'm gonna have these three hot girls that had time to make themselves look really nice, and they're gonna be swarming around me, never more than like five feet away. And I'm a freaking ruin, some 80s horror movie victim that survived a run-in with, I dunno, whatever scary killers use knives or axes or razors on their fingers.

We're approaching Professor Talbott's house like skidding off a cliff in slow motion. Sadie and Hazel are gonna dump me like some carcass from the battlefield and Mary's gonna *freak*.

Nah, who am I kidding? She probably didn't think about me all that much over the years and here I come, a fun little memory covered in blood. She'll be sweet and kinda distant, and she'll pity me because I survived Camp Psycho Axe Murder 3, but my ugliness right now is gonna turn me into a pity case or a joke.

Yeah, maybe it's stupid to be this vain about how you look when you've been sliced open and your arm is infected and it's your first day in 1921, but that's how it is.

Sitting here in this car, chugging along down a much earlier version of Court Street, the memories start to come back. I walked out of the woods near my cousin's house in 1997 and into Mary's yard. Her mom welcomed me like I'd always been one of the girls, and she put me in one of Mary's dresses and took us all to an autumn fair. We were sitting on a blanket in a park in New Stafford, three kids that didn't know they were almost teenagers. Whispering in each other's ears, doing lots of giggling. Nettie asking me out on Mary's behalf. Nervously holding hands for the first time. Sneaking off to a grove of trees at the edge of the park. Our first kiss as the twilight faded into a bright carnival night. The sweetest night of my life.

So many firsts that day, but I think the biggest one probably wasn't even the pre-teen love between me and Mary. The thing I really had to come to grips with that day was that I was in 1915.

Then, as quickly as I'd gotten every beautiful thing I'd ever wanted, it was gone. But once I saw Kenny's savage face, I knew I had to give everything up to keep Mary safe. I didn't know how he'd followed me, but I knew that there was no way we'd ever be safe or happy. So I charged at him, attacked him, threw him back across the veil. And I knew he'd be back. So I had to say goodbye - the hardest thing I've ever done - and leave Mary crying in that old abandoned house while I followed him back.

He didn't seem to remember what had happened - not consciously, anyway. But I got the worst beating of my life that night, my head split open on the bannister, my face black and blue and puffy.

I was trapped in 1997 again, and this time it was for good - but so was Kenny - and that meant Mary was safe.

I had a *monster* crush on her the following summer - it was one of those things where she was the only thing I saw when my eyes were closed. Every time I blinked my eyes, she was there. She was there when I went to the grocery store, she was there when my parents cooked out and had their friends over. When I spent the night with my cousin Kelsey and her friends, she was practically in the room. When I went to bed at night, when I woke up in the morning, *right there*. Her gorgeous, sweet face, always in my dreams, always in the warm fantasies that kept me laying in bed for hours. Maybe in the future I'd see her again, and some magical storybook thing would happen with us. Always a maybe, always over the next horizon.

I guess puberty makes you crazy. Eventually, it went away. In hindsight, I was glad - the torture was just too much. And besides, I couldn't bear to be so deeply in love with her when she probably hated my guts for leaving her. She probably moved on.

So yeah, I'm keeping Sadie close today. She's my safety blanket. I'm a nervous wreck.

"Aw, it can't be *that* bad, can it?" Hazel asks. We're about a half a block away.

"I think there's a lot of history," Sadie tells her.

A look of revelation dawns on Hazel's face. "Aaaah, now I begin to see. Well, it's none of my beeswax, but if you're curious, I think that girl's mighty tore up about something that happened between the two of you."

"She is?" I clench my fists with dread and guilt.

"Sure seemed that way to me," Hazel replies, then shrugs. "But I'm not gonna poke my nose in. If she's got something to say, I'll let her say it."

"You don't need to feel that way," I tell her. "We're buds, right? Thanks for sharing, by the way."

A warm glow of appreciation fills Hazel's cheeks. "Anything I can do to help."

Sadie gives me a *here we go* look. "You ready?"

I sigh. "No."

"I won't leave your side." Sadie's eyes are locked on mine. "They'll have to pry me off with a tire iron."

I clutch her arm softly with both hands, give her a smile with all my gratitude in it.

I was right the first time. Mary freaks out.

She and Nettie are coming up the sidewalk when Hazel pulls along the curb. Mary sees me and her hands fly up over her face. All you can see is huge brown eyes above her fingertips.

I probably look like a picture from Rotten.com or The Many Faces of Death or something. I mean yeah, I'm covered in blood - and in quite a bit of pain - but it could be a lot worse, right? It's just a nasty cut. It's not like I'm, ya know, *dying*.

"Oh my god!" They're waiting when the car pulls up. "*Courtney!!*"

The car rattles as Hazel shifts the parking brake. The girls pull open the door before she can shut the motor off.

"It's not as bad as it looks!" Sadie assures them, getting out behind Hazel and helping me. "She's jake. We just need to get that wound cleaned up and dressed, and let the poor thing take a bath. She'll be right as rain, won't you, Courtney?"

"Oh yeah, totally."

If you're anything like me, you have a natural reflex in situations like these. I actually have to stop myself from answering with inappropriate jokes about zombies, or jokes about movies, or jokes about video games. I'm feeling this desperate need to release hours of tension with gallows humor, but my brain keeps rejecting all my possibilities and I'm discovering that all my humor is tied up with references nobody here is gonna understand.

Understandable joke: 1.

Oh, there we go, I got a hit.

Mary and Nettie make their way around the car, dressed all pretty in blouses and knee-length skirts and Oxfords. Oh, they're so much more gorgeous than I could have imagined. The need to deflect their intimidating beauty with humor intensifies.

"What on Earth happened!?" Mary demands.

I give her a one-sided smirk, raise my eyebrows. "You think *this* is bad? You should see what I did to the army of evil assassins they sent to kill me."

Silence. The street is still.

Then a long snort from Sadie, and a wild cackle. She's shaking hard with laughter, the back of her hand on her mouth. Nettie smiles very slowly as the joke sinks in. Mary's mouth falls open a little.

"*Courtney!*" She shouts. "How could you possibly make some frightful joke? You're *hurt!*"

"Why, you haven't changed at all, you silly goose! Not even a little bit!" Nettie's grinning now. "Oh, how I've missed you." She comes up and kisses me and hugs me as close as she can without hurting my wound.

I shine love and affection on her. "I've missed you too, sweetie, you have no idea."

"Come on," Nettie offers. "Let's get you inside and have a look at that."

Mary stares helplessly, mouth a little ajar. There's so much she wants to say, but she's got no idea what to say or how to say it.

Behind me, Hazel: "Don't worry, Mary. If she can crack a joke, she's alright."

Nettie and Hazel each take one of my bags from the car. The older woman from the porch comes down to meet me when I step onto the sidewalk. Her salt-and-pepper hair is pulled back in a rather severe bun, and she wears an almost Victorian-style brown calico dress that drops to her ankles. She offers me a warm smile full of kindness and puts her palms on my cheeks. She has an oddly youthful face.

"We meet at last. Welcome home, Courtney."

I give her the most grateful smile I'm able to muster while my brain is caught, hiccuping, on who she could be. Have I seen her before? Am I forgetting something important?

"This is my Aunt Lizzy." Nettie is behind me, lifting the strap of my backpack onto one shoulder. "Professor Elizabeth Talbott."

"If you insist, though I am retired," the older lady supplies. "You're welcome to call me Aunt Lizzy - you girls practically grew up together, and you've been in the picture quite a while - though Elizabeth is fine, if you prefer."

"Oh, um. Elizabeth." I smile. "Thank you so much."

She pats my cheek with one hand, a little wrinkled but still very soft. She lowers her voice, a bit conspiratorially. "Now, if you're anything like me, you probably want to get yourself washed off a bit before all the fussing starts. Am I right?"

"Yes, *please!*"

She smiles a sort of *I knew it* smile. "Your room is ready for you upstairs, first door on the left. The washroom is just past that."

"My...room?" Wow. I lost track of myself in all the chaos. I get this sensation like I'm flying off a cliff when I realize that I never once thought about where I was gonna stay.

"Ah, I suppose nobody told you. You'll be staying with me for the time being."

These situations are awkward enough to navigate when you're fully rested and you still have most of your blood. Sadie darts a carefully neutral glance between me and Elizabeth. There's a hint of eager disappointment in her eyes that makes me wonder if she'd planned for me to stay with her.

I try to form a sentence, tell her I don't have money or anything. "I-I...but I don't...I can't-"

"Come along, child." Elizabeth turns toward the house. "You're not going to be able to articulate much of anything until you've had some rest. Being thrown through a versal aperture would rob just about anybody of their wits."

Sadie helps me up the porch steps and through the front door. Elizabeth's house is cool and breezy inside, and it smells sweet and cozy, like fresh laundry and wood. The floor is paneled in slats of rich hardwood, and a few strange devices sit in the parlor. They kinda look like telescopes, but with dials and gears and strange symbols. They look really steampunk; I wonder what they're for.

"It's okay, Sadie," I tell her as I step onto the stairs. "I can handle the stairs. It's just a stupid cut. I'm not about to make you carry me all the way up."

"You're *sure?*" She looks skeptical. "I can tell you're lightheaded. I really don't mind - you're not the least bit heavy. *And* I'm already mad at myself without you falling down the stairs and breaking something."

She's right. I put my left hand against the wall and the world spins like a dryer.

"That's what I thought." Sadie smiles. She pulls herself in close - really close. She wraps her arm firmly around my waist and very quietly tells me: "I'm not about to let anything else happen to you."

My stomach goes topsy-turvy.

I feel Mary staring hard in our direction. Tension in the air, heavy silence between her and Nettie. I dare not look back. *Oh, god. What did I come bleeding into?*

"Oh, Sadie? Just a minute." Hazel sets my bag down and comes up the stairs behind us. She hands Sadie a small brassy telescope about the width of a dime, then nods at my wound. "Keep an eye on that for me, would you, darling?"

"Sure thing," she says a little uncertainly. She helps me get upstairs and into the bathroom so I can wash myself off in the sink. I feel a hundred percent better seeing my pale skin again, watching the dark blood and filth spiral down the drain, but Sadie stares at my cut with a vaguely worried expression the whole time.

"Now, then." She takes a towel and gently helps to dry me off. "Let's get you lying down so we can get that wound dressed."

My curiosity is getting the best of me. "Hey, so...what's that little scope thingy for? The thing Hazel gave you."

"Huh? Oh. I think it can see infection, or something. She just wants to make sure your cut heals right."

See infection? Like a portable microscope? Wow. "I hope it works - that would be really awesome. Because it kinda *feels* infected, actually."

She stops. "It does?"

"Yeah," I admit, wondering why Sadie sounds freaked out. "But I'm sure it'll be fine once I disinfect it and everything."

"Y-yeah, sure. Of course it will." She starts helping me back toward the sunlit bedroom that Elizabeth set aside for me. Not to worry, right? I've been hurt before, and I know how to apply disinfectant and keep a wound dry. I may not be a doctor, but I have eighty years more medical knowledge than anyone here. Plus, I'm caught up on all my boosters - tetanus, hepatitis B. I'm sure I'm more than a match for any infection.

So I really don't get why she's staring at my wound like it's an open casket.

Two

"Those scattered few who survive the Blackstead sometimes wonder if they ever left the forest at all; even if the survivor physically escapes its clutches, she will remain haunted by her experiences in the forest for as long as she lives."
-Sorceress Hazel Morrison,
The Blackstead Forest, Official Conclave Report
March, 1922

Five years. I've spent five years looking for Courtney. It's why I learned divination, and why Nettie followed me and started learning arcana. I've spent five years studying, scrying. Catching murky glimpses. Fragments of words. Split-second snapshots, too fleeting to make sense. I pushed myself hard, became really good. Then I became *powerful*. I could turn my eye anywhere, see anything, watch people and hear conversations as if I was there with them. Clear, sharp, vivid. But Courtney was always too far away. I could *almost* see her. *Almost* talk to her. I *almost* knew things about her life. Almost.

Five years of morning daydreams, late night anguish. Five years of wondering if I'd ever see her again. Five years of imagining our reunion.

Then one day, right as I'm about to start college, she falls out of the sky and into my lap like a carton of busted eggs.

Nettie and I get to Autumn Grove, only to find out that I just missed Courtney by a few hours. Five years of searching, waiting, dreaming, studying, and I'm just a couple of hours short. It's as if I'm falling to the floor, and before I can even shatter, I'm caught. Miss

Morrison and Sadie Van Tassel come calling late in the evening with all kinds of wild stories. Not only is Courtney still nearby, but they think they can fetch her home with our help. I'm over the moon!

Sadie is our age, a college freshman just like us. We might even end up being pals. But it seems she knows Courtney - and what's more, they got to be really good friends. The poor thing is all alone here so I'm trying my darndest not to be sore at her, even if she acts as if she's got some kind of claim on Courtney. But the more I watch her, the more I come to see that she's not like those girls who want to make everything a competition. She's always looking at me, always so modest when Courtney gets mentioned, and always so timid and sad once she finds out how long Nettie and I have known her. Those self-sacrificing manners, that smile of hers, all that pep - Sadie reminds me so much of Courtney. I see the same loneliness on both of them. Sadie cares an awful lot about her, too. She was mighty hurt when Courtney got ripped away from her - a lot worse than she lets on - and I'm an empath, so I'd know! She's not pushing it in our faces, bragging about what a gay time they had or anything like that. She just wants Courtney back, same as me, so I can't bring myself to hate her. But I'm a little jealous of her, and I hate myself for it.

The worst part is that Sadie *does* have some claim on Courtney. They became best pals, both of them alone, both of them damaged - two peas in a pod. With Courtney all alone here for the first time, Sadie was all she had, too. They confided in each other, trusted each other. I imagine they were even more shocked than Nettie and me when they found out we would be here.

But the rub was that Courtney was close, and she might be coming home in the morning! I was so excited; how could I possibly sleep? So Nettie and I went to bed, and I lay there all night staring at the ceiling, listening to the clock in my bedroom as it ticked away the slow hours.

Then, about three-thirty in the morning, something happens.

I must have finally drifted off, because I'm lying there with that queer floating sensation you get when you're just barely asleep. That's when it hits me, a sizzling pain right up my arm and shoulder, like spilling hot oil out of a red-hot skillet on my bare skin, a white-hot knife slicing into muscle. I come awake instantly, sucking in a breath and whimpering pathetically into my pillow. *Criminy, that hurt!* Why, I can't remember the last time *anything* hurt that much! I'm whining and moaning and on the edge of tears, but I'm trying to hold it in because I don't want to wake Nettie.

Too late - my door opens, very silently, a few minutes later. There she is, like clockwork, peeking her frazzled head into my room.

"What happened, Mary?" Nettie whispers. "Are you all right?"

I sit up, clutching my right arm. "It's the darndest thing. One minute I was asleep, and the next it felt as if I'd rolled over onto a hot grill."

She comes in, goes around me, and sits down next to my pillows. "Let's have a look."

My soft bedside lamp comes on with a little click, and Nettie turns to look at my shoulder.

"Sorry to be a baby," I tell her. "I probably just pulled a muscle."

She frowns. "Doesn't look like any pulled muscle I've ever seen." She gets a hand mirror and holds it up so I can see. Sure enough, there's a little red mark running up the top of my arm to my shoulder, no more than a few inches long. It's not the sort of thing you'd notice unless you looked closely, but I see it clearly enough. "What on Earth could that be? You haven't any scars or birthmarks on your arms."

"I haven't a clue," I confess. "If I'd hurt my arm recently, I'd have known it."

"Does it still hurt?"

"Like the devil."

"Well, you want me to get you anything?" she offers. "Glass of water? A sip out of Aunt Lizzy's laudanum bottle?" she grins.

"Nah, I'm jake. I'm sorry I woke you up."

She rubs the wound-that-isn't-a-wound with her soft hand, then kisses it. "Come get me if it gets worse, okay?"

"Sure thing. Thanks, Nettie."

She pats my knee and leaves the room. I pull the shoulder of my nightgown back and give it another look in the lamplight. Just a red line, razor straight, like an ink pen. It's a sharp ache, and then scorching hot, back and forth by turns, and sometimes it gets deep, bone-throbbing cold before going back to sharp again. When I focus on the wound, on the pain, I'm overcome with the most eerie feeling all over. Something is all wrong.

Whenever I close my eyes, all I see is Courtney's face. It's not surprising, since I cast that oracle this evening, and I saw her clear as day. But somehow this is different; I hear her breathing hard and I'm stabbed with a sense of panic. Traces of other things, too - car headlamps, a cold cruel face, a bunch of big fellas? It's all in flashes, like someone running a projector in slow motion.

I sit a moment, gently trying to grab hold of something in the flurry of images. Sometimes my arm gets numb and tingly and I squeeze my fist, trying to relieve the discomfort. The whole time, very gradually, a sense of dread falling over me. Reluctance, horror, a feeling that I have to do the most terrifying thing in the world, all by myself. Darkness all around, hard to get a clear sense of where I am, but I haven't any trouble *feeling* what's around.

I snap out of it, look at my clock. I've been sitting here like this since Nettie left the room, and that was fifteen minutes ago. The mark on my arm is getting darker now, turning to faint blue ink instead of red, but the pain is fading. It's just a sort of dull, distant cold feeling now. Maybe I'll turn the light off and try to get some sleep.

As I roll over, the conversation from last night comes back to me. All of us sitting around the coffee table, planning what was to be done. Aunt Lizzy and Miss Morrison had spotted two versal apertures in a twenty-mile radius, and the closest one by far was inside the Blackstead Forest. I confess that I don't know much about those woods, but they've a fearsome, evil reputation. Bad things happen there, people see things that shouldn't exist. People disappear. But Aunt Lizzy said that the only way to get Courtney back for good was for her to go through one of those apertures, and that meant going into the Blackstead. Somehow, deep inside, I knew it was true. The conversation made everyone a little bit grim, but Aunt Lizzy never expressed any doubt that Courtney would be all right. So when I conjured the oracle and made contact with Courtney, Hazel told her to go out there.

I was such a sorry fish. All I could think about was all the things I wanted to say, all backed up in my throat. How Courtney felt a sense of awe seeing me, a sense of wonder and forgotten feelings, but she didn't know what to say, either. I suppose we hadn't much time, anyhow. Maybe that was what stopped me shy of saying much of anything.

But the conversation moved along and swept me away from personal thoughts. Hazel and Sadie would go back and get a few hours' sleep while Courtney made the transit, then come back over here early in the morning for a peek through the versocular. Once Courtney was on this side of the veil, and once we'd located her, they'd go pick her up. Easy enough. The only thing was, when I asked to go with them to fetch Courtney, Hazel and Aunt Lizzy wouldn't let me. They said it "might be too dangerous," and that only an arcane like Sadie could handle herself. I was annoyed - what was so special about Sadie, anyhow? Had she really gotten in a fight with those toughs? Had she really been attacked, just like Courtney? And if it was so dangerous, why did they send Courtney into the heart of that frightful place all alone?

Sadie was tore up about it, too. She came over to me, a little bashful; maybe she was afraid I'd chew her head off. But she leaned in close and murmured a promise - "Don't worry, Mary. I'll bring her right back, safe and sound."

That kid makes it awful hard for a person to hate her.

But now something else is bothering me. This mark on my arm isn't a normal wound; I'd bet my life on it. And these images, impressions, feelings I'm getting. Are they important? Where are they coming from?

One of the very first things every diviner learns is *always trust yourself*.

Pretty soon I don't need to concentrate anymore. Pictures arrive on their own, with ever-increasing clarity. You know how, on a quiet evening, you can hear someone's motor coming from all the way up the street? First you're not even sure you hear anything at all, then you barely hear it, and then it grows louder. This is similar. At first it's only flashes of sound and images and feelings, but all these things become clearer, longer, more frequent. Soon I'm able to piece together enough details to make sense of what I'm looking at.

A girl my age, way outside the city limits, all alone and scared to death. She trudges up a dark hill, following the white glow of the full moon, and finally watches it emerge through the gnarled trees. A winding trail ahead leads away into a thick black forest, vast beyond comprehension. Just ahead, the ground dips very slightly; it has some sort of significance for her, and the sight of it frightens her. All around, the forest is dead still, dead silent, alive with shadows. Eyes play tricks, things move just out of sight, and when you look, nothing is there. She creeps into the dip in the trail and looks off to her right, into the woods. Something long and winding, like an enormous snake, lay piled under decades of leaves. On a tree next to it, two marks carved into the bark with a knife - an M with an arrow through it and a C crossed out with an X. That long snake under the leaves is actually a very old road, a road that hasn't been used by a living person in decades, maybe centuries. The markings on the trees aren't fresh, but they don't look old, either; it's difficult to make any guesses about their age in this light.

This seems familiar...these markings, the woods, something. I've never been to this place myself, but something is ringing a bell. What is it? *Think, Mary.*

The images come faster now, and they're fluttering by faster than if I were actually watching in person. I've seen this kind of thing happen once or twice before, practicing on Nettie. What I'm seeing is a memory, something that's already happened by now.

About fifty feet from the trail, a flimsy little wire fence, knee-high. Beyond that, uncharted wilderness. I feel - *she* feels - naked. I wish I had some kind of weapon, a knife, anything. She's got a dull old combat knife from a military surplus store, straight-bladed with a black handle, *but I left that back in my apartment like a genius. And now I'm bleeding because someone else* didn't *leave their knife at home. That psychopath asshole brought his grandpappy's hunting knife from Vietnam and bragged to me about killing college girls with it. Killing* me *with it.*

Oh, god. The words, the mental voice. Courtney! That's why all this seemed familiar - Hazel described this place last night when she gave directions.

Suddenly there's a connection between us, and it happens the instant everything tumbles into place. The next thing I know, the next ten minutes rush into my head.

I experience them in about two or three seconds.

Courtney

I've dropped my messenger bags and purse in the back, and I'm getting ready to slide into the driver's seat when I see it. Remember the Slipknot-mobile I told you about? Well, it's wedged across the exit from my apartment complex, stopping anyone from leaving. It's one of those long boats from the late 60s or early 70s, faded red and tricked out with a noise-polluting stereo system and those ghetto springs that make your car bounce when you rollin' up in the hood with your skuzzy white trash homies. Everyone like to pretend they Snoop Dee-Oh-Double-G. The doors are wide open like a tailgate party, and this screamo metal shit growls out of the sound system in the trunk. A crowd of people loiter around in a cloud of smoke, and cigarettes glow on and off in the fading twilight.

Awesome. They've blocked me in to make me confront them. Today keeps getting better and better.

I wait a second, hoping they haven't seen me and that they'll get bored and leave, but they aren't going anywhere. Occasional laughter rises up around the car as a counterpoint to the ongoing sounds of someone having bone surgery without anesthetic - played in hi-def stereo with a subwoofer. I heave a sigh. Alright, I might as well get this over with.

I start my car, back out, and pull up to the trailer trash checkpoint. I've got my light aluminum baseball bat in the trunk - I bought it for self-defense and I've never used it - but I decide not to use it now, either. Half of these meth dealers are well over six feet tall and built like linebackers - they'd have my bat out of my hands as soon as I swung it. And then, goodnight - it's already in their hands, so why not beat me to death? They could even claim self-defense. No, I'm better off not giving them things to hit me with - they've already got plenty.

As I pull up, those cigarette cherries bloom as everyone takes one last drag, puts them out, and gets ready for tonight's entertainment. Derek brought Krystal and about six of their fucktard friends, and this is what they came for. I told you that Stanhope is a shithole, right? Well, it just goes to show how lame that town is when you spend your week looking forward to driving the hour to Autumn Grove to attack a sophomore. *Big doins tonight - load up all the kinfolk n' go down-err-n' stab a college girl to death.* I take one last breath of the clean air in my car and get out to face them. I can't be sitting down when they approach.

The street light comes on as I step into the flat cloud of cheap cigarette smoke. Like I'm in some sadistic fight to the death for entertainment.

"Well, well," Derek says, stepping out of the shadows. "Look who decided to show up."

He looks more reptilian - or insectoid - every time I see him. Jet black hair, unwashed and oily, drapes over one side of a bony face. Swarthy, greasy skin that shines in the floodlight. Cold, empty, alien eyes without a trace of empathy or compassion, the kind that sci-fi makeup designers spend a fortune trying to recreate with contacts. Tendons and sinew and a big Adam's apple that bulges out of his throat like a huge codpiece. He's not much taller than me.

I curl my lip. "Sorry. I know you said to meet you on the playground after school, but I had stuff to do."

Someone snickers.

"Krystal put up with a lotta shit from you," he says in a lazy drawl. "You and your Barbie friends fucked with her, told everyone about her private shit, and now you're stealing her clothes and shit."

None of that is even remotely true. She was never around enough for me to 'fuck with,' and besides, all that implies a level of intimacy we never had. I really don't even know her that well. And Tiffany and her friends barely breathed a word about her; they honestly thought she was beneath their notice.

But that doesn't matter to Derek. Krystal has spent weeks carefully crafting me into an evil chimera of Pol Pot, Hitler, Lizzie Borden, Elizabeth Bathory, and Rasputin, so now these filth actually think they've got a reason to hurt me.

The only thing worse than a loser meth dealer is a loser meth dealer with a crusade. Now he's got a way to vindicate himself with what he thinks is some higher purpose, all while he gets an easy outlet for his psychopathic tendencies. He's probably shining inside - I bet he's all like, *'I can finally justify breathing everyone else's good oxygen!'*

Well, I'll play along as much as I can. If I can buy enough time, maybe someone will come along and tell this greaseball to move.

I turn away, looking right at Krystal. She huddles over by the car, hair dyed motley strips of jet black, hot pink, neon green, and white. The black and the white come together in a skunklike pattern down one side of her head. She's got cakey foundation, rouged cheeks, and fire engine red eye shadow that goes to her eyebrows. She picked up this style - if that's what you want to call it - right before we split up. When I asked about it, she said it was called 'Scene.' I asked her whether it was a scene of violence or drug deals or teen pregnancy or chemical spills. She didn't respond.

Right now, she's got an interesting cocktail of emotions on her face. Deep in her eyes, a little tiny bit of excitement and schadenfreude. It's probably fun for a small-town girl to get out once in a while and see a good ol' knock-down-drag-out melee in a parking lot that isn't Wal-Mart. But those are fairly weak emotions - mostly she feels a bit put on the spot, a bit embarrassed (I'm not sure why), and there's a growing hint of concern in her expression.

"Hey Krystal," I ask her, very casually. My cavalier tone hides my organs going stiff and shivering. I realize that my chances of getting out of this unharmed - even alive - aren't good. "You're saying I have your top, right? Just out of curiosity, how many times have you been over to look for it?"

She stammers, then looks imploringly at Derek. After a second, he speaks for her. "You know damn well she's been asking really nice since you got out for spring. She only came over once to look for it and you chased her out-"

That's totally absurd, and I have to resist laughing in his cigarette-browned face. It would only make *me* look stupid, like yelling into a hurricane and telling it to fuck off back out to sea. But you see what's happening, don't you? She won't answer me because she knows she's been over here *three* times - on the pretense of looking for her skanky top - but she didn't look around much because she wanted to hang around trying to manipulate me into...I don't know. Begging her not to leave or something. The skanky top doesn't exist - it's a decoy, an imaginary pretext to get into my company or to incite an act of violence. Whatever he does to me in this parking lot, they'll forget all about the top afterwards. It's a ruse, and everyone knows it.

I may not laugh, but I grin. "Alright. Why are you *really* here? Why did you drive an hour to come see me? Were you really that bored back in Stanhope? Or is there some reason you brought six big strapping meth factories? Some *big job* that needs some *big men?*"

Little moans. *"Ooo!"*

"She just call us-?"

"You gonna take that shit, bro?"

And now he stares - this is the part he likes. He stands there leering at me - the leer of rapists and playground bullies everywhere. That open-mouthed smile that would look like simple childish joy if there were any humanity in the eyes. But the eyes are dead, gray. Cadaverous. Half-lidded, like the Xanax is just kicking in. And deep in his expression of frozen dead amusement, a flicker of the blackest hatred. The seconds tick by.

"Come on, Derek," Krystal says. "We made our point. She's not worth the hassle."

He ignores her, looking happy without looking human. Some sick fantasy plays out behind his eyeballs, some horrific sight that only he can see.

Maybe this is what Krystal meant by 'Scene.'

A dry click shatters the quiet. A tiny glint next to his hip - a big hunting knife, held low, down against his leg. I don't know why he's not just brandishing it like, '*AhAAA!* Have at you, knave!' He might as well. There's no point in hiding it like the Unabomber or something.

"You're right," he says, very calmly. His smile widens a bit; his eyes stay dead. "There is a big job we came for. But speaking of big jobs..." He holds the hunting knife up in his fist, points it at me kinda awkwardly. "If you give me a big blow job, I might let you walk outta here."

His goons laugh. "Yeah, bro!"

"Me too!"

"And me!"

Here we go. He's getting down to business.

I lift my eyebrows. "How about a counteroffer? If you let me walk outta here, I might leave enough of your dick behind for you to be able to *have* a blow job."

The primate moans rise around me again. "Ooooooo!" It sounds like a couple of them came from behind me this time. This isn't good. They're gonna surround me.

Derek doesn't even blink at what I said - his face is a cold, clammy mask.

"Derek, seriously! Come on!" Krystal implores him. "Let's just go! I don't wanna get in trouble."

Another tense moment of silence as he glares at me. Then a presence behind me, the smell of man-grease and testosterone. Too late.

Some ape with cold slimy skin and coarse red hair grabs my arms, pins them behind me. "I got her! Get her, bro!"

This is where things get tricky. I'm gonna have to stay *really* calm - as calm as this scumbag in front of me - if I want a chance of walking away in one piece. And timing is critical. I can't even flinch until the perfect moment, or this gorilla behind me will know what I'm trying to do.

Stay chill, Courtney. You got this.

I hope.

Slime Bucket holds his knife, plays with it. It's a thick curved blade, six inches long and nickel-plated. It's got bits of white crust on the blade - no doubt he's used this same knife to cut coke and who knows how many other things.

He fingers it, plays with it, stares at me. Gnats and mosquitoes swarm in and out of the headlights. My car runs behind me, the A/C kicking on and off, the motor going louder, then softer.

Then he makes a disgusted sorta face, steps up, and winds back. He's holding the blade low; he's gonna try to get me in the stomach. I *really* don't want to get stabbed in the stomach.

Krystal moans. "No..."

I wait for him to lunge in...

And slip my right arm free at the last second. Grab my captor's arm, swing him around.

Fire across my shoulder, and then a scream - but not mine. It's an anguished cry from behind me.

"Owww! You stabbed me, faggot!!"

A few scattered laughs, but when I turn around, Derek actually has to pull his knife out of his friend. He got the big ape under the armpit. He screams and yells over and over.

"Ah, shit! Ah, fuck! Aaaah!"

Nobody really cares about me anymore, at least for the moment. Derek helplessly looks back and forth between me and his injured lackey until the cries ruin the mood. All his friends are gathered around the stab victim as he whines and moans.

"He's hurt pretty bad, dude," one says. "You got him good. He's bleedin' everywhere, bro."

"Ah, shit! Ah, fuck, man! I'm gonna die! I'm gonna fuckin' die."

That oaf might be a real crybaby, but I can't fault him completely. I don't know what was on that blade - whether it was just drugs or what - but I think the slice down my shoulder burns a lot more than it should. Even if that knife was dull - and I don't think it was the sharpest - it wouldn't feel like someone rubbed Icy Hot in the wound. It hurts worse with every second that goes by, and it's bleeding more every time I look at it. It's only a cut on the arm, but it's starting to bleed like he nicked a vein.

I'm not exactly an anatomy expert or anything, but I don't think there are any major veins where he got me. And I don't think the trace amounts of drugs on that filthy knife are enough to make me start gushing blood.

"Ahhha! Derek? Derek! Fuck, man...dude, I think I need to go to the hospital..."

One of the goons leaning over him looks at Derek. "He's right, bro. He ain't lookin too good."

I've got my left hand clamped over my own wound, ignoring the fact that I shouldn't be touching it with my bare skin. The contact burn is nothing compared to the horrible fire erupting inside this thing. I'm clenching my teeth against it, glaring defiance at him.

He points his bloody knife at me. It drips onto the pavement, through the headlights. "Saved by the bell, bitch. You better run, cause I'm comin' for you. Next time, you're fuckin' dead, Barbie."

Saved by the bell? Did I slip and fall into a bad high school movie from the mid-80s? Do I at least get the cute Molly Ringwald outfit with the pink sweater?

"You'll never see me again, dickbrain," I tell him. But he's already headed for his car. His friends are getting more and more frantic as they haul their casualty into the front seat. In moments, they're roaring outta there like one of those skuzzy-looking redneck shows from the 70s with loud cars and good ol' boys. Screams from the car - "You're dead, bitch!"

Once they're out of sight, I double over in agony. This is easily the most painful cut I've ever had. Did he poison his knife when he planned to stab me with it? Honestly, I wouldn't put it past him. But if he'd poisoned his knife, I'd already be woozy or weak or something, and I'm not. It just hurts like freakin crazy, burning and icy at the same time. And deep, somehow, even though I can't really explain what I mean.

I examine the wound. I'd swear he only grazed me and it wasn't that bad, but this thing is a good six inches long now. I know I didn't just see it wrong - if he'd given me a six-inch cut with that ugly thing, I'd have known it. So my brain struggles against the impossible - the cut must have grown, somehow.

Then again, I've been in two different realities today, eighty years apart, and my best friends talked to me via telepathy from the 1920s.

Alright, so maybe nothing's impossible. But this thing is *horrible*. Like, if I went to the hospital with it, I'd probably have to get stitches.

The thought of going to the hospital rolls my stomach up with dread. Something deep inside is telling me that if I went to the hospital, I'd die there. And that's when it occurs to me that it's where that greasy smelly oaf is going, since he got stabbed in the line of duty trying to kill me.

So the only sane thing to do when you've got a six-inch death trench up your arm - spewing blood like crazy and burning like you doctored it with ammonia and antifreeze - is to get to that haunted forest and look for an ancient road that'll take you to an interdimensional portal. I mean, use your common sense. But first things first - I have to improvise a tourniquet before I bleed to death.

I clench my teeth against the pain and get back to my car. Open my door, pop the trunk - I think I've got an old t-shirt or sheet or something back here. I left my hoodie inside the car, and I'm only wearing a plain tank top right now, so at least that shitlord didn't ruin any of my clothes.

In my trunk, an oversized white t-shirt - some musty XXL shirt with a faded beer logo on it, turned inside out. I think my cousin Kelsey might've left this in here forever ago, and I always forget to throw it away. Pull it out and wrap it around my arm as neatly as I can manage. Use my left hand and teeth to cinch it as tight as I can. Pull it until I yell from the pain. There.

Fuck, ow. That hurts. And I'm sure this thing isn't exactly sanitary, but honestly I don't care too much about infection right now. Something tells me that germs are the least of my worries. I'm about to go into the Blackstead - you know, the woods nobody ever comes out of? And this death wound is still bleeding, even through the tourniquet.

Half-grunt, half-sigh, all frustration. I get back in the driver's seat, shift the stick, and get out of this freakin parking lot before this disgusting universe can think of some other way to kill me.

Mary

The mark on my arm is exactly where Courtney's cut is! That monster wasn't lying in the precognition I had earlier today - he really *did* try to kill her! Why, she never did a thing to him! But at least Courtney was clever and got a nasty gash instead of a ruptured heart or a belly wound. She drove off, down around the edge of town and out toward the Blackstead Forest, and the bleeding got worse and worse.

Now I'm finally catching up with myself again as she forces her steps onto that old road, approaches that worthless little wire fence. She stops, thinking of how everyone who crossed this fence never came back, and she's overcome with terrified panic. Far away in the trees ahead, a flicker of sickly white light, gone in a flash. A breeze picks up, but she can't feel it down here on the forest floor. It hisses in the trees but it sounds more like a whisper, a voice. Words.

I'm frozen in place, my stomach tied in knots. My fists are clenched, white knuckles showing, and I want nothing more than to scream and run so fast all the leaves will fly out from under me, and I'll slip and fall five times and trip and roll down the trail. I want to scream *and scream and burn up the road like a street racer, never letting off the gas until I get back to campus. The thought of pulling a Fast and the Furious is a nice, comforting human thought, the only thought keeping me from screaming myself hoarse and going insane.*

But what that Hazel chick said is true, and I know it's true because I feel it inside and I've been watching it happen for a while now. If I haul ass out of these woods and drive off, I might not even make it back to town. This place, this reality, is closing in. Everything is ending. I don't know what's ahead of me, but I know that behind me is certain death. I'm being backed into this, and the only remote chance I have is going into these woods.

Fuck my life. I swallow and step over the toy fence. *Time to join the missing. Time to vanish.*

I clench my eyes shut, wishing I didn't have to live this memory, but I'm ashamed as soon as I think it. Courtney lived this. If Courtney did it, I have to do it. I must know what happened to her.

My heart is beating faster and the terror rises in my chest, and all I can hope is that she survived. I don't know what I'll do if I have to watch her die *and* experience her death. My mind will snap like a piece of candy. And I've some deep sense that if Courtney dies, I die with her.

Everything speeds up. Down the trail, dead quiet, then flashes in the trees. Eventually it's not my eyes playing tricks on me anymore. There's a tiny white light, floating among the trees in the distance, sickly pale like a corpse. The low roar of the wind morphs into distant echoes of fiddle music.

Fiddles. Like in the stories. Terror rises inside me like every hair rising on a cat's back. Because I know what it is. It's real. A low roar of fright fills my eardrums, and I run faster through the woods.

The trail winds around - is that a hill? It's not all that big, and I scramble up toward the top. Rocks, where are the rocks? Only a glade. A dark glade, sticks poking out of the ground, straight. Hang on, those aren't sticks. This grove is really dark, like there's something more than shadows.

The rocks, I see them, but they're up the hill from me. This wasn't the top.

Something eight feet tall turns around in my direction. The flat, sharp brim of a 17th century Pilgrim hat, like a blade in the dark. Before I can move, before I can even react, the face is turning to look at me. White mummified flesh turns the face into a frozen death mask. Holes in the darkness where eyes used to be, darker than black. And a huge gaping hole in the bottom. A mouth, frozen open forever in a soundless howl, darkness flowing out of it like a spring of pure horror. It turns and my brain is screaming panic and it sees me-

I scream. Cry. Bury my head in the pillow. I don't know what it is, but I know that no human was ever meant to see it.

Courtney is running up the hill, mind gone with fright. *Stones at the top of the hill. Gotta get the stones.* She's not even thinking about what will happen if the stones aren't there. She mustn't. She knows she's seconds from death, and if the stones aren't there...this must be the terrifying fate that awaits anyone venturing into these cursed woods.

Then, a strange sort of *popping* sensation across my entire being. Almost the way your ears pop when you're riding a train downhill, as if I can hear the world again, sense it again. Reality is *more real* than it was.

Courtney. She's arrived.

"Mary?"

I scream out loud, a jumble of flying arms and legs as Nettie's sudden voice startles me back into the wall.

"Why, darling! Whatever is the matter?"

She's coming to comfort me and it's only Nettie, but in this half-twilight awareness I'm still terrified of being touched. I cringe away, like someone touching a live wire.

"Courtney. She's here. Courtney's here."

I fumble for the lamp. Soon I hear Elizabeth padding down the hallway.

"Why, she's scared half to death!" Nettie complains as the light comes on. "I don't know what got into her!"

The light brings the room to life, to human familiarity, and it starts to ground me. Aunt Lizzy appears in the doorway, and I jump a little at the sight of her.

"Mary," Lizzy asks. "You say Courtney's here? Did she cross the threshold?"

My teeth start chattering and I begin to shiver. I can only nod. Nettie approaches slowly, sits down next to me. She reaches toward me, touches me, pulls me close.

"There, darling. It's all right now."

"She...Courtney-she-"

"You saw it, didn't you? Courtney's transit?" Lizzy flips the light switch in the hallway. She looks at Nettie, who's quite confused. "Mary's a diviner, remember? Some diviners are more natural at it than others, and it just so happens Mary's got a rather unique connection to Courtney."

"Aaaaaah," Nettie says softly. "I think I begin to see."

"Indeed," Lizzy says. "You take care of Mary. I'll go down and take a peep."

"Sh-she's out there all alone," I stammer. "I have to go tell Miss Morrison right away."

Lizzy stops, looks at me. I expect her to refuse, say she'll go instead, but she just nods. "Very well. At least let me have a look first, before you go running off in the dark."

"I'll go with her," Nettie offers.

Lizzy nods. "All right. Meet me in the living room once you're both dressed."

Through the versocular, Courtney looks much larger, much clearer. The information next to her looks like it's from some old textbook.

VERSAL TRANSIT COMPLETE.
SERVANT LANGUISH — TRANQUILITY DAWN.
SUBJECT PRESENCE: 100%.
SUBJECT RESONANCE: 100%.
SUBJECT ARCHETYPE: RESIDENT — ARC TRANQUILITY.
2 MINUTES 18 SECONDS UNTIL APERTURE SEALED.

"This means she can't go back? Ever?" I ask.

Lizzy shakes her head. "She's crossed the Rubicon. I hope she's ready to live here."

"We'll stick by her," Nettie promises. "We'll make her one of us in no time."

Nettie and I breeze out of the house in the gray predawn gloom, making our way through the fog as quick as we can. Hazel Morrison's house is no more than a block and a half away, but the walk feels like it takes ages. I notice every single step, and we're tense and rigid. We don't talk much.

My stomach is thrumming nervously when I climb Hazel's porch steps and knock softly on the door. Quiet footsteps, and then Sadie's face peeks through the door. She smiles when she sees us.

"Mary, Nettie." She's whispering, her voice muffled even further by the mist. "Please, come in."

We step into Hazel's spicy-smelling, warm-toned front parlor; it's so cool and peaceful and quiet this early in the morning. Hazel's house is so lovely; I wish I could stay for longer. Sadie pulls a shawl closer about herself and shuts the door quietly behind us.

"Why, you've barely slept a wink," Sadie comments.

I shake my head. Nettie makes a so-so motion with her hand.

"Me neither," Sadie confesses. "This whole thing has me on pins and needles."

"That's why we came," Nettie says. "Courtney's here."

Sadie's calm vanishes. "She is?"

A tiny creak at the top of the stairs, like the floor settling.

"She completed transit probably twenty, twenty-five minutes ago," Nettie elaborates. "The aperture sealed behind her."

"Then she's ours," Hazel announces from the stairway, arms crossed over her nightgown. "At last."

"Sorry if we woke you-" Sadie and I say it at the same time, then grin at each other.

"Oh, heavens no," Hazel waves it off. "I've never been able to sleep in a crisis, and I've had my share."

"Miss Morrison?" I ask. "There's something else. Courtney's in trouble. I saw...I saw..." My heart starts beating faster as I remember all the dreadful things in that vision.

"What did you see, Mary?" Hazel quietly comes downstairs. "What happened?"

"I don't...whatever it was, I-" I swallow loudly in the quiet parlor. "Something was after her."

Sadie looks concerned. "Mary, darling, you're as white as a sheet!"

"And scared half to death," Hazel notes. "Whatever she saw was deeply traumatic. All right, girls, thank you for coming to tell us. We'll take it from here. Sadie, as soon as you're dressed, let's get you armed. We don't know exactly what we're walking into, but I know darn well we're not leaving without Courtney."

Sadie pales a little, but nods. "All right."

"A-armed?" I ask.

Hazel smirks. "Why, sure. If Courtney *does* have unwanted suitors, it's our job to tell 'em to scram, right?"

Nettie and Sadie both grin. Every last one of these girls is screwy.

"You sure you don't want a hand?" Nettie offers.

"We'll be all right, but thanks," Hazel says. "We're a team, and you two have been wonderful. I'd like you to get back over to Professor Talbott's house and make a bed for Courtney. We don't know what kind of shape she'll be in after a dangerous transit, and if I know Talbott, she'll want to keep Courtney close."

Sadie offers us a little smile. Regretful, afraid, determined, brave, all layered like a wedding cake. A surge of affection for this pretty, courageous girl wells up in my chest, and I embrace her. It's all pretty sudden, and it catches her off guard at first. But once she collects herself, she embraces me in earnest.

"We'll bring her home," she assures me quietly. "I promise."

I give her one last squeeze and then we make an agreement with our eyes.

"Please be careful out there," I tell them both.

"Don't worry, we will," Hazel promises. "We'll be back in just a little while."

So that's that, then. Nettie and I start back toward Aunt Lizzy's house - our new home - just as the first cold light of dawn begins to spread through the fog. Some bone-deep part of me begins to feel tired, just as real work begins. It's cruel and spiteful of my body to act this way. Though I suppose I'd be reluctant to fall asleep anyhow; I'm so scared I'll remember something - *anything* - I saw in those terrible woods.

Three

Wednesday
September 7, 1921

8:07 a.m.

Sadie

"Oh, Marian, I wish you <u>would</u> tell me! As you said, we have been the closest of friends for so many years - the greater portion of our lives! You'll never rid yourself of my companionship so easily! You yourself have spoken of my fierce loyalty on many occasions! Which leads me to what I wish to say. Do not fear my outrage, and do not fear giving me false hope. Ever since I lost my only precious daughter to miscarriage, I have felt that a part of me was gone, never to return. And since that black day, my thoughts have wandered in strange places, asking strange questions, and for years I thought <u>myself</u> mad. <u>Please</u> know, my dearest one, that if you give me nothing else with your strange tale, you will <u>most</u> <u>certainly</u> give me peace on <u>that</u> score. The thought that some of my strange notions might be rooted in solid fact - and not my own madness - would be of <u>enormous</u> comfort to me.

So, let me get to brass tacks. Mother to mother, I ask you plainly - <u>do you believe my daughter yet lives</u>?? You mention a young woman of your own acquaintance, and it is plain you care for her. Does she remind you of me? Let me set your mind at ease immediately: I wish to be initiated into all your mysteries and otherworldly knowledge. I earnestly wish for you to share these strange secrets with me, those whose burden gives you such apprehension. Consider my interest to be genuine and enthusiastic - I wish to be your student and perhaps even your collaborator.

If you are certain that my daughter is truly dead and nothing of her remains, then you know I will let go of any wasted endeavor. But Marian, if she lives, if by some miracle she was stolen away by the fairies instead of dead in my arms, <u>you</u> <u>must</u> <u>tell</u> <u>me</u>! And if you were to aid me and guide me in this search, no matter how futile, no matter how remote the chances of success, then I will still be happy I had a chance, however slim.

I remain, ever your most devoted and affectionate,

--Jennie"

-Jennie Ashford, letter to Marian Carlyle,
December 1915

Mary comes upstairs a few minutes after I get Courtney settled into her bed, hovering like a ghost outside her door until I tell her to come in. Unless Courtney tells me she doesn't want Mary around, it's not my place to keep her away. I'm a little worried that Mary will be a sour egg, giving me filthy looks or making mean little jabs, but she's been a darling. She and I fall into a strange kind of synergy when we're taking care of Courtney; Mary is always out of my way when I go to do something, and I'm always out of hers. If I need something, she's already on her way to get it for me. We always seem to be on the same page.

Courtney is in a frightful lot of pain. I know she is. She might be able to fool some people with that brave face of hers, or that silly wit, but I know better. Mary does, too. Courtney starts getting worse as soon as I get her in bed. Until now, she's been fighting every moment, her face set in a grim mask of composure. But something relaxes her, the room, the bed, the electric fan blowing on her face. Maybe even me or Mary. But after she gets settled, she starts getting pale, beads of sweat standing out on her forehead. She closes her eyes a lot, takes short little breaths, teeth clenched inside pressed lips.

"I brought some stuff for...*that*. There's a tube of Neosporin and some Band-Aids in my bag." She points to the foot of the bed, where I put her brown canvas bag. "If I knew I'd need it this soon, I'd have brought more. Or maybe, like...worn some armor."

Once I've removed Courtney's filthy tourniquet, Mary quietly asks, "May I?", and just points at the cut. She acts like she's had some experience with first aid, but when I ask her, she only shakes her head.

"I haven't any training or anything like that." She smiles softly. "I just know the patient."

Poor Courtney is absolutely lying there in one of her tank tops, nervous and embarrassed to have us taking care of her. She's too sweet to tell us to go, too shy to relax completely. Courtney's just the prettiest thing, and she's so hard to resist when she blushes and bites her lip all nervous like that. She's so kissable. I wonder if Mary notices me blushing? I wonder if she'd be sore if she did.

Mary cleans and dresses that wound with an angel's touch, using the supplies we rummaged out of Courtney's bag. She's gentle and kind, talking very softly as she treats the injury. Courtney doesn't even flinch under her care. And Mary looks as if she's come back to something warm and familiar, smiling as they talk, occasionally touching Courtney with a lingering hand. If you must know, I can't help feeling a bit jealous. They've gone right back to old routines, reminiscing about things I didn't get to share with them. I start to feel the bruised ache of sadness deep inside. I feel like an outsider.

Just as I'm getting lost in my gloom, Courtney says, "I wish Sadie had been there. She'd have totally fit right in with us."

Mary looks at me, half-smiling as she remembers some distant happy occasion, and then smiles. "Why, I think you're right. She'd have had a gay time with us."

And then Courtney starts laughing and wincing and laughing through the pain. Mary and I exchange a baffled look.

"Oh, my god," Courtney moans. "I should've known someone would say that."

"Say what, dear?" I ask.

Courtney rests laughing eyes on me. "*Everything* is gay when *I'm* around."

It takes us another few minutes to work out that, in the future Courtney comes from, "gay" doesn't mean "happy" anymore. Mary smiles and rolls her eyes and says that it seems she remembered learning this before, and Courtney's stream of wise cracks has got me laughing into my hands.

"Try to get some rest, you little nut." Mary grins at her. "One of us will come back to check on you in a little while." She pauses, softly touching Courtney's hand. "I'm awfully glad you're here, darling."

I smooth Courtney's soft blonde hair back from her forehead, wishing I didn't have to leave her side. "Same here. Awfully glad."

She just glows at us, smiles through her deathly pallor. "Yeah. Me too."

Before I leave, I pull out the little brass scope Hazel gave me and peek at Courtney's wound. Before Mary bandaged it up, it looked like a regular cut - sharp, clean. It looked as if it would heal nicely; no infection that I could see, either. But now that I look at it through the scope, I see a whole different picture. The same clean cut is festering with colonies of black spores. I've never seen anything like it before. When I say the stuff is black, I mean that it's *nothingness*. It absorbs light, gives nothing back. It's dark space, turning her wound into a bottomless chasm. It is not of this world.

I'm just glad that I'm able to hide my shock, to bluff like everything is all right. But I must give something away, a little startled twitch or something, because Mary catches it, glances at me. I hand her the scope without saying anything. She doesn't hide her alarm as well as I do; her face falls, and one little hand flies up to cover her mouth.

"What's up?" Courtney asks faintly, her head resting on the headboard.

I give her a flat smile. "Hazel just wanted me to take a peek with this silly old thing, that's all. I think it's broken. Try to get some rest."

Even though I haven't known Courtney as long as Mary and Nettie have, I still know that look on her face. I hear her gears clicking, see a line of witty comebacks and pointed questions fluttering past those sharp blue eyes. She wants to make some horrid joke about it, or ask some dreadful question like when we're gonna amputate her arm, but I think she's just too darn tired. Because she's certainly not dumb.

"Okay." She looks right through me. "I'll try."

Nettie and Hazel and Elizabeth are sitting in the parlor when Mary and I come back downstairs. Halfway down, Mary stops me with a hand on my shoulder.

"Say, what *was* that stuff, anyhow?"

I look a little downcast. "Maybe I should just let Hazel give you the dope. She's the one who knows about it."

"Give her the dope on what?" Hazel asks over a glass of iced tea. I answer by holding up the brass scope.

"Ah." Hazel sets her glass down. "I was just getting to that. Have a seat, girls."

Two hours ago

The sky glows with the coming sunrise when we finally get to the woods and start the long climb up those winding trails. Before we left Hazel's house early that morning, she gave me two long daggers with a gunmetal steel finish, about the size of bayonets. They're solid and heavy in my lap, and there's something comforting in their thick weight. I'm a little nervous about the silly things, but part of me keeps wanting to hold them. I'm always easing them out of their scabbards, twirling them like a master. I don't understand - how am I doing this? I've never held a dagger or a bayonet or anything before. Could it be some funny property of the daggers themselves?

Hazel drives with calm confidence; she must know just where she's going. I don't think it's a show, either. Her face is calm, relaxed, but her gray eyes are fixed like a steel trap on the dirt road ahead. There's a couple of times I glance at her and see her fixated on something a thousand miles away. Sometimes her face changes ever so slightly, as if she's watching something terrible happen and she's powerless to stop it. In those moments, she clenches the steering wheel really tight with one hand or both, knuckles white, tiny micro-spasms in her arms like she's having a nightmare.

"Hazel?" I ask her very gently, as we turn a curve on the trail. "Are you all right?"

"Hmm? Oh!" Head darting around, she answers a little too fast. "Just ducky. Why do you ask?"

"Oh. Nothing, really. You just...seem far away. And not happy."

She looks at me a moment, weighing something in her mind, then takes a long, slow breath. "Well. I suppose you and I have already been through a lot together. And if we're watching each other's backs, you deserve to know if I'm up to scratch. Well, the truth is, I was in the War."

"Oh, yes," I remember. "Hodges mentioned it."

"Yes. So, I guess if I'm ever staring off and acting funny, usually that's why."

"So you...fought?" I ask carefully. "In the trenches and everything?"

"Sometimes, but I wasn't with the infantry. I was with the American Arcane Expedition; we were an independent command attached to the AEF."

I listen in awe. I didn't know any of this.

"You mean the arcane circles fight in wars?"

Hazel makes a sour face. "Not usually, though it's been happening more. The German circles stayed out of it in the beginning, but once the British blockades started making life harder inside Germany, a lot of their circles offered their services. They started arriving on the battlefield about 1916, and that's when things got nasty." We bounce over a big rock and she winces. "The Germans are some of the best arcanists in Europe - sophisticated thaumaturgy, way ahead on theory and practice. They're big on electromagnetism, seismology." Shakes her head, a little disgusted. "Biphasic metallurgy, for crying out loud. Who ever heard of such a crazy thing?" Sigh. "But they came in and started making everyone's lives hell. That brought the British circles into the war, and they weren't ready for what Jerry had. Kept the Allies on the back foot and didn't let up."

She pauses, slowing the car to round a sharp curve, then continues.

"Anyhow, long story short, I got there in July of 1918, and a lot of the whoopee was over by then, at least on the arcane side. The French and British squabbled over us for a while - kept us running in circles so we couldn't get anything done. Finally, General McClure -

the lady in charge of the American arcane effort - got sick of it and told 'em to go to hell. By then, I was already attached to the Royal Sussex up near Ypres, and they'd just made me a company commander. My British boss liked me and was trying hard to get me a real commission." She heaves a sigh. "McClure picked that moment - right as I was getting comfortable - to bring me back down to rendezvous with my brigade. So me and my company ended up outside of Soissons."

My mouth is dry; I've heard of that town. There was a big battle there - Chateau-Thierry or something. "Was-were you...you know, scared?"

She smiles a little. "Well, I was twenty-three, just out of undergrad myself, and I guess I was a little cocky. Hell, all of us American kids figured we had something to prove - a lot of us in college or just out of it, fresh-faced, eager. We hadn't seen the war up close, and we figured all the Brits needed was us to come show 'em how it was done." She snorts. "Turned out the Krauts had a few rounds of fight left in them."

"What happened?"

She smiles. "Well, we're almost there, so I won't have time to tell you right now, but let's just say the moral of the story is that generals love it when people throw their lives away and catch them when they bounce back. They love it even more when you throw your life away and hit Fritz in the face."

My head is swimming. "Is that...why Hodges called you that name yesterday? The...Blood..."

"The Bloodstaff, yes," she answers. "The Krauts gave me that one. Not much of a mystery there." She bobs her head toward the metallic red staff in the back seat.

"Jeepers," I breathe, all in wonder.

"Aw, just a bunch of hooey," she waves it off. "Still, if it helped us end that filthy mess, I guess it was worth going." The sun peeks above the horizon behind us, casting pale orange light on the faces of a thousand leaves. Hazel squints ahead as we stop in a clearing. "I think that's our girl." She pulls the parking brake. "And get those daggers ready. I think we have a problem."

"I still don't know what on Earth I saw out there." My eyes are far away. Mary, Nettie, and Elizabeth listen intently as Hazel and I tell our story. "And the more I think about it, the less it makes sense, and the less I *want* to think about it."

"What was it?" Nettie asks.

I shake my head very slowly. "At first glance, just a fella...kinda hunched over, shuffling around. But he only looked like a fella for a second. He was...covered in something. Some kind of inky black stuff that you don't see until you blink. Then it's burned into your eyes, like a bright light." I gulp. "Courtney...she was on the ground, just ahead of me. But I didn't get a good look at her, because that thing was walking toward her. He - that is to say, *it*, because I don't think it was a man - was all wrong. People don't move...the way he - *it* - moved. Sometimes there was no face, a-and other times, I don't know. Big black eyebrows, deep shadows over the eyes. Sometimes his arm would sorta rotate around and he'd have a big curved knife in it." I stop, remembering the glass of iced tea in front of me. I take a big sip.

Hazel takes over, eyes narrowed as she remembers. "It seemed to lean over Courtney even before it reached her, keeping that knife clenched in its fist the whole time. I'm no expert on this stuff, but it looked to me like a lesser vampiric revenant."

Elizabeth is white as a sheet, and each word she speaks is no more than a quiet breath. "Dear God. *Here?!*"

"As I said, it's not something I'd bet money on, but that was the first thing I thought of. We scared it off with some projectiles before it got near Courtney, but we were cutting it a little close for my taste. That thing would have made a meal out of her if we'd been another few minutes too late."

Mary's face crumbles with horror. Nettie takes her hand, grim-faced and silent. Hazel hadn't told me just how much danger Courtney was in, how close a shave it was, and the terror feels like a stone in my chest.

I resume the tale. "I ran to check on Courtney, and Hazel made sure the thing was gone. That was when I saw all the blood." I shudder. "I was scared plumb to death. I thought we'd lost her."

"Is that how Courtney got the...black stuff?" Mary asks quietly. "In her wound? From the...thing you mentioned?" She's awfully pale. Her eyes are half-open, and she's swaying like she's dizzy.

Hazel looks at me. "Did you find voidtoxin in the wound?"

I glance helplessly between them. "I...*think* that's what I saw."

She quietly holds out her hand for the little scope, and I give it to her. She rotates something on the brass pipe, presses a button somewhere, then looks through it.

"Aw, hell," she says quietly. "She's crawling with the stuff. I'm afraid this is no good." She's a little paler than she was a minute ago. "But no, Mary. I don't believe that's how

Courtney contracted it. She had to be exposed to it during her transit somehow. Usually the transmission is through direct contact."

"Hang on," I tell her. "That thing we saw in the woods. If it was one of those...vampiric-whatchacallits, then how come it just looked like a fella?"

Hazel gives me a tiny nod. "Whoever attacked Courtney before she got to the woods, his intention to murder an innocent person was what followed her through the veil - not the man himself. Any creature under the anomaly's control could have picked up on it and assumed his shape, possibly to help it hunt prey. Like Courtney."

Mary shades her eyes with a hand, and everything she does is slow. Her face is starting to turn an oatmeal color.

"I still don't get it," Nettie bursts in. "What *is* this voidtoxin stuff?"

"Deadly," Hazel replies after a moment, looking at me. "Aphotic poison, rare but lethal. It comes from extraversal space. It means a long, miserable death and even worse after, unless it's dealt with quickly. Saving Courtney might require finding a...*creative* solution."

"How long?" Mary's voice is weak, barely audible. "How long does Courtney have?"

"With the way *she* fights?" Hazel speculates. "Maybe another thirty hours."

"...to live?" I ask helplessly.

Her only reply is a grave expression.

Mary's eyes are closed, and she's teetering. "We must..." She swallows. "We must do...someth-" And then her eyes roll back and she falls over onto Nettie.

"Mary?" Nettie bats her cheeks. "Mary!"

Hazel's around the coffee table, touching the back of her hand to Mary's forehead.

"Miss Morrison?" Nettie's face is heavy with fear of death. "Whatever Courtney has...do you think it's catching?"

Hazel says nothing at first, just takes Mary's wrist very gently in her hand. She checks her pulse with a finger, looks into her face. Her gaze moves down, delicate fingers turning Mary's arm. Mary's wearing a short-sleeved summer dress, much like mine and Nettie's, only hers is soft pink. Hazel touches her short cotton sleeve, moves it back with a finger. Nettie and I draw a gasp together; Mary's upper arm is powder white, and right in the middle, a slender blue-black line.

Just like Courtney's wound. Same place, same shape.

"No, Nettie," Hazel says tonelessly. "I don't believe so." She reaches for the small scope and hands it to me. The fish-eye bubble of the lens shows a vertical line of night-black emptiness about two inches long, running from Mary's shoulder to her bicep.

"How did you know?" My voice is almost a whisper.

"I didn't," she says. "And this changes everything."

"How so?" Nettie asks, voice hoarse, holding Mary's head.

"Because evidently they're linked somehow. If one dies, they both die." She looks up at me, eyes sick with horror. "And they could both be dead within the hour."

Four

Sadie

"...From a dose (of voidtoxin) such as this, animasepsis occurs within minutes, attacking the immune system and interfering with the body's ability to heal. This results in excessive blood loss and considerable pain. Such wounds are difficult to staunch, and death by exsanguination is a risk. Typically, however, the wound stops bleeding once the toxin reaches the inner theric body and devotes itself to attacking the central theric systems. Hence, in earlier times, "the Executioner's Repose" referred to the moment when an animaseptic wound stopped bleeding; this was because once voidtoxin reaches the inner theric body, its progress is virtually impossible to halt. Once this stage is reached, the patient has between six to twelve hours to live. The only treatment known to save a patient at the inner theric stage of infection is a bolus dose of concentrated holy aspect. However, this alone generally proves fatal, due to the volatility of a holy/void reaction. A human body can rarely sustain that amount of violent trauma and survive."
-*Chirac's Manual of Extraversal Medicine*, Fourth Edition
Verse: Citadel Ivory

Hazel calls it *animasepsis* - it's when your theric body gets poisoned. It's not common, but it's been known to happen. Symptoms depend on what kind of toxin it is. Voidtoxin, or entropotoxin, is rare and usually fatal. Treating it is difficult; doctors who have managed to treat it had to get really inventive. The problem is, we don't have a doctor. Johnny Forsythe would be the first person Hazel would ask, but he's in Cincinnati, taking Hodges to the Seven Towers Conclave.

All we have is an arcanist and a versologist, and all *they've* got are a couple of college girls with a lot of heart and no real knowledge about how to save their friends.

Mary's with Courtney now, side by side in the same bed, dying together from the same horrific poison. It was Hazel's idea to move her next to Courtney so it would be easier to watch them. After all, they're connected somehow - we must assume that what's done to one will affect the other.

Connected. I rub my eyes, squashing a yawn behind my fist. It's been a long night. Before that, it was a long day. Mentally, I'm worlds away from where I was this time yesterday morning, which was worlds away from where I was a week ago.

Nettie and Hazel talk quietly over by the window, discussing arcane formulae or something. Elizabeth lurks outside the door, occasionally casting them a look of disapproval but saying nothing. Hazel's skill with channeling could be the only thing that saves Courtney and Mary. I'm feeling frayed and irritable and I can't tell how much of it is being tired, how much is being scared to death about Courtney, and how much of it is this stupid thing about their connection. As I sit here in the shining quiet of this lovely morning, I must ask myself, honestly - am I angry that I'm not lying beside Courtney, dying with her, instead of Mary? Am I angry that *I'm* not the one with this 'connection?' Maybe I'm just angry that she's finally here and she's still dying. Getting here was supposed to make her safe, not kill her faster. I don't really have what you'd call a temper, but it's all a load of bull and it's making me really darn mad.

Nothing has made sense in days. I seriously doubt anything is gonna start making sense anytime soon, not when I'm this tired.

"No other abjuration formula can be altered to work on an individual, you see. At least none that I know well." Hazel holds a book that looks like a bible some preacher's wife might have, except that it's wrapped in a book cover of sturdy brown canvas. It's worn and frayed, stained with splotches of oil and old blood and lord knows what else; this must be her field grimoire from the war. It's got a few snap-buttons and canvas straps that must have made it easier to carry with the rest of her gear when she was in the trenches. "Most of these are area abjurations, and anyway I think these two are our best bet to start with. Cross of St. Gallen, which is an area abjuration but it's flexible enough for us to adapt; and Shield of Roskilde, which is a personal abjuration designed for a single target."

"None for an individual person? Really?" Nettie asks, puzzled. "Seems like the first thing you'd need if you were fighting Huns."

Hazel's soft gray eyes look distant and glazed this morning; the skin underneath them is starting to sag and turn a sickly color. "Oh, of course, let me clarify: I've plenty of field abjurations in here that you can use on a single target, and I picked up most of them in France. Usually they're kinetic resonance to keep you safe against bullets and shrapnel, or thermophasic in case the Jerries start shelling you with high explosive. Then there's Number 50s, which are a little of both; I've a few of those pre-made. But none of that's gonna do squat against voidtoxin."

"What will?" I sit down on the foot of the bed.

"That's what we're gonna try to find out," Nettie says quietly.

It's such a gorgeous sight, your first time seeing a skilled arcanist go to work. I'll remember this for the rest of my life, even as tired as I am. I just wish it wasn't under such frightful circumstances.

I know what you're thinking - *Hang on, Sadie, how could this be your first time seeing a channeler go to work? Just yesterday, you watched Hazel fight Hodges' goons. Heck, you're arcane yourself, aren't you?* Both of those are true. But first off, being a natural arcane is a whole different kettle of fish; whatever you unleash is spontaneous. You feel the energy building in you, and then you feel what happens when you let go of it. That's it. There's power, sure, but no real sense of wonder. Besides, Hazel and Pearse fought with aspected weapons yesterday, not conjured formulae, so that doesn't count, either. And the one reaction she did use was pre-configured in her staff; it was a simple matter of recalling it and casting it. It simply *happened,* and I'd never have known it went off if not for feeling the surge of power in my bones or hearing Chisel Face scream when his arm snapped like a twig in three different places.

But this is different. Hazel holds her staff, shining metallic the color of blood, in her left hand. On her right, she wears a fingerless leather gauntlet laced up the inside with old brown army string. At the tip of her exposed index finger is a shiny silver cap, almost like a thimble. It's so bright and shiny it almost glows white, and I have to squint to look at it.

She plants her staff on the floor and holds it, and I hear a dull roar in my ears - like when you go down the side of a mountain - when she focuses her energy. A perfect glowing circle of dull silver appears around her feet and expands a couple of yards out in all directions. The circle looks almost like a projection of some kind, hovering above the floor, slowly rotating around her ankles. Every move she makes with her index finger appears inside it, becoming part of the slowly spinning projection.

She starts with her finger in the air, pointing left, then dart to the right, left, up, down, up. Five points, quick. As she traces the lines in front of her, they appear in the circle spinning around her ankles and form a strange glimmering geometric design, a bit like a maltese cross. The whole display turns brighter each time her finger touches the "edge" of the circle, so that by the end it's as bright as the sunlight on the floor around it. After a moment of letting the reaction build, she holds her hand out, palm up, and lifts the circle into the air. With a little flick of her hand, the projected circle spins and shrinks, appearing on her chrome fingertip, where it gets brighter. Then she reaches forward, pointing it at Courtney. Some blurry light floats just off the tip of that finger, like when your eyes are watery and you can't focus. She moves it down over Courtney's chest, then makes a quick stirring motion with her finger.

A dull *thud* noise in my head. Suddenly the room is clear and normal again, and it's only now I realize there was a kind of high-pitched...*singing,* almost, all around; a pleasant tingly feeling in my chest, like cool air on a spring morning. But now that it's gone, everything feels dull and flat and there's a bland taste in my mouth.

Courtney cringes and whimpers in her sleep, rolling her head over and burying her face in Mary's shoulder. Oh, it hurts me so, watching her suffer. I go to her, awkwardly putting my hand on her ankle. She calms almost as soon as I touch her; how much is she aware of?

Hazel watches Courtney and Mary carefully. "Nettie? The therascope - any change?"

Nettie squints through the funny little brass tube, rotating the end, focusing on Courtney's injury. Then her face drops in surprise. "Why...yes! I believe so. Looks like...five percent reduction in voidtoxin mass."

Hazel gives her a crestfallen look. "Only *five percent?!* Hell, that was a caliber six reaction!"

"What does that mean?" I ask.

"It means it's the most powerful version of that formula we can cast." Elizabeth leans on the doorway. "Am I right in assuming that's what you are, Hazel? Caliber six?"

"Yes," Hazel sounds a little defeated. "I've got two, maybe three more of those in me before I pass out. I might be able to get a fourth one if I drain all my charge crystals, but I doubt it."

"An arcanist can't cast a reaction more powerful than their own caliber, you see," Elizabeth tells me. "And it's never wise to push your limits too much. Otherwise, you can suffer brain damage or even stop your own heart."

"What about me?" Nettie volunteers. "Could I try?"

"Nettie, you've barely reached caliber one," Elizabeth replies. "Trying to push that reaction any higher could kill you."

"Well, we must do *something!*" she protests, casting a watery glance at Mary. "We're running out of time!"

"I can still try a Bastion of Roskilde, just to see," Hazel assures her quietly, but her face is heavy with doubt. "I'll try caliber three as a test. You can observe and tell me if you see any change."

"All right." Nettie sounds dubious.

Hazel places her staff on the floor and, once again, a floating circle expands around her ankles. She sketches a slightly different design this time, six points, and the reaction feels solid in my teeth when she lets it go. It fastens right into Courtney and is gone as soon as it's cast. Nettie peeks through the scope again, giving them a good, long look.

"That bad, huh?" Hazel asks after a moment.

"No change..." Nettie protests. "But why?"

"It was a long shot, anyhow," Hazel sits heavily on the windowsill. "Roskilde is more of a combat shield or a protection against injury."

"B-but...hey, last time...Mary responded point zero five percent better to St. Gallen than Courtney did. What if we tried it directly on her? Sort of...sent the energy the other way?"

Hazel shakes her head, staring at the floor. "Point zero five is barely anything. And casting it with Mary as a target will just insulate the effect. It's as if you hit Mary with a mallet and tried to knock Courtney off the bed. Courtney's the conduit, probably since she's the one with the wound."

"But we can't-"

"Nettie," Elizabeth says gently, stepping into the room. "It's a dead end. Please, let the woman think."

It's quiet in here. Birds chirp and flutter outside the window.

An idea drops into my head like a coin hitting the floor.

"Say, Hazel," I begin. "Didn't you say earlier that each formula has a, um..." I snap my fingers. "An element? An...axis of some kind?"

She rubs her eye. "Yes, that's right. A resonance axis, the primary element in any formula."

"And what elements were in the first one? The...cross one?"

"Cross of St. Gallen?" She glances at the ceiling in thought. "Cryo, subkinetic, and a bit of holy."

"And the second one?" I press.

"Roskilde is two thirds kinetic, one third electromagnetic."

"So, does that mean Courtney responded to something in the first reaction that was absent in the second?"

Some pep returns to Hazel's face. "Perhaps cryo or holy. And since voidtoxin isn't native to physical space and doesn't have physical properties, I'm gonna go out on a limb and guess that it wouldn't respond to cryo. So that just leaves-"

"Holy," Nettie finishes. "It's one of the only known extraphysical elements. There's using the old bean, Sadie! We try a formula with a holy resonance. Have you any of those?"

Hazel winces. "I'm afraid not. Holy-based formulae haven't been in common use since the mid-18th century, and I'm afraid I don't know any except St. Gallen."

"Have you any at home?" I ask. "In your library?"

She shakes her head. "Most of my books are on theory or artifact lore. I'd need to go back a few hundred years, and we'd have to visit the library in Cincinnati for that."

Mary catches a little breath, moans miserably in her sleep.

"So there's nothing we can do?" I ask, crushed. "We just sit and watch them fade away?"

"Not necessarily," Hazel replies. "I happen to have an artifact with entirely holy properties, and I have it with me right now."

My hopes soar, and Nettie and I share an open-mouthed look of excitement.

"And the catch?" Elizabeth crosses her arms.

"The catch is that it's the Jewel of Brynnhilde."

Elizabeth shrugs and shakes her head.

"Well, I'm glad not to have you chiding me, Professor," Hazel says wryly. "The Jewel of Brynnhilde is a Viking Age artifact, circa ninth century. Legend states that it belonged to the valkyrie Brynnhilde, and she wore it for centuries. But nobody else has been able to bring the gem to life since she passed away; it simply hasn't responded. Countless people have worn the jewel over the last thousand years and none have awakened its powers." She shrugs. "Most people think it's just a story."

"Sounds apocryphal to me," Elizabeth agrees.

"And to everyone else." Hazel gets up, goes to her bag in the corner. "But readings indicate the presence of dormant holy energy. I think that's what it's made of. And if that's the case, it could at least help us. Maybe it could ward off some of the toxin's worst effects, stabilize them at the very least, give us time to find a cure."

"Could we try?" I ask quickly, standing up. Nettie gives her a fiercely hopeful look.

"I think we've very little left to lose, don't you?" Hazel produces a small, velvet jewelry bag from her knapsack. She plunges her fingers in, produces a sparkling white diamond about the size of a blueberry. It's been made into a pendant, attached to a delicate silver chain. "However, before we try, there are things you should know. There's a small possibility that there might be...consequences." She holds up the jewel, sparkling and lovely in the morning sun, and studies it. "Sadie and Nettie will have to share the decision on Courtney's behalf."

"Consequences?" Elizabeth peers over the wiry rim of her glasses. "I thought you said it was a dead artifact, just a lot of folklore and a few specks of dormant energy."

"I never said it was a dead artifact," Hazel corrects her. "I said that since the original owner passed away, nobody has been able to awaken it."

"You're splitting hairs, Morrison," Elizabeth chides. "If a thousand years of queens and princesses haven't been able to awaken this artifact, it's probably a safe bet that a Displaced college girl from Arc Servant won't be able to, either."

She sighs. "Yes," she says patiently. "But I never said that was my main concern. Please, Prof, let me finish." She leans back against the wall, takes a deep breath. "The most likely scenario is that it simply does nothing. But there's a small risk of a reactive blast. Holy and aphotic are opposite elements, you see - the inert holy energy could interact with the voidtoxin and cause a theric explosion. A blast like that could kill her on the spot."

"And Mary with her," Nettie says quietly. "Can we minimize the risk?"

Hazel nods. "I'll avoid touching the toxin directly and hope that her body can insulate her from any possible reaction. Aside from that, she's wearing two different abjurations now, and that should hopefully protect her from the worst."

Courtney and Mary huddle together, pale and bony. Mary's breaths are shallow and infrequent, Courtney's even more so. Courtney's ginger blonde hair spills over her pretty face, and her skin is sallow and gray. Death is on her, approaching quickly.

"Hazel…" I ask quietly. "Just one more thing. In the very worst case scenario, what would happen to Courtney if the jewel…*worked?*"

"Like the sources suggest?" She blinks, clearly not expecting the question. "Well…I believe she might become a vessel for the valkyrie Brynnhilde's essence. What that means, I wish I could say for certain. Some have called that essence "the valkyrie's gift", or referred to being "chosen", and believed that the subject would become a valkyrie like Brynnhilde herself."

"So...a transformation of some kind?"

"According to the saga," Hazel states. "As for myself, I think she might become a natural arcane like you, Sadie; and probably one of great power. But yes, I think it would involve some kind of transformation on the theric level. If she survived, she would probably be bound to the jewel for life. But again, I can only guess. We've nothing more concrete than some old medieval legends, I'm afraid."

Nettie and I share a long look. "And Mary?" I ask.

"Why, I doubt it would affect her one way or another," Hazel says. "Unless it killed Courtney. Then we'd probably lose them both."

Silence. A motor car goes chugging up the street.

"Let's do it," I say decisively. "She hasn't long, and it's the last chance we've got."

Nettie nods slowly at me. "Courtney wouldn't hesitate; she'd want us to try it, and Mary would too." She takes a deep, nervous breath, then looks at Elizabeth. "I agree with Sadie. Let's do it."

Elizabeth takes off her glasses, rubs her eyes. "Well, I won't be the one to tell Marian Carlyle her daughter died because I didn't try every last thing I could." She nods. "Very well. Let's go ahead, then."

Hazel holds the pendant dangling from her fist like one of those murderous ball-and-chains in a fairy tale, and she's got a death-sentence look in her eyes. I don't think she quite believes what she told us about those low odds.

"All right," she says quietly, turning toward the bed. "Here we go."

Courtney slips closer to death every second; she looks worse every time I look at her. They're on their sides, facing each other; Mary's cuddled up in Courtney's chest, whimpering and moaning. Courtney's fists are clenched white, twitching occasionally. Are they completely unconscious, or are they dreaming? What do they see? Whatever it is, I doubt it's pleasant, judging by the suffering etched in their faces. What did my Courtney ever do to deserve suffering like this? What did either of them do?

My own fist clenches. This was no accident; someone did this to them. This voidtoxin stuff is no accident, either - why, Hazel said herself that it doesn't appear in nature. It's pure cruelty and hatred. One madman tried to kill her with a knife, and this filthy poison is the work of some other lunatic.

If Courtney dies...

My eyes burn with tears. If Courtney dies, there will be a reckoning. I will find these disgusting monsters, and I will inflict more suffering on them than they can possibly imagine. And I will savor every drop.

"Sadie? Would you help me move her, please?"

"Oh, sure."

We roll Courtney onto her back, pull her up, and Hazel is careful not to let the jewel touch her. I lift her darling head onto her pillows, then stop to wipe a lock of her beautiful hair off her forehead. Her lips are purple, and the bags under her eyes look like bruises. I don't know what I'll do if this doesn't work, if we can't save her. It seems a silly thing to try and save a girl's life with a diamond instead of rushing her to the hospital, but she was beyond normal aid from the moment she was wounded.

Please. Brynnhilde, or whoever you are. Please be in there. Please help my Courtney. She doesn't deserve to die this way.

Nettie crosses the room, seizes my hand, squeezes it, and stands close to me. I take a deep, nervous breath. Our best friends are dying and all we've got is each other, and all our hopes for saving them are tied up in a piece of medieval jewelry.

Go on, have a weirder day than this. Just try.

Silence fills the room from wall to wall, thick enough to stick a fork in. Hazel stands over them, pendant dangling from her fist, and takes one last deep breath. "Sorry, Courtney. This might hurt, sweetie."

Hazel tenderly lifts Courtney's head and slips the pendant around her neck, holding the jewel above her chest until the last moment. Then she drops it and jumps back a step.

Nothing.

Nettie's fingers begin to shiver in my hand. Hazel watches, fist against her mouth. Elizabeth is behind the door frame; I can't see her.

"Damn it, no," Hazel whispers. "God dammit, you have to do something."

The stupid thing sits there looking pretty, and Courtney pants in short breaths like a dying dog. Hazel pulls out her therascope, lifts it to her eye.

Her eyebrows rise in alarm. "My god! Sa-"

Courtney heaves herself off the bed, back arched. She lingers above the sheets for a long second before she starts twitching like someone getting fried in the electric chair. Like someone being hanged.

"Sadie! Nettie! Hold her down!" Hazel's voice pierces the silence, clear and decisive. It's a completely different voice, and she's a different woman. This is Captain Morrison, and she's back on the Western Front all over again. Her commanding voice dispels fear, fills you with resolve. This is the voice you run to when everyone else is running away, the one that gives you strength when bullets rip the air and shells are raining death all around you. This voice will keep you alive and in one piece, get you back home again.

Nettie and I are moving before we even realize. I'm falling across Courtney, holding the arm closest to the wall, and Nettie's on the other side. It's all we can do to keep her from flying completely off the bed. Elizabeth rushes in, holding her ankles.

Hazel drops her bag by the bed and produces a tiny bottle with lavender-colored liquid in it.

"She's going into cardiac arrest! Her heart's gonna rupture if we don't get this animasedative in her." She pulls a cork stopper off with her teeth and spits it onto the floor. "Sadie! Use your knee to hold her arm. Get her head back and her mouth open."

The decisiveness in her voice helps me climb over my seizing best friend and - somehow - hold her down. I get my hands around her face, hold her mouth open.

"Got it!" My voice is loud and shrill.

Hazel pours the little vial into her mouth. Almost on contact, Courtney begins to calm.

"It's working," Nettie says.

"Not outta the woods yet, girls," Hazel reminds us. "Talk to me - how's the wound look?"

I turn Courtney's arm; the cut is bright and hot like it's on fire underneath the skin. "Red like cherry candy, glowing hot. And her fever's picked up, too!"

"Mary's too," Nettie says over the tussle. "The mark was black a minute ago, but now it looks like red ink."

"Good," Hazel replies. "Keep holding them! As soon as Courtney calms down, we-"

But Courtney's already stopped. One moment she's bobbing up and down like someone holding a live wire, and the next she's perfectly still.

I look over. "Um, Hazel?"

She leans over. "Sadie! Check her pulse!"

Horrified, I scramble to do as she says. I get my finger on the dip in her neck, feel around. I can't find a pulse.

"I don't understand, I can't-"

Hazel crowds in, leaning across Nettie, presses two fingers to Courtney's throat. "Damn it!! Girls, get back."

Numbly, I back up and climb off the foot of the bed. Dull fear crawls across my scalp. Courtney isn't breathing.

Hazel stretches her arms, flexes her fingers, then weaves her hands, one around another, in a series of strange gestures. She traces short designs in the air, then taps the side of her fist against her staff. Every time her gauntlet touches the metal, it makes a queer little sparking sound. My hair stands on end, too, like static electricity on a cold day. Then she pulls something from the air, weaves it around her hand, and touches the middle of Courtney's chest with her fist.

Courtney seizes again, just once, back arching off the bed, then flops down. Mary, lying next to her and barely breathing, moves in a slow, languid mockery of Courtney. Hazel must be using electricity to shock Courtney's heart somehow.

"Come on, honey, *come on!*" Again with the rapid-fire hand gestures, an even longer pull, then an electrified fist to Courtney's chest. She seizes even higher off the bed, then flops onto the mattress. Hazel pushes the fingers of her bare left hand into Courtney's throat, desperately searching for a pulse. After a moment, Hazel stumbles back, staff clattering out of her hands. Her face shocked and horrified, like she's been shot. She falls back against the wall, crumples to the floor.

Elizabeth slowly, reluctantly, lets go of Courtney's ankles. Her lip trembles, eyes filling up.

And Courtney is still. She lays on her side, eyes closed, her pretty hair spilling over her face and across the white sheets. Seeing her there on the bed, my heart feels like it's being wrung out like a wet rag. I stumble toward her, my legs moving on their own. She's still, but not peaceful. Suffering twists her features, and her eyebrows are suspended above her lovely face in a pleading expression.

Nettie looks at me, eyes wild. "What else are we missing? What else haven't we tried?"

I stumble to the bed, reach out, touch Courtney's soft cheeks. She's so still. My angel, my best friend. Just a little while ago, her eyes sparkled with life and wit and laughter. And now she's still. No breath, no life.

I jerk my hand away like I just touched a hot stove. This is all wrong. So terribly wrong.

This can't be happening.

She can't be...

My face twists into an ugly grimace, and I scream. It's long and feral and bloodcurdling, and tears go spilling out of my eyes.

No.

Another scream, and I leap onto her. I know what I must do, even if it kills me.

"Sadie..." Elizabeth's voice is no more than a quavering whisper. "Please. She's gone."

But I'm not hearing it. I touch both hands to Courtney's chest and close my eyes. Immediately, a dark void opens in my mind and I'm completely focused. I'm able to channel energy through my arms and into her body.

"Sadie?" Hazel's voice, very quiet. Then she turns frantic. "Sadie, *no!*"

My essence glows white, surging out of me and into her. In this dark place, I can see things I couldn't before. Courtney's motionless body. Her mortally wounded anima, lying still.

That horrific wound, clean and empty of toxin. That pendant at her throat, dull like the first gray light of morning.

The toxin is gone. And next to her, Mary glows a very soft pink, slowly fading. It's now or never.

I sink my hands into Courtney's liquid essence, and it feels like sticking my hands into a sinkful of tepid water. Her energy rises very slightly into my hands, and our essences mingle as I let mine trickle into hers. In my second sight, my energy is a glowing stream of white rivulets trickling toward the middle of her chest. The tiny river winds and curves as it makes its way through her, following pathways I can't see. Finally, it reaches her heart.

And explodes in blinding white light.

Underneath me, Courtney surges up again, just like when Hazel shocked her. But this time, her eyes fly open and she sucks a ragged breath into her lungs. The diamond catches the sunlight, absorbs it, magnifies it, and casts it across the room. The jewel, gray and indifferent moments ago, is as bright as the sun. Her heart starts pounding.

There's a commotion in the room as Hazel and Nettie scramble. I withdraw my anima back into myself, forever mixed with a little bit of Courtney's. My world reels; I'm woozy like I suddenly lost a great deal of blood.

And I'm more relieved than I can possibly say.

Courtney's eyes are even bluer now than they were before, glowing like some sunlit tropical sea, insane with energy and wonder.

"Sadie?" She mumbles. "What th-...am I dead?"

I'm smiling bigger than I ever have in my life. A single tear trickles off my cheek and falls onto hers. "Why, no, dearest. I don't believe you are."

Her face calms, passing through an expression of gratitude before her eyes roll back and she collapses onto the pillow. My fingers gently search her for a pulse; this time it's loud and strong. I slump, resting on her a moment, lightheaded and dizzy and oh, so relieved. Next to me, Mary's face is calm and peaceful again, and a slight rosy hue is returning to her milky cheeks.

"Sadie, I don't-" Nettie talks very quietly as she approaches. "What on Earth did you do?"

"Something really stupid." Hazel speaks quietly, approaching with her staff. "Very stupid and very brave. Sadie offered up her own life to save theirs."

I look at her, trying to stay focused with a woozy head. "But I'm still alive...right?"

She nods slowly, then breaks into tear-streaked laughter. "Yes, you silly girl. Bound to her for life, probably, but alive."

"This is a miracle," Elizabeth breathes.

"Why, yes, Professor," Hazel agrees, looking at me with something almost like rapture. "That's exactly what it is, but I think it's even more than that."

"What do you mean?" Nettie asks.

Hazel dabs her eyes with a handkerchief. "If the sagas are anything to go by, you must realize the essence of the valkyrie Brynnhilde isn't a bandage." Her smile has faded somewhat. "It's a partnership."

Elizabeth massages her forehead. "This is precisely what I meant when I asked if there was a catch, Hazel."

"I'm only just now remembering the full text, myself." Hazel wearily slumps onto the windowsill. "When the diamond got really bright, that's what jogged my memory. There's a poetic verse in *Eddas of the Folkvangr Valkyrja*, and it seems to point to some sort of...*contract*. Some quest or charge willingly taken."

"Why, that's a hell of a detail to overlook," Elizabeth says bluntly. "What kind of quest or contract are we talking, here? Is the girl going to have to ride off to slay the World Serpent or some other such nonsense?"

Hazel smiles wearily and shakes her head. "No, Prof, I don't think so. But I do believe she will be driven by this woman's influence, and while I'm fairly sure Brynnhilde was good and honorable and all that, I've no idea what her actual personality was like."

I rub my eyes. Lordy, I'm tired. "So, are you saying she could make Courtney a different person? Like, really mean or something?"

"I don't think so, honey," Hazel replies, leaning her head on the window frame. "In the Eddas, it said that Brynnhilde would 'flare once again to brilliant life' at the 'first sound of the battle-horn.' I'm fairly certain Courtney will be herself unless someone's foolish enough to attack her, or more importantly, any of you. That's when I believe Courtney might be in real danger."

"Then we must endeavor to keep the girl away from battle-horns and any other kind of horn that might wake up your..." Elizabeth makes a flippant gesture in the air as she searches for a word. "Shield-maiden or war-maiden or what have you."

"We should certainly keep an eye on her," Hazel says gravely. "I've studied that jewel for some time but I never truly thought I'd see it awakened. Courtney will most likely be her old self, but with a great deal more power."

"How much power?" Nettie sounds a little fearful.

"I'll take a look at her with a therascope in a bit," Hazel replies. "Then we'll have a better idea. But a girl your age with that much power is automatically a bull in a china closet. What's in her heart is quite irrelevant, because her youth alone is the most dangerous factor of all."

The room goes quiet, except for the birds outside and the soft ticking of Courtney's bedside clock. This conversation is quite serious, but I feel myself nodding off. Hazel notices.

"Now that you girls have had enough whoopee to last you the entire academic year, it's time for you to rest."

Oh, what wonderful news. I'll just reach in Courtney's bag and help myself to some of her comfy clothes, then curl up next to her. Maybe just take a little nap...

Interlude - An Unbreakable Bond

Hazel

"People always talk about the girls and their high resonance caliber, as if that's what makes or breaks a person when things get dangerous. But it's not. Why, if you could take one of those caliber ten arcanists from the old legends, you'd find that they're nothing on their own. What keeps you alive and gets you through hard times is the bond you share with your friends, and how do you measure the resonance caliber of a bond? You can't. And no crazy old artifact can give you that, either."
-Alice Thatcher, *Memoirs of an Accidental Aspect,* 1927

Time passes differently in Courtney's bedroom. The *lek-lek-lek* of the little clock on the nightstand belongs more to the room than to time itself. The air is quiet, sun-drenched, peaceful. Shimmering trees wave outside the window and sunshine spills over the dark wood floor. Professor Talbott gave her a real gift when she gave her this room, though I think the good professor's got a soft spot for this kid.

Talbott and I stand together near the doorway, looking at the four of them piled on the queen-size bed. Courtney sleeps in underwear and a white tank top she brought with her; ABERCROMBIE is emblazoned across the front in red sparkly letters. Mary sleeps next to her in a short nightgown, facing her; the two almost seem to comfort each other in sleep. Sadie was exhausted after that reckless stunt she pulled, so she simply stripped to her underwear and borrowed one of Courtney's tank tops, something with *PINK Victoria's Secret* written across the front. After putting that on, she curled up behind Courtney, wrapped her arms around her, and promptly fell asleep. Over on the other side of the bed, Nettie lay in a nightgown, head cradled on her arm, next to Mary.

"Just look at them," Elizabeth says in wonder. "Why, I've never seen the like of that in all my days. The way they're together like that, so peaceful, so comfortable. They've such a natural way with each other, don't they?"

"Yes," I agree. "Though I think they have even more than that, now."

She looks at me. "What exactly happened here, Hazel?"

I shake my head wearily. "I wish I could say for certain. As you said, it was a miracle, but...so much more, too. I've seen a lot of things this morning that I didn't even know were possible."

"That makes two of us, I suppose," Elizabeth sighs. "What shall become of Sadie?"

"I suppose only time will tell. My readings show that she's still got ninety-seven percent of her original anima; she only lost a tiny piece in bringing Courtney back, then received some of Courtney's in return. But the two are bound now, inseparably. It could be years and years before we know the full extent of what that means." I lean on my staff. "She could have a sympathetic binding with Courtney, much as Mary has, or so much more. I just don't know."

"And Courtney?" she asks.

I sigh. "Another matter entirely. Sadie's anima transfusion jumpstarted that diamond. It was just a pretty rock, but now it's blazing like the sun. It's been awakened, beyond any doubt."

"And what does that mean for the girl?" Elizabeth presses. "Aside from that business about the contract or what have you."

"She's not the same kid that came through the versal aperture. That girl, the Displaced, died this morning. She was reborn as something else. What that means for her, what it might cost her, I couldn't guess. Though…" I lift my eyebrows, rub the back of my tired neck. "I got a look with the therascope, and it's just as I predicted. Not only is she a Type A, but she's a caliber eight as well."

"Good lord," Elizabeth breathes in amazement. "That is exceptionally rare, isn't it?"

"Rare? Hell, I didn't think it was even *possible*."

"Does she have an aspect?" Elizabeth presses.

I draw a deep breath. "Holy."

Her eyebrows lift in wonder, and she's silent for a moment.

"Isn't that also rare?" she asks slowly.

I nod. "You don't see much holy aspect these days. She's a living relic of another age."

Elizabeth shakes her head in wonder. "My god. What sort of fairy tale is this, Hazel?"

"I wish I knew," I tell her, "so I could make sure these kids get a happy ending."

We're silent for a moment. Courtney's little bedside clock happily marks time in this timeless room.

Elizabeth adjusts her glasses. "I tell you, this just beats all. Something has been at work their whole lives, behind the scenes. They come together as if by fate, acting as one mind, and miracles happen. And now look at them - closer than sisters."

"What happened this morning brought them together, that's for sure," I admit. "They're probably inseparable for life now."

"An unbreakable bond has been forged." Elizabeth nods. "Most young people at least wait until college begins before embarking on these kinds of lifelong relationships."

I smirk. "Well, I suppose I can't scold them. Patience has never been my strong suit, either."

She returns the smirk, regarding me out of the corner of her eye. "That's why you're a bad influence, Morrison. And you're barely any older than they are, which makes you a worse influence still."

"Why, Professor, what frightful slander!" I place a hand on my chest. "I'm a paragon of feminine virtue, the very best role model for decent young ladies."

She rolls her eyes. "Uh-huh. I see that going off to fight the Hun has not cured your strange delusions. Come along, you lunatic, and let these girls sleep in peace."

Professor Talbott is one difficult woman to argue with.

I stop at the front door, turn, and look at her.

"Now, are you sure you wouldn't like me to stay and watch the girls with you? Those rotten cowards could come calling any time-"

"And I told you to get yourself home and get some sleep, Hazel Morrison." Elizabeth smiles wryly. "I remember a very young Braddock senior who bit off more classes than she could chew. She would wade heroically into her assignments and very bravely fall dead asleep in the library."

"That was one time, Prof," I remind her with a roll of my eyes. "Okay, twice."

She smirks; her sharp grin reminds me of Nettie. "When those girls wake up, they're going to need you. Lord knows I won't be able to give them the answers or guidance they need. Even the great Captain 'Bloodstaff' Morrison, Conqueror of Soissons, still needs rest every once in a while. You're no use to anybody if you collapse from exhaustion."

"But what if they *do* come around?" I can't help but ask.

She picks up a double-barreled shotgun from beside the door, holds it in both hands. With her round, wire-framed lenses and long brown calico dress, she looks like some frontier school marm getting ready for an Apache raid. "Then that spineless insect Kluivert can come back and clean what's left of them off my porch."

I grin. Her eyes are hard and gray like concrete - I don't doubt her for an instant.

"All right, well, I did leave an extra caliber six Cross of St. Gallen on Courtney's bedroom; I seriously doubt any of them are getting through that. I also put a Number 50 shield on Courtney's door and another Number 50 here on the front door, just have Nettie activate them-"

"Yes, Hazel, I know," she assures me. "And don't worry. If they come up and start attacking my house, I'll just telephone the police. They'll have an awfully hard time explaining why they're trying to kidnap a college girl. They'll be dragged off to jail or the asylum."

I nod and sigh. "Right, of course. Well, just...call me up right away if you need me, all right?"

"Yes, Hazel, yes! Go get some sleep. You've put the freshmen to bed and now it's your turn! Now shoo!"

"Okay, okay." I turn and look at her on the way out. "Thank you, Professor. For taking care of Courtney."

"Of course." Her face softens. "I always suspected I might be taking that girl in someday, so this has always been her home as far as I'm concerned."

Too bad not everyone sees it that way. And too bad it takes more than a few Number 50s to make someone leave well enough alone.

I should have laid myself right down on that couch and told Elizabeth Talbott that if she didn't like it, she could just go chase herself, because I wasn't gonna let those girls out of my sight.

Hindsight is all about "should have."

Interlude - Message From Howgrave

Knights of Augustine, Main Lodge
Autumn Grove, Ohio.

Friday, September 9, 1921.
2:31 AM.

Awoke at 2:23 a.m.; found Eastwicke lurking in the hallway in the dark. Challenge; password given. Asked him why he had returned at such an hour; no response. After fifteen or twenty seconds of silence, Eastwicke said the following: "Get rid of the girl. Reverend Howgrave is watching. He is aware of all that transpires. If the girl is allowed to remain within the town, Reverend Howgrave shall bring the gospel of Silence to Autumn Grove. You have one day."

I asked Eastwicke where Pearse had gone, where the information had come from; he did not respond. He soon turned and left the way he had come, closing the door behind him. I confess to being deeply unsettled. When I gathered my effects and went to follow him moments later, he was gone as if he had never been there at all.

Recommend immediate search for Eastwicke and Pearse as soon as daylight permits. As for "the girl", if he refers to the Displaced, it is not our task to do the bidding of Howgrave or anyone else, or trifle with Displaced persons or other such trivialities. The Knights are not an errand service.

What this message portends, I could not guess. If the Blackstead Anomaly - using the name of the seventeenth century Puritan fanatic Howgrave - has awakened, it is certainly beyond the power of the Knights of Augustine to challenge. Contingencies must be sought, up to and including abandoning this verse.

Personal note: If Reginald Kluivert decides to act based on this information, he shall do so without my assistance. I should sooner surrender myself to the Seven Towers Conclave than to assist in any further meddling - we have done quite enough damage already. Now is the time to deliver healing to those innocent souls harmed by the ignorance and brutality of our brethren, and to beg their forgiveness. The mere fact that Howgrave seeks this young woman's capture is proof enough of her innocence.

D. Melville, Chamberlain of the Hall.

Five

Friday
September 9, 1921
11:29 a.m.

Courtney

"The modern age of arcanology might look very different - or might never have begun at all - if the Middle Ages had not come to the rescue one sunny morning September of 1921."
- Edith Winthrop, *Flapper Sorcery: American Arcanology in the 1920s*

"What do you do when the treatment is as deadly as the disease? Well, you sleep it off and then get up and play video games, I reckon."
-Helen Cooksey, letter to Alice Thatcher, 1923

It's morning.

The sun is warm on the sheets, and a wire fan is blowing a lovely breeze in my face - almost too cool. It flaps the curtains, smells like clean laundry and sunshine. I squint and shade my eyes with the back of my hand while my aching pupils get used to the light. When I can finally open them, the first thing I see is the mahogany wood floor glowing in the sunshine.

I'm wearing a short white nightgown, trimmed with lace around the bodice and shoulders. The nightgown - or maybe it's a slip - is really delicate and feminine. I'm in the same cozy bed I remember, a big queen-size bed next to the wall.

1921. It wasn't a dream.

Thank goodness.

My head is a soup of memory fragments: agony, love, tears. So freaking much has happened to me, and I have a hard time making any sense of it.

As my fingers explore the silky lace on the shoulder straps, I notice a fine silver chain around my neck. A beautiful diamond dangles from it, about the size of a blueberry. When I take it in my fingers and look at it, it catches the sunlight and throws it back on the surrounding walls in a dazzling, twirling panorama. Thousands of tiny lights spread across the room, sparkling and dancing with every little move I make. The display is deep and expansive, vast as the night sky; when you gaze into it, it feels like staring out into space. And the gem is twice as bright as the sun coming through the window, almost shining with a light of its own. Watching the countless lights dancing across the room is making me dizzy, so I close my eyes, lean back against the headboard. I ground myself, then open them again.

Doing my best to avoid looking at the telescopic display on the wall, I take one last look at the gem. It's cut beautifully, the outside covered in countless facets. It's definitely the most valuable thing I've ever touched; it's the kind of rich girl jewelry you see ads for in *Vogue*. This thing has to be insanely expensive. So why am *I* wearing it?

It's mounted in a slender setting of dark silver, solid and heavy as iron, but way more elegant. And the whole piece has this dense solidity to it. It weighs as much as any other piece of jewelry, but just below the surface of my awareness, it feels heavy. *Really* heavy. As I lay here in bed in the sunlight, gazing at this gorgeous diamond, I feel lighter and happier than I can ever remember.

"Well good morning, shell shock!"

I startle. That sounds like-

"...Sadie?"

She's grinning at me from a chair by the window, sitting on crossed legs, wearing my Victoria's Secret tank top. She's got my cherry red Game Boy SP in her hands and my white earbuds in her ears. A huge grin splits my face at the sight of her.

"Oh, golly." She looks embarrassed as she pulls the earbuds out. She bites a lip and glances at the tank top she's wearing. "I hope you don't mind me borrowing your stuff."

I'm beaming at her; I don't think I've ever been this happy. "Are you *kidding?* Sweetie, what's mine is yours; you don't even have to ask. It looks awesome on you, by the way."

Her face fills with warm happiness again. She's off the chair and flopping onto my bed in one move. "Gosh, Courtney, you're a doll. Thanks a bunch." She scoots closer.

"You can always use my stuff. Always. You're my Ride or Die." I smirk, hold out my fist.

She tilts her head. "Ride or Die?"

"Yeah, like, ya know. My girl, the one I trust. No matter what comes at us, we face it together, side by side. Always."

Before, when I was lying here sick, I thought about everything Sadie had done for me. There's a lot I decided to tell her. I just hoped it wouldn't be too forward. I guess we'll find out.

My smirk relaxes into a smile. "My bestie. Best friend, I mean. I hope that's not too, ya know. Forward, or whatever."

She beams at me. "Why, of course we're best friends, you little nut! Right from the start! And I like the other thing you said...Ride or Die?"

I grin. "Ride or Die."

She holds her fist next to mine. I tap hers on top, and she awkwardly reciprocates. We share a grin. I should've known better than to doubt Sadie.

"What are you playing?" I ask, nodding at the Game Boy.

"Oh, um..." She flips it upside down. "Zelda?"

"Oh, *A Link to the Past!* Best game *ever?*"

"I don't really understand what's happening," she confides. "When the screen came on, I chose 'continue' instead of 'new game' and just started playing around. I still don't really know how to play, and I think I'm kind of a poor fish at it."

"You'll pick it up," I assure her. "Playing my save was a good choice - I just started it not too long ago. Maybe you can beat the second dungeon for me. It's pretty easy."

"Oh...why, I can certainly try. Maybe you could show me."

"Yeah, definitely! Whenever you want."

She scoots closer, her face lighting up. "Oh, I am *so* awfully glad to see you awake. How are you feeling?"

That's a good question - I'm not really sure. Euphorically happy, to start with. The colors here in this room are the brightest, most saturated colors I've ever seen. The mahogany floor glows a rich reddish brown, and the leaves sparkling outside the window bleed bright emerald. Come to think of it, wasn't it this way before, when I phased over at lunchtime with Sadie? And it's not just the colors. It's knowing that I'm here on this quiet beautiful morning in 1921. It's real. It actually happened.

I'm with Sadie, too. It looks like all the hurt and suffering and heartache wasn't for nothing. I made it. I'm really here.

But aside from being happy, I feel...*different*. I'm coursing with new life, from the inside out. And somehow I'm getting the sense that that's not just a metaphor. I feel like me, but...*more*, too. A little cuter, a little happier, a little more pep. Wait... "pep?" I've never used that word in my life. Maybe I picked it up from one of the girls. But under all that, there's something...*brilliant* inside me. It's like a bright, white-gold light. I seriously feel like I could get up and run a mile, despite the fact that I'm not fully a hundred percent.

Oh, yeah...that god-awful terrible wound. I look for the horrendously painful cut on my shoulder...and it's not there. I look hard, running my fingers across my shoulder, and finally find the tiny hairline scar where it was. Wait, *tiny hairline scar?!* That thing was *huge!* How the hell did it not leave some jagged mark down my arm? And if this thing has already healed and scarred, then I must have been out for a *long* time.

"I-I'm not sure," I tell her. "Wait, how long was I out?"

"Why, you slept the better part of two days. But you sure needed it, poor darling, after all you've been through."

"Two days..." No gouge like mine could possibly heal in two days. "I thought for sure it was more like, I dunno, two *weeks.*"

"Nah. Hazel said that when you woke up you'd be full of pep and you'd be climbing over yourself to get out of bed. But she made me swear not to let you until she's made sure you took the integration okay."

"Wait, the *integration?*" I blink. "That sounds...scary."

"Oh, right, I was asking." She leans in. "How are you feeling?"

"Oh, um...kinda like...a different person? But still kinda me? If that makes any sense?"

Her eyes sparkle. "That's probably because you are. Different, I mean."

"How?"

"You've been through a lot. I guess we both have." She shuts the Game Boy. She's gotten awfully comfortable with the tech I brought along, and for some reason I find that incredibly endearing. "You said you felt like a different person? Well, that might be because...you're part *me* now."

"Wait, huh?"

"Hoo, boy." She squints one eye, scratches her head. "Maybe I should telephone Hazel, make her explain it."

I shake my head, stop her with a reaching hand. "Oh no, you speak my language; you're doing great. I just...help me understand what you mean."

"Okay. Well, you see, you...died." She winces.

I blink. "I *died.*"

"I'm afraid so. I don't understand it either, but your heart stopped and you weren't breathing."

Her words are working deep within me. I don't quite remember what she's talking about, but I think I'm close. A vague memory of deep, horrendous pain like a huge frozen stone in my chest, stabbing knives in my lungs. I guess it's not the weirdest thing in the world; sometimes people die in the emergency room or in the ICU and get resuscitated. But I've got the creeping suspicion that this isn't the same at all. I mean, come on. Why would anything *ever* be normal? I feel like Vermeer ate a bubble gum pouch full of LSD, watched *Lord of the Rings* with a soundtrack done by Nine Inch Nails, and I'm living in the painting he made right afterwards.

"In order to cure the voidtoxin - the horrible black stuff in your wound that was killing you - Hazel gave you some old Viking diamond or something." She points to my chest. "That one."

I look down at it, shimmering beautifully in the morning sunshine.

"It killed the toxin, but in the process it killed you, too. She said there was sort of an explosion, and...it was too much for your body to take, and you died right there on the bed. I watched the whole thing." She swallows. "Oh, Courtney, it was *terrible*. I didn't handle it well."

A memory of a spear going through my heart, the worst pain I've ever felt. Was that the same thing?

I feel an emotional ache creeping into my eyes, and I reach out and take her hand. "What happened?"

"I...don't know. I don't know what came over me, but I was taken by a sudden need to pour some part of myself into you. Hazel called it an 'anima transfusion' and said that it was stupid and it could have killed me. But it didn't." She smiles. "It only took a small piece of my life force - or whatever they call it - to get your heart beating again."

A dim memory, tunnelvision. Out of nowhere, I woke up with pain like a steel pipe through my chest, and Sadie was sitting on top of me. I remember she was crying for some reason, a single tear dropping onto my face. But she was smiling. And then...nothing. The next thing I know, I'm right here, waking up.

Someone called her "the Arbalest." I heard it, clear as day. Or did I make that up? I can't even tell what really happened.

"You mean you-" I pause and look at her, stricken. "You...gave up some part of yourself for *me?!*"

Her eyes grow soft and sad. "I don't miss it. I feel just fine. Why, I'd have given everything if it meant keeping you alive."

Nobody has ever said anything like this to me. Nobody has ever *done* anything like this for me. I want to cry and smack her and hug her and kiss her and hold her close for hours, all at once.

"Why, Sadie?" I ask quietly, a little accusingly. "Why would you do that?"

She gazes into my face. "Do you really need to ask?"

And in that moment of silence, my stomach flips like a roller coaster.

"Besides," she smirks. "It wasn't a complete loss. Hazel says I made off with part of *your* anima too. Though she still isn't sure how much."

I blink stupidly. Then I start laughing.

"Okay," I say, finally. "I think I can live with that."

"She says we're 'bound for life' now. Something about a 'blood entanglement' or some such thing. Whatever I did seems to have made us closer somehow, and the process is irreversible."

Aaaah. Now I get what she meant by "you're part me." That's kinda badass. I sit up in bed, lifted by enthusiasm.

"Well, that sounds pretty awesome, actually. I can *totally* live with being part New York hottie."

A red flush creeps up her cheeks, and she giggles.

"And yeah," I tell her. "I *do* feel closer to you. I already felt like we had a freaky amount of chemistry, but now we're like...solid, you know? And really, really close. Like we're not one person, exactly, but we're kinda *partly* one person? And we've got this..."

"Synergy. Yeah." She smiles softly at me, and her eyes twinkle. She's so pretty. I look down; I'm still holding her hand. It's soft and delicate, exactly the size of mine. Her glance falls to the bed and she blushes a little. But she doesn't pull away.

"You should see yourself, Courtney," she says quietly. "I've always thought you were awful pretty, but now you're...*radiant*."

I wonder what she means, and I wonder what I'll see when I look in the mirror. I'm half curious, half scared. But I'm also frozen in place by her breathless words, her pretty candy-red lips. Was I right, back in my old universe? Did she actually find me attractive? I thought I was just being stupid.

But we're a long way from simple affection or attraction. Her slender blue eyes are heavy with love and conviction. Lifelong certainty. Marriage vows are sworn on whatever is between us right now, the kinds of marriages that don't end.

I always thought fate was a silly concept, but now I'm starting to believe. Everything that led me here has been too eerie. Sadie immediately became my best friend, and when I was banished she fought like crazy to get me back. She gave part of herself to save me. And now I'm only in 1921 - I'm only *alive* - because of her.

If I admitted to myself how I feel about her right now, it would show up on my face like newsprint. All the blood would rush to my brain, my cheeks would turn scarlet red, my pupils would flash and dilate and I'd get a cornered look in my eyes. It would all be too intense and my gaze would skitter onto the floor, which would be like taking a red marker and writing PLEASE ASK ME OUT on my forehead. Or I would look up at her, meet her eyes, and some mysterious force would take over and I'd become an NPC in my own life, and then everything would happen all by itself.

I close my eyes, take a deep breath. Zen. *Get a hold of yourself, Courtney.*

A knock on the door frame makes us both jump, and our hands fly back like rubber bands.

"I hope I'm not interrupting," Mary says softly, half-hiding behind the door frame with an uneasy look on her face that says *I'm* totally *interrupting*. The door has been open this whole time, and my mind frantically scans the last few minutes of conversation, hoping I didn't say something I'd have rather kept private.

Our voices - mine and Sadie's - roll over each other. "God, no, come in!"

I feel like I've been doused in kerosene and set on fire as Mary makes her way in; everything's burning all over. I hope I don't look like the street urchin caught in a stranger's kitchen with food everywhere. Mary looks lovely this morning; her soft round face glows from lots of rest. She's wearing a little white shift like mine, and she comes and sits on the bed with me and Sadie. Once she's on the bed with us, all her awkwardness evaporates and she smiles happily.

"I was just telling Courtney about some of what happened, what we had to do to save her."

Mary folds her legs under her and glances at me for the first time. Her lips fall open a little bit; they're soft and red and delicious like cherry gum. She gives me a really vulnerable, doe-in-the-headlights look with those big, round pupils of hers. A warm, rosy blush rises into her milky white cheeks. She suddenly catches herself, shaking off whatever headspace she was in, and looks at Sadie.

"I still don't believe it myself," she says. "I thought things couldn't get any weirder, what with all the versology stuff and Courtney being banished out of existence. Then all I remember is talking to you and Nettie and Miss Morrison, and all at once I started getting frightfully hot. Then weak. I thought I might be coming down with the flu or getting a heat stroke, but then everything blanked out." She stares at the bed, pondering. "I seem to remember lying in bed, hot and sweaty and having the most frightful dreams."

"We put you here in bed with Courtney, to monitor you," Sadie says.

"Oh," Mary says, looking at me, then looking away. "I think I partly remember that. I wasn't sure if it was real." She absently touches the square red Game Boy, spins it around on the sheets.

"Yeah, you totally can't make this stuff up," I agree.

"Just to make an index," Sadie starts counting on her fingers. "Courtney doesn't belong in one reality, so she phases over here on accident, then gets kicked back out again by some goons." She flicks a second finger. "Hazel is a wizardess, and apparently I am too. We have a wizard battle with those goons when they come to my house." Another finger. "We use a telescope that can see into other realities to guide Courtney out to some scary woods, but she gets attacked on the way, then almost gets killed by corpses in the forest." Four fingers. "A nasty black poison from in between realities gets in her wound like a leech and sucks out her life - and makes *you* sick, Mary. That is, until we cure it with a thousand-year-old magical diamond, which kills her too, but then I bring her back from the dead by giving her part of my life force." A thumb. "And apparently now she's part...valkyrie. And part Sadie. And you two have always been half-each other, which is why you got sick at the same time. Did I miss anything?"

Mary ponders. "I think that pretty much sums it up, don't you?"

I squeeze my eyes shut, rub my temples. "Alright, so besides the fact that I haven't hit enough acid this morning for that to even *begin* to make sense, there's also the part where I didn't actually know half of that."

They both look at me, a little shocked. Even Mary, who seems like she's doing her best to avoid looking at me this morning. Maybe she's pissed at me for some reason.

"Which part?" Sadie asks.

"Uh, well, there's the part where I was stabbed, for one thing." I squint. "I *so* do not remember that, by the way. Is that how I got *that?*" I point at where the wound was.

They share a look.

"Why, yeah," Sadie says. "Apparently the voidtoxin, too."

"Who attacked me?"

"Oh. Him." Mary looks revolted. "Some fella that had it out for you," Mary says. "Someone that knew an old girlfriend of yours?"

Derek. Who else?

I roll my eyes. "Of course it was - so freakin obvious. I'm so glad I never slept with her. But anyway," I look at Mary. "I got *you* sick, too?"

Sadie breaks in. "No, no. *You* didn't get her sick, Courtney. Hazel called it a 'sympathetic affliction' or something. Anything that happens to one of you on the theric level happens to both of you."

"Oh, I didn't know that," Mary says quietly. "That must have been why I had that horrible pain in the middle of the night." She rubs her arm.

"Wait, you felt me get stabbed?" I ask. "Cut, whatever."

"I think so," she says softly. "I had a mark on me all morning, right where your wound was, and I must have passed out when you did."

"Ohhhhh." It all makes sense now. All this happened to her because of me. Talk about unfair. "I'm *so* sorry, Mary. Is that why you're pissed at me or whatever? Cause I totally don't blame you-"

"Wait, huh?" Mary's eyes are big and lovely, the color of cocoa in the sunshine. "I'm not..."

Sadie smiles mischievously, pats Mary's knee. "It's jake, Mary. But what I wanna know is," she gestures between us. "How did you two end up with this connection?"

We look at each other, wide-eyed and baffled.

Mary shrugs a little. "Why, I guess we've always been-"

A sudden pounding at the door booms through the house. We jump.

"That doesn't sound good." Mary looks out into the hall.

Sadie glances at me. "It's probably not."

Oh, *shit*. Those old fund-raising LARP douchebags - I'd totally forgotten about them. Hazel said she arrested that tool with the monocle thing on his eye, but what about the other two - the wrinkled sack of lung cancer and the meathead? Could they have run back to the Benevolent Order of Assless Chaps and gotten more of their creepy friends? They totally knew where I'd be and when I'd be there, which is a lot more than *I* knew. If it was that easy to stalk me once, they could definitely do it again. And if they wanted me gone before, they're gonna be *SO* pissed now that I'm back here with this Viking Bling of Resurrection.

But I feel a little safer now. Remember how I told you that this diamond felt heavy somehow? Something tells me they aren't just gonna banish me like that again. They can't. They have no idea what they're up against, and they're seriously about to get their asses handed to them. I have no idea how I know that - I just do. These guys are about to get owned.

I'm gonna end this bullshit, once and for all. Nobody's gonna mess with me or my friends ever again.

I narrow my eyes and smirk. "Let's get dressed."

Six

Courtney

"If Reginald Kluivert had been flexible and adaptable enough to rid himself of the superstitions of his native verse and to seek confirmation of Eastwicke's strange report, he might have discovered enough self-control to avoid a confrontation in September of 1921. Not only did Kluivert fail to respect his chosen opponents, but his attack on their home also strengthened their resolve and created enemies where none had existed a month before. However, his true blunders were his disregard for gathering reliable intelligence (which might have alerted him to the presence of the remanifested valkyrie Brynnhilde) and a disastrous underestimation of his adversary, Captain Hazel Morrison."

-J.M. Devon, *Taming the Frontier: The Decline of Rogue Circles in America 1900-1945*

Mary wants to go downstairs first, in case it's them at the door; they don't know her yet.

She's got a point, even though I hate the thought of any of my friends getting in their crosshairs, Mary especially. I desperately hope that psycho rapist or that old gnarled pervert aren't down there. I will fucking lose it.

Mary runs off to get some clothes while Sadie and I plunder my backpack for quick outfits. Soon I'm back in jean shorts, Chucks, and an Abercrombie t-shirt. Sadie grabs jean shorts, my dark purple Chucks - yeah, I have two pairs and I brought them both - and my Ataris t-shirt. My stuff fits her every bit as well as it does me. I stop to give her a quick look.

She slouches a little, looks embarrassed. "Gee, I bet I look dumb-"

I raise my eyebrows. "Are you kidding?! You look *hot* in my stuff! Honestly, girl, is there *nothing* you can't rock?"

Her embarrassment turns into a flush of pleasure.

Mary comes down the hallway in a plain short-sleeved summer dress. She gives me and Sadie an uneasy look, and her eyes are hot when they linger on our exposed legs.

"You sure you still wanna go first?" I ask her.

"Oh. Right, yes." And she turns and heads downstairs.

"I could get used to this." Sadie flashes me a wicked little smirk. "I feel like such a naughty vamp."

"It works for you."

Sadie goes back to her corner by the window long enough to pick up two shortswords from the floor next to her chair. The swords are a shiny dark gunmetal gray, and she twirls them like a pro.

"Whoa!" My mouth falls open. "You didn't tell me you had shortswords! Or that you were like a freakin expert with them."

"Oh, these belong to Hazel," she says in an offhanded tone. "She loaned 'em to me the morning we went out to pick you up."

"God," I breathe. "It's gonna take me forever to get caught up."

Rising voices of argument reach us upstairs; whoever is on the front porch isn't happy. The landing at the bottom of the stairs is near the front door, and soon the conversation becomes all too clear.

An older man is talking on the porch. He's got the kind of clear, smooth voice you could imagine from someone on the radio. "Professor Talbott, you know that we respect your pioneering work in versology. But the rules must apply to everyone, regardless of status or accomplishments."

"And who made these rules, exactly?" Elizabeth asks testily, standing in the front door, arms crossed. Nettie stands grimly beside her. "Who decided on them, voted on them, had a say? Because you know who else makes rules and comes around to kidnap young women? Brigands. Bandits, highwaymen, thieves, cutthroats-"

"Please, Professor. Calm down."

Elizabeth's voice goes up a notch. "You come to *my* home *telling me* to give up a young woman in my care, then you *dare* tell *me* to calm down?!"

"We're all trying to be civil here," the man says, his tone placating. "The young woman is dangerous. We've explained this. Give us the Displaced, and we'll be on our way."

"On your way to where?" Elizabeth's tone is scorching. "Are you finally going back to your native verse? What was it...somewhere in Arc Hierophant, correct?"

Silence for a moment. When the old man speaks again, he's quiet and menacing. "You should choose your words more carefully, Professor."

"I have a better idea." Elizabeth reaches down next to the door, seizes a double-barreled shotgun. She breaks it open, checks it; two slugs are loaded in the barrels. She snaps it back together; men murmur and shuffle on the porch. "How about you pack up your circus and leave, Kluivert, before I scatter you all over the street?"

The girls and I share a fearful look. Tension and discomfort crawl up my spine. But deep inside, another feeling begins to rise; a bloodthirsty eagerness I've never felt before. Something in me is saying *let me at these fuckers, and I will break every last one of them in half.* It's totally foreign, like someone else's thought downloaded into my head. I've said things like that before, but I've never felt this kind of intense craving for a fight, this hot, dark taste that's in my throat.

"Now let's all be civilized," the man named Kluivert says. "This isn't Dodge City."

"No," Elizabeth agrees. "You're right. There's law here. Nettie, go telephone the police, would you?"

"I'm afraid that's no use, madam," another man says. He's got a shrill, nasal voice that I find really annoying. "You see, we've already planted obscurations around the perimeter. What goes on here will be quite invisible and inaudible to non-arcane persons."

"Kluivert, you sleazy pimp." Elizabeth's eyes are venomous. "You really are nothing more than a common thug."

Mary has edged into sight of the door and is looking out. A moment of tense quiet, then a scattering of men's voices.

"We'll require *her*, too," Kluivert points. "That one there. She's got some kind of deep connection with that Displaced. We'll need to take her for observation."

Mary's face freezes in alarm. Nettie stands protectively in front of her, her face grim.

"Like hell you will," Elizabeth hisses. She lifts the shotgun. "The first one through this door gets a buckshot facial."

"This needn't turn ugly, Professor," Kluivert continues calmly. "Just give us the girls and we'll be on our way. It's for the greater good."

Something inside me rises and stretches like an athlete that's been in bed for days. There's another awareness in me, almost like another person. She - the other person is definitely a woman - *really* needs to break some heads. I get a sense that war was this chick's whole life for a long time. War and dangerous errands, destroying evil things beyond the abilities of mortals. And she's as jittery and impatient as a hyperactive third grader stuck inside on a rainy day. She's ready.

What the hell happened to me? Who is this chick?

Let go, Courtney, a voice says inside me. *And I'll show you.*

I - no, *we* - look at Mary, huddling next to Nettie. Outside, men talk about scanning for shields and abjurations, and what kind of firepower they'll need to knock a hole in the wall and get her. Mary, who never did anything to anyone.

Sadie and I exchange a grim look. "I'm gonna end this," I tell her.

She nods once. "I'm with you."

I might have worried for Sadie before this morning, but something is different with us now. I *know* she can take care of herself, and I *know* she's ridiculously powerful. With this Viking chick, I know things in a hazy sort of intellectual way, like I know that water is made of hydrogen and oxygen. But with Sadie, I feel things in my bones.

'You're part me, now.' Wow, okay. Whatever, I guess. No time to worry about it now.

The shotgun wasn't the only thing that Elizabeth had next to the door. A black steel pipe, a good three feet long, is propped by the doorway. In an instant, I know that it's what I need. I step off the landing, grab the pipe, and appear in the doorway next to Elizabeth.

The other chick in me takes a single glance, counts ten men. Wow, that's a lot of guys. All of them in suits and ties and vests, wavy hair and round glasses, wingtip shoes and ironed slacks. So this is the Knights of Augustine.

"You want me?!" I throw open the screen door. "You should be careful what you wish for."

Elizabeth hisses my name in alarm as I step onto the porch. An aging man stands in front, maybe early seventies. Sandy brown hair, thinning and combed back really neat, slick with pomade cream. His navy blue necktie is flanked with plain black suspenders, tucked neatly into his trousers. But it's his eyes that catch me. They're the kind of scary, hypnotic eyes you see in old pictures in a psychology textbook, or in one of those traveling carnival acts where the guy calls himself "The Marvelous" and then something ending with an -o. High thick eyebrows, dark pupils, and an intense, commanding stare. He wears round pince-nez glasses with a gold wire rim, and I'm not sure if they humanize him or make him look creepier.

The chick inside my head - or wherever she is - gives me an evil grin. She thinks this is gonna be fun. The words that come out of me are mine, though.

"You know what I can't stand about men?" I ask them, almost casually. "You always shove your way through life, expecting everyone else to move out of the way for you. You get an idea in your head and then you act like you're the only expert there is. You know *so fucking much*, don't you?" My smirk is like a dagger, and it stays out of my eyes. "Well, I know a few things, too. I know for a fact you're not here to protect anyone. Where were you when Mary was dying from voidtoxin? She got it because *I* got it, and *I* only got it because that douchebag with the monocle banished me." I level him with a cold stare. "And yeah, we survived, by the way. Thank you for asking."

Silence. They're all a little stunned, like a comic shop full of guys when you walk in and start talking about Warhammer or something. A totally random thought occurs to me. I look around at this collection of nerdy douchebags - and I don't mean good nerdy, I mean these guys are fucking *dweebs* - and I realize I could take them. Almost instinctively, I feel a rough estimation of their power. It's about average for arcanists, maybe a tiny bit above average if I look at Kluivert. But *I* am something else entirely. I look around inside myself and feel all the ways that I'm a total badass and how I could take all these guys out in like fifteen seconds, and I get the sense that I'm only beginning to scratch the surface. Some immense power rises up out of my inner sight.

Holy shit. I always wanted to be able to protect myself, but I never imagined feeling like *this*.

I look right into Kluivert's scary eyes. "There's just one thing I don't get. I thought gay guys were supposed to be all, like, stylish? Probably just a stereotype, though - I mean-" I laugh. "you guys are totally *not* Will and Grace material. Maybe you're a new thing, like...Queer Eye for the Displaced Girl."

Kluivert snaps out of it, fixes me with a serious look. "You really need to come along with us, Miss."

"*Oh!*" My eyes light up. I turn around and exchange a hilarious look with Sadie. "*Ohh!* Yeah, I've heard that one already. Let's see...there was some meathead rapist, a mummy with lung cancer, and some assclown with a monocle. They banished me - which is kinda like rape, if you think about it. You know, an act of violence against someone who didn't consent?" My smile is fading. "It basically killed me. And all because a bunch of fucktards couldn't take no for an answer."

"And how!" Sadie exclaims.

His expression darkens. "Regardless of these accusations, you must still-"

I cut him off with a hot glare. "I've known *so many men* like you. You're all nothing more than a bunch of old perverts and rapists and cowards, and you're only here to cop some cheap feels, strip us naked, and get your rocks off because no woman on Earth will have anything to do with you. Probably not a lot of guys, either - maybe that's why you're so pissed off."

Sadie cackles. I can almost hear Mary's jaw hitting the floor.

His nostrils flare, big caverns full of nose hairs. Before I know what's happening, he backhands me, hard. Stars explode in my eyes. My nose feels chlorinated, like I got pool water in it, and I taste fresh blood in my mouth. Inside the house, someone gasps.

"Watch your words, you little harlot," Kluivert says dangerously. "You will come along and obey, or else."

Sadie was right. I *am* different. A week ago, my chest would be thick with tears right now, and I'd be seconds away from bawling my eyes out. That trauma is still in me, that raw nerve Kenny left; men yelling at me - or hurting me - would leave me messed up for years. And while I still feel it somewhere deep inside, it's like a forgotten holiday decoration in the attic. All I'm aware of now is a tingly numbness, some dangerous force coming awake. I let my head come back up, let my eyes find Kluivert's. He's puffed up with righteous anger, used to being obeyed, but something in him flinches just a tiny bit when he sees my eyes.

That chick inside my head, I feel her just kinda look at me. *Let's ruin his world.*

Let's.

So I backhand *him* with the pipe. It's all in slow motion - his cheekbone shattering, his glasses crunching like a cough drop. His face caving in, blood and spittle flying out of his mouth, before he spins and falls back onto his men. And I somehow instinctively know that they'll be on me in a second, so I gotta split.

One of Kluivert's men pulls something out of a pouch. By the time I realize I need to move, my muscles have already fired. I'm flying forward off the porch, tumbling end over end in the air, before I land in a crouch in the middle of the street.

I just did a somersault over a bunch of guys, flew fifteen or twenty feet, and landed like a ninja. What the hell did Hazel *do to me?!*

"Cuff her!" The guy with the nasal, nails-on-chalkboard voice points at me. One of them lobs something at me; some kind of a plain, shiny bracelet with a steel finish. I bat it aside with a flick of my metal bar. There's a pathetic little hiss and the thing goes flying off, hitting the street and busting like a cheap ornament. The instant I hit it - or it hit *me* - a little shock surged into my arm. I think whatever they threw at me was supposed to restrain me, but I drained its power and shattered it instead.

I look at the dumbass who threw it. "Your toys suck."

Astonished hope dawns in Elizabeth's eyes. Nettie and Mary turn to look at me like I'm a different person.

Two more men closer to the street, one with a wand and the other with a gauntlet, grit their teeth and make rapid gestures. I don't know what they're doing, but I'm not taking chances. A surge of energy takes over, throwing me forward like a bullet. I land, whirling, smash one guy's arm. Then whirl the other way, crushing the other man's elbow.

Sadie splits the air with a shout.

"*Yeah!!* Attagirl, Courtney! Knock the *tar* out of 'em!"

I twirl again; someone else is behind me with an old canvas bag, ready to stuff it over my head. I smash his arm with a wet crunch, letting my inertia spin me around to pulverize his knee. He screams in my ear; it sounds really strange in the peaceful street.

It's dead quiet and all I can hear is the intimate sound of bones breaking, men screaming, spells failing. So this is what battle feels like. Part of me is getting nauseous from the disgusting way it sounds, how it feels. But that *other* girl sharing my space is amped up, liberated. These guys are starting to bleed everywhere and it's making me sick at my stomach, and I'm carrying that around while my adrenaline and reflexes move and guide me. It almost feels like I'm a video game character and she's the one with the controller.

But I'm not *totally* under her control. Every time I act, every time I swing this awkward pipe, *I'm* the one insisting on arms, legs. *Her* first reaction is to kill. This whole no-murder thing is me overriding this...automatic programming, or whatever it is.

Life happens a tenth of a second at a time. I'm making big decisions based on vague impulses - the sense of where people are around me, notions of objects they carry, vague feelings about what kind of properties those objects have. The canvas sack the guy had? I don't know what it was; all I know is that it felt *dark and heavy*. Thirsty. Like sucking on a dry blanket. I feel like it's some kind of abjurative object, something to muffle my powers or shut me up or something.

My powers. I can't believe I just said that. That's one of those things everyone in my generation says half-ironically on TV.

The men on the porch are on their way down here. Sadie and Nettie take advantage and follow them onto the street. Sadie twirls her swords, her face splitting in a razor-sharp grin as she looks for a challenger. Nettie's wearing a fingerless gauntlet now; I've never seen it before. It's a beaten-up thing made of old dark leather, and it's got a tarnished coin or a medallion or something on the back of the hand. She cinches the string on the inside of her forearm, securing it, and glares at the men swarming around us.

Oh, we're about to party.

These guys are all around now, moving. Someone comes at Sadie from about twenty feet away. She's got hot venom in her eyes, and she swings one of her shortswords. The projected force hits him like a baseball bat - *whump* - and he flies back, hitting the street with a roll, gasping for breath. Sadie grins in astonishment.

Her swords can hit guys from like twenty feet away? Oh, that is *seriously* awesome.

Another man comes running into the street, holding two blunt, straight objects, like tiny staves. He jabs them in her direction before I can even shout a warning. The staves thrust a heavy wave of force at her with a kind of *whuf* sound. She turns just in time, crossing her blades in the air; it sounds like a rock hitting a car door. She swings back, the man deflects. I feel the force inside my chest, like something whipping by at thousands of miles an hour.

"This doesn't need to get ugly, sweetie pie." His deep voice makes me cringe; there's something cold and inhuman about it, like a man that could beat his wife to death without batting an eye.

Sadie casts him a look of hateful contempt. "Aw, so's your old man!" Then she twirls her shortswords and lunges forward with both at once. The baton-wielder parries with just one of his staves, but the blow knocks him off balance. Sadie wastes no time - her powerful right-handed backswing takes him across the throat. A streak of blood flies out of the wound and the man topples backward, landing on the sidewalk, eyes wide, bleeding to death.

You wanna know the funny thing? I really don't care anymore, not after what these men did to me. Not with what they're trying to do - right now - to me and my friends. The violence exploding around me, these men dying - I don't feel an ounce of horror or sympathy. Though which one of us *truly* doesn't give a shit - me or *her* - I couldn't say, at least not at the moment.

Nettie clenches her gauntleted fist and punches the ground. A solid metal feeling stabs into the air in front of her, and I feel it in my bones, hard and solid. A shield of some kind. Sadie's right behind her, searching for threats.

"Courtney!" Nettie yells. "That thing looks like trouble!"

She points away, across the street. Some desk clerk over by College Green, dark hair slicked back, white office shirt and vest and glasses, is struggling with something. He's got this huge medieval crossbow thing, one foot planted on the front, and he's straining to pull it back with both hands. My intuition says that thing was *not* meant for him, and the way he's struggling in shirtsleeves and tie, I'd say that's pretty obvious. But before I can do anything, he pulls the bolt into place and aims it with a triumphant grin. First he aims at me, but then his grin turns malicious and he aims it at Nettie.

I know everything in a glance. I know that crossbow - or maybe it's an arbalest or something - is ridiculously powerful. Exactly how powerful, I'm not sure - but I know it'll probably blow Nettie's shield apart, and then whatever force is left over will blast her and Sadie back onto the sidewalk. How bad it'll hurt them, I have no idea. But I've gotta do something.

I could throw this pipe at him, but he's about thirty feet away, and at that distance I'm not entirely sure I can hit him. If I miss, I could hit someone outside this obscuration field or whatever. *And* I'll be unarmed in the middle of a fight. Only one feasible option pops into my head. I almost groan.

You're shitting me, I tell my companion.

Yeah, it'll suck, she says. *But it's the only way to make sure Sadie and Nettie are safe.*

Ugh, fuck this.

The man's grin widens, eyes alight with malice, and he moves his hand under the lever. When he squeezes that metal bar on the bottom side, the arbalest will fire.

I'm moving before I can even think about it - leaping, diving, rolling up in front of Nettie. Somewhere, the girls all yell, one after another, some variation of *"Courtney, no, what are you doing!?"*

Too late. The desk jockey squeezes the handle. *Snik.*

The world erupts in light and a roar of noise.

The flash of light fades. My eyes throb as they adjust to the normal morning sunlight. I'm lying on my side and spasms of pain flinch across my chest when I pick myself up off the street. That explosive blast hurt; it felt like being hit in the stomach with a giant Nerf bat.

But the real impact was on what Sadie called the theric level - it feels like I just stepped into the ring with a heavyweight boxer that knew how to beat up my soul instead of my head. Most of the pain and bruising is *inside* somehow, on another level of my being, but believe me when I say it's just as real.

But even though it hurt, *sh*e shrugs it off like it's nothing. I slowly get up, rolling the stiffness out of my neck.

"Ow."

The crossbowman's eyes bulge, lips shaking like he's trying to form words. He's wearing a look of astonished dread, like he expected that thing to blow me in half. He quickly leans down, loading another bolt into the mechanism. This one glows deep red.

Nuh-uh. We're not gonna find out what *that* one does.

I start toward him. On my way, I lift my awkward metal pipe, twirl it gracefully in my hand, testing its weight. That same instinct tells me exactly how to throw it; how to use my arm, how to position my body. I know just how it'll fly; I can see it in my head. I can *feel* every move it'll make from here to its target before I even lift it.

I could do so much better with a nice dagger or throwing axe, but a steel pipe will have to do. And that's weird because I've never actually thrown any of those things - not successfully, anyway. You should have seen me when I was a kid and I tried to throw knives and hatchets. I don't think I hit a target once. Mud puddles? Nailed those. But only when I wasn't aiming for them.

He struggles more and more frantically, whining and making noises of alarmed frustration like, "come on, you blasted thing, come on!" I come at him, faster and faster, then I wind back and give it a perfect throw. End over end, sailing through the air, just like I imagined. The end of the bar hits him in the windpipe, sending him flying off his feet. The pipe falls, bouncing and clanging on the sidewalk where he stood. The crossbow flies out of his hands too; I jump forward and catch it, not wanting to see it damaged. It's awfully big, even for a medieval arbalest; I look tiny holding it, like one of those anime girls with the crazy huge weapons. The wood has gone dull over the years, but if it really is centuries old then it definitely doesn't look it. With a little touching up, this thing would look like a museum piece.

Something keeps nagging me. *Arbalest, arbalest.* Where have I been hearing about arbalests lately?

"Displaced!" A man's shout, from the porch. "It's over!"

The nasal guy with the ratty face has a black revolver planted against Elizabeth's temple. On the sidewalk some brute with a fedora grips Mary by one arm, holding the same kind of gun against her head. Terror rises in my chest. Elizabeth's face is bleak with fury, but Mary is wide-eyed, terrified.

Those fucking bastards. *Mary. Please don't let them hurt Mary. I won't be able to handle it. I can't.*

"Drop that weapon!" Ratman shouts. "Put it down, slowly, then step back!"

Sadie turns and throws me an uncertain glance. Nettie watches nervously as the remaining Knights move to surround them.

"This is your last warning, Displaced. Drop the weapon and step back. You and your doll-faced friend can come with us, or we can shoot her in the head and you can come with us anyway. But the longer you wait, the more fun we're gonna have with her."

God dammit. I don't see that I have much of a choice. Even with all my new abilities, I still can't get to Mary in time to save her from a gunshot to the head. They've got me. I set the crossbow down, then watch them approach with venom in my eyes. I step back, hands up. Another short man in a waistcoat starts coming my way with one of those bracelets I broke earlier. I can feel it now - the bracelet. It gives off the stifling, dry feeling like the canvas bag earlier, except a lot colder and more concentrated.

It stops arcane abilities dead, Brynnhilde tells me. *It's a one-person nullification field. I'm not actually sure what'll happen if they put that thing on you, but I'm pretty sure you won't be able to defend yourself.*

I'll be defenseless, at the mercy of men. Again. And not just me this time - Mary, too. Dread and terror, like a dark shock down my spine. But what can I possibly do? I look over at Mary, my darling Mary. Now that my adrenaline is starting to cool, I see the look of helplessness on her adorable face when she looks at me, and it feels like these brutes have my heart in their hands. If I don't cooperate, they'll crush it. Guilt washes over me like a tide.

"You too, sweetheart! Drop those knives. And you with the glove, take it off and drop it!"

I'm already defenseless.

I swallow the hot tears that threaten to come back. Looks like it's over. I thought I could just make a brave stand and everything would be okay. Stupid me.

It's all my fault. Everything that's about to happen, it's all me. And that's the thing I really don't think I can handle.

The man with the bracelet slows, then stops altogether, looking past me. Then everyone's eyes drift down the street. I search their faces a moment, suspecting a trick, but then I turn and look, too.

An indistinct figure about a hundred feet away, moving quickly toward me on the sunlit street. Long olive trench coat, swaying back and forth, wide open in the front. On the collar, gold pins; one says "U.S.", the other, two crossed staves over a flat book. On each shoulder of the coat, another pin – the silver twin bars of a US Army captain. A plain mocha blouse, dark green military pants, laced up knee-high boots. Gingerbread hair, pulled back in a loose bun.

Black Colt 1911 in one hand, bloody crimson staff in the other. Death in her eyes.

Sadie's face lights up like a floodlight.

Hazel.

"How about you sonsabitches pick on somebody your own size!?"

Our attackers' faces drop.

"Morrison!" Ratman calls. "That's far enough!"

But Hazel moves faster now - she twirls her staff, shoving it lengthwise in front of her as she walks.

Revolvers flash; the men open fire. Terror stabs my heart - they really shot at her! Their bullets bounce away with a sound like rocks thrown at leather. Hazel lowers her staff, raises her black 1911. I watch her like I'd watch an oncoming train. She's not really gonna shoot that thing...is she?

Cl-pow! One shot rings out, then two more. *Cl-pow, cl-pow!* Each deafening gunshot tears down the street, ripping the stiff quiet as it goes.

The bullets rip into Mary's attacker, staggering him, one after another. After a long, terrible moment, he falls backwards, three dark bloody holes in his chest. Mary screams.

Well, I guess that answers *that.*

Kluivert wobbles to his feet on Elizabeth's porch, swaying, face covered in blood. Elizabeth seizes her shotgun with the speed of a much younger woman and bashes Ratman in the face with the butt stock, then approaches Kluivert, driving the barrels into his chest. But something tells me that, even wounded as he is, he could still be dangerous.

I bend quickly, seizing the crossbow. Now I remember where I heard "arbalest."

"Sadie!" I shout. "Catch!"

She turns swiftly, catching it out of the air. Her hands are moving as soon as she touches it, sliding back the mechanism, steadying the bolt, aiming the weapon. Then she stops, giving the arbalest a puzzled look like *how the hell did I do that?!*

"Courtney!" Hazel's eyes are soft with worry as she approaches. "Darling, get to Mary, keep her safe. I don't know what Kluivert's got up his sleeve."

I nod and take off down the street.

Behind me, she calls out: "Sadie, Nettie! Turn and face them, side to side - I won't let 'em get around you. Nettie, conjure your best force barrier, push forward. Sadie, get ready to fire. I'll cover you."

Mary's shocked and dazed when I reach her.

"Mary! Sweetie, are you alright?"

She lunges, clinging to me. I hold her, drawing a breath of relief, careful to stay between her and the rest of these thugs.

"I gotcha," I tell her softly.

"Courtney." Her voice is heavy with alarm. She's looking behind me.

Three more are closing on me, grim-faced, smiling. They look like low-ranking gangsters from some mafia movie. The one in front of me holds some oversized revolver at his waist, pointing at my chest. White button-up shirt, mouse-colored fedora, one of those disgusting pencil-thin mustaches. The leering, triumphant grin on his face reminds me of Derek.

"It's over, ginger," he says around a toothpick. What is it with asshole bullies and toothpicks? Kenny loved those things, too. "Time to come back with us. And if you come along like a nice girl, I promise to give it to you slow and easy. You might even enjoy it."

That's the grossest thing I've ever heard in my life.

I have to remind myself that this is actually real, and I'm not in some old gangster movie. If I let the unreality of the situation take over, I could slip up and get one of us hurt.

This chick - her name is Brynnhilde, I know that now - has got some *Bourne Identity* thing going on, and she feeds information right into my brain. The guy on the left is a common thug and enforcer. He knows how to use that truncheon from experience - he's beaten his share of women and may have gotten a few gigs as extra muscle, loansharking, that sort of thing. The guy on the right has been in and out of prison, running on the outer edge of violent street gangs most of his life. And the guy in front of me has seen the beginnings of military service but went home early, either as a deserter or a dishonorable discharge, or even just an injury in basic training. He wasn't in long enough to train the streets out of the way he uses a firearm. He's also a bit of a sociopath - I can see that in the cruel blankness behind his eyes.

How do you know all this?! I demand. *That's all really specific. Are you some kind of seer?*

Nah, nothing like that. Just experience. This is all basic stuff you can learn to spot with enough practice.

Well, what should I do? I ask. *Two of them have guns, and they look like they're ready to use them.*

You got this, she assures me. *I'll show you. You came with a whole lot of fancy moves for me to work with; I never imagined that my first remanifestation would have such an arsenal! They'll never see any of this coming.*

I have absolutely no idea what she means, and even though this whole conversation is happening inside my head in a hundredth of a second, she wants to get into action as soon as possible. I'm with her on that.

I launch a roundhouse kick at the man in front of me, knocking the gun clear of his hand. I let my momentum carry me around one more time, then crouch and sweep his legs out from under him.

Okay, *that's* new. I've played a lot of fighting games, and I've watched a lot of martial arts movies. I even had those basic karate classes from friends in junior high, but that was it. I've never actually *learned* any of those moves. Everything I'm doing is something I've seen before, but I never learned how to do any of it with my own body.

Before I died - or I guess I should say, before the real me *died,* Brynnhilde says, *I promised that I'd make a warrior out of an artist or priestess or scholar, as long as she had the fire and the bravery to become my successor. And I meant it. If you've spent enough time watching warriors in battle or in combat, then it's stored inside you and I can use it.*

Okay, that's pretty awesome. Let's see what else we can do.

Once he's on his way down, I stay low, twirling behind Truncheon. Then up, hooking my arms through his. I brace.

Just like clockwork - *bang, bang!* Two revolver shots from Red Vest, right in the chest. Before the shooter can get his bearings, I throw Truncheon forward onto him, knocking them both to the ground. Then it's just a matter of walking over and kicking the gun out of his hand.

Cold confidence in the heat of battle. That must be Brynnhilde, too.

By now, Toothpick is getting up, looking between his gun and Mary. Brynnhilde is urging me to make an example of him, propelling my muscles forward before I have time to think about it. There's no time to reflect, and only the most basic thought runs in the background like a stream of code while my body moves to act.

I'm on him, giving him a high side-kick to the face, sending him sprawling to the sidewalk. And then I see him laughing. I tilt my head at him a little, narrowing my eyes. It's a gesture that says *what's so funny?*, but it's so *not me* that I'm a little alarmed. It's kinda scary having a stranger share your body, especially when she's better at murder than you've ever been at anything in your life.

"Heh." He finishes laughing. "Pearse said you skirts were some grade-A ass, but he never told me how choice *you* were, ginger. Or how juicy *she* is; *that* is one sweet piece of pie." He leers at Mary from the ground. "I promise to be extra easy with her if you just come along quiet. I won't hurt her, on my word. Unless she asks me to." He wears a toothy grin, the kind of reptilian smile you only see on scary, perverted old men looking at porn in out-of-the-way convenience stores. The kind of smile they give you when they're standing in a back corner and never take their eyes off you for an instant, when you know they're just waiting to get you somewhere the security cameras can't see.

He's friends with Pearse. The same one that put a hand down my shirt, the one that would've done so much worse if he'd had a chance. The memory bubbles up like hot bile in my throat.

If he lays a finger on Mary, I swear I'll chop his arm off. I give him another swift kick to the side of the head, laying him out on the bricks.

"Courtney, behind you!" Nettie, yelling.

I swivel. Red Vest is up. Four more Knights, moving away from the action, are rallying around him. I guess I was moving too fast to notice before, but these guys are all armed. All of them. Whether it's aspected weapons or regular ones, everyone's carrying something. One man in front of me carries a double-barrel stagecoach shotgun, and another one's got a semi-auto pump shotgun. One of them has a humongous nickel-plated revolver that looks like it would explode your head like a watermelon, and one in front, looking right at me, carries a mace. The wooden handle is about two feet long, and it's got a long spiked head of blackened iron. An orange-ish aura floats around it, like the glowing belly of a furnace.

"A fiery mace?" I ask out loud, to no one in particular. "Seriously?"

He hears me and gives me a cold smile. "To smite fiendish witches like you and your coven of whores."

I just, I can't even. He sounds too much like that crazy backwoods preacher - the one that used to come to campus once a year and stand around on street corners screaming at random chicks about wickedness and temptation.

Well, even being part of a fiendish whore coven won't protect you from a blast from one of those shotguns, or being blown open by Sir Chastity and his *+5 Bane of Girl Cooties*. And I don't know how long Toothpick will stay dazed from my slick moves. Time to bounce.

I don't look away. "Mary, back up. Keep your eyes on them."

She nods. We back around Toothpick, who's slowly coming out of his daze. I feel Sadie and Nettie coming up behind me, and Hazel behind them. Somehow I *feel* Hazel's staff now, solid and satisfying, like strength in my bones.

"Let's play this real careful, girls," Hazel says quietly. She's holding her staff horizontally at her waist. "These fellas wanna make some heroic last stand, but that's three of the Knights in that group. We can't let them get away or we'll never see the end of this."

Sadie's got her crossbow aimed at them. "What do we do?"

"Mary?" Hazel asks. She hands her a long, shiny black scope, like you'd see on a small rifle. "Look them over. Tell me what we're up against."

Mary seems uncertain, but takes the scope. She slowly raises it to her eye, then lifts her eyebrows in astonishment. "Wow."

"Wow...good?" Nettie asks. "Or wow bad?"

"Wow, as in...I've never used one of these before," Mary replies. She pauses, then adds. "Okay, Hazel. There's a fella named Petrie over there, caliber three. He's the one with the red hot cudgel, like a stove. That thing is a caliber five fire-aspected mace with force projection. Emmett is a caliber four, and he's projected a caliber four subkinetic shield around them. The other one is just a caliber one, and your therascope thinks he might be an alchemist."

"And they're backing up," Nettie says tersely.

"They're gonna make a run for it," Hazel realizes. Without taking her eyes off the group, she pulls her 1911 out of its holster and hands it to me. Numb and surprised - I'm not sure why she's handing me her gun - I throw my pole onto the street and take it. It's cold and a lot heavier than I expected.

"How are you with a gun, Courtney?"

"Uhhmm...I've shot them before. Little ones. I'm not an expert or anything."

"Well, there's nothin' simpler than a gun, honey. Point at the bad guy and shoot him, that's all you need to remember. I've put a fresh mag in there - that's seven rounds, plus the one in the chamber. Both hands on the grip - yeah, like that. Not so stiff, loosen your arms, bend your elbows - attagirl. Alright, when I give you the signal, I want you to empty your mag at those bastards. Sadie and I will handle the rest. Okay?"

Um. "Yeah, sure. Okay."

"I'm gonna have to maintain a shield in case they let loose with one of those street sweepers. Nettie, you too, honey. Can you use that gauntlet to conjure an E/M shield for us?"

"Um, caliber one, at best," Nettie says doubtfully.

"That will be enough. Any E/M resonance will help us greatly. I'll handle most of the shielding - I just need that E/M to interfere with some of what they'll throw at us. You and I together will do just fine." She takes a quick look at us. "I'm relying on you girls, okay? Alright, Courtney. Squeeze that grip good - she kicks hard. And Sadie? Get ready to fire on my command."

Sadie nods, deadly serious as she aims down the sight of her crossbow. She's got that glowing red bolt loaded - it's a lot brighter than that mace over there. Nettie crouches, puts her fist against the bricks; after a moment, a funny sensation goes through my skin and my hair, like static electricity.

The street has gone silent except for the groans of wounded men. Over on the porch, Elizabeth watches with frozen calm as she holds her shotgun to Kluivert's face. Down here with me and the girls, the tension is so thick you could cut it. Until now we've been too focused on surviving one moment to the next. But now everything's quiet and it's starting to sink in that any one of those men could fire, anytime they wanted, and all kinds of things could happen.

"Courtney," Hazel says. "Give 'em hell."

Whew. Okay. Squeeze the grip hard, ignore the rough spikes against my hand. Aim down the sight, right at that douchebag with the mace...

Cl-pow!

The gun flies back, hard, almost hits me in the face. Holy shit! *'She kicks hard'* is an understatement. I get this image of one of those cannons in the movies, rolling across the deck of a ship after they fire.

Over in their huddle, a wiry, balding man flinches. Alright, I made a dent. Let's try again. Raise the gun, bend the elbows, relax, grip hard.

Cl-pow!

Cl-pow! Cl-pow!

Each shot tells. At first, the bullets hit his shield with a little *plink.* You could barely hear it. Now, every round makes a louder impact. *Plank. Plank.* It's starting to sound like I'm shooting through electrified glass. The guy with the combover winces in pain.

"A couple more, Courtney! You're doing good!"

Cl-pow! Plisk.

Cl-pow! Plosh.

The shield fails. Ultrathin pieces of air, like the thinnest ice, shatter and fly away into the breeze, then evaporate. The middle-aged guy with the combover falls over, yelling and cradling his arm.

I don't know what I expected. Maybe I thought they'd get dismayed and surrender, or that we'd be able to just mop up somehow.

Instead, the guy with the stagecoach shotgun fires.

A fiery blast erupts from both barrels, and the deep roar goes through my bones. Hazel's red staff is up, and bits of buckshot glow blue and orange as they hit her shield. Hazel's knuckles are white, her teeth clenched, as she takes the impact of the blast. Nettie whimpers and jolts back a bit from the impact but maintains her position. The buckshot hitting our shield makes a bunch of high-pitched *clank* sounds, like the impact of a hundred hammers on solid steel.

The sounds have barely started to fade when Hazel's voice rises above the chaos. "*Now, Sadie! Fire!*"

Snik.

BOOOOOOM.

A deafening roar. The ground shakes, and a blast of heat and wind rolls back over us, blowing bits of dirt in our faces. Mary squeals, and I turn and cover her with my body. The group of men are right on top of where the bomb detonated, and the blast tosses them into the air like flaming toys. Trails of smoke follow them across the sky and down the street, where they land in piles of charred, burning wreckage. Their screams were short - they died away fast.

We slowly uncover each other, and I think we're all a little bit reluctant to stand up and look at what we did. But we can't see much from this distance; a black heap of bones and grease smolder on a rise about a hundred feet away. Little columns of smoke from down the street hint at where the others landed, and that smoke rolls away from us, down the hill toward the river.

And we don't say anything for a second. I think we're all too stunned. Hazel is the first to recover. She steps over and gently takes the 1911 from my hands, pops the magazine, and changes it for a fresh one. Then she makes her way back to Elizabeth's porch. She strides up the steps and over to Kluivert, clicking the hammer on her gun as she shoves it into his temple.

"It's your lucky day," she tells him.

"How do you figure?" He's wearing a filthy expression. His shattered face is a mess of blood and bruises and deep cuts.

"You get to live." She slaps a cuff on his wrist, then slugs him in the face, sends him flying.

He's dazed for a moment, blinking and dabbing at his mouth. He gives her a crafty look through narrowed eyelids. "How do you think this will look when it goes to trial at your Conclave? They'll have you in front of a firing squad, Morrison."

"Naw, I don't think so," she replies easily. "That's a hell of a stunt you tried to pull, coming to someone's house with a gang of hired thugs, giving them aspected weapons and turning them loose on a buncha kids. *Kids.* You've gotta be the stupidest wannabe gangster I've ever seen. You went looking for war but you weren't ready for it."

"Nobody imagined you'd get that worthless diamond working, turn your Displaced into some freak out of a Viking myth."

Ouch.

"Or that you'd just happen to have some kid who miraculously attuned with Svendmeyer's Arbalest," he goes on. "I wonder what other aces you've got up your sleeve, Morrison."

Sadie and I exchange a curious look.

Hazel smirks. "And that's why you got cut to pieces. You barely gather any intelligence at all, and you charge in fueled by your own misogynist arrogance. They're only young girls, how could they hurt a bunch of big professional woman-beaters?" She leans down, hauls him up by the collar in a single move. She shoves his head to the side with the barrel of her Colt, forcing his eyes in my direction. "You convinced yourself it was an easy prize so you went all in, and look what happened. You lost *everything*. Your little stag club, your freedom, everything. You're finished."

She presses her Colt into his face hard enough to bruise, and he flinches. "Get a good look, Kluivert. *That's* no myth. That girl is as real as anything, flesh and blood and *feelings* and a *LIFE!* One *you* tried to ruin - *lives*, more than one, you tried to ruin! This is what happens to kidnappers and rapists, Kluivert." Her voice goes dark and deadly quiet. *"Remember it."*

She shoves his head away with the barrel of her pistol, then holsters it.

I take one last look around. The fight is over, and the wounded are seeing to each other. Nobody's in any mood to mess with us anymore. Sadie and Nettie come up and engulf me in a hug. I hold them close, squeezing them as my adrenaline fades into fear and nausea and shaking nerves. Mary runs up, tears streaming from her eyes. The three of us hold her, hold each other. All I can feel is sunshine, warm on my clothes. All I can smell is the sweet, lovely smell of girl hair.

Sadie puts her hands on my cheeks. "Are you alright?"

I glance at the blood and carnage on the street, quickly close my eyes, swallow the rising bile. I feel tired, bruised, beaten. Spiritually, too, like I just read a thousand homophobic forum threads while someone pounded me with their fists. But oddly enough, that pale gold light is still inside me, coursing through my veins, and I know that no matter how worn down I feel, I'm okay. They're gonna need to try harder than that now.

But I think human Courtney and valkyrie Courtney still have different feelings. Maybe I'll integrate eventually.

I smile at Sadie, touch her cheek. "You're so selfless, asking me how I'm feeling when you were the one that had to--the one that, you know." I pause, draw a shuddering breath. "Sadie, I'm so sorry."

"It's jake, Courtney. Really." Her eyes are alive. "Somehow it doesn't bother me. I know what I did, and...well...I can live with it. I don't know why, but I can. They were only here to hurt my friends and me, so I took the shot. I'd take it again."

I grab her, pull her close for a moment. "I don't deserve you," I tell her quietly.

She holds me close. "That's a load of bull and you know it."

Finally, I step back and look at Nettie.

"Next time you feel like stepping in front of a cannon, tell me ahead of time," she says, grinning. "I'll get you set up with a traveling circus so you can at least earn a few clams for the trouble."

I grin. "I oughtta smack you." And she laughs as I hug her.

"I'm glad you're okay, Courtney," Nettie says quietly. "Please don't pull a stupid stunt like that again. You had me worried plumb to death."

We kiss each other on the face, and I turn to look at Mary. Her lips tremble with tears. She raises her hand, clenches her fist, then lowers it. Then the dam breaks, washing her face away in a flood of sobs. She seizes me, clinging hard and squeezing me.

"Hey, it's okay, it's over now," I tell her as soothingly as I can. "You're safe. Nobody will ever hurt you while I'm around. Ever." Sadie and Nettie crowd close, arms around her, comforting her.

She sniffs, an ugly ripping sound in the gloomy quiet. "That's just what I'm worried about, you little fool."

"What do you mean?" I ask quietly.

Sniff. "I mean *you*. You've got these...*gifts*, now. And I'm worried to death that you're gonna keep taking long chances to save me, or save one of us, until-" Sniff. "Until you do something *really* stupid and get yourself killed." She holds me close again, crying on my shoulder. "You stupid, stupid girl."

I share an awkward look with Sadie and Nettie, then put my chin on her shoulder. "I'm sorry. I didn't...this is ne-"

Mary seizes me in a sudden kiss. It's firm, worried, relieved - the kind of kiss you can't give someone unless you've been in love with them your whole life. It only lasts a few seconds, and I'm just starting to realize what's happening when she pulls away. Her head is back on my shoulder before I can even look at her. My stomach plunges and I feel a warm blush rising to my cheeks. *Th-that was...nice...*

Sadie and Nettie and I share a look of confused astonishment. Things get quiet for a minute. Mary knew she was gonna make things awkward and that's why she hid her face. I'm totally speechless, and my stomach is still rolling around in my torso from that kiss. I kinda want more.

Sadie recovers first.

"Mary, listen to me," Sadie says, taking Mary's face in her hands. "Courtney will never be alone as long as I draw breath. You hear me? I will protect her. I will watch over her, always." She gives Mary a pointed look, and Mary nods. Sadie looks at me. "Ride or die. That's how we roll."

I grin at her, and the tears, the nerves, spill out of me too. I sniffle and squeeze Sadie and Mary, and Nettie holds us close.

Mary sniffles and pulls away after a moment, giving me a sunny smile. She spreads a hand, wiping her eyes with the tip of a finger.

"You're a darn good egg, Sadie. Thank you." Her eyes dart back to me. "Still...I'll feel a lot better about Courtney's safety once I can do a better job of protecting myself. I think it's time I learned how to do that. The less I'm in danger, the less Courtney will have to protect me."

"Maybe we all should," I agree. "Like, together. Whatever I did today was just pure instinct. But that's not good enough. I don't want it to be on accident. We should all find what we're good at and use that to back each other up. I want us *all* to be badass. Together."

Sadie grins, nods. "I like the sound of that. A team."

"Why, that's a good idea," Nettie says. "If we're alone, we'll be safe. But together…"

"Nobody stands a chance," Mary says, her soft face unusually serious.

"Exactly," I smile at her. I can't think of anything better to do, so I lay my hand down flat in the air. "Girl squad."

Mary places hers on mine, and gives me a warm, loving smile.

"Till the end." Sadie's, on Mary's.

Nettie grins, slapping her hand on Sadie's. "We'll be the meanest janes in this whole damn town. The big-timers and fraternity boys will all learn to fear us. Courtney and Sadie don't pull their punches."

And there's a strength in the air between us, charged and ready.

Something important has happened.

It's the beginning.

Epilogue

Courtney

The corpses are still smoldering, and black smoke spirals into the sky.

People have arrived from three Conclaves - the Seven Towers, New Amsterdam, and even one from Massachusetts Bay - to help round up the Knights, make arrests, and disband them. Too bad they didn't get here like, I dunno, yesterday. It would have been nice if a bunch of college chicks that were *totally unprepared for this* didn't have to do *everything*.

A few men pull bandannas over their faces as they reach the carnage. I rest an elbow on my knee, curl my fingers against my forehead. "Are we ever gonna have a normal life?"

They wind back and toss buckets of water; a big black cloud rolls off in a hiss of steam. The men cough and wave away the cloying stench of charred mobster.

"Gosh, I hope so," Nettie says quietly. "Why, if I have to deal with stuff like this every day, I'll go batty."

Hazel and Elizabeth are over on the street talking to someone I've never seen before, a tall, elegant black man in a fine bowler hat and finely-cut dark suit. He carries himself with antique grace, like an aristocrat that walked out of an old painting. Watching him feels like a nostalgic echo, like those Christmases when I was little and they brought out the horse-drawn carriages, or like walking into a building closed up since the 1880s, perfectly preserved inside. Elizabeth glances over at us and places her hand on his arm; the two exchange a quick word, and she makes her way back over to us.

"Don't you lazybones ever do anything?" She rests fists on her hips, and a smirk creases one side of her face. It makes her look like Nettie. "Why, I don't believe I've ever seen a group of layabouts like the four of you."

It hits me sideways, and I'm stammering. I'm looking at them and they're looking at me and I'm getting to my feet with a head full of swirling guilt. Sadie's about to follow.

"She's just razzing you, you silly geese," Nettie says, pulling me back down with a weary smile. "That's her way of saying we've been too busy lately."

Sadie and I share a quick, embarrassed look and say "...oh..." at the same time.

"Honestly, Courtney." Elizabeth shakes her head with a grin. "You come back from the dead, and the first thing you do after you wake up is charge in and thrash a good fifteen men in single combat. I hope you at least plan on getting a bit of rest before you conquer the world." She heaves a breath. "You too, Sadie Van Tassel! If you're looking for medals for bravery, I'm sure we could find you some without your having to risk your neck for them."

Sadie offers her a weary smile.

I smirk. "That depends on if they finally got the message. And besides, it's not like we were alone. I had help."

"That's what worries me," she says, looking us over. Before any of us can respond, she reaches into a pocket in her dress. "Hold out your hands. I have something for you."

So we put our hands out. She drops a small piece of cherry candy in each palm. I look at mine a little stupidly.

"It'll make you feel better, child," Elizabeth says. "A gift from my mentalist friend over there. Girls, meet Dr. Holmes of the Massachusetts Bay Arcane Assembly. He's an alienist and a Professor of Abnormal Behavior at Harvard."

The dandy with the polished black cane looks directly at me and tips his bowler hat, a kindly expression on his face. We all wave; I return the friendly smile and pop the candy in my mouth. It's one of those old-fashioned cherry cough drops, the kind that tastes more like candy; it's a richer, sweeter flavor than the kind I always had as a kid. It tingles just a little bit on my tongue and for an instant, my thoughts are scrambled and I can't focus. But it's gone so fast that I'm not sure I felt anything at all. My friends suck on theirs, relaxing a little.

Elizabeth nods once, satisfied about something. "Good."

I squint. "Wait, why good?"

"That candy contains a trauma-inhibiting reaction. It will protect you from being scarred by what happened here today."

Oh, my goodness. I never even thought about that - we *would* have been scarred, wouldn't we? All of us! I exchange a look of amazement with Sadie. God, what *isn't* possible? It's gonna take me a while to get caught up. My brain is still skipping like a record on the part where Mary kissed me.

"Say, Aunt Lizzy," Nettie asks around her candy. "What's gonna happen with all those Augustine goons now?"

Elizabeth glances down the street, where Hazel and Dr. Holmes are conversing. Around them, a few volunteers - I'm assuming acquaintances of Holmes - are rounding up the

Knights who took part in the attack. They're all wearing those silvery bracelets and looking different shades of angry.

"Well, as I understand it, they're to be disbanded, and the lot of them are to be shipped off to Cincinnati for trial by Conclave. That is, except those few that are wanted by New Amsterdam or Massachusetts Bay. I believe that's why Holmes came out here from New York - to see what he could do to help your friend Dr. Forsythe close up shop. But as it happened, he arrived just a few moments too late to come to your aid when they came after Courtney and Mary." She takes off her wire-rimmed glasses, rubs an eye. "But there's one other matter. Hazel Morrison and Dr. Holmes have agreed that Sadie should receive the crossbow she used today, with all its equipment, immediately."

Sadie and I share an excited look.

"When something like this happens," she elaborates, "which is almost unprecedented in our country, the possessions of the rogue circle go into interim care of a local arcanist until it's decided what's to be done with them. Hazel has taken custody of all of it for the time being, and she insisted you have it, Sadie."

"Golly, that's fantastic!" She beams. "But...why me? Aren't I just some kid that got tied up in all this?"

"Hardly, my dear," Elizabeth smirks. "You're naturally aspected and you have the misfortune of - in an instant - becoming known to several large Conclaves at once. But to put it bluntly, you're being given the crossbow because it attuned to you."

"Attuned?" Mary asks.

"Yes. You see, most artifacts can be used by most people, more or less successfully, depending on a great many factors. But some artifacts resonate so perfectly with the essence of a particular person that they're considered to be attuned. For lack of a better way to describe it, the crossbow *likes* Sadie. They're a perfect match."

"So that explains why you just grabbed it out of the air and you had it ready to fire again in like a half a second," I remark.

"Exactly, Courtney," Elizabeth says.

"A monumental feat for any arcanist." A male voice. Our heads whip around and we're halfway to our feet before we know what we're doing. Elizabeth falls back a step, and Hazel swings her staff into a defensive position, ready for combat. There's a man on the sidewalk, wearing a bowtie and round glasses. He stops and lifts his hands, showing us that he means no harm. He looks oddly youthful, like a man who hit about forty and stopped aging, but his white hair and deep-set eyes suggest he's a lot older. How the hell did he sneak up on us like that?

He pauses, making sure we understand his peaceful intentions, and looks back at Sadie. "As I said, immediate attunement to one of the Eleven Masterworks - you've made history today, young lady. That is a groundbreaking achievement for any arcanist, in any age. But one so young, and of such power - one need not be a diviner to see that you are destined for great deeds."

"And who are you?" Aunt Lizzy asks.

"Ah, forgive me. I snuck up on you - old habit, I'm afraid." He doffs his hat. "Darius Melville, Chamberlain of the Hall, Knights of Augustine. At your service." He gazes sadly at the blood and carnage on the street, and his face turns cold when he sees the remaining Knights being led away into custody. They regard him with astonishment, shock, and outrage. Whoever this guy is, they didn't expect to see him, and they're not too happy about it.

"Eleven Masterworks?" Sadie asks.

"Indeed! You've heard of 'The Clockwork Magister?'"

Sadie and Nettie glance at each other, shake their heads. "Ah, then please, allow me. The 'Clockwork Magister' is the name given to the late eighteenth century Swedish artificer Gustav Svendmeyer. He equaled the genius of Leonardo DaVinci, but fortunately far exceeded him in realizing inventions." Melville points at Sadie's crossbow. "The crossbow you hold originally dates from the fourteenth century, and at that time it was plain and unremarkable. Artificers tinkered with it over the years, but it was little more than a plaything before Svendmeyer got his hands on it. It was he who transformed it into a work of breathtaking genius."

Sadie is quiet as she stares at it, like she's trying to puzzle out its secrets for herself.

"You are a kinetic aspect, are you not?"

Sadie nods.

"Perfect. The crossbow's true genius lies in its ability to channel your own theric energy seamlessly into its projectiles, with no loss of energy at all. One hundred percent conductivity. When fired, it will channel all caliber seven of your power for a millisecond, then release it in one gigantic explosion on impact. All this with no drain on you." He smiles. "The arcanist who wields this weapon may do so without stopping, so long as she has ammunition."

Sadie gives us excited looks.

Melville gives us the warm look of a teacher whose students share his enthusiasm. "Its name is *Siegebreaker*, and it's yours. Congratulations, Miss Van Tassel."

"Siegebreaker?" I grin. "Okay, that is *seriously* awesome."

"Melville, old man, is that you?" Dr. Holmes approaches with Hazel.

The white-haired guy walks up and gives Holmes a smile and a handshake.

"You two are acquainted?" Lizzy asks.

"Only in passing," Dr. Holmes says. His voice is a quiet baritone. "We met at a thaumaturgy conference in Cambridge some years back; oh, that must have been before the war, am I right?"

The Augustinian nods, smiling as he remembers. "Seems so long ago, now. But I would like you to know that I've not come seeking mercy or clemency. My brethren have committed an atrocity today - and not the first, it seems." He gives me a devastated look. "I know that talk is cheap and the words of a Knight of Augustine mean little, but I do wish to say that I am sorry I couldn't prevent what Hodges and Pearse did to you, child. Believe me, I did try; I argued with all my might, I raged and even threatened to resign, and yet I could not change their course."

"And...what?" Hazel asks. "The shit show that happened this morning - I assume you sat that out, too?"

Melville nods gravely. "I did indeed, though not idly." He reaches into his jacket and withdraws a scroll and a key. "You see, when Kluivert marched down here like some petty warlord, I planned to simply lock him and his lackeys out of the Augustinian Hall and turn these over to the Seven Towers along with myself. But before I left the Hall, I noticed something most remarkable." He turns his gaze on us, and he almost looks...amazed? "Two Type A arcanes, one caliber eight and one caliber seven, side by side with friends and family. Fighting with great courage, defending their home against interlopers. And that's when I realized...if those young ladies have not yet formed a circle, they jolly well should. So in thinking of your futures, I decided to gift these to you, instead."

He comes up to me, gives me a ceremonial bow, and hands me the scroll and key. "I present you, young Miss, with the deed and keys to the building known as the Augustine Hall, to be your new home and headquarters whenever you band together with these remarkable friends of yours. Should you rally together in such a way, this college and this town may sleep peacefully. None need fear the likes of the Knights of Augustine again."

I stand, awestruck and humbled, and take them from him.

"Why, Melville?" Hazel crosses her arms. "Why play the Judas and help us?"

He straightens up and gives her a serious look. "For simpler reasons than you might imagine, Captain Morrison. I'm doing it because it's *right*. And because any little thing I might do to help ease the suffering my brethren have caused, I will do. This is not why the Knights of Augustine were formed, and God help me, I will not let our last act be one of infamy." He leans on a silver-tipped cane and holds himself with a dignified air. "I would have come earlier and lent you my aid in your fight, but I swore an oath never to raise my hand against my brothers. It is an oath I regret, but an oath nonetheless, and while I may not break it, I will do everything short of it. I shall testify in court and open Augustine Hall, with all its treasures, to these young ladies here, should you allow it. It is the very least I can do."

The girls and I share a dumbfounded look. Even Hazel's speechless. Of all the things that might have happened in the aftermath of this street brawl, none of us could've seen *this* coming.

"Wow…" I'm absolutely shocked. "Th-thank you."

"No," he says warmly. "Thank *you*, for all the great things you will do. The hand of destiny lays upon all of you, but especially you, Courtney Ashford. You shine with a brightness and courage I never could have imagined before meeting you. Mark my words, dear girl - the fates themselves shall tremble at your deeds."

So in all the epic things he just said, I keep getting hung up on one stupid little detail. "Ashford," I say quietly. "I've seen that name before. Is that…supposed to be me?"

Melville gives Hazel a look of amusement and surprise. "She doesn't know her own provenance?"

Hazel looks annoyed. "As it *happens*, I was paying her a visit to discuss that very subject, but then Kluivert and his desperados showed up. It sorta threw a wrench in my plans."

His smile fades a little, but doesn't go away. "Ah. I do apologize, Sorceress. I meant no offense. Then, if I might give her one last gift…" He turns to look at me. "Yes. That is the name you were meant to have, the name that was waiting on you. When I saw you in the therascope, it already showed you as Courtney Ashford. Your integration is complete."

Hazel is terse. "What that means in English, Courtney, is that every Displaced leaves a hole when they're forced into Exile. That hole still contains everything that's supposed to be yours - name, family, documents, all kinds of things. When you're restored to your Sanctuary - that is, the verse you're supposed to be in - those things become yours again. The verse returns them to you. That's why you appear as Courtney Ashford in Melville's therascope."

The girls turn joyful, excited smiles on me.

"*Oh*, Courtney, how *wonderful!*" Mary beams. "You're finally here now, with us, a hundred percent!"

"And there's more," Hazel says. "I've a great deal to tell you about your new abilities, about the kind of power you wield. But that can wait until later on, once you've had a chance to catch your breath."

The kind of power I wield? The way she's talking, it sounds like what I just did was only the beginnings of what I can do. Excitement rises in my chest. Oh, this is seriously awesome.

"The one important detail I should probably share with you now," Hazel begins. "Is your age."

I blink. "My...age?"

"Yes. Time flows differently between Verse Tranquility Dawn, which is this verse, and Verse Servant Languish, which is your Exile verse. When all was said and done, you'd become two years older than Mary or Nettie. That's two years older than you were supposed to be."

I squeeze my eyes shut, trying to unravel this. But I think she's right. When we were kids, we were all the same age. But I've already been in college for two years. How did I just randomly get two years older than them?

"Oh, good heavens." Dr. Holmes gives me a sympathetic look. "Not a time differential, too! On top of everything else?"

Hazel nods. "Unfortunately, yes. But the good news is that coming back here fixed your anima - fast. It started fixing it that first day you phased over, when you were with Sadie. Once you re-attuned, you lost those two years you weren't supposed to have. You're back on track now."

Nettie blinks. "Are you saying she got younger?!"

Hazel smiles a bit. "Why, yes. I suppose I am. She's returned to the age she's supposed to be, which is eighteen. Like all of you."

The girls gape at me in open-mouthed astonishment. My mouth hangs open, too - I haven't eaten anything in days and my brain doesn't work. Okay, I'm...*eighteen* now. And not twenty. It kinda doesn't sink in, even though some deeper part of me is starting to realize it's true.

Elizabeth seems pensive; she seems unfazed by the mindfuck I was just given. "Mr. Melville, you say that Courtney is destined for great things. Does that explain why Pearse and Kluivert wanted her gone?"

Melville's smile fades. "I believe so, Professor. Somehow, the Blackstead Anomaly - the one they call Reverend Howgrave - got his hooks into them, or at the very least, into Pearse. Then he preyed upon all the base prejudices in our order and stoked them to gain control over as many as he could. From there, it was a simple matter of using the Knights to keep Miss Ashford away from the versal threshold."

"What for?" Hazel asks, incredulous.

Melville looks at me. "As I said. The hand of destiny lies heavily upon these young ladies, but Howgrave - the so-called 'Tricorne Man,' is especially terrified of *you*, my dear. He saw what you were capable of long before your first phase." He gets serious. "Do be careful, for I fear you might hear from him again, and much sooner than any of us would like. His fear of you will torment him constantly, and he will continue to seek your banishment. Or your death."

Terror shoots through every nerve in my body.

"The Tricorne Man." My voice sounds shrill in my ears. "I've heard that legend before. That's what his name is? How...grave?" For some reason, that name freaks me out, like *really* bad. Saying it out loud makes it worse.

He nods solemnly. "It is."

Nettie gives me a curious glance. "I'm surprised you'd know that, Courtney."

"Yeah," I reply. "I worked in the Archives. I know all kinds of crazy stuff."

"That was the name given to him back in the eighteenth century by the first settlers in this area," Melville goes on. "They preferred it over his real name, for a variety of reasons, and even I admit that I don't like the sound of his proper name. It makes me uneasy."

At least I'm not the only one. Silence for a moment; a breeze kicks up.

"The eighteenth century," Mary ponders. "You aren't saying some crazy man has been living out there since colonial times?"

Elizabeth's face is a pensive mask, and Hazel looks grim. They're both quieter than usual.

"To be honest with you," Melville replies, "I'm not entirely certain. Some believe he is the same man, while others say there have been a host of followers that have taken the title to keep the legend alive. Knowing what I know about dark energy, however, it is entirely likely that Reverend Howgrave has extended his life indefinitely by sacrificing that which makes us alive to begin with."

"You mean anima?" Mary asks.

"Precisely. If it *is* the same person, then he stopped being a *person* long ago, and now continues to exist in some horrific imitation of the life he once lived. He would now be little more than a mummified corpse held together with pure dark energy and hatred."

A chill goes down my spine, and my arms freeze into goosebumps. For some reason, this conversation is scaring the *fuck* out of me, and I still have no idea why. The girls and I exchange worried glances and scoot a little closer to each other.

Mr. Melville turns to Hazel again. "Whatever fate lies in store for me, I will not resist. But should I be allowed to remain at liberty, I promise to do all in my power to watch over you. All of you." He looks at Aunt Lizzy. "These young ladies have come to Braddock College for an education. Allowing them to pursue their studies in safety should be our top priority. Don't you agree, Professor?"

Aunt Lizzy's face has lightened. "I do indeed, Mr. Melville."

Hazel and Dr. Holmes share an inquisitive look, like they're asking each other something. Finally, Hazel shrugs. "What the hell. The paddy wagons are all full, and I'm buried in paperwork anyhow. Alright, Melville, you win. I'll list you as 'assisting Conclave agents in the line of duty' or something." Then she turns to us with a little grin and a wink. "And I'll recommend that these four troublemakers have their pick from all confiscated material, for educational purposes, with the aim of establishing a student circle at Braddock College."

The girls and I share a look of dumbfounded excitement.

Hazel gives us a sunny, mischievous smile. "Congratulations, acolytes. As of right now, you're real arcanists."

We turn joyful looks on each other, bursting with excitement. Sadie squeals, and we all hug in one big pile.

It looks like our plans to become badass together just became official.

Melville watches the girls file into the house, then sighs. "Ah, to be that age again. Just starting college - what an adventure everything was." He turns to Hazel. "I'm afraid there is another matter."

Hazel's eyes narrow. "Chisel Face and Eastwicke. They're still out there."

"Quite so, Captain. And more, still."

"More?" Elizabeth asks. "Good lord, what else?"

Melville's eyes linger on the house, as if he's making sure none of the girls will overhear this conversation. "While my former brothers' theories and methods were hopelessly outdated, I'm afraid they *were* right about one thing. It seems that something did follow Miss Ashford across the versal threshold."

Dr. Holmes shares a frightened look with Hazel and Elizabeth. "Considering that you used the word 'something' and not 'some*one*', I believe it safe to assume we're talking about a revenant of some kind?"

Melville nods grimly. "It does seem likely, old fellow. Tell me, Professor. Captain. Have you any idea if anyone on the other side wanted to hurt Miss Ashford?"

Hazel snickers. "Everyone and their cousin. She was in the terminal phase of a resonance purge when she finally made it through that aperture, and she was more dead than alive when we found her. I imagine there were quite a few people laying for her."

Elizabeth narrows her eyes thoughtfully. "It seems I remember hearing something, years ago. My niece, Lenora, was planning to keep Courtney and share guardianship with Marian Carlyle - Mary's mother. The day Courtney arrived in their care, they interviewed her and discovered that she was not safe at home. Courtney often mentioned that her false father threatened to kill her, and in deadly earnest, for he often backed up these threats with severe beatings."

Melville and Holmes share a horrified look.

"Poor child," Holmes says quietly.

"Sadly, there's more," Elizabeth goes on. "She would have stayed with my niece - in 1915 - but something pursued her there as well. It tracked the girls down one afternoon and began threatening Mary. Courtney earnestly believed her false father had found her, and that she must return to Exile to keep this beast from wandering. She believed it was the only way Mary would be safe."

"She fell on her sword," Melville says quietly.

"Precisely," Elizabeth says. "The sort of man who could project a revenant to chase a twelve or thirteen-year-old girl into Sanctuary is not the sort of man to take it lightly that she escaped again, even as an adult."

"You believe this false father is projecting such a revenant again?" Holmes asks.

"I believe so," Melville says ominously. "Over the last forty-eight hours, a greater revenant has been manifesting in the Blackstead, absorbing dark-aspected energy."

"And once it absorbs enough aphotic aspect to take form, it'll come this way," Hazel realizes.

Melville nods. "That is my fear."

Elizabeth makes a wry face. "Things got complicated rather quickly, didn't they?"

"I'll send a telegram back to Cincinnati," Hazel assures her. "See if the Home Office will send us some reinforcements. A greater revenant is a threat to everyone in town."

"Then I hope they send help," Melville says. "Because none of us are powerful enough to challenge it alone."

Elizabeth's face is bleak. "It'll kill every one of our girls."

"Not just them," Hazel says quietly. "A greater revenant might kill everyone in town if it felt like it, depending on the rage that fuels it. And it sounds like that fella's got enough rage to keep going long after Courtney is dead."

"Well, that was more whoopee than I expected to have in a year," Sadie remarks as we step into my bedroom.

"And how," I reply. We grin at each other.

"Are you done being a heroine for now?" she asks. "Because I'm *totally* done being a heroine for now." She smirks even more, probably hoping I'd notice her using my words, too.

"*Totally,* honey. Absitively, posilutely."

She hugs me tight, gives me a soft kiss on the cheek. I return it.

She steps back, smiles into my eyes. "Well, I suppose we'd better go get something to eat, hadn't we?"

Oh, god. I forgot all about food. Ugh, now I'm so hungry that I'm not hungry anymore, it just hurts.

"Yeah, probably."

So we start gathering up our clothes so we can get changed.

"I kinda hate to take it off," Sadie confesses, looking at herself wearing my clothes in the tall mirror. "I feel so daring and vampish."

"It's yours whenever you wanna wear it," I tell her. "Anything you want."

"I may take you up on that, darling." With a final regretful sigh, she pulls my t-shirt over her head, then stands in front of the mirror while she folds it. She's wearing one of those old-fashioned bras, the longish kind that stretch down to the bottom of your ribs. It's a copper penny sort of color, and it looks nice with her flawless pale skin. She catches me looking and shrinks just a little.

"Sorry," she says quickly. "I didn't think you'd mind if I just…"

"Oh, no, not at all." I fumble a little. "I was just looking at your bra. I was wondering if I'd have to get rid of mine now."

"I don't see what for." She places my t-shirt neatly back in my backpack and peeks inside for a second. She pulls out my plain white bra, looks at it. "Nobody's gonna see it. But we're about the same size, right? You're always welcome to borrow one of mine if you need to."

"Thanks, Sadie. You're a doll."

"What are best pals for?" She winks. "Speaking of clothes - are you absolutely ready to be one of us?"

I chew my lip. In all the turmoil, I'd almost forgotten how different everything would be.

"It's gonna be a huge adjustment for me," I admit. "Though I guess I am the same age as everyone again." Maybe I should write a book - *101 Things Nobody Should Ever Have to Say Out Loud.*

"Oh, you'll love being modern - why, before you know it, you'll forget you were ever anything else."

With guidance from Mary and Nettie, Elizabeth had gotten me a couple of outfits to get me started, and Sadie finds them in the wardrobe. She strips me to my bra and panties, then starts dressing me. The garter belt goes on over my panties and garter straps dangle around my thighs. Sadie hands me a soft pair of sheer, flesh-toned silk stockings; they're tricky to get on and she kinda has to help me arrange them around my feet and teach me how to coax them over my legs. Once they're up around my thighs, she shows me how to attach them to the garter straps so they'll stay up. I feel like one of those pin-up model chicks and I'm curious to see what I look like; I start toward the mirror.

"Not yet, missy," she says with a little smile. "Let's wait till you're done."

Sadie holds up a breezy knee-length summer dress; it's a pale mint green color with rounded, cream-colored lapels. The look she gives me is a question mark.

"It's cute," I agree, nodding a little. It doesn't seem real; my brain still doesn't accept that I'm the one that's gonna be wearing it.

So she brings it over and helps me slide into it. It falls comfortably into place around my shoulders, and it's soft and cool when it swishes around my knees. This is *so weird*.

"Now you just need some shoes," Sadie says. "Mary and Nettie weren't very bold with their choices, but your style is a bit minimalist anyhow."

Sadie pulls open the wardrobe and looks at the two pairs of shoes along the bottom.

"What about those brown mary janes?" I ask.

"Oh, these?" She grabs them, holds them up.

I nod.

The brand new leather heels are about as stiff as I'd imagine, but I manage to get them on. Once I fix the straps, I stand up.

Sadie beams, then happily presses the palms of her hands together next to her face. "Why, aren't you a sight for sore eyes! Modern clothes look so natural on you!"

"Really?" I ask nervously. I still feel every article of clothing on my body, the soft airy dress, the stockings hot in the sun and bunching tight around my knees, the sensible brown pumps that make me look like an actress in a silent film.

"Definitely," she replies. "What was that you said to me the day we met? *You look so natural, like you're really from the 20s!*" She grins. "Well, now I get to say it to you."

I don't know why that's making me blush so hard, but it is. I try to bite off the grin that swallows my face.

"Do you want me to wear makeup or anything?"

"Not unless you want to, since we're only getting lunch," she says. "Though I saw you brought some along, and that's good, since you'll want to make a habit of wearing it most of the time if you don't already."

"Gotcha." I really don't wear it often, if I don't have to. It also doesn't help that Kenny just happened to be fuming mad every time I wore makeup. Maybe it made him insecure, or maybe it made him jealous, I don't know. I guess after a while I just sorta became afraid to put it on, and when I reached college, I had to get over how dangerous and rebellious it felt to wear it. Now I'm starting to get the urge to.

"Though..." Sadie reaches in my messenger bag, hands me my shiny little silver hoop earrings. "You can certainly wear these."

So I put them in.

"Now," she says proudly. "Feast your eyes!"

I nervously approach the tall mirror, feeling like I'm about to meet a stranger. And sure enough, I don't recognize her.

I'm so pretty that my breath catches; I can't believe it's me I'm looking at. I'm a living ghost of another time, an unspeakably old photograph brought to life. An actual real live flapper. I feel beautiful. Actually, no, I feel a little bit sexy. A rosy blush touches my cheeks and I look even prettier. Sadie comes up behind me and puts my familiar silver necklace around my neck. The three little gem-encrusted hoops sit just below my collarbone, draped just above the diamond pendant.

The photo from the yearbook flashes in my head, the blonde girl, a dress just like this one. This necklace.

"Oh, my god," I breathe, my hand going to my chest.

Sadie was right. It's me. The girl in the yearbook is me.

I feel woozy.

And that's when everything falls in on me. This is really 1921. *I'm actually here*, and I'm actually a part of it. It's my world, the *real world*. And I can never, ever go back to 2004, because 2004 doesn't exist; it's as real as some D&D world, or Middle-Earth, or something.

A verse is nothing less than everything that exists, and from the perspective of that verse, it's all that exists.

The girl in the yearbook is me. I'm Courtney Ashford, Class of 1925. Soon *I'll* be the one making memories in sepia-toned photographs from some distant time, hidden in the musty pages of antique yearbooks from long ago.

I clutch my necklaces against the thrill coursing through me. Then I glance into my eyes, daring and excited, and turn to follow my friends out onto the street, into a world of Model Ts and silent films and flappers.

Flappers like me.

AUTHOR'S NOTE

Like all good fiction, this novel is inspired by a true story. The sorcery and versology are all just for fun, but this tale really did begin in my university archives in 2004. Like Courtney, I was taken captive by college yearbooks from long ago, I wandered my campus in the 1920s, and I spent time with real people. This went on for a while, and I didn't want to come back. Whatever the reason for my journey, it stayed with me; I was never the same. I was haunted by my experience for about ten years, until I started working on the narrative you hold in your hand. While most of this is fiction, it's about a time and place that really was, and it's inspired by real people who made the most treasured memories of their lives there.

As you've seen, cultural expectations and norms in Arc Tranquility are a bit different than in our own world (which I've referred to as Verse: Servant Languish). If you're well-versed in fashion, you probably noticed that I took liberties with the clothes, giving a lot of my characters outfits more appropriate for 1926 or 1927, despite the novel taking place in 1921. That was just a matter of preference.

The big one, though: when I started this novel, I imagined a lot of people would be eager to point out that lesbian relationships were taboo in the 1920s - which they were, in our own world. That's why the world that Mary and Nettie call home is technically a separate reality, with very different properties. And there, same-sex relationships are quite common. Verse: Tranquility Dawn also has a very different history than our own world, which I might explore later on. But regarding historical (in)accuracy, all I can tell you is that this novel is the product of five years of authorship and fifteen years of research - all of it geared not toward giving my characters the same home my great-grandparents lived in, but the home they *deserve*.

SPECIAL THANKS

This novel owes its existence to a small group of the most amazing people I've ever known. Seriously - without them, I'd still be dorking out on social media about my own half-conceptualized universe and characters, and it would be sad and pathetic because none of those characters or places would have made it out of a folder in my hard drive.

First, my wife, Lindsay, who never gave up on me. From the moment I said "I think I'd like to turn scotch-soaked regrets in the dead of night into a novel" she was with me all the way. She put up with my incessant babble about character development, let me play my nostalgia-infused pop punk mixes in the car, and got excited with me about our characters and their shenanigans. And she never let me give up, because this novel became as important to her as it is to me, and she wanted it in her hands. I owe you everything, darling.

Second, Jorden Ridenhour and Dave Horner - the best pals a girl could ever ask for. Jorden has been with me through the beginning of this long ride. He somehow became a connoisseur of fine literature without becoming pretentious, and I have no idea how he managed that, but that's *exactly* the kind of eye I needed. Without his tireless work editing this novel, I'd have released something truly awful. He and Dave were the first fans I ever had, and part of this mention is to thank them for that. Like, seriously - those people who tell you to just write for yourself without caring what other people think? I wish *I* could be like that. I need someone to share my stories with, someone to get excited with me, and Dave and Jorden did exactly that. From the moment they started reading, they pounced on this story, fell in love with the characters and their world, and stormed my inbox, clawing and screaming for the next chapter. I honestly couldn't have kept going without you guys loving this as much as you did. Dave Horner is himself a talented author and he's been with me every step of the way. If I got stuck, he was there to help get me out of the mud and on my way again. He's also one of my closest friends and an incredible co-author I had the privilege of working with on our 1920s crossover novel, *Underground*. I hope one day we can share that novel with the world, because I've honestly never had so much fun writing anything in my life. Without you guys, I probably never would have even mentioned *The Flapper Covenant* to anyone, let alone finished it. I owe you the world.

And my beautiful friends and beta readers, so few and so valuable!! Nicole, my college bestie and roommate, who had a front-row seat for my month-and-a-half long existential thing in 2004, and who eagerly alpha-read an early version of this novel despite her life being on fire. Nicole also posts about this book everywhere she can, whenever she can find an opening to do so. It means the world. Bobby Kinkela, who played D&D with me in college and who has been a dear and loyal friend ever since - and I know because you stepped up and took the Beta Reader Challenge. Thanks, Bobby. Finally, Tibor and Annemiek Van Wingerden, some of my oldest and best friends, the two that never gave up on me, no matter how weird and closed-off I get, and who loved my novel probably more than I deserved. I love you both.

Some of my biggest thanks go to my fans. My best friend, Gia Lynne Moffitt, hadn't arrived in my life when I first went to publication - but I wish she had been. She read an early version of this novel and became an instant fan - and one of my most loyal ones. She has tirelessly (and ravenously) gone to countless online book groups to proselytize this book - not just for my sake, but because it's genuinely become one of her favorite novels. Thank you for falling so deeply in love with the experience of this novel, the world, and the girls. Thanks also to Mike, Disva, Greg, Emily, and Kris for freaking out as much as you did over this novel, for becoming real fans, for all the amazing things you've written online, for getting so excited. I seriously can't thank you all enough.

Social media. A huge thank you to Althea of *Althea is Reading* for all the help and attention she's given to this novel. Althea took time out of her blogging schedule for a humongous interview (and as you can see, I talk a lot) and has mentioned me several times when she totally didn't have to. Also a big thanks to Jo Havens (author of *The Blood We*

Spill), Icantreadstraight, and all my awesome Bookstagrammer friends for reading and reviewing me on faith alone even when I was basically a nobody. I still don't think you realize how much your enjoyment of the story helped me personally and how much your Bookstagram reviews helped me with exposure. You've helped put this story in front of people who'd never have found it if not for you, and I'm so deeply grateful. You've seriously been so helpful.

Finally, a special thanks to the Ohio University Archives and Special Collections for so many things - but most specifically for materials I was able to research during my time at OU, as well as for making so many collections available online.

Lastly, a warm thanks to you, dear reader, for joining me on this adventure. I humbly hope it's given you some joy, and I hope you stick with me and the girls through the completion of the tale. I promise that we won't let you down.

-Cassie
August 9, 2021.

Made in the USA
Coppell, TX
20 February 2022

73862317R10239